FINAL APPROACH

"Riveting...Nance's knowledge of the subject stands him in good stead....A tale of suspense that is both thoughtful and satisfying."

—Air & Space

"A smoothly written fictional look at some real and rather frightening industry problems. Best read on the train."

—Kirkus Reviews

"A first-rate technical detective story...Keep[s] readers in suspense...This nonmilitary techno-thriller is a sure winner."

—Publishers Weekly

FINAL APPROACH

John J. Nance

FAWCETT CREST · NEW YORK

A Fawcett Crest Book
Published by Ballantine Books
Copyright © 1990 by John J. Nance

The fictional major U.S. airline, North America Air, which appears in this work, does not exist. Its background, structure, route system, management, and philosophy have all been fabricated for dramatic purposes, and bear no resemblance or relation to any certified U.S. airline operating now or in the past. This fictional airline should not be confused with the newly certificated North American Airlines of New York City, which began operations in 1990.

Library of Congress Catalog Card Number: 90-41140

ISBN 0-449-22035-4

This edition published by arrangement with Crown Publishers, Inc.

Manufactured in the United States of America

First Ballantine Books Edition: March 1992

Cover photo © 1991, John Terence Turner, FPG International Corp.

15 14 13 12 11 10 9 8 7 6

To My Mother, Margrette Nance Lynch,
Who laid the foundation,

and

To my Aunt, Martha Nance Kanowsky,
My first editor.

ACKNOWLEDGMENTS

Without all those folks at the NTSB who helped by example and otherwise over the years (some 300 dedicated pros who try to do so much with so little), this story could not have come to life with such "real" people against a background of such vivid reality.

Without all my fellow airline professionals who spend their lives trying to achieve perfect safety in an industry that never before realized it was based on the performance of human beings, the human struggles reflected here would not be credible.

1

A lightning flash blinded Dr. Mark Weiss momentarily through the rain-smeared windshield, illuminating his wife Kimberly in the passenger seat of the family's station wagon as she turned in his direction. A rumble of thunder followed in rapid succession.

"Honey, we don't have a choice. Dad may not . . ." Kim stopped, choking on the recognition that her father's heart attack several hours before on a Dallas golf course had left him at death's door.

"I know, but I still wish we could wait. This is a lousy night to be traveling anywhere." Mark found her hand and squeezed it gently.

For nearly an hour the nighttime thunderstorm had whipped the Missouri countryside, swelling the streams and threatening to block their path to Kansas City's International Airport, a delay they couldn't afford: the last flight to Dallas was already preparing for departure.

Mark felt the gusting winds competing with him for control as he maneuvered along the crown of the rain-slicked rural road, his concentration divided by the nagging worry over the last-minute reservations he'd made on Flight 170 for Kim and the boys. He hated the thought of them flying alone. They always seemed so vulnerable.

Kim squeezed his hand in return, a flicker of a smile crossing her face. She knew he had to stay for his Saturday meeting.

Mark was very good at helping others overcome all sorts of fears and phobias in his practice as a clinical psychologist, yet Kim knew how quickly he turned into a basket case of anxiety when *his* family flew anywhere without him. Working with airline people had made it worse. For two years he had treated the traumatized employees of a major East Coast airline sliding toward bankruptcy. Kim knew the plight of those people was on his mind. Tomorrow's meeting was an attempt to renew the foundation grant which had kept the program going.

"I should be able to join you in Dallas tomorrow by six," he said simply.

Kim studied her husband of seven years as she reached into the backseat to collar six-year-old Aaron, who had hit the breaking point listening to the marathon wailing of his four-year-old brother.

"Mom! Greg won't shut up!"

"Both of you quiet down! I mean it!" Kim commanded. Greg was reacting to the tension in the air. So was Aaron, for that matter, but he was handling it differently—firing a steady barrage of questions at his father and waving his favorite toy, a plastic jet fighter, a replica of the F-15, on which Mark had stenciled the name Aaron had given it: "Millennium Falcon."

"That's the airport, right Daddy?" Aaron strained at his seatbelt, waiting for an answer, a wide-eyed look of excitement on his face.

In the distance, sodium-vapor lights were bathing Kansas City International with an orange glow, barely visible now between the urgent swipes of the windshield wipers as they fought a pitched battle against a sea of rain. In the foreground, Mark could almost make out the ghostly apparition of virga—hanging wisps of rain showers on rapidly descending columns of moisture-laden air—an indicator of violent downdrafts.

"Daddy?" Aaron was demanding an answer.

"Yes, Son, that's the airport," he managed, turning to Kim. "What was the departure time again?"

"10:05."

"And it's now . . . ?"

"9:40."

"I don't know if we'll make it or not," he said, "but we'll sure try." Mark pressed the accelerator down a bit harder as another burst of lightning caught the distant outline of a TWA maintenance hangar, the distinctive aroma of fresh rain filling the car.

* * *

Beneath Gate 12 in the North America Airlines terminal, in an operations area never seen by passengers, Captain Pete Kaminsky stood in front of the pilots' bulletin board, shaking his head in resigned exasperation.

"Not again!" he said to no one in particular, unaware a fellow captain had stopped to peruse the same piece of paper that had caught his eye.

"You talking about the latest memo?"

Pete turned in the direction of the question, somewhat startled. The man's face was unfamiliar. "Yes, I was."

"More of the same. Now we're supposed to report, in writing no less, if we dare overrule maintenance and refuse to fly a broken airplane. In other words, you suckers fly anything maintenance says to fly, or we'll make your lives miserable."

Pete looked closely at his counterpart, startled by the sneer on the man's face as he continued, tapping the memo angrily with his uniform cap. "Look at this phrase. Anyone who ends each note to us with bullshit like—'compliance is mandatory and failure to comply will be met with severe disciplinary action, up to and including termination' is not fit to lead professionals in any field. I've had it with their threats."

Pete looked closely at the offensive phrase, startled he had overlooked it before. "I . . . guess I'm so used to seeing those words, I didn't even notice them this time."

"Everything we get from this goddamn company has that phrase in it." The man put on his captain's hat as he turned and scooped up his rectangular flight bag, opening the door to the hallway before hesitating and glancing back at Kaminsky, whose name he did not know. "You headed out?"

"Yeah," Pete answered. "You just come in?"

"Yep. Goin' home after four days on the road. Watch it out there, it's pretty bumpy. Thunderstorm cells were showing up on our radar in all directions."

"That's encouraging," Pete replied with a friendly snort, noticing a smile cross the other captain's face as he held the door with his shoulder and gave Pete a small wave with his free hand.

"Have a good one."

"Thanks."

Pete turned and moved farther into the crew room, feeling suddenly tired and depressed as he headed for the stack of pilot mailboxes lining one wall, pawing through the memos and technical revisions in his pigeonhole. He had fought hard to become an airline captain, and the position meant the world to him. At the age of forty-eight, his captaincy marked the apex of his professional accomplishments. He was proud of his four stripes—he loved his job—but he couldn't deny something was missing.

The crew room itself was depressing—heavily worn easy chairs and a stained rug allegedly designed by Halston. It had belonged to Braniff before their first bankruptcy in 1982, typically opulent with oak paneling, leather seats, South American tapestries on the walls, and even a huge console color television, long since broken. Now it was North America's, and therefore neglected. There was no money to be spent on flight crews in the midst of the competitive wars spawned by airline deregulation, so what had been a showplace was now a dowdy dump. Even the various hanging TV monitors displaying arriving and departing flights were in bad repair, their images dim and flickering.

"Hey Pete, what're you flying tonight?"

A fellow captain's voice wafted across the room, a pilot Pete had roomed with years ago in Minneapolis when they were both fresh out of the Air Force and making the grand total of four hundred dollars a month—barely paying for food, yet ecstatic to be airline pilots for North America. Those had been happy days.

"The infamous Flight 170 sequence. The Dallas Everywhere," Pete shot back, a broad smile on his face. "Tonight the milk run to DFW through at least a couple of tornadoes, tomorrow the New York death march through Memphis, Nashville, Washington, and points north. But neither rain nor sleet nor snow nor dark of night shall stay this carrier from its appointed rounds."

"Nor lack of airworthiness, apparently." His friend pointed to another posted copy of the memo, and Pete nodded without comment as he moved on toward the sitting area and the closed glass partition which lined the wall at the far end of the room, separating the operations men from the pilots. His first officer/copilot, Jean Simonson, had already left to begin her walk-around inspection of the Boeing 737 they would be flying to Dallas. His job was to sign the flight plan, review the weather, and then go fly. The flying part he still loved. The rite of passage through the crew room at the beginning of each trip, however, had become a trek through a swamp of lousy attitudes, diminishing outlooks, possible furloughs, base closures, and relocations, and letters about red ink—oceans of red ink—as North America hemorrhaged money. The fact was, his airline was in serious trouble, fighting competition from new-entry airlines by slashing operational budgets, fares, and personnel. It was depressing—almost as depressing as trying to talk to the glowering, overweight, angry operations agent, Mike Balzer, who was looking disgustedly at him from the other side of the operations desk.

"Awright, Captain, here's the packet."

Pete looked the man in the eye, noting the hatred there, and wondering how long it had taken old Balzer to come to loathe everyone on the pilot side of the window. Balzer's attitude was legend among North America's crews. He seemed to hate everyone.

The agent reinserted his cigar and backed up, sliding the glass partition closed with a perfunctory bang as another drumroll of thunder shuddered through the crew room. Pete Kaminsky sighed and buttoned his impressive blue coat with the four gold stripes on each sleeve as he put on his hat with the "scrambled eggs" of gold braid on the bill. With long-practiced familiarity he checked the gate number of his flight on the TV monitor one last time, picked up his rectangular "brain bag" map case, and pushed open the heavy door to the rain-swept ramp beyond.

"Where are *you* sitting, Daddy?" Aaron Weiss watched his father's face for the answer as Mark tightened the seatbelt around his son in the left window seat of row 12.

"I'm not, Aaron. I'm staying here until tomorrow. Remember?"

"Oh yeah. Will Uncle Bill be in Dallas?"

Kimberly Weiss settled into 12B next to their older son while Mark wrestled her carry-on bag into the crowded overhead compartment. They had been among the last to board.

"Yes, Aaron, Uncle Bill will be there to meet us. Greg, sit down."

The four-year-old rubbed his eyes and hugged his mother from the edge of seat 12C as she looked up at his worried father, who had leaned down to kiss them good-bye.

"We'll be okay, Mark. Really."

"Call me? As soon as you get to the hospital?"

"Okay."

"And if your brother isn't at the gate, call me immediately."

"He will be. Stop worrying. One of us will meet you at the airport in Dallas tomorrow night." She raised up to kiss him, then motioned him on, watching half-amused as he backed up the aisle waving to her and the boys, then turned and moved toward the exit.

He had just the right balance now, she thought, between the look of experience and the hint of youth: a few wrinkles around his eyes and a forelock of sandy hair set over a broad, rectangular face. She was proud of him, and proud of herself for choosing such a good-looking, gentle husband. Strong and gentle—and protective.

"Kansas City clearance delivery, North America 170 to Dallas with information bravo."

A disembodied voice on the overhead cockpit speakers replied to First Officer Jean Simonson's request with a familiar litany:

"ATC clears North America 170 to the Dallas–Fort Worth Airport as filed. On departure fly runway heading for radar vectors, climb to 5,000, expect flight level three-five-zero ten minutes after departure, departure control one-twenty-six-six, squawk two-six-six-five."

Mark Weiss had already made the decision to stick his head into the small 737 cockpit before he got to the front of the aircraft, slipping in quietly as Jean read back the clearance she had hastily scribbled on a notepad. As a private pilot with less than a hundred flight hours, he was well aware of the gulf between his own flight knowledge and that of airline pilots, but there was a camaraderie that cut across the lines, a unisex brotherhood whose rite of admission was an FAA-issued pilot's license of whatever grade.

The atmosphere of a commercial airline cockpit was technologically intoxicating, the impressive little compartment a siren song, luring him to take a closer look every time he boarded an airliner—especially at night, with the soft glow of myriad dials and instruments all within a fingertip's reach of the two pilots in the two-person cockpit, and the important hum of electronic cooling fans blending with the distant whine of hydraulic pumps. Who could fail to be impressed by such a place? A feeling of awe washed over him now as Jean Simonson and Pete Kaminsky noticed him in the doorway, the aroma of fresh coffee wafting from a cup in the captain's hand.

"Hello!" Pete Kaminsky never tired of showing off his "office," but too many passengers feigned sophisticated disinterest. "Been up front in one of these birds before?"

"A few times, yes. I fly little Cessnas, though. All this seems overwhelming."

Kaminsky extended a huge right hand somewhat awkwardly from his left seat position.

"I'm ex–Air Force, but I started in Cessnas too, although it was a long time ago."

Mark shook the captain's hand, noting subconsciously how tiny the cockpit looked in comparison to the size of the fellow. As a psychologist, he had always been fascinated by personalities and the relationships between powerful, headstrong people working in such a small space under what he knew were often high-pressure conditions. Kaminsky's physical dimensions made the contrast even more acute.

"Is this wild weather going to be a problem?" Mark asked the question tentatively while nodding a greeting to Jean, but Pete knew instantly what he meant.

"In other words, are we going to fly in this stuff?" Kaminsky smiled at Weiss, who looked a tad sheepish. "Don't worry. We'll go ahead and push back from the gate on time, but we're going to swivel around at the end of the runway and take a hard look at this with our radar. If I see any red on that scope—in other words, if I don't see a clear path out of here—we're staying on the ground." Pete considered his visitor's level of expertise. "You may already know this, but on this digital radar, anything that shows up in red is severe weather, and we avoid severe weather like the plague."

Mark nodded, and Pete Kaminsky watched his eyes as they swept appreciatively over the instrument panel. Pete decided not to mention the nearby tornado watch. There was an awkward silence, and Pete filled it at last. "What takes you to Dallas tonight?"

"Oh, I'm not going with you," Mark began, gesturing to the cabin behind them, "but my wife and two little boys are on board. My father-in-law just had a heart attack in Dallas. He's in critical condition."

"Sorry to hear that." Kaminsky studied the concerned look on Weiss's face. He knew the meaning behind it. He had stood in other cockpit doorways himself years ago, trying to find a diplomatic way of asking a fellow airman to be extra cautious with those he loved—a concern long since a thing of the past.

"Don't worry. We'll take very good care of them. We may be forced to make on-time departures from the gate, but there's no force in hell that's gonna get me off the ground if I don't like the weather—and I'll tell you, right now I don't like the weather."

Mark thanked them and made his exit, moving slowly up the jetway and eventually appearing on the other side of the rain-washed terminal windows at Gate 14 as the senior flight attendant appeared in the cockpit door with a cup of tea for the copilot, her silver hair in stark contrast to Jean's young face, her half-lens reading glasses hanging precariously on the tip of her nose, the computer list of first-class passengers in her hand.

"How ya doing, Barb?" Pete asked with a friendly smile.

Barbara Shubert, mother of three, grandmother of six, private pilot, and twenty-four-year veteran with the airline, smiled and peered over the top of her glasses, a top sergeant inspecting her troops. "Fine, Pete. Sorry I didn't say hello when you two came aboard. We've been battling maintenance for a replacement oxygen bottle in the back."

"Need my help?"

She shook her head. "Not this time. They finally surrendered."

Barbara turned away to greet a late-boarding passenger as Jean reached behind her to pull the folding cockpit door shut for a private discussion.

"Pete, I've got a problem with number three main tire."

"Oh?" The captain looked startled. They had been sitting together in the cockpit for nearly ten minutes. Why had she waited this long to say something about a maintenance problem?

"I found two deep cuts on my walk-around and called maintenance. This character comes out with a disgusted attitude, takes a quick look, and says, 'Honey, you'd better learn something about tires, there's nothing in the world wrong with this one,' and walks off. I followed him back to the maintenance office to talk to the supervisor, and it turns out this jerk *is* the supervisor."

Pete shifted in his seat, trying to find a diplomatic way to reply, but Jean raised her hand to stop him.

"I know what you're going to say, I already know. If the damn supervisor won't agree it needs changing, we haven't got a leg to stand on. I just wanted you to know what happened so if the tire blows out on us, you'll know why."

Pete nodded and shifted his gaze out the windscreen, noticing Mark Weiss as he stood on the other side of the heavy plate-glass window, looking lonely. Suddenly Pete felt lonely, too. Lonely and old.

"There was a time, Jean, when all a captain had to do was tell them once to change it, and it would be changed. Period."

"I know. I read. Even with a wing missing we couldn't ground the airplane without management approval. We don't control a damn thing anymore."

Pete Kaminsky felt an unfamiliar wave of anger welling up in his stomach at the invasion of his cockpit by the reality of the tawdry shell his once-proud company had become. He drew himself up and half-swiveled toward Jean, his right index finger raised in the air and a feigned, half-maniacal look on his face.

"The hell we *can't* control things, Jean. I may have to let this airplane be pushed back on time, but like I told the man, we aren't flying anywhere until *we* decide it's safe!"

The sound of the gate agent closing the Boeing 737's forward entrance door punctuated his words.

2

Thunder from somewhere above the airport almost covered the crisp sound of the airline reservationist's voice. Flight 255, she confirmed, was on time. Kell Martinson thanked her and punched the disconnect button, turning off the speaker and the remote microphone—the odd image of an otherwise perfectly sane man talking to his car's sun visor flickering across his mind as silence returned to the cushioned interior of the Riviera.

On the other side of the windshield the sheets of rain had decreased to a mere downpour, but the junior U.S. senator from the state of Kansas was still having trouble making out the moving shapes of buses and rental-car shuttles through the rain-smeared glass as they darted back and forth in front of him on the semicircular airport drive, each pursuing some appointed round at the North America terminal. Officially he was supposed to be at his family's old farmhouse near Salina, Kansas, not splashing through a traffic jam at the Kansas City Airport. Since he wasn't officially there, he couldn't afford to be seen, which was why he couldn't meet his inbound administrative assistant at the gate when her flight arrived in fifteen minutes. His face was too familiar to midwesterners. She would have to find him at the curb.

Feeling warm and insulated in his own high-tech cocoon, its windows opaque from the falling rain, Senator Martinson sat there for a moment in thought—his still-youthful face bathed in the greenish glow of the Riviera's computerized dashboard. He loved his car, but he'd really bought it for the touch-sensitive computer screen system—a consistent purchase, he felt, for a

10

pilot-senator from an aviation state like Kansas, who was already a well-teased lover of electronic gadgets. Cynthia Collins, the legislative aide who would be arriving shortly, delighted in needling him about his "toys"—as much, he suspected, as he enjoyed her taunting. She had labeled his new Riviera a "Star Wars" car, and greeted the installation of his mobile speakerphone with the suggestion that he should go all the way and have the cellular equipment surgically implanted. His suggestion in response had caused her to blush—while hurriedly closing his office door.

Now the thought of Cynthia sitting in a darkened airliner cabin at the exact moment, quite possibly engaged in unprofessional thoughts about him, filled his mind. Her flight would have already started its descent—dropping right into the middle of the thunderstorms making up a small line moving east across the Kansas-Missouri border. That realization shook him out of his reverie. The fury of that advancing cold front had worried him for the last two hours as he drove beneath it into Kansas City from Wichita, nearly two hundred miles to the southwest. Cynthia Elizabeth Collins—who permitted the diminutive "Cindy" when they were alone—was not a confident flyer, and her flight would be bumpy tonight.

Kell put the car in gear and left the terminal drive, deciding to wait out the remaining quarter hour somewhere within view of the runway. It seemed a bit silly, but no pilot in love with flying ever tired of watching airplanes land, and he was no exception. Kell drove past the airport hotel and headed toward the ramp operations area along Burns Street, intending to park close to the fence near the general aviation ramp where he had arrived in private airplanes many times in past years. The sight of an airline-crew shuttle bus approaching the security gate just ahead gave him another idea, however, and as the bus driver activated the automatic gate with a radio control, Kell cut his headlights and glided up behind it, shadowing the lumbering bus as it moved through. A bit dangerous, he thought. It would be embarrassing to get caught, but at least leaving the area would be no problem—the gate opened automatically for departing cars. Wichita's airport had the same system.

Once inside, Kell broke off to the right, keeping out of the bus driver's rain-splattered mirrors as he found a parking place along Ottawa Avenue, a spot with a commanding view of Runway 19. He switched off the engine, childishly proud of beating the security system, yet aware that if *he* could do so with such ease, so could a terrorist or saboteur.

To his right, a giant Air Force C-5B sat on the air cargo ramp, bathed in lights, its huge cargo doors open, loading or unloading something important, Kell figured. He could see security guards around the nose of the 747-sized airplane, and large trucks were parked at the far end. Strange, he thought, to see the Military Airlift Command's largest transport at Kansas City's commercial airport. Kell made a mental note to ask what was going on when he got back to Washington, just out of curiosity. He had access to such information as a member of the Senate Armed Services Committee.

With a start he looked at the security guards more closely, wondering if he was too close for *their* comfort. If they were Air Force security police, they had no sense of humor when it came to unauthorized cars, even those driven by unauthorized senators. The C-5B was at least 800 yards away, however, and none of the security team seemed to be looking his way.

Kell read 10:06 P.M. on his watch as he reached to the glove compartment to pull out a hand-held scanner radio from within, punching the digital VHF frequency of Kansas City approach control into the control pad—a frequency copied from one of his aeronautical charts earlier in the day. The sound of a pilot's voice filled the car's interior almost instantly.

"Kansas City approach, North America 255 with you, out of 19,000 now for one-zero thousand."

Perfect timing! The flight was Cindy's.

Kell looked across the runway into the murky night sky with a happy rush of anticipation at the thought of spending the next two days in her arms. Cindy his aide; Cindy his lover.

"North America 170, roger, taxi to Runway 19, altimeter 29.23."

Captain Pete Kaminsky pushed the two thrust levers forward, careful not to exceed a reasonable power setting for taxiing as he manipulated the nose wheel steering tiller located next to his left knee.

He glanced at Jean as she extended the wing flaps to the takeoff setting and began reading the before-takeoff checklist, waiting for his responses. Such routines were vital in preventing human error, Pete thought, but they became too familiar as well. He remembered the chilling cockpit voice tape from a Delta 727 takeoff crash in Dallas a few years back—the pilot's voice confirming the flaps were set for takeoff when in fact they were still up. Someone had answered without looking.

"Takeoff warning horn?"

"Checked."

"Speed brake lever?"

"Detent."

Airline pilots officially never made mistakes, but Pete could remember dozens he'd committed over the years. There was a private little ritual he had begun in Vietnam long ago while trying to survive as a fighter pilot in the F-4. It was a quiet, private incantation at the end of each flight, an implied thank-you to a higher power: "Well, I cheated death again!" Pete chuckled out loud, startling Jean. In airline flying you weren't so much cheating death as cheating human nature. The phrase, he knew, should be: "Thank God I got through another one without doing anything stupid that I have to admit to."

The smell of more fresh coffee brewing in the forward galley of the 737 wafted through the vent in the closed cockpit door, a warm and cozy aroma in contrast to the wild and inhospitable night outside. The wind had picked up again, and the taxiway surface in front of them was wet and glistening, the bright lights of the Boeing illuminating the soaked grass and taxiway signs more effectively than they lit the tarmac. Pete suddenly noticed a cardboard box on the taxiway ahead, and began edging the 737 to one side to avoid sucking it into an engine. Off to the right a ghostly row of air cargo buildings lurked in the mist, along with the incongruous sight of an Air Force C-5 filling the north end of the ramp. Off to the left stretched an expanse of mowed grass, battered down by the heavy rain of the previous hour. And all around them, as the radar showed all too clearly, was an angry swarm of thunderstorm cells.

"Kansas City tower, Central West 1880 with you at the marker."

In the darkened interior of the Kansas City air-traffic-control tower, Carl Sellers turned his attention to the approaching flight, this one a commuter, a small twin-engine turboprop Metroliner checking in on final approach. Carl could see the rotating beacons of the aircraft in the distance as he keyed the microphone.

"Central West 1880, cleared to land. Winds two-four-zero at one-six knots, gusts to two-zero."

"Cleared to land."

Carl looked at another round of lightning flashes, then at the wind gauge, and over to the airport windshear detector display, noting that none of the warning lights was on. Strange, he thought. A night of wild weather like this usually tweaks at least one of the windshear detectors. Maybe it isn't as wild out there as it looks.

"Kansas City tower, North America 170. Looks like a large cardboard box has blown onto the taxiway just behind where we are now. You might want to get someone out to pick it up before an engine eats it." Pete felt a twinge of worry. The FAA was violating pilots for any comments not absolutely required while the aircraft was in motion under 10,000 feet. But this *was* business. It should be permissible.

"Thanks 170, we'll take care of it."

Sellers picked up the phone to the airport police and explained the box, pleased that a squad car almost immediately headed onto the taxiway to get it.

Standing by the glass at Gate 14, Mark Weiss stiffened for a moment at the sight of a squad car racing past the terminal and onto the taxiway, seemingly chasing after his family's flight with blue-and-red lights flashing. From his vantage point he could see the 737 as it reached the end of the inside taxiway and turned 90 degrees toward the approach end of the runway—traditionally called the "hammerhead." As he'd promised, the captain began pivoting the jet around to the left, apparently looking at the weather with his radar. As Mark watched, the squad car stopped short of the hammerhead and began sweeping the taxiway with its searchlight.

The telltale signature of a major storm cell approaching—the intense splotch of red inside a larger area of yellow on the digital color radar—gave Pete Kaminsky all the justification he needed to keep Flight 170 on the ground for a while.

"Tower, North America 170. We've finished our look at the weather and I think we'll hold our position for a little while if we're not in anyone's way."

The voice came back in their headsets without hesitation.

"No problem, 170."

Jean pointed to another spot of red showing on the radar scope off to the south. "That one's going to be in our way on climb out if we don't get a left turn."

Pete nodded. He had seen that type of display many times before. Sometimes they even developed a little hook on the end—the unmistakable signature of a tornado.

"I'd expect some possible shear, don't you think?" Jean was pressing her nose to the right cockpit window, watching the landing lights of the Metroliner now about a mile out.

"Looks likely. That thunderstorm cell's no more than 3 miles to the northwest."

As Pete spoke, the lights of the small commuter bobbled downward, then up slightly, the red position light on the left wingtip indicating the pilots were beginning to fight with gusty winds. The cylindrical shape of the small craft was not yet visible, but the lights marked its passage as it came over the threshold of Runway 19 and dropped suddenly, the nose coming up at a sharp angle, left wing down, then up, the sound of increasing power audible even in the 737 cockpit.

"Jesus!"

Jean and Pete reacted as one, both willing their fellow airman back into control, watching with relief as the lights stabilized and settled to the runway in a smooth landing.

"Lord," Pete said, breaking the tense silence. "They looked like they were going to lose it."

In the tower, Carl Sellers had not been looking at the Metroliner. He had been straining with the field glasses to see the cardboard box in the police car's searchlight as the officer swept the taxiway. The call from the Metroliner captain was a surprise that didn't fully register.

"Uh, tower, Central 18 . . . uh, Central West 1880. That, ah . . . it's gusty out there on final."

Carl couldn't see the near panic on the faces of the two young pilots, the captain in his early twenties, with less than two thousand hours of flying time and more than the normal level of adrenaline. He couldn't tell they had neither the experience nor the training to recognize what they had just encountered, nor the presence of mind to put the right words forward to describe it. All he had was the phrase "gusty out there on final."

"Roger, Central West, understand. Thanks for the report. Call ground control when clear, 121.8. Good night."

"Roger" was the only response, followed by a blinding streak of light somewhere behind the slowing Metroliner, a huge lightning bolt accompanied by a nearly instantaneous bone-rattling thunderclap, which shook the tower windows with a vengeance. As the echo of the thunderclap died down, Carl could hear the instrument landing system alarm sounding.

"I think it got the ILS shack." The voice of the ground controller in the tower alongside Carl Sellers was followed by the airport police officer calling on his car radio in a voice nearly an octave higher than normal: "Ground, airport 16, that almost got me! I think it hit the ILS shed right in front of my position."

The controller had already acknowledged the officer's call sign as Carl reached for the phone to alert their standby maintenance technician. At that moment, another bolt hit to the south of the airport, and still another to the north as the tie line from the radar room—RAPCON—rang again.

"Carl? Shipping you North America 255 with a call at the marker. He's nine out for Runway 19."

"Thanks." Carl managed the reply, racing his mind to stay up with the increasing pace, marginally aware that someone was asking something of him from his left.

"What?"

"Could you alert maintenance? I've got a problem with airport squad car 16 out there."

"Right."

"Tower, North America 170, that lightning strike was right along 19 and that cell is moving overhead. I recommend you wave off our inbound company." Pete Kaminsky's voice was unknown to Sellers, but his concern was clear. But "waving off" an inbound flight exceeded his authority. He could report the conditions, but if the runway was clear and operable, to land or not was the pilot's prerogative. Even if he saw a tornado moving across the field, the rules said he couldn't formally shut down the runway.

"Hello?"

The voice on the end of the phone startled Carl for a moment. He had momentarily forgotten whom he was calling.

"Maintenance?"

"Well, I'm off duty, but yes, it's me."

"ILS is in alarm and I think we just took a lightning strike on the shack. I need you out there."

"Which runway?"

The answer was forming in his mind but had not yet crossed his lips when the radio speaker crackled to life again.

"Kansas City tower, North America 255 at the marker and in the rain, ILS seems inoperative but we've got the field."

Carl hit the transmit button, holding the phone to one side for a second. "Roger 255, ILS is in alarm, you're cleared visual, cleared to land Runway 19, winds two-four-zero at one-six, gusts to two-five. A Metroliner reported gusty winds on final several minutes ago. Altimeter 29.23."

The words had tumbled out with impressive speed and efficiency. All they *should* have been told, they *had* been told. But there was something more. There was something in the back of his head that he should have said. What was it?

"Hello up there, this is maintenance, you there?"

Carl put the phone back to his ear. "Sorry. What did you need?"

"Which runway? One-nine?"

"Right."

"I'll go take a look." The line went dead. One less distraction. Carl ran a quick mental check of where he was, and it all seemed complete. Almost.

"Goddamn tower isn't going to do anything!" Pete had watched the bright lights of inbound Flight 255, a North America Airbus 320 now 6 miles out, the steady beams playing visual games with the heavy clouds and vertical streamers of precipitation marching toward the airport. He keyed his microphone, still on tower frequency. "North America 255, this is North America 170 on the ground. That's pretty wild weather you're getting into. We just had a lightning strike along the runway. Recommend you wave it off."

A voice began to say something and stopped in midsyllable, the microphone obviously released. Another male voice followed within seconds, a voice Pete recognized with certainty.

"Thanks, 170, but I believe we can handle it."

Jean turned to Pete with a question in her eyes.

"I'll be damned," he said. "That's Dick Timson. What's he doing on the line tonight?"

"You mean our chief pilot?" Jean added.

"Yeah." Pete chuckled slightly. "They do let the head eagle out of the cage every now and then."

The two pilots watched the approaching Airbus 320, conjuring mental images of its cockpit, which was a technical marvel with cathode-ray tubes—essentially TV displays—replacing the traditional round-dial gauges. The aircraft was flown by space-shuttle-style side-stick controllers, which replaced the control yokes for both captain and copilot. The A320 was a thing of technological beauty, with a fly-by-wire electronic flight-control system that simply would not allow a pilot to stall it.

"Dammit. Dick's going to try to land in this crap, big as life!"

"You know him?"

Pete looked at Jean, belatedly remembering the "sterile cockpit" rule, the FAA's punitive view of nonessential pilot comments, and held his finger to his lips, his eyes rolling momentarily toward the tiny microphone that fed their voices to the cockpit voice recorder. She nodded.

The bright landing lights which marked the position of North America 255 were now less than 5 miles out, and as Pete Kaminsky and Jean Simonson watched in amazement, they began to drop below the usual glide path which airplanes normally followed to the runway. At first the deviation was subtle, so much so that neither Jean nor Pete was sure anything was wrong, but within seconds it was apparent that Timson's airplane was settling to the ground at a dangerous descent rate, the nose and landing lights canting upward, indicating an attempt to climb, the airplane still too far out for the sound of the engines to reach the 737 cockpit.

"Is he below glide slope?" Jean's eyes were glued to the side window, watching incredulously as the Airbus's landing lights dropped below the level of distant groves of tall oak and sycamore trees which formed picturesque windbreaks on the farmland north of the airport.

"He sure is," Pete replied. There was, they both knew, a major freeway out there in the dark: Interstate 29, covered with cars and trucks unaware of the aerospace behemoth screaming at them at far too low an altitude.

"They gotta get up. Climb!" Pete was leaning halfway across the cockpit, the sterile-cockpit rule forgotten, straining to see, watching as the lights of the oncoming Airbus seemed to stabilize behind the trees in the distance, hanging there for seconds which ticked by with the unhurried, torturous pace of passing hours. Pete's mind rebelled at the idea he could be watching a crash in progress. That simply couldn't happen, although he knew intellectually it could—and had in other places at other times when technologically sophisticated aircraft had tangled with windshear in thunderstorms. It looked for all the world, Pete thought, like Timson had flown into a microburst. But surely he could fly out of it. Those lights had to climb . . . had to rise!

Just when it seemed the surrealism of what they were watching had gone too far to believe, Flight 255 rose above the tree line, the Airbus's screaming engines pushing it back to a safe altitude, the aircraft finally crossing the approach lights of Runway 19 as it climbed steeply, the powerful twin beams from the landing lights cutting upward into the misty skies like something out of a Steven Spielberg movie.

"I was afraid he was going to get in trouble out there. Dick's a good pilot—he knows better than to fly into stuff like that." Pete said the words quietly, his voice drowned out suddenly by the approaching engine noise, his eyes following the huge machine as it passed in front of them, the sound of both turbojets at full power literally shaking the smaller Boeing 737.

"Good Lord, Pete, he was below the tree line!" Jean's eyes were glued to the Airbus as it flew overhead. A stiff wind from the northwest replaced the vibration of the passing Airbus, shaking the 737 gently as thunderstorm-generated gusts moved their airspeed needles slightly, then died down.

"Two-fifty-five's going around. Severe microburst on final." The strained voice from the cockpit of the North America Airbus echoed in the ears of the 737 pilots and the control tower simultaneously.

"North America 255, what are your intentions?" Tower controller Carl Sellers acknowledged the go-around call from the Airbus with a logical question. Now the airplane was over the middle of the airport, apparently leveling off at about 1,500 feet. Obviously they had experienced a close encounter with windshear, and they'd probably want to go out and enter a holding pattern somewhere, letting the storm blow through. That was what Carl expected, so what he heard next made no sense.

"Tower, North America 255 would like a closed pattern.

We'll come right back around for another visual approach to Runway one-nine."

A closed pattern meant they wanted to make a U-turn, fly back parallel to the runway, and immediately turn back to land on the same runway. That was unbelievable. They had flown through what they themselves called a severe microburst. Now they wanted to do it again?

"What's he up to, Pete?" Jean asked in the cockpit of North America 170.

"Be damned if I know, but I'd bet that microburst is still out there. Did you feel it a moment ago?"

"Yeah."

The white taillights of the 320 could be seen banking to the right as Timson or his copilot turned the big jet. The two of them watched in silence as the Airbus made its way back toward the north.

"The wind's died down. Maybe he knows what he's doing." Jean Simonson had pushed her face almost over the forward glare shield, cupping her left hand to block the instrument lights as she tried to figure out what the pilots of Flight 255 were thinking. She watched as the Airbus reached a point approximately a mile north of the runway and began a steep right turn back in their direction. Their 737 sat on the hammerhead just to the left of the approach end of Runway 19, the right side of the cabin visible to the approaching flight crew.

"Jeez, that's going to be tight." Jean seemed stunned, and Pete imagined he was speaking for both of them as they watched the progress of the descending airliner, mentally calculating its trajectory as it turned rapidly back to the east and south in a continuous arc on its turn to final approach.

"North America 255, cleared to land, Runway one-nine." The voice of the tower controller cut in suddenly, but there was no reply from 255.

Now the Airbus 320 was turning back toward them, the landing lights sweeping like a slow-motion scythe, moving clockwise horizontally through the air—pointing east, then coming through southeast and illuminating their airplane as the 737 sat pointing west, their right side now bathed in the lights from the Airbus. To Pete, the 320 seemed to hang there for a moment, no longer moving to the right in their field of vision, the lights almost painful in their eyes. The moment arrived when the lights should be swinging by them, and it was he who first realized no such movement had occurred.

"God! What's he doing!"

The landing lights were much closer than before, but they were dropping again, this time dangerously close to the runway, and aimed right at Pete's airplane. Suddenly the 320 seemed to nose down sharply, the landing lights pointing out the altered flight path, the turn stopped, the aircraft getting close enough to hear again.

"Pete . . ."

It was more of a choking sound than a word that emerged from the captain's seat, but it accompanied Pete Kaminsky's emergency decision to jam the two throttles of his 737 to the firewall. His right hand shot forward, gathering thrust levers on the way, reacting to the unbelievable specter which simply was not moving out of their window. The Airbus had dropped, the nose had come up again, the huge airliner stopped its descent mere feet off the ground and less than a quarter mile away. The landing lights of the onrushing craft had them bracketed as Pete and Jean saw the airplane roll to wings level, its nose coming up, but looming larger with every split second as it came straight at them.

What had been a puzzlement had now become a clear and present danger. They had to thrust themselves and their passengers out of the way!

Jean seemed transfixed, her mind calculating the changing trajectory of the machine behind the glaring lights now flooding her window with bluc-white light, the sound of distant engines becoming less distant, their own engines just beginning the eight-to ten-second process of winding up to full power.

In the control tower, Carl Sellers was still puzzling over a power interruption that had scrambled his radar display and dimmed the lights for a split second. Now he heard a half-verbal sound of amazement from someone to his left. He dropped the field glasses again and looked toward the end of Runway 19, his mind rapidly assimilating the obvious fact that North America 255 was coming down in the wrong place. There wasn't time for comment. There was nothing he could say on the radio in time—the aircraft was too close to the 737! It was one of those incredible moments in which the reality of an impossible sight is essentially rejected by the brain because it couldn't be happening, even though it is.

In the cabin of Flight 170, Kimberly Weiss had noticed bright lights to her right, across the aisle. Now they were blinding, streaming through the window as other passengers turned their heads in curiosity. She could tell they were dropping in her perspective, the changing shadows cast by the beams of light stabbing across the passenger seats from thirty-two windows confirmed that. Several people had lit illicit cigarettes on the nonsmoking flight, and there was enough stagnant smoke to make the scene unreal, as if thirty-two small spotlights were being panned up across an avant-garde theater set, hesitating, and starting ever so slowly to pan down again, all the while getting brighter. And there was sound—the sound of engines getting louder. She realized the 737's engines were revving up as well, and she also knew enough about flying and airports to realize one other essential fact: whatever was approaching was airborne and at high speed.

As Kimberly watched with rising alarm, the 737 began to move forward, barely, slowly.

The ultimate nightmare of trying to run from an approaching horror but not being able to move was upon them, and Pete felt a helplessness like none he had ever experienced. The sudden rush of power from the accelerating engines had begun thrusting them forward. All he needed was a few seconds, but the sound of the screaming machine to their right had become deafening, the noise of a powerful engine passing just above the fuselage becoming almost enough to mask the sounds and the feeling of immense force which suddenly gripped the cockpit as the right main wheels of the Airbus bit into the fuselage of Flight 170 at about window level, collapsing the skin and ribs and stringers of the right side instantly as the tires exploded, their relatively thin rubber casings crushed and breached by the Boeing 737's disintegrating structure, the main struts also collapsing and folding backward as they raked through the cabin, obliterating rows 17 through 20, along with the occupants at the top and left side of the fuselage, the left main gear and lower fuselage of the Airbus collapsing the vertical tail and rear cabin area. The force of the energy exchange shoved the smaller aircraft to the left and robbed the Airbus of speed and acceleration, the lower aft fuselage contacting and shredding the aft cabin and fuselage of the Boeing, the right horizontal stabilizer and tail assembly tearing open the number three fuel tank and propelling its contents of kerosene into what was left of the Boeing cabin, splashing it left and right as the ample supply of sparks from grinding metal ignited the fluid into a fireball. The main fuselage of the Airbus—ripped open beneath, landing gear gone, tail destroyed along with any hope of aerodynamic control—pitched forward, still moving at over 100 knots as it trailed debris and seats and the ruined bodies of numerous occupants of Flight 170.

Airport police officer Brian Harlow had just left the taxiway in his squad car after picking up the soggy cardboard box when a flash and a horrendous noise told him instantly something had happened at the north end of his airport. As he looked in abject disbelief, the outline of a twin-engine jetliner trailing sparks and flames shot over the top of the 737 like a circus tiger leaping through a flaming hoop, its trajectory gently arcing down, the nose pointing at the surface of the taxiway, then impacting it nose wheel first as the nose section whipped up and out of view, the wings and aft fuselage telescoping, flames erupting everywhere.

Now the Airbus was a shapeless mass of fire and debris tumbling past his position beside the taxiway, the fuselage and wings of the Airbus 320 rumbling by with an ungodly sound, spewing fuel and flames and pieces. When the roiling mess had passed by, leaving him untouched, Officer Harlow looked to the right and realized the 737 was no longer there.

Sitting to one side of the runway, Senator Kell Martinson had been puzzled by the gyrations, and then the go-around which terminated Flight 255's first approach. He had heard the radio call about the microburst, but obviously the pilot had it under control. Kell had watched passively then as the Airbus reversed course, letting his eyes rest on the runway, waiting for Cindy's flight to touch down and roll past his position, decelerating normally with thrust reversers operating and mist flying. As soon as they turn off the runway, he thought, I'll head for the terminal.

With his mind on pleasant thoughts, Kell did not notice the lights of the 320 as they dropped below the image of the 737 to his far right. He did not hear the initial crunch of metal, or see the explosion of igniting kerosene until his field of vision was

filled with flame and fragmenting wreckage filling the night with
kinetic horror mere yards in front of him along the taxiway. And
at that moment, his mind simply refused to accept the impossible
image. Such things were not supposed to happen.

His world instantly in flames, Captain Pete Kaminsky was
unaware that the cockpit had been neatly sheared from the disintegrating structure of the 737, nor did he realize that he and
Jean had been pivoted almost exactly 180 degrees to face the
raging fire that was roaring inches from their still-intact windscreen. Pete struggled to let instinct and training guide him.
Emergency evacuation. He needed to evacuate his passengers.
He found the engine fuel and start cutoff levers and moved them
to the off position, grabbing then for the intercom receiver with
his right hand at the same moment he felt cold air on the back
of his neck and struggled to turn around. He was about to tell
Jean to unstrap and get back to the cabin to make sure the doors
were opened and emergency slides deployed when his eyes finally focused on the void behind them. There was no cabin.
There was nothing there but runway lights. Jagged metal stringers and shards of aluminum plating bordered the bewildering
picture, and the infrared heat from the fire in front of them
burned into his neck through the glass. He unstrapped his seatbelt, not realizing until that moment that he was lying against
the left windows. Jean was hanging in her seat above him. The
airplane must have rolled over on its left side, he thought.

But where *was* his airplane?

Pete pulled himself out of the seat, his large hands reaching
up to help Jean release her seatbelt. She dropped heavily, supported by Pete's arms as she grabbed with her left hand for
something metallic to hold on to. Pete noticed her right arm
then: it was blood-smeared and hanging uselessly at her side.

With Jean's feet now on what had been the left hand wall of
the small entry alcove to the cockpit, the two pilots faced the
abyss behind them.

With the flames licking at his severed cockpit, Pete realized
they would have to jump to the ground—and now. Holding his
copilot tightly as she clung to him with her left arm, they
launched into the void, brushing sharp metal in the process,
landing unscathed at the foot of the flames. There were sounds—

the sounds of fire and wind and liquids hissing on hot metal—
but otherwise it was deathly quiet, as if nothing were amiss.

Pete and Jean stumbled back, staying clear of the debris. It
was then that his internal compass realigned itself. Until that
moment he had not understood. The raging inferno which had
appeared outside his windscreen wasn't Dick Timson's airplane.
It was his own. It was the funeral pyre of Flight 170's cabin,
and as he looked in disbelief, Pete could see the outline of burning seats and window frames on the eastern side of the hammerhead.

"No!" It had begun as a whisper and risen to a scream in his
throat as the big man started forward, searching the flames for
his passengers. Where were they? He had to help. Pete Kaminsky began running around the south side of the wreckage, seeing
the trail of debris, most of it on fire. There was wreckage to his
right, a dark mass of twisted metal, and from that direction,
over the noise of a distant siren now starting to wail, he could
hear a voice. His pace quickened as he skirted the burning mid-
section and headed for that sound, hearing other human sounds
now from the eerie scene, unidentifiable noises of pain and confusion.

The ruined tail of the 737 was on his left, the flaming remains
of the shattered cabin in between. But seats had been dragged
out of the wreckage by the Airbus as it crashed through, and he
thought he could see people safely standing on the far side of
the tail, which was not in flames. Maybe people had survived.
Maybe they all had made it. In the distance the fireball that
marked the main wreck of Flight 255 flared as bright as daylight,
illuminating the mass of twisted seats and injured people he was
approaching.

Standing at the window of Gate 14, the initial eruption of fire
and flame had flared in the corner of Mark Weiss's vision, then
in his mind. Something had happened at the far end of Runway
19, the last place he had seen Kim's flight waiting for the weather
to clear—waiting for a safe time to take off. His head jerked
automatically in that direction, his eyes taking in the sight of a
tailless fuselage and wing assembly arcing to the taxiway surface
in what seemed like a slow-motion special effects shot. He saw
the nose impact and crumble, the wings begin to fold forward,
and the rear fuselage begin to flip over, all of it disappearing

behind a curtain of flame as what was rapidly becoming a fireball splayed out along the concrete surface, sliding and bouncing and flaring as it skidded to a halt, a grotesque inferno of ruined machinery and humanity to the north of the terminal.

Mark had no recollection of following the North America agent through the door to the jetway, or of literally pushing the woman down as he ran at full speed to the end of the boarding ramp and yanked open the door, rushing down the steps and frantically looking around for something to drive. A baggage tug idled in front of him, and he leapt onto it, forcing it into gear, accelerating as fast as he could, oblivious to the four baggage carts banging and spilling boxes behind him, and unaware of the rising sounds of sirens and motors as fire trucks left their enclosures, police cars roared onto the field and Klaxons blared in the distance. He only knew he had to get to Kim and the boys. Whatever had happened had been too close to them.

Recklessly, he shot down the ramp on the unstable tug, selecting the far entrance to the parallel taxiways, dodging debris and taking to the marshy grass at one point, heading as fast as he could for the hammerhead. There was much flaming debris behind him and along the concrete taxiway, but there was something more chilling in front of him. Where the hammerhead had held the 737, there was now the scattered burning remains of an airplane.

Brian Harlow regained his senses within seconds of the crash and put his squad car in forward gear, accelerating directly to where the 737 had been. His radio exploded in sound and fury, radio calls electronically lacing a delicate web of coordination between the fire and police and rescue personnel as men and women scrambled into vehicles and raced toward the scene.

Harlow, however, was the first to respond, accelerator to the floor for a second until caution prevailed, causing him to slow up. He approached the darkest area in front of the wreckage with his foot on the brake, but not hard enough. A large chunk of metal bounced off the front grill as he slammed the brake pedal to the floor and threw the steering wheel to the left to avoid what appeared to be a person lying in front of him. Harlow backed up slightly and turned, illuminating the figure, then struggled to get the gearshift into park again. He tumbled out, running to the man caught in his headlights and realizing at once that he was far too late.

Harlow stood in shock for a second, finally forcing himself into motion once again. More equipment was arriving now, people alighting from fire trucks and rescue trucks in all directions. He moved on toward the dark shapes between him and the fire that was consuming the main part of the wreckage. Holding his flashlight more like an instrument of protection than detection, he walked slowly ahead, picking his way past the crushed forms of several passengers still strapped into their three-place seat assembly, stepping carefully over other human remains that he was rapidly learning not to examine too closely, and headed for a lone figure sitting on the concrete.

Harlow shone his light on the woman as she looked up at him. She was young and attractive, blond hair and face streaked by sooty smudges and splotches of blood, but otherwise physically intact. Harlow's eyes took in the shape of her exposed breasts and her flat stomach, his eyes automatically roaming to her waist and her shapely hips, covered now only by a torn pair of panties, her legs bare and smudged as well, a thoroughly incongruous image amidst such a gruesome scene of death and destruction. It registered that her clothes had been torn off in the trauma of the crash, and that he was looking at a disaster victim who needed his help. But all his training as a policeman was pushed aside by the frantic need to deny the horror of the situation, to find something good and comfortable and acceptable in his nightmare, and her femininity was exactly that.

She was trying to speak to him over the noise, but he couldn't hear. Harlow leaned down, careful not to touch her, not trusting himself suddenly, straining to hear her tiny, confused voice.

"My baby. My baby is here . . . but . . . I can't find him."

Harlow saw the detached look in her eyes and watched her dreamy, confused gestures.

"Where, ma'am?"

She looked into his eyes and bit her lower lip, her right hand flailing the air absently.

"I . . . uh . . . was holding him." She looked down slowly at her left arm and stared at it for a second as Harlow recognized the symptoms of shock.

"He's only two months old, you know," she said in a sing-song voice, suddenly strong, then dropped her tone once again, looking up at him wide-eyed and chewing her lip once more. "I was holding him tight. They said I had to hold him on my lap. I had him . . . here. Where is he? Do you know where he is?"

She held a small blanket, or what was left of a blanket, tightly in her left hand, gesturing as she spoke. Harlow followed her gesture, looking around, moving his flashlight back and forth, trying to find the child quickly and realizing at the same time that the distraught young mother was sitting many yards from where the 737 had been hit.

Harlow looked at the inferno in the distance and knew instinctively her baby was gone. He had obviously not been in an infant seat, nor had he been restrained by a seatbelt. She had made the fatal mistake of trying to simply hold him in her arms, and for a baby, Harlow knew, that was a death sentence in any crash.

"We'll find him." He spoke the lie gently, helping her to her feet, holding her tenderly. "Let's go now." Harlow smelled the plastic aroma of an airliner cabin mingled with the odor of acrid smoke in her hair as he gave her his jacket and walked her to the safety of the squad car.

They had been in row 12.

Mark kept that thought turning over and over in his frantic mind as he struggled to function, guiding the little tug to a halt near the central portion of the flaming wreckage, seeing the severed cockpit and noting with a flicker of hope that the section in flames began at the front of the wing box, substantially behind row 12.

But where was row 12? Mark saw the dark mass of wreckage and seats to his left. There were people standing around, looking dazed, and others—obviously rescuers—dashing onto the scene. The wail of sirens was rising by the second in the distance, flashing red-and-blue lights joining the eerie orange glare of burning machinery. He could see some survivors silhouetted now by the flames. The section in front of him was not burning. Could Kim and the boys be there? They were here, somewhere, and they must be safe. He willed them to be safe.

Mark dodged dark shapes on the concrete as he sprinted toward the spot he had seen, finding several people struggling to get out of passenger seats which had been scattered around like the toys of an angry child. He ran figure to figure, seat to seat, looking into faces, pulling up the edges of sharp metal panels to peer beneath, pulling at other debris and struggling to identify the bodies of those who hadn't made it, making sure he did not recognize them. Someone was working on a victim to his right, kneeling and giving CPR to a small form on the concrete. With his heart in his throat, Mark pushed close enough to see, realizing the size was close to Aaron's. But it was a little girl in a blue dress—and she was not responding.

Twenty yards or so ahead of him, Mark saw part of the torn sidewall of the 737's fuselage, a 15-foot-square section sitting like a gently curved, broken shell on top of a mass of debris, and still containing an unbroken row of windows. As he moved toward it, the top of the seat row could be seen under the end closest to him, the garish light of the fire behind him reflecting off various angles of metal and glass. He knelt beside the exposed armrest, finding the little tag, struggling to see the numbers. The light was flickering all around him, but it wasn't quite enough. He had to let his eyes focus, fighting the growing panic, staring at what seemed to be an eight . . . no, a one and . . . what? A three? Mark cupped his hands, trying to reflect more light onto the tag, and in a quick flash recognized the tiny numbers as a one and a three. Row 13. The row behind his family.

Mark Weiss began moving with increased urgency around the side of the panel, trying unsuccessfully to lift the heavy-gauge aluminum, slicing his hands in the process and not caring, kneeling, dashing to another location and peering under, yelling for help and pushing hard to move it.

Finally the panel yielded a few inches as he shoved, exposing something beneath the edge as a fireman appeared from nowhere with a powerful flashlight. Mark grabbed the light from his hand and dropped to the panel's surface again, peering beneath, seeing several human forms in a jumble of material. He reached underneath, finding a hand and arm, feeling in vain for a pulse and realizing he could pull whoever it was closer to the edge by pulling gently on the arm—her arm. It was a woman; her polished fingernails shone in the light for a moment as Mark positioned himself to haul her out. Gently but steadily he pulled, feeling the form begin to move, tugging as carefully as he could, and realizing the hand was limp. He dropped again, shining the light beneath the panel's edge, trying to see her face and realizing that he had been avoiding a look at the ring he had felt on one of her lifeless fingers.

With an emptiness as large as the galaxy, he shone the light on a diamond wedding ring, a small solitaire set on a platinum band, encircling the finger on which he had placed it so many happy years ago.

Jean had tried to follow Pete and keep him safe. He was too distraught, but the big man had waded into the debris, trying to save his passengers, finding body after body amidst the few survivors and the rescuers who were increasing in number by the minute. Jean had let him go, moving into the wreckage on her own and taking charge of another area, hardly noticing the intense pain of her dislocated shoulder, working with one of the flight attendants to comfort people and move them away from the flames. From somewhere a bloodied Barbara Shubert appeared, her shredded uniform evidence of her brush with death in the forward jump seat. Jean hugged her for an instant before resuming her frantic efforts in what was becoming a massively confused situation on top of a Dantesque nightmare. The initial quiet had given way to a cacophony of sounds and sirens, screams and moans, yelled orders and blaring two-way radios, accompanied by the background rumble of flames and crackling metal.

With the searing heat of the central wreckage of his airplane behind him, Pete kept moving, holding injured people until he could attract the attention of a fireman, giving orders, tenderly placing limp hands on quiet chests when it was too late, and moving slowly toward a small clump of debris at the edge of the taxiway. There were two people there, one kneeling and a fireman helping, a flashlight in the kneeling man's hand. Pete came up to them and followed their gaze to the limp hand and arm protruding from the wreckage. He looked in the man's tearful eyes—staring into an abyss of hollowness and pain—and recognized him as the fellow pilot whose family he had promised to protect. As the fireman grabbed for him, the bleeding captain sank to his knees, struggling to speak, the enormity of it washing over him.

"I'm . . . I'm so . . . sorry. I'm so sorry! I tried . . . I . . ."

Mark Weiss looked up at Pete with an expression beyond description—beyond anguish—the broken remains of something small and plastic in his hands, a scarred and twisted model of the F-15 fighter bearing a hand-printed name on the side which was still barely readable: "Millennium Falcon."

3

Friday, October 12, Washington, D.C.

A flowing river of colored leaves surged across the divided roadway in front of him on a wave of autumn wind, the late-evening landscape painted by the soft brush of greenish streetlamps and the glare of incandescent headlights as Joe Wallingford turned onto the Suitland Parkway, headed for home. It was 11:25 P.M. and he was mentally exhausted. Fridays at the National Transportation Safety Board tended to do that to him— the usual last-minute rush punctuated by a thousand unplanned interruptions. He supposed it was the same in any business.

Joe accelerated and headed east, his mind chewing over the raging battle among the staff. He would have to convince the Board members to use some incendiary testimony from a New England commuter crash, and he hated the process—and hated politics. Nineteen years of such nonsense was making him cynical. He knew the symptoms.

Joe reached over and switched on the radio, tuning it to an easy-listening station. The window should be down, he told himself. Can't enjoy a night like this with the window up. He worked the crank, feeling the cool breeze flood the car, breathing the aroma of fall and forests along the tree-lined suburban motorway. It was a beautiful evening, and surprisingly so. The city looked magnificent. He had noted that as he pulled out of the garage at 800 Independence ten minutes ago and turned toward the stark white facade of the U.S. Capitol bathed in spotlights, the sound of wind-blown leaves scraping lightly over concrete filling his ears as he paused at the curb, waiting for traffic that wasn't there—luxuriating in the empty streets.

Joe took the exit ramp to Branch Avenue, mentally reminding

himself of the comforting fact that his packed bag was in the trunk behind him. He had "the duty" for the next few days. If there was an aviation accident significant enough to require a Washington-based investigation, Joe would lead the "Go Team" as the IIC—the investigator-in-charge. And as always, if he needed the bag, it was ready to go in an instant, packed with duplicates of almost everything he had in his bathroom at home. He had adopted the habit of acquiring two of everything many years ago when he first joined the NTSB. It had been a family joke: don't ever give Joe just one tie or one shaver. Give him two of everything—one for home, one for the infamous bag. Before their divorce, Brenda had done just that. In fact, he corrected himself, she still did, sending him two little electronic alarm clocks for his birthday back in June.

The inviting thought of a crackling fire, the leaves blowing across his patio, and a Moselle wine he had been saving caused him to smile. That was an evening to look forward to—but the beeping noise that began coursing through his consciousness at that exact moment was not.

Joe shook his head, sighing disgustedly before launching an emphatic "Damn!" at the road ahead. He reached to his side and found the offending electronic device, pushing the silence button harder than necessary. The rest of the world called them pagers or beepers, but NTSB Go Team members had been carrying them for decades, and still used the original name: Bellboy. Whatever you called it, Joe thought, they were a damned nuisance that could shatter a relaxed evening in an instant.

Joe spotted a phone booth along the road ahead and stopped to call the FAA command post, hearing the first details of what had just happened in Kansas City. He reversed course immediately.

Within twenty minutes he was back in the basement parking lot beneath the FAA building, the return trip a barely remembered sequence of blurred images, the terrible situation unfolding in Kansas City on his mind, a scene of broken airplanes and broken bodies, images in gruesome detail which were all too familiar from past experience. There was no question about scrambling the Go Team. This accident was obviously too big and too important to be left to any of the NTSB's undermanned, underfunded field offices.

Joe draped his topcoat over the first chair by the door as he entered the FAA command post on the ninth floor at flank speed, a nod of recognition greeting him from the sole occupant, an FAA technician he knew only as Wally.

"What do we have so far?" Joe asked.

Wally filled him in on the details, confirming that the NTSB's field man, Rich Carloni, was driving to the scene from Kansas City, the death toll would be fearful, and the airline's operations control center in Dallas was in gear and waiting for the NTSB's call. "They're assembling their team to join you in Kansas City." Wally paused to take a deep breath and check some notes on an ink-covered legal pad.

"Lord." Joe shook his head. "You know we almost scrambled the team to Florida this afternoon?"

"Yeah, I heard about that. Boeing 737, older version, blew a hole in its cabin south of Key West?"

"Correct. But it was a cargo flight—Miami Air was the carrier—and they got it down safely. The NTSB chairman decided not to send us. We'll have our regional office do the report."

"Ah, one other thing." Wally seemed hesitant, and the pause caught Joe's curiosity.

"Yeah?"

"When I talked to the tower controller, at first he kept saying he—the 320, I suppose—flew into a microburst. Then he corrected himself and said they didn't have a clue what happened. The Airbus was turning to a visual final approach and just lost it. I asked him about the windshear, and he says 'I'm probably wrong . . . forget I mentioned it.' "

"You know his name?"

"A fellow named Sellers, Carl Sellers. He sounded terrified."

Joe nodded. "How *about* the weather?"

"There were thunderstorms in the vicinity, and windshear had been reported. I don't have details though."

"Thanks for that much, Wally. It just might be significant."

Joe realized he had been leaning on the edge of the man's desk, energetically rubbing his forehead, his muscular, almost wiry body slumping slightly from fatigue. There would be no time to shower and change before heading for the airport, and that bothered him. Joe cared about his appearance, the result of never being quite handsome enough to just coast on good looks. With his green eyes and ruddy complexion, his dark hair cut short and carefully combed, his penchant for crisp shirts and pressed suits made him an imposing figure in a sea of slightly wrinkled clothes and striped ties.

"I need to get my people in motion," Joe said at last as he straightened up. "Can we get the Gulfstream?" The image of the FAA's twin-engine turboprop Gulfstream I and the newer pure-jet Gulfstream III flashed across his mind's eye. Both were kept just a few miles away, in the FAA's hangar at Washington National Airport, and the FAA was bound to help the NTSB with such emergency transportation.

"Well . . ." The duty controller looked embarrassed. "Our illustrious associate administrator has standing orders that we can't commit either Gulfstream without his personal approval, so we're trying to chase him down."

"He doesn't have a Bellboy?"

"He does, but he keeps turning it off. We think he's at a late dinner. Should have him on the line in a few minutes—I hope."

Wallingford paused for a second, considering the difficulty of getting the Go Team to Kansas City without one of the FAA airplanes. The last commercial flights of the evening had all left National already. If they had to wait for the next one, the team wouldn't be able to get there until late morning, and that was too long to wait.

"Tell him we really need it."

"No problem, I'm sure. I'll try to set up a three A.M. departure, and I'll call you on the beeper again if we can't meet that deadline. We'll take care of Mr. Associate Dictator Caldwell."

Joe thanked him and took the briefing sheet, heading for the door and his office. There were nine Go Team members to notify, plus one Board member, after which he would begin the process of contacting the various so-called interested parties. North America Airlines, Airbus Industrie, the FAA, the Air Line Pilots Association (ALPA), and the engine manufacturer would have to be called, and each would be sending preselected employees to join the NTSB team. Joe looked at his watch as he pushed open the door to the stairwell. It was going to be a sleepless night.

Senator Kell Martinson had stood in shock beside his car for what seemed an eternity, but in fact was less than five minutes. Fire and destruction lay before him everywhere, it seemed. There was no way to prepare for what had just happened—the mind-numbing realization that the steep turning approach (which he had thought a bit odd) had been a suicidal maneuver.

Cindy was in that inferno somewhere. He stared dumbstruck at the burning wreckage as he tried to grasp that horrid reality. His aide—his lover—had been on board that airplane.

The panicked feeling of being in exactly the wrong place at the wrong moment overtook him—a hunted feeling, like the mindless, urgent need a child feels suddenly to flee a dark and scary room. Kell jumped behind the wheel and put the car in drive, roaring past the startled figure of a man who had to leap to one side to get out of the way. Heading the car toward the security gate, he braked to a halt for a few seconds to let it open, then raced through, clawing for the anonymity of the highway. He had to get out of there. Get back to Kansas. Get to the house in Salina.

Rich Carloni angrily twirled the dial again, searching in vain for a radio station with news of the crash. Only the potpourri of rock music, elevator music, country music, and talk shows spilled from the speakers. Disgusting! Without a phone or a two-way, he had no idea what was happening ahead as he raced up the freeway toward Kansas City Airport, and the apprehension over how to proceed once he got there was knotting his stomach. It was one thing to pick up the remains of two or three people smashed into hamburger by a private plane crash—he'd already done that several times in his eight months as an accident investigator with the Board. It was another thing entirely, however, to deal with a major airline crash—something he'd never experienced.

The exit ramp for the airport was coming up fast, more visible now that the heavy rain had stopped. The windshield wipers began an awful squawking sound, and Rich snapped them off as his mind raced forward to the question of where to go on the airport property. Should he drive first to the tower, or should he go through one of the gates directly to the scene? He decided on the latter. The airport police would be the primary controlling agency for now.

He rocketed through an intersection near the Marriott, ignoring the stop sign, heading for one of the entrances to the airport ramp where he braked to a halt long enough to flash his ID at the officer who had just arrived to guard the gate.

"I'm from the NTSB. Where will I find your chief?"

The officer took a close look at the identification card before answering. "Go between these two buildings, sir, then turn left on the grass in front of the parallel taxiways. Be careful, that's where most of the wreckage is, on both surfaces. You'll see several squad cars right there. Captain Baldwin is in there somewhere."

"Thanks." Rich accelerated through the gate, following the instructions until he had passed between the two hangars, suddenly finding himself nose-to-nose with an incredible mass of burning wreckage and mangled metal. "Jesus Christ!" His words had been spoken out loud, but they drowned in the tidal wave of sounds that met his ears now—the noise of frenzied activity amidst the macabre scene before him.

There was debris strewn everywhere. Debris and bodies. He could see several in his headlights before he swung the car to the left, following the grassy strip adjacent to the taxiway as instructed until the police cars came into view. He put on the parking brake and got out, thoroughly shaken, as one of the officers came over with a questioning look, appearing surrealistically in his headlights out of a swirl of smoke.

"Who are *you*?"

"Carloni from the NTSB." The answer took extreme effort. Half his consciousness was captured by the scope of the wreckage, which seemed to be everywhere.

"Good. Chuck Baldwin, airport police." The man extended his hand and Rich shook it weakly. "Okay, Carloni, this is your show. I've got eight men out here, and three more coming in. Command post is in North America operations at the terminal for right now. Tower is the backup. I'll brief you on the frequencies available on our hand-held radios, the ambulance and injured situation, et cetera, as you want it. I assume this will bring in a team from Washington?"

"Yes. Yes it will. They're, uh, probably on the way. I don't have an arrival time."

Baldwin waved his Kellite flashlight toward the south end of the field. "The plane that was landing? A few got out from the front section, which broke off—the first-class section forward. Nothing but bodies down in this area. The plane it hit was back at the other end on the hammerhead. We've got more survivors out of that one. Both pilots, a couple of flight attendants, about two dozen passengers.'' Baldwin paused, noting the glazed look in Carloni's eyes. "You with me? I know this is a hell of a mess . . .''

Rich looked at the airport police captain for a moment, trying to overcome his shock and think clearly. This wasn't a crash, it was a holocaust. What in the world should they do first?

"Hey? Your name is . . . Carloni?''

"Yeah.''

"Snap out of it, Mr. Carloni. You're in charge. My department is here to help, but something this big . . . well, I'm not going to make the decisions on something this big with the NTSB here. So, what do you want us to do?''

The officer was dead serious, and intimidating. In his early fifties, probably ex-military, in control and waiting for an intelligent answer from the shorter, twenty-nine-year-old federal hotshot standing before him. Rich was the one legally in command, and the one expected to swing into action. But he had never felt so inadequate, alone, and out of place.

"Is this the newsroom?'' The voice was deep and gruff, but the words were clearly enunciated.

"Yes.'' The reporter said it sharply. With a major story breaking in Kansas City, all she needed was another time-wasting phone call.

"Did anyone on that airplane from Washington, Flight 255, get out alive?''

"We don't have that information yet, sir. Who is this?''

"Don't matter. Listen carefully: this crash wasn't no accident.''

She froze for a second, wondering if this was a prank. "What do you mean by that? What do you know?''

"The whole story. I heard them plotting it. D'you know that Congressman Larry Wilkins was on that airplane?''

The reporter hadn't known that. Wilkins had been in office less than a year and was already widely disliked on Capitol Hill. He was a determined right-wing extremist with a scary agenda trying to masquerade as a responsible Republican, but it was standard knowledge he had grown up with a white supremacist philosophy. He had built a small empire of car dealerships while being groomed for politics by a shadowy collection of powerful, wealthy Southerners based in New Orleans—a group with ties to elements as diverse as the Ku Klux Klan and Lyndon La-Rouche's rabid crowd. But somehow, for some strange combination of reasons she couldn't fathom, Wilkins had scrubbed his public image well enough to win election from one of the Louisiana districts.

"He was on 255? From Washington? How do you know?"

"I just do. And he's dead, isn't he?"

She hesitated. The word from Kansas City was that no ambulances had made Code 3, lights-and-siren runs from the wreckage of 255. That seemed to indicate that no one got out, but it was too early to confirm. That was not reliable information.

"I don't know."

"Yeah, he's dead. The airplane was brought down. I can't tell you exactly what it was they monkeyed with in Washington, but I can tell you it weren't no accident."

"Who is this?"

"Forget it, little girl, I told you it don't matter who this is. Just remember *what* I told you." The line was dead in an instant, but it took her nearly a minute to replace the handset, carefully and slowly, as if it were a snake. Her editor was 20 feet away, framed by the plate-glass window at the Cable News Network facilities in Atlanta, which occupied several floors of a spectacular glass-and-steel office-hotel complex known originally as the Omni. Their newsroom overlooked the enclosed courtyard, contained within a soaring atrium.

The reporter made her decision, walking briskly to her editor, who listened intently before picking up a phone to consult with his boss at home, all three of them trying to decide whether to sit on the call, report it to the authorities, or report it to the world.

"How could it be sabotage? One landing airplane hit another one on the ground!"

"I don't know. All I know is what he said . . . that it wasn't an accident . . . something about monkeying with the airplane in D.C."

"Was Wilkins really on board?" The editor swung around, addressing a young man several desks away. "Jerry? Call Wilkins's AA in Washington at home. You have the number?" The man nodded, already digging for the name of the congressman's administrative assistant—AA in political shorthand.

The editor turned back to his reporter, three more staffers now gathered around them. "Even if he *was* on the airplane . . . even if he's dead . . . unless somebody can tell us this is an unnatural crash, I don't see how we can use it."

Through the din of background noise in the newsroom a young woman hurried toward the editor's desk holding a freshly ripped page of Associated Press wire copy, her approach unnoticed until she placed it in his hands.

"Thanks." He looked at the copy and whistled softly. "Oh boy! Either our mystery man's been active, or something else is going on. Listen to this:

> " '*Washington, D.C.*—Among the victims reported to be on North America Flight 255, which crashed into another North America flight Friday evening in Kansas City, was a highly controversial U.S. congressman recently elected from Louisiana. Congressman Larry Wilkins, a self-described ultraconservative and past associate of Lyndon LaRouche, was en route to Kansas City to deliver a speech, according to his office. Wilkins's fate has not been confirmed, but an anonymous phone call to wire service offices within an hour of the crash alleged that the crash was not an accident. The caller claimed that Mr. Wilkins's flight was deliberately sabotaged by a person or persons who intended to assassinate him. The FBI has been notified of the phone call, and has begun an investigation. There is no word yet from the FAA or the NTSB on the possible causes of the crash, but . . .' et cetera, et cetera."

The editor looked up at his companions, silently polling the group.

"Everyone's gonna be airing this now. We'd better go with it."

Pete Kaminsky had fought the paramedics off for what seemed like an eternity as they appeared from nowhere and tried to put him in an ambulance ahead of his passengers. At one point he had spotted Jean, her uniform shirt drenched in blood, her arm hanging limp, yet still working with people. He had helped get her into an ambulance, trying to stem her violent shaking, a result of exposure, pain, and the trauma of what she had experienced, hugging her for reassurance before they closed the door. Finally there was no one left to help, and he had to succumb to the medics, the numbing ride to the hospital as unreal as what had come before, his admission to the emergency room another fight—there were other patients to treat before him.

"Captain, you're bleeding at the forehead, you may have a concussion, and you could have internal injuries."

"Take care of the others first."

"Sir . . ."

"I'm okay. I'll wait."

Behind him were two gurneys covered with sheets, one bloodstained. Pete realized their occupants were beyond help. A team of doctors and nurses was working feverishly on someone to his left, a crash victim who had gone into cardiac arrest.

And in the room beside him a young doctor in a rumpled tuxedo was working on someone Pete could barely see. The patient was wearing a white shirt with epaulets and stripes on the shoulders—a male, judging by the exposed arm. The man was alive, but quiet and unconscious, if Pete had overheard the doctor correctly. He realized with a curious, cold feeling in his stomach that the man had to be one of the pilots from the Airbus. He tried to lift up on one elbow, a sharp, stabbing pain protesting the action. Straining, struggling, trying to count the stripes on those epaulets through the door and past the rapidly moving figures working to save the man's life, Pete lifted himself even higher, the pain reaching new levels that he was determined to ignore. The doctor moved aside at last, only to be replaced by the starched white frock of a nurse, who finally stepped away herself for a split second, leaving Pete a clear view of the shoulder stripes on the patient's torn shirt, the stripes which represent a pilot's rank.

There were four. It was the captain of Flight 255. Thank God, Pete said to himself. At least Dick had made it.

As Pete Kaminsky was being coaxed into the ambulance just after midnight, a member of the airport fire department was positioning himself with a fire hose to wash down spilled and unburned jet fuel near the mauled tail section of the 737 which had been partially crushed and folded and had separated from the main fuselage. Most of the fuel-fed fire had incinerated seats and occupants in the main fuselage during the minutes following the impact of the marauding Airbus. The tail had not burned, but the twisted structure that had been the aft cabin area bore little resemblance to an airplane, with jagged pieces of aluminum jutting everywhere, reflecting in staccato bursts the red-and-blue flashes from the galaxy of rescue-vehicle beacons, the ruined section seemingly lost in the noise of engines and shouted orders that obscured what the fireman now thought he heard from within.

The man laid down the nozzle of the hose and moved forward, ear cocked, sure what he had heard was an echo. But it got louder as he approached, the sound of someone, a female, trying to yell for help but not managing much volume above the din surrounding them. He selected a likely foothold—a punctured gap in the silver skin which formed a wall before him—and tried to mount it, but there was no handhold that wouldn't slice through his heavy gloves, and he had to back off.

The voice was definitely there now, and definitely female, coming from somewhere within the twisted jumble of metal. He stabbed the beam of his powerful flashlight at the mess but could see nothing. One thing, however, was now certain: someone was alive in there. Someone they had all missed before.

"Hang on! I hear you! I'm coming!" He screamed the words as loudly as he could while dashing around to the other side, playing the flashlight through the wreckage, spotting seat fabric and what looked like a limp arm deep within. Obviously not the source of the voice. At last he found a foothold *and* a handhold, clambering up as carefully as he could, shocked at the razor-sharp edge on the metal stringers. Against his better judgment, he quickly tossed his fire hat away in order to maneuver his head through the twisted structure, wiggling and dodging and climbing steadily until the voice seemed close enough to track. He shone his light once again into the interior, into what appeared to be an impossible cage of shredded metal reeking of jet fuel just waiting for an ignition source. Why it hadn't already burned, he couldn't understand. Apparently the fire in the main section had been kept away by the wind.

There. To the right of a greenish piece of serrated metal, a face, a moving face, eyes staring back at him, pleading in the process.

"Can you hear me?"

There was a long pause, and then an answer, as if the owner of the voice couldn't quite believe someone had finally come.

"Yes."

"Are you injured?"

"I . . . we can't move. There . . . we're . . . six of us here. All hurt. Several are unconscious, bleeding badly. One may be dead, I can't tell . . . he's not moving or talking. We can't move. My leg's trapped. There's a piece of metal in it, and I can't get free. I'm afraid to try. Please . . . please get us out. You're going to have to come in, though."

"Okay, I'm going to get help here immediately."

"Mister . . . ?"

"Yes. I'm here."

"We're all soaked in gas."

Her sentence froze his stomach, confirming what he had already not wanted to admit: he was climbing around inside a primed firebomb.

"There're big puddles everywhere in here. It's burning my skin and some got in my eyes. Please don't light anything. We're soaked."

The fireman carefully pulled his two-way radio from a coat pocket, taking pains not to strike metal against metal, wondering if he even dared hit the transmit button to call for help. This was going to be a dangerous race . . . and a nightmare.

Joe Wallingford arrived at the FAA hangar on the north end of Washington National Airport at 2:45 A.M., only to find it dark, unoccupied, and locked, the FAA's Gulfstreams unmanned inside and members of the NTSB Go Team standing around in confusion. Infuriated but controlled, Joe found a pay phone and dialed the FAA command post back in the city, knowing instinctively what had happened the second a sheepish and apologetic Wally came on the line.

"Joe, I'm terribly sorry, but Caldwell said you can't use either airplane. He wouldn't tell me why."

"Thanks a hell of a lot for letting me know."

Joe half slammed the receiver back in its cradle as Andy Wallace, one of his investigators and a human-factors expert, approached the booth.

"What's wrong, Joe?"

"We're orphaned, that's what. Damned duty officer assured me we'd get the Gulfstream for a three A.M. departure, and Bill Caldwell has refused the request. We've gotta go commercial."

"Oh, no."

"Yeah. Wonderful start." Joe shook his head in disgust, his mind already racing over plan B. "Let's round up everyone. I'll run over to the terminal and get us booked and ticketed on whatever's first out to Kansas City. You get the bags all loaded into one vehicle, if someone has a pickup or camper?"

"One of us does."

"Good. After I get the tickets, I'll come back here and get you and we'll go get the bags checked. Maybe you should send everyone to a restaurant to wait it out while you wait for me here. We can't get out of here till six A.M. at the earliest."

"They're gonna be thrilled."

"Aren't we all."

Joe drove the half mile to the main terminal, working to control his temper. Caldwell had been uncooperative before, but this was too much. Yet Bill Caldwell was a powerful man. Any protesting Joe could do would have to be done carefully through NTSB Chairman Dean Farris, who was friendly with Caldwell. Not only would they be at least three hours late getting to Kansas City now, but the trip would also cost the NTSB budget several thousand dollars. The public just assumed the NTSB's job was important enough to justify adequate funds and interagency governmental cooperation. The public would be shocked to know the truth, he muttered to himself.

Joe flipped his NTSB badge at an airport police officer to explain the presence of his car at the curb and dashed inside, startled by the relative silence of the deserted terminal in the wee hours of morning—National by day was a familiar swarm of human activity and noise. The earliest flight to Kansas City was on North America at 6 A.M., and Joe booked the nine seats he needed in coach with the lone ticket agent on duty, using his own American Express card. By 5:30 A.M. the team had assembled in the departure lounge, boarding the empty Boeing 727 early with the help of a solicitous gate agent, the pilots coming back before departure to share worried assessments of the ho-

locaust in Kansas City. The captain, a younger pilot in his late
thirties, lingered until the last minute, pumping Joe for information he didn't have, until his flight engineer found them.
"Captain, is this gentleman the NTSB team leader?"

"Yeah, he is." The captain, looking puzzled, introduced Joe
to his second officer.

"I just got a call from our operations, and they wanted me to
relay a message from the FAA command center to the Go Team
leader. Uh . . . ." The pilot consulted a hastily scribbled note in
his hand. "Two items: a Rich Carloni will meet you on arrival
in Kansas City, and six passengers have been found alive but
trapped in the wreckage of the 737, and rescue efforts are underway. The message also said to relay to Joe . . . is that you?"
Joe nodded. "Relay to Joe that Wally apologizes again."

"Thanks," Joe said simply, offering no further explanation
to the curious second officer, who obviously would have liked
to hear one.

"Mr. Wallingford, as an NTSB man, you're welcome to ride
on the flight deck in my jump seat if you'd like."

"Thanks, but not this morning. Too much to do."

"Let me know if you change your mind." The captain turned
to go, then stopped himself, leaning back over the seat in Joe's
direction. "You did know that the captain on the Airbus was
our chief pilot, didn't you?"

Joe Wallingford was startled, as was Andy Wallace, who had
overheard. "Really?"

"Yeah. Dick Timson. Had to fly the trip yesterday because,
just before departure, he suspended the captain who was scheduled to fly it out of Dallas to D.C. and Kansas City."

With that, the captain moved quickly up the aisle, dodging
and greeting passengers before disappearing into the cockpit of
the Boeing 727.

The noise of footsteps on the wooden parquet tiles of the
Kansas City terminal had been a constant din all night long.
Now it was 5 A.M. central daylight time according to his watch,
and once more the door to the room swung open.

Mark felt strangely calm now, more aware of the plush sur-
roundings each time another grim-faced airline representative
entered or left the North America Club, trying to speak in hushed

tones while escorting clergymen and physicians to the various collections of pitiful humans within.

Mark Weiss had dealt with grief before, personally, clinically, and distantly. He was trained, but the training was worthless to him now. He longed for some form of unconsciousness, but had fought every attempt by well-meaning doctors to sedate him. He had let them bandage his cut hands, but no more. Crash or no crash, Kim's father still hung near death in Dallas, other family members now insulating him against any word of the horror in Kansas City. Kim's mother was stronger than Mark had expected, taking the news of her daughter's and grandsons' deaths in stride and staying at her husband's bedside. Mark's brother-in-law had relayed that report an hour ago. No one knew what to do. Should Mark fly to them, or vice versa? What kept yanking his mind around was the continuous thought that he must ask Kim, and the jolting realization of where she was, where *he* was, and what had happened. Like a computer caught in an endless loop, the nightmare continued.

"Mr. Weiss?"

Yet another sad-eyed man had knelt beside him, this one probably a minister. He didn't want to be rude, but he didn't want strangers around him right now. "I'm . . . okay. Please. Leave . . . leave me alone a while."

The man disappeared as quickly as he had come, dissolving somewhere in the crowd of grieving relatives and friends, some of them sobbing uncontrollably, others in various states of agitation and shock. It had been mass confusion for hours.

Mark found himself memorizing the boardroomlike features of the club room, the polished chrome chair rails and oak tables, the soft colors and fabrics, a leather-covered couch and silent television in one corner, and the galaxy of small ceiling spotlights someone had turned down to their lowest setting.

Through the numbness and the mental pain that kept ricocheting back and forth in his head like lightning strikes through a black night, Mark remembered the captain of Kim's flight . . . the big fellow he had talked to in the cockpit and who had approached him in tears on the bloody taxiway. They were all victims. But of what? He would have to know. He couldn't accept this. He had to know.

* * *

It was 6:12 A.M. eastern standard time and still dark when the Washington Monument passed Joe's window on the right-hand side of the Boeing 727 as they lifted off to the north from Washington National. He glanced down at the infamous Fourteenth Street Bridge as the powerful engines boosted them safely over the structure, remembering with excessive clarity the snowy day in 1982 when a brightly colored Boeing 737 belonging to a now-defunct carrier called Air Florida had limped off the same runway with only 75 percent power and ice on its wings—a flight that ended on impact with the Fourteenth Street Bridge. That had been a brutal accident to investigate in many ways.

The thought jolted him back to reality and what lay ahead. The bridge was behind them now. On any normal takeoff it disappeared hundreds of feet below within seconds, as it had with this takeoff, and as soon as they achieved a safe altitude, Joe resolved to turn his fatigued mind to organizing their actions on arrival in Kansas City. The problems they'd encountered getting out of D.C.—an aggravation he didn't need—were merely a distraction from the main event. The world in Kansas City was effectively in flames, and that was a reality with which they would have to deal instantly on arrival.

One member of the Go Team had been glued to a pocket radio. There was, he reported, an allegation of sabotage floating around, and apparently the job of removing the people trapped in the 737 was developing into a major problem. Memories of the 1987 Continental crash in Denver and half-frozen survivors hanging upside down for hours awaiting rescue crossed Joe's mind. Those images and others began to blend into a fuzz as the sound of the slipstream of high-speed air on the other side of the 727's metal skin set up a lulling white noise, a mental anesthetic, blotting out consciousness.

Joe opened his eyes suddenly and realized with disgust that he had fallen asleep, his watch confirming the passage of forty-five minutes, a vague memory of a voice calling his name.

"Joe, are you awake?"

The confusing sight of a beautiful female face framed by a soft cascade of auburn hair loomed before him, an alluring image of softness with a concerned look, and for a few seconds he failed to recognize Dr. Susan Kelly, the newest member of the NTSB, who had come aboard at the last minute.

"Yes?"

"I'm Susan Kelly, remember?"

"Oh, lord. Sorry, Doctor." Joe lurched forward in the aisle seat, formulating apologies for losing control and falling asleep.

Joe had seen her take a seat in first class and figured she had booked the flight by herself, paying for the extra luxury. Not even Board members could get reimbursement for the extra first-class fare.

"When you get a few minutes, I want to compare notes. I'll come back in a little while." She smiled thinly and stood up, her neatly pressed skirt brushing his arm as she turned and headed back to the forward cabin, followed by Joe's eyes, absently appreciating how attractive and well proportioned she was.

And untouchable. She was a Board member; Joe was staff.

He got to his feet and headed back to the rear lavatories, determined to resurrect himself. It was embarrassing to be caught napping, literally and figuratively, by one of the members, though he was glad she wanted to talk. He had been curious about her ever since the appointment was announced, though technically oriented nuts-and-bolts investigators like Joe were supposed to be unimpressed with anyone from squishy scientific areas such as psychology.

In many respects, Dr. Kelly's appointment was a lucky break for the staffers—a highly qualified aviation psychologist with a reservoir of respect among the airlines themselves and a foundation of political support which made her dangerous to cross, even for Chairman Farris. To Joe, she had seemed excessively standoffish in their few meetings around the Board offices, and her first-class ticket and patrician demeanor did nothing to dilute the image. In any event, he thought, it was a relief to have anyone along other than Farris.

Joe dried off his face, combed his hair again, and straightened his tie before leaving the lavatory, making his way forward through the cabin as the flight attendants struggled to serve a plastic breakfast.

He pulled out a notebook and tried to organize his thoughts while wolfing down the food, finishing just as Dr. Kelly returned to the cabin, taking an empty aisle seat across from him.

"Do you have any more details?"

A flight attendant passed between them, interrupting his response.

"All we have, Doctor—"

"Susan, please," she said, smiling slightly. An assessment of what was and was not proper flashed through his fatigued cerebral cortex, balancing the risks of accepting her invitation to call her by her first name. What the hell, he concluded.

"Okay, Susan. All we know is that the Airbus 320 was making a turning final approach, and for some reason he lost altitude prematurely and slammed into a 737 waiting for takeoff at the end of the runway. We have over a hundred fatalities, but some survivors, including, possibly, some of the crew members, and there are reports of some passengers still trapped in the wreckage. The captain of the Airbus, I'm told, was the chief pilot of this airline, and he apparently reported windshear on his first attempt to land, broke off the approach, and was coming back to try it again."

She nodded. "This is my first field investigation, as you probably know. I'm going to have a lot of questions."

They discussed what lay ahead, and what each of them would be doing on arrival. There were five NTSB members, and one of them almost always accompanied the Go Team to the crash site. It was true that the investigator-in-charge (who was always a professional staff member, not a Board member) was fully in charge of everything the NTSB team did in the field, and it was also true that even Board members were supposed to take orders from the IIC during such trips. But a Board member was still a presidentially appointed 2,000-pound gorilla compared to a professional staffer. Although, Joe mused, that was a terrible simile in Susan's case. With clear blue, wide-set eyes and a disarmingly direct gaze, a cultured and soothing voice, and a professional and businesslike manner, she was really quite attractive. Fewer than thirty-five of her forty-six years could be read in the slight crinkles around her eyes. At the office she wore her hair back, favoring understated glasses and conservative outfits, all of which failed to defuse what had struck Joe as an incongruous smoldering femininity just below the surface. Brenda, his ex-wife, had been like that. She could undo her hair, take off her glasses, and transform herself like a butterfly from the very image of a cool businesswoman into a very sexy lady. It always fascinated him how women could do that. Men, by contrast, were always the same old shoe, whether stuffed into overalls or a tuxedo.

4

Saturday morning, October 13

"Yes sir, I'm quite sure. No one by the name of Cynthia Collins has been admitted. I have the entire list right here." It had been a long shot, and it was the last hospital. Kell Martinson thanked her and broke the connection, looking up at last from the open phone booth in the darkened highway rest area where he had been standing for the better part of an hour—his cellular car phone out of range and useless so far from an urban area. A radio newscast had mentioned survivors from *both* airliners, and suddenly he had felt hope, but now it was gone. If Cindy wasn't in a hospital, she wasn't alive. He had been right all along.

Senator Martinson reentered the interstate with a growing knot of guilt in his stomach. He had run like a coward, and it was tearing him apart.

It was nearly two hours before he negotiated the cloverleaf ramp at the interchange of I-70 and I-135 near Salina, heading south and then west in pitch blackness over the familiar country roads which led to the farm. Finally his headlights illuminated the arched entryway his grandfather had built so many years ago, the half mile to the house littered with leaves and grass and puddles of wind-whipped water which told a tale of the thunderstorms that had passed within the previous hour.

It was good to see the house again. For all his eight years in Washington the farm had remained his home, though he could spend less than two months a year there. Their long-time family friends on the farm next door, the Carmichaels, had become his housekeepers and caretakers in his absence, keeping the farm perpetually ready for him. The grand old two-story structure loomed in front of him now, the solitary porch light spilling over the veranda.

He switched off the engine and got out, stepping into a different world of crisp rural silence. The stars were showing to the west and the north, the storm front having moved on to the east. A formation of cumulus clouds, backlighted by the moon, was soaring across the sky. He could hear the windmill in the distance churning the darkness, caught in the teeth of the same stiff breeze that had been his boyhood companion in this place. The wind seemed mournful, now, though—reminiscent of the sad night in 1983 when his mother had passed away in a Salina hospital, a year after his father's fatal heart attack. He had returned to the house alone that night in the wee hours, feeling her loss very deeply. There had been thunderstorms then, too, booming and rumbling away in the background as he sat until dawn in her old rocking chair near the front window, listening to her laughter echo through his mind, and feeling secure in the warmth of his memory of her. It was all still there—*she* was still there—but just out of reach. Like an electric light whose switch you can't quite locate in the dark.

He took a deep breath at last and climbed the front steps, turned the key, and snapped on the living room light, noticing the blinking message indicator on the answering machine by the telephone as he headed to the back room to crank up the central heat. Only a few local people and his staff had the number, but tonight the messages could wait.

Kell's great-grandfather had been a successful St. Louis merchant, a self-made man who had followed the railroads west a decade after the Civil War, following the well-worn Oregon Trail from St. Joseph, Missouri, with high hopes of reaching Oregon, but settling instead on the dusty great plains near Salina. His son—Kell's grandfather—had also stayed, building this house in 1905 at the age of twenty-three, all of it with his own talented hands. The house had risen from the flat Kansas prairie like a small palace, a two-story, Victorian-style home with a curved stairway, a gabled and turreted roofline, some gingerbread trim under the eaves, and a sparkling coat of white paint, which had been maintained by the family even during the dust bowl–days of the depression. The interior had been renovated numerous times in the decades since, and the old house and the surrounding land were thoroughly up-to-date now, with a satellite dish antenna in the back and an added metal chimney showing through the roof (the result of adding a small free-standing fireplace to the upstairs study). Yet the image of the Martinson homestead was still that of a grand old turn-of-the-century rural mansion, with its history firmly rooted in the early days of central Kansas and the Martinson clan.

The feeling of being at home and at peace was strongest here, Kell thought. Washington and Wichita were places he lived, but this was where he belonged. The ticking of the grandfather clock in the front hall reverberating off the oak floors or the creak of the timbers in the house as they gave slightly under the force of a rising wind were sounds that had remained the same all through his life. They were a constant, and a balm to the pain he was feeling now—pain mixed with fatigue as sleep overtook him at last.

Kell awoke suddenly, realizing he had been dozing at the kitchen table with his head in his hands. He glanced at his watch, reading 6:03 A.M., and moved to the television set, snapping on the satellite dish translator and the TV, checking to see if it was tuned to CNN. Their logo flashed on the screen, followed by the introduction of a newsman visible in a box next to the anchor's image in Atlanta, live from Kansas City Airport.

His stomach was tightly clenched in an instant. The crash had seemed like a horrible nightmare, but here it was again in garish color, the aircraft wreckage illuminated by searchlights serving as a backdrop for the man's report. There were 141 known dead, and 38 survivors so far, including the pilots from both aircraft. But there was a desperate rescue going on with as many as 6 survivors trapped in the wreckage of one airliner. Kell tensed at the news, until the reporter confirmed it was the departing flight—the 737—that held the trapped passengers. Cindy could not be among them.

The bodies of victims had not been removed from the crash site pending arrival of the NTSB team, who were said to be on their way from Washington. They would, the correspondent promised, hold a preliminary news conference later in the day, and that would be reported on the evening news. Suddenly the image of grieving people covered the screen as a background to the reporter's words. Apparently a camera crew in Dallas had caught the looks of utter disbelief and agony on the faces of friends and relatives who had come to Dallas–Fort Worth International Airport to pick up those who had never left the Kansas City taxiway. Kell winced at the camera's voyeuristic intrusion. An airline representative was trying his best to move the people into a private room and away from the camera, but the camera followed them, and in the faces of the relatives who stood confused and uncertain before the lens, Kell recognized expressions of the same fear mixed with agonized hope he had felt several hours before as he had searched the Kansas City hospitals by phone, frantically trying to find Cindy listed as injured and alive rather than the alternative.

The reporter in Kansas City was back on the screen, holding a microphone in his left hand, his hair whipped by a cold breeze, and wearing a black raincoat glistening with moisture from the gray skies overhead.

"With the crash of North American 255 only hours old, there is only speculation this morning over whether thunderstorms, sabotage, an engine fire, or something else brought down this sophisticated new Airbus 320 as the captain made his second try at the runway last night. We do know his first landing attempt had to be aborted because of dangerous wind currents pilots call 'windshear.' " The screen dissolved then to a prerecorded report on microbursts with graphic pictures of downward-moving columns of air striking the ground and radiating high-speed wind currents away from the center in all directions. A narrator explained how an airplane flying through the middle would travel from a headwind instantly into a tailwind, and how the resulting loss of forward wind speed over the wings could cause the airplane to stall, and drop.

Kell ached for some coffee or something to drink, but he would not let himself move—as if hanging on to every word might somehow resurrect hope for Cindy, though he knew better.

The reporter returned to the screen. "As for the report of an engine fire, at least one eyewitness has said he saw the aircraft on fire, or trailing sparks from the engines, just before impact. But there is another, more sinister possibility. Within hours of the crash, reports began circulating that controversial congressman Larry Wilkins, of Louisiana, was on board the flight from Washington, and that the crash was not an accident, but was the result of sabotage aimed at killing the congressman."

Kell Martinson's mind snapped to attention. It wasn't just the mention of a fellow member of Congress, it was *which* member of Congress. Wilkins! A new cascade of conflicting thoughts raced through Kell's mind at high speed. Larry Wilkins was an embarrassment to the dignity of the Congress, and Kell had said so publicly, getting caught up in a controversy he hadn't needed to create. Cindy had been furious.

Cindy! The thought that she had perished on the same airplane—that he had watched the fascist bastard from Louisiana die in the same wreckage—infuriated him. It was as if Wilkins's presence in the twisted rubble somehow desecrated her memory.

The newsman was still talking, and Kell suppressed his shock to listen.

". . . from what we've learned. The NTSB's first representative on the scene has refused comment, but we have learned that Kansas City Airport police are already investigating the presence of an unauthorized car in the vicinity of the crash site moments before the disaster. The car was described as a late-model luxury car with Kansas plates. It nearly ran down an airline employee as it left the cargo ramp area, as I say, moments after the crash. The man who had to jump out of its way could not get the license number, but he did see that it was a Kansas license plate, and he described the car as either a silver Pontiac Grand Am or a Buick Riviera."

Senator Kell Martinson was on the edge of his chair now, thoroughly rattled, remembering from some recess of his memory the image of a man leaping out of his way back at the airport. He strained to hear more from the announcer. What had he said? The man didn't get the license plate? That was it. Thank God! But evidence of any unauthorized car would keep the rumor of sabotage going, and the FBI would go crazy until they found the car. His car. And him.

"Jesus Christ!" Kell flung the words softly to the figure on the TV screen as the reporter resumed his report: "We've talked with officials of the airline, and now I have with me Mr. Bill Rustigan, who is station manager for North America Airlines here in Kansas City." A tall, nearly bald man in a wrinkled business suit moved forward in response, a look of great uncertainty on his face.

"Mr. Rustigan, I understand there were quite a few friends and relatives of both the inbound and outbound passengers here in the terminal when the crash occurred. What were you able to do for them? How do you handle this sort of thing?''

Rustigan thought the question over slowly before answering. "Well, you can plan, but this has never happened to us before. We tried to get all the affected people into a conference room near Gate 14, and that was difficult because they were wandering all over the place in shock. One man even took one of our cargo tugs and dashed to the scene to look for his wife and kids.''

"Once you got everyone in one place, what did you do?'' the reporter, a young newsman named Dawson, asked.

The station manager looked at Dawson in disbelief. "What *can* you do? We sit with them, we try to help them deal with this, call other relatives . . . make some effort to hand them off to friends or relatives. We try not to leave them by themselves. That would be totally inhumane. I mean, you do the best you can, right? It's a horrible shock.'' Rustigan gestured toward the runway, his right arm dropping loudly to his side again. "One second someone you love is leaving or arriving on a routine trip on the safest form of public transportation, and the next . . .'' He gestured behind him again. "I'll promise you this. We'll stick with each and every one of them as long as they need us. I have a bunch of our people—agents, flight attendants, pilots, cargo handlers, and so on—sitting with the victims' families. We're all hurting. We lost some of our people, too.''

North America's morning flight from Washington nosed into Kansas City's Gate 9 at 7:14 A.M. central time, the flight crew fighting knotted stomachs at the sight of burned airplane wreckage in the distance as they turned off the east-west runway. In the cabin, Joe Wallingford and the members of the NTSB Go Team had looked out in silence as they passed, noses pressed to the frosty Plexiglas windows, their minds and metabolisms already gearing up for the challenges ahead.

Out of habit, Joe positioned his NTSB identification badge on his suit-coat pocket before leaving his seat, filing out with the tidal wave of other passengers when the turn came for his row to leave. Dr. Kelly would already be out the door, he figured. He was wrong. She was waiting for him when he came through first class.

"Joe, what's first? The media?''

He shook his head. "I don't think so. They may be there, but we can't say anything yet."

"Isn't that my job?" She asked the question with what sounded like an edge in her voice, or perhaps, Joe thought, I'm too tired to judge.

"That's your call, Doctor. It's just that we don't have anything to say officially right now."

"No, you didn't understand me. *When* we decide to speak to them, shouldn't I do the talking?"

Joe smiled at her and nodded. "Yeah, when it's time and you feel comfortable doing so."

Susan followed him into the jetway and up toward the terminal, both of them somewhat startled at the disheveled young man who caught them halfway.

"Mr. Wallingford?" He inspected Joe's badge, recognizing the name. "Ah, good. I'm Rich Carloni, your field man."

Joe put down his briefcase and shook Carloni's hand, aware of other passengers beginning to push around them. Susan stayed in place behind him. "Rich, glad you're here. This is Doctor Susan Kelly, one of the Board members."

Carloni reached out his hand, stretching past Joe and almost tripping on the down-slanted floor of the jetway. "Member Kelly? I'm glad to meet you."

"Why don't we move on and you can brief us on the way," Joe suggested.

Carloni's hand went up, motioning them to stay in place and to move to one side of the crowded passageway. "I need to tell you . . . the media's all cranked up just outside the exit here waiting for you."

"How . . . ?" Joe asked, only mildly concerned.

"I don't know. I didn't tell them when you were coming, but they figured out you were on this flight. It is, as you might guess, a zoo around here. They're everywhere, even clamoring to get cameras into the rescue scene at the end of the runway."

Joe looked at Carloni, taking in the deep blue-black crescents under his eyes, the smudges on his coat and face, his uncombed hair—all in contrast to his carefully tied necktie, which had not been loosened. He had obviously been working his tail off.

"Recommendations?" Joe asked, looking him straight in the eye.

"None. I just didn't want you to get blindsided."

"We appreciate that." Joe glanced at Susan Kelly, who was nodding.

On Joe's cue they resumed walking, emerging into the glare of a half dozen TV lights, squinting at the brightness, Joe shaking his head in the negative at the several offered microphones, yet nodding in as friendly a manner as he could while following Carloni. Carloni led them beyond a ticket counter to an unmarked wooden door, which opened into a small office with Spartan furnishings and the curious smell of stamp-pad ink.

"I thought I'd better brief you here. The VIP lounge is in use for the, ah . . . victims' families," Carloni said.

Joe motioned Susan to a chair, which she refused. He put down his briefcase then and leaned on the nearest desk as Rich Carloni took a deep breath.

"Okay. First, the airport fire department rescue crews are having an awful time with the survivors in the 737. There were two rows toward the back . . . the structure just sort of folded around them, the floor cracked open, and they're so tangled up in heavy, sharp metal, there's no way to get them out without cutting in there piece by piece, or slowly pulling the pieces apart. Problem is, all of them are soaked in kerosene, and one mistake . . ."

Joe nodded and glanced at Susan, who was expressionless.

Carloni searched Joe's face for a second before continuing.

"It looks like of the six, only four may be alive, and they're badly injured. We may be running out of time."

Joe raised his hand slightly and Carloni stopped. "Rich, don't take this wrong, but since we have no authority over the rescue crews, unless there's anything the Go Team needs to do in that rescue effort, let's get the other matters out of the way."

"Sorry, Mr. Wallingford. I just came from there, and it's . . . it's very wrenching. There are children involved."

"What's the status of wreckage security and distribution?" Joe asked, shifting the subject rapidly.

"Most of the pieces, both large and small, are confined to the outer and inner taxiways alongside Runway 19, and the hammerhead area. Some pieces ended up on the runway. The front fuselage and cockpit section of the Airbus ended up in the grass halfway between the taxiways and the runway, and that, fortunately, didn't burn. The pilot and copilot, two flight attendants, and twelve passengers came out of that section alive. I know we don't have much time, but just so you know, the heroics of the two surviving flight attendants in getting the people away from the wreckage was something else! No one else on the Airbus made it. We have all the bodies that were thrown free marked and covered but not moved, waiting for you. My orders, in accordance with the handbook, were that the police not allow a single piece of wreckage to be moved except to pull out survivors. I think they've complied. The airport manager, by the way, wanted me to tell you he needs his runway open again as soon as possible."

Joe snorted. "It may be days. He has another runway, we just landed on it."

"There's a big Air Force plane trapped down there, and I guess the crew is giving him a hard time, but I told him we couldn't commit to when the wreckage could be moved."

"You told him right," Joe confirmed. "Have you had time to make any ground arrangements?"

"Yes. All done." Carloni pulled a packet of papers from his coat pocket. "The manager of the Marriott here on the airport property came out hours ago and has helped set everything up. We have the main ballroom as the headquarters, and the phones will be in about now. I reserved fifteen rooms; I didn't know who was coming, so there are no names attached. I've also got portable cellular phones for all of you rented from a rental-car counter. They're expensive, but they'll keep everyone on line and in touch. There are four rented minivans parked at the hotel and one parked at the curb here, and the airport police have already given me flight-line passes for them. Ah, I also rented one small conference room for interviews."

Carloni continued as Joe made notes, impressed with all the young investigator had accomplished.

"How about passenger lists, survivor lists, hospitals, all that?" Joe asked.

Carloni shook his head disgustedly. "North America's command and control here is nonexistent. They're in mass confusion. A fellow named Rustigan is their station manager, and he's been so emotionally thwacked by all this, he makes promises but forgets them."

"The lists, then?"

"Promised, but I haven't seen anything yet."

The door to the office fairly burst open, revealing a disgusted

Andy Wallace. "*There* you are! Joe, I've just come from baggage claim . . . these idiots have lost half our damn bags, including the field kit."

"Wonderful."

"Yeah. They're going back to the aircraft to check. The flight goes on to San Francisco. If they're not there, they didn't make it on in D.C."

Joe looked at Susan, who was shaking her head as well, then back at Andy. "File the reports, Andy, then get everyone over to the hotel and start rounding up the incoming team members from North America, Airbus, FAA, the Air Line Pilots Association—all of the parties who're sending people. Stay in charge until I get there. Schedule an organizational meeting with just us staffers"—Joe stopped and glanced at Susan Kelly with a small grin—"plus the Board members at, say, nine A.M. Let's tell the media, if Dr. Kelly agrees, that we'll do a conference for them around noon, and a briefing of all the parties at two P.M."

Andy reached for the doorknob, but Joe stopped him.

"Andy, if you need to change any times, do it. Those are initial targets."

Andy Wallace smiled at Joe, appreciating the trust. His style of command under pressure had endeared Joe Wallingford to everyone. He was considerate, and that meant something.

Joe wanted an initial tour of the wreckage, but for ten minutes more he and Carloni compared notes, Rich doing most of the talking, relating his actions and the problems that were already getting in the way of an orderly investigation.

They left at Joe's signal, getting into the rented minivan and entering the flight line, Carloni using a borrowed police radio to get clearance from ground control to enter the ramp area and taxiway.

It was familiar, but it never became routine, looking in person at the immediate aftermath of a major air disaster. Susan was silent, her eyes intent on the scores of tarps covering the bodies of the dead, all of whom had been left in place.

"My God," she said softly.

"The tail of the 320 is relatively intact," Rich told them. "I imagine the voice and flight recorders will be found easily. Same for the 737 when the people are finally pulled out, though there won't be a lot to read on those tapes, I suppose. They just were unfortunate to have been in the way.''

They passed the separated forward section of the Airbus, which had been flung to the side as the aircraft disintegrated, and, weaving to avoid other clumps of wreckage, finally approached a confused mass of emergency vehicles, empty ambulances, cherry pickers, maintenance stands, and fire trucks surrounding a mass of jumbled aerospace metal with the remains of a 737 tail fin stabbing the murky air, the emblem of North America Airlines blaring its presence with the same incongruous impact of brightly colored plumage marking the fallen carcass of a dead bird.

Rich shook his head in disgust. ''Would you believe North America sent a paint-sprayer crew out here before dawn to paint out their name and logo?''

''Standard procedure,'' Joe replied with a snort. ''Every airline lists that in their emergency response checklists as one of the most vital duties.''

''Unbelievable,'' Rich said quietly. ''As if people will be too stupid to know whose airplanes crashed here. I had the cops escort them out of here—at least until the survivors are rescued, for God's sake!''

They got out then, walking toward the glut of firemen and other emergency personnel standing restlessly around the wreck, many of them holding fire extinguishers—a fire-fighting-foam truck mere feet away, its nozzle manned and ready to shoot fire suppressant onto the wreck—and the survivors—at the first hint of a spark.

A tired and dirty chief, whom Joe estimated to be six foot four, stood with a walkie-talkie, exuding authority but saying nothing before they approached. Joe introduced himself, and the chief explained the frustrating difficulty of having to use great care to pull away the heavier structural pieces, cutting others, all with a hydraulic tool called the Jaws of Life, which was designed to work in such conditions, its gasoline generator placed a safe distance from the flammable wreckage.

''You can't use torches or saws, right?''

''You've got it. We light a cutting torch or create sparks with a saw, we'll lose all of them in there. We have to be damn careful using Jaws, too, foaming the area we're working in.''

''How are they doing in there?''

The big man looked at Joe, a look of great sadness and empathy. "God, it's been hard. There are six of them. One was dead by the time they were discovered. At least he's not moving, but we haven't been able to get a stethoscope in yet. The one who kept yelling and finally got herself heard is a young college girl, I think in her twenties, who's got a . . . a . . . metal rod literally through her leg, impaling her. She's unbelievable. She's been guiding us in calmly. One of the doctors managed to get several hypos of morphine in, and she's worked on her seatmates, a seven-year-old boy and his four-year-old sister, who're both in bad shape. We may lose them."

"How about the others?" Susan asked.

"A husband and wife. She's unconscious; he's been hysterical and in pain, trying to get to his kids, and afraid he's going to lose his wife. He's not cooperating at all. The two little kids are his. We think his wife may be close to death, but until a doctor gets in there, we can't tell."

Joe turned away and nearly fell over a tall man in a business suit who had appeared unannounced behind them. The fellow extended his hand, identifying himself as an FBI agent assigned to investigate the accident.

"Where do you want to talk, Agent . . . was it Jamison?"

"Yes sir. Chet Jamison. I'll ride back with you."

The startlingly loud report of brittle metal reaching the breaking point filled the air suddenly, and all eyes whirled back toward the wreckage in apprehension.

Deep within the aerospace prison which held her, Linda Ellis heard the noise as a distant sound which forced her mind back toward reality as she opened her eyes and stared at the gray daylight filtering in, a bit more of it now, she thought, than before. The morphine had made her head feel fuzzy as it dulled the pain, and she had to struggle to think as she watched the outlines of worried rescuers laboring behind the jungle of metal, so close yet still out of reach. There had been a noise . . . one of them was saying something, and she strained to pay attention.

"Hang in there, Linda. We've got another major piece out of the way. We'll be able to get a doctor in there in a few minutes."

Linda looked to her left at the contorted face of the little girl in the middle seat. Linda had been in an aisle seat, the little girl . . . what was her name? Jill. That was it. Jill was four, and her brother was seven. Jill had been in the middle seat. Their parents were across the aisle . . . somewhere. Too much debris separated them. Linda had tried to reach the father, who kept yelling. She had tried to give him the hypodermic needle with the painkiller, but she couldn't get her arm through.

Jill was unconscious again. With a start Linda felt for her wrist and found a pulse. The brother—she had forgotten his name again—was holding his sister's shoulder and crying softly. Jill closed her eyes and repeated the same phrase she had clung to for so long. "I will survive this. We will survive this. We *will* survive this!"

It was so cold. So very cold. The men trying to reach them had a machine blowing warm air into the area, but it wasn't enough. She had tried to think of fires and fireplaces, imagine herself in front of the family fireplace in Austin or on a sunny beach, but it didn't work. She was freezing, and Jill's father kept yelling that they were all going to die of hypothermia.

At least she had found the milk. Her eyes had hurt so badly from the fuel that covered her, but part of the wreckage holding her prisoner was from the plane's galley, and there had been an unopened milk carton by her side. She had poured it in her eyes—rubbed the milk in her eyes—and they felt much better. God had sent her the milk. That meant she was supposed to survive. She had to survive. It was her duty. The milk carton proved it.

"How much longer?" She heard Jill's father yell the question, and the same answer as before came back from the faceless forms above. "Soon." Always soon. Soon was becoming an eternity. The fuzziness returned and the University of Missouri sophomore felt herself surrendering to it. She would sleep awhile. Soon they would be out, and safe.

5

Saturday morning, October 13

North America 135 was the first Saturday flight in from Dallas, a point not lost on most members of the media, who had positioned themselves to meet it. Passengers with no connection to the crash and grieving family members alike emerged from the jetway unprepared, blinking into the confusing glare of TV lights, a forest of camera lenses recording their varied expressions.

Among the first wave, Bill Deason, a harried-looking man in his thirties, emerged with only a topcoat, read the Gate 10 sign quickly, and turned right, hurrying past several gates before finding the appropriate door he had noted on his hastily copied instructions. He pushed his way inside, past a departing priest, and immediately spotted his brother-in-law sitting alone near a corner in the club room. Mark Weiss heard his name as Bill approached and nodded weakly, both of them standing for a few seconds in awkward silence before Bill hugged Mark, a gesture that at any other time might have been embarrassing to the two men, but in the pain of the moment was merely a background to the tears cascading from both faces.

As the passengers continued to flow into the terminal from the Dallas flight, a North America executive emerged with a contingent of other airline personnel behind, each escorting family members of those lost or injured in the crash. Two buses waited at the curb, exhaust fumes curling around their undercarriages in the moisture-laden air, one bound for the hospital with the relatives of survivors, the other with instructions to proceed to a nearby hotel, where the airline would help make arrangements for such painful tasks as body identification and shipment.

When the other passengers had all emerged, a lone figure stepped out of the jetway, her face a haunted study in panic and grief, her clothes stylish but hastily donned. She wore the telltale signs of tears instead of makeup and carried only a handbag, and to one curious reporter, there was something strange and wrenching about the nervous self-consciousness with which she tried to move across the gate area as anonymously as possible, avoiding both of the buses and heading instead for a taxi stand, where she disappeared quickly into the first cab in line. Mrs. Richard Timson repeated the name of the hospital to the cabby and sank back in the seat, her mind racing—her badly injured pilot husband some 12 miles away. The taxi sped toward the freeway past the airport hotel where at that moment Joe Wallingford was beginning the task of organizing the NTSB's search for the answer to the burning question on everyone's mind: Why?

In the small conference room at the Marriott, Dr. Susan Kelly was fighting hard to concentrate—to keep the awful images of the crash site from controlling her mind and her feelings. The agony of the kids in the wreckage kept pulling her away. She had not seen their faces, of course, but she could feel their agony. This was not what she had imagined accident investigation would be.

She had watched Joe Wallingford with growing admiration as he assembled the staffers and went over a short, concise list of priorities and assignments. Each staff member was to head up one or another of the investigatory groups, but there were immediate things to be done, and areas to emphasize.

"As fast as possible," Joe was saying to one of them, "I want the flight and voice recorders out of the Airbus. We have allegations of sabotage of an airliner with a sophisticated electronic flight-control system, and most of you know there have already been worries that strong electronic signals might interfere with such a control system. The FAA has issued guidelines to keep the Airbus 320 a minimum distance away from powerful microwave transmitters and other such radio sources, so we'll need all the information we can get about that, as well as about the so-called mystery car somebody saw leaving the cargo area."

"God, Joe, is sabotage really a possibility?" Barbara Rawlson, chairman of the systems group, was shaking her head and looking incredulous.

"Who knows, Barb. Let's just make sure we account for the entire flight-control system quickly. Were there any strange devices? Could anyone have tampered with it? That sort of thing."

Joe looked at some notes on a steno pad before continuing. "Now, of course we've also got the horrifying possibility that something went wrong in the side-stick controls or the flight-control computers, and the plane crashed itself."

"Why horrifying, Joe?" Susan asked. It was the first question she had managed, and Joe seemed slightly startled, though pleased.

"Well, the Airbus is very sensitive to this type of problem. They went way out ahead of everyone with this new electronic-control technology in the 320, and they would be horrified themselves if anyone started seriously thinking that with so much redundancy and so many backups, the flight-control system could malfunction. They insist it can't happen, and so far we've no reason to believe otherwise."

"Until now."

"Well, maybe until now. Maybe not," Joe said, looking Susan in the eye long enough so that she found herself averting her gaze, a reaction which puzzled her. He was in his element here, she knew, and she was only learning. Perhaps that was it, but it made her feel insecure and vulnerable, and she had spent her professional life fighting vulnerability.

"Okay," Joe continued, turning back to Barbara, "we have windshear, possible sabotage, possible flight-control malfunction, and as always, possible human error of some sort, which is Andy's bailiwick. Andy, what's the status of the crew?"

Andy Wallace had functioned as Joe's right-hand man many times before, even when he held an equal position to the other staff members on field investigations. Joe could always rely on him. No political backstabbing, and no laziness. Andy was always ahead of the game.

"The captain of the Airbus is named Richard Timson, chief pilot for North America and a staff vice-president. He survived with a bad concussion and some internal injuries, plus a damaged hand. He's in serious condition, but he'll make it. The doctors tell me it will be tomorrow at the earliest before he can talk to us."

"How about the copilot?"

"Fighting for his life. Massive cranial damage."

They covered several other items before Joe tapped the table with his pen and gave them all an exceptionally serious look. "Warning: I expect and demand that each and every one of you, and those people from the airline, FAA, ALPA, Airbus, and so on who are assigned to your groups, go absolutely by the book when around the wreckage. That means gloves at all times, hard hats when appropriate, and absolutely no chances taken. *You* may not mind slicing your hand open, but consider that the piece of metal which bites you may carry blood cells from an accident victim infected with AIDS, or some other disease. I will not tolerate any risk taking. Understood?" Joe looked sequentially at everyone but Susan, each staff member nodding in turn.

"Okay. It's now 9:10 A.M. The main organizational meeting is at 2 P.M., and Susan has agreed that we'll hold a preliminary press briefing at noon in the main ballroom. Keep your phone charged and on, keep me informed, especially about the rescue out there, and let's get moving. We've got a major puzzle to solve, and I guarantee political pressure will be flowing in on this one."

Joe stood up and Susan caught his arm. "Political pressure?"

He smiled at her and nodded. "Through experience I've learned that unless we find a clear-cut reason, all the parties are going to start jockeying for self-protective positions. Airbus will hope for pilot error or windshear, the airline will vote for anything that doesn't reflect on them, and everyone else will be protecting their own turf. It always happens, and it does nothing but interfere with what we're here to do."

"Which is find out what happened."

"Exactly. Not lay the blame."

For her would-be rescuers, noon came rapidly, but for Linda Ellis, time had stretched into an agonizing eternity, a purgatory of sorts, though more light had fallen on them now. Jill's mother was dead. Linda had never seen her, but her husband had at some point checked for his wife's pulse and realized there wasn't one any longer. His anguished shriek was even louder than his previous noisy protests and oaths of frustration. His chest was apparently pinned so firmly that he could move even less than Linda. She felt for him, but she had long since decided that when they got out of this and recovered, she was going to tell him what she thought of his whining behavior through the long hours.

Those thoughts now evaporated as his sobbing touched her deeply; the tragedy that had overtaken his poor family was completely unbearable.

Jill was still alive. God only knew how, Linda thought. Her blood loss must have been stemmed by some sort of clotting or cauterizing action, but logic dictated that she shouldn't have lasted twenty minutes with such severe injuries. Linda had given her another morphine shot, struggling against her own rising agony to turn far enough to reach her little arm. Her brother, Jimmy, was easier—he could hold out his arm for Linda to reach. She had sung to them for a while earlier, until she too drifted off again, a tendency she was trying to fight now that their rescuers had almost broken through. There were several more metal bars in front of her, but already a doctor was wiggling his way toward them, and at long last he was beside her, his face next to her ear as he assessed little Jill's condition, deciding that they would have to do some emergency surgery right there before moving her an inch.

The doctor told Linda they would cut the bar impaling her leg on both ends and pull her out in a crane-mounted sling with the thing still in place, then remove it in the hospital. Her neck hurt too, but she wiggled fingers and toes on command, and the doctor seemed relieved.

"In ten minutes or so, Linda. In ten minutes. It's just about over." She felt herself beginning to believe him. For so many hours they had lied gentle, desperate lies to her, but now maybe she could believe they'd make it. There was open gray sky above them now, and plenty of warm air, and even an intravenous needle in her arm she had barely noticed.

The North America air cargo manager had barely begun to accept the scope of the disaster, which had isolated his cargo ramp overnight. All the taxiways leading to the one operational runway were covered with debris from the shattered North America flights. No airplanes could get in or out, which meant he also had to deal with the continued unwanted presence of a gigantic Air Force cargo plane in front of his building. The morning, in other words, had been doubly bizarre even before the phone rang. Now there was a high-ranking military commander on the other end asking for the commander of the cargo jet outside, as if military aircraft didn't have communication radios. Hugh Billingsly wrote down the telephone number and headed outside. He would have loved to examine a C-5, the free world's largest airplane, but the Air Force people who had materialized the previous evening to load and guard the airplane were in no mood to be giving tours. One of the tired and humorless young air policemen fingered his M-16 and watched Billingsly carefully while his partner delivered the message to the cockpit some four stories above the concrete. No one was being allowed within 100 feet of the giant transport.

Within five minutes a thoroughly fatigued young Air Force major appeared in the doorway, returning with Billingsly to use his telephone. The major stopped dialing suddenly and looked at his host apologetically. "I, uh, wonder if you could step outside the office for a few minutes, sir?"

It was his office, but Billingsly complied, even more puzzled.

"Major Archer here in Kansas City, Colonel." The number had finally answered. No identification of where it was, or what it was, other than somewhere in the Washington, D.C., area. The slip of paper had said "Call Colonel Wallace."

"You're blockaded, they tell me," the colonel said.

"Yes sir. The crash left debris spread over both taxiways and Runway 19 out here. I've been after the airport manager almost hourly over one of the radios to get the runway cleared off so we can taxi by, but he can't move until the NTSB gives the okay, and I'm told they may take days."

"That load must get out of there, Major. It's due in Kwajalein, and it's a security risk as long as it sits at a civilian airport."

"Sir, I *know* that." He had been in touch with his command structure, MAC's 22nd Air Force command post at Travis Air Force Base in California, all night. Wasn't the man aware of that?

"Major, of course I don't want you to endanger your airplane, but we have to get that load out of there in the next few hours."

"Sir, I'll coordinate with my leaders again at Travis, and they can talk to headquarters at Scott, but—"

"Major, we're the DOD customer, and the customer is telling you to get your ass in gear and find a way out of there. There are reasons for forcing this issue that I simply cannot go into over a nonsecure line. Do it safely, but do it. Is that clear?''

"Would the Colonel please tell me how?''

"Dammit, you're in command there. Use your head, use creativity, diplomacy, affrontery; beg, demand, or cajole, whatever it takes. Just get airborne.'' The colonel chuckled sarcastically. "Hell, throw your weight around. You've got 750,000 pounds of it.''

"Yes *sir*, Colonel, sir. And how high would you like me to jump?'' The reply was a bone-weary attempt at sarcasm in answer to the colonel's weak attempt at humor.

"All the way to Kwajalein.''

The colonel ended the call, and Major Archer stood there shaking his head in disbelief. How the hell was one lowly Air Force pilot going to force the NTSB and the manager of a major commercial airport to do *his* bidding? And why the hell was it so urgent? If there was a war going on, he wasn't aware of it. Whatever was in the hold of his airplane—whatever the huge, self-propelled vehicle with the oversized rectangular body contained—the contractor's people and the government officials responsible for it obviously wanted it out of Kansas City in a hurry, and with no fanfare. He could see their tactics clearly. If any feathers got ruffled in the process of forcing their will on Kansas City International, it would be the aircraft commander's fault. His fault.

Yet, he had his orders.

Joe watched the media people coalesce into an audience the moment Dr. Kelly mounted the platform at one end of the ballroom, a forest of cameras and microphones arrayed before her. They had talked urgently for ten minutes about what could and could not be said at this point. Joe knew she was nervous and trying not to show it, but she could handle it, he felt sure. That was the most valuable service a Board member could perform in the field: keeping the media focus off the staff.

"Ladies and gentlemen, I'm Dr. Susan Kelly, one of the five Board members of the National Transportation Safety Board, and this is a very brief, preliminary news conference to acquaint you with our procedures and ground rules, and what we will be doing in probing the facts of this tragedy.''

The media ranks had grown by 2 P.M. to nearly eighty, and

it was a bit frightening. Susan worked on controlling the speed of her delivery, the tendency to rush being her lifelong reaction to public speaking.

"First, we are not here to make any quick determination of cause. We will examine wreckage, send some things for analysis, eventually authorize the removal and cleanup of parts now closing the north-south runway, and interview witnesses, but under no circumstances will any of us speculate about what might have happened. As you probably know, it could take upward of a year before we release any formal findings. The National Transportation Safety Board has a congressional mandate to find the probable cause in each air accident, and that is for one purpose: to prevent whatever happened from happening again. We are *not* here to assess blame."

"So what do you have so far? Could this have been sabotage?" The voice came from a balding print reporter in the forward row.

"Well, all we have are the same basics that *you* have. We just got here a few hours ago. We will be investigating engines, structures, systems, operations, air traffic control, weather, human factors, maintenance and records, and any other aspect deemed important. These are the principal group divisions."

A hand shot up in the middle of the throng, and Susan pointed to the man.

"Dr. Kelly, you mentioned air traffic control—is it possible this was a controller error?"

Susan looked at the crowded room, working to suppress butterflies. One false step—one false statement—and she would make herself look idiotic in the eyes of the professional staff. She was aware of Joe Wallingford hovering off to one side. He was Mr. NTSB among the staff, but she was the new kid in the executive suite, and winging it, despite all the preparation.

"At this stage of an investigation, you rule nothing in and you rule nothing out. Anything is within the realm of possibility. In every investigation, one of the groups is labeled the air-traffic-control group. That's a standard practice, regardless of the facts of the crash. They will be looking into these areas as a matter of routine."

"But," the man continued, "is controller error a possibility?"

Susan tried to effect a smile, but it wasn't coming out quite right. "We just don't know, and we can't characterize *any* potential causal factor as either possible or not possible in the first few days. What we have here are two airliners in pieces on the ground, and a lot of people dead and injured. We're here to find out why. Right now, we don't know why. That answer your question?"

Another hand went up and a female journalist got to her feet, asking whether the electronic flight controls could have been at fault, the very question neither Airbus nor Susan really wanted to hear just yet. Susan deflected the question—awkwardly, she thought—but more followed, asking for the very speculation and conclusions she had told them she could not provide.

Questions about the possibility of sabotage, an assassination plot against Larry Wilkins, continued. The FBI would have to help them with that, she told them. Next question.

Susan finally reached the point she had promised herself she would not reach, letting her voice catch on too many "uhs," flashing the signal of uncertainty at the throng of reporters, an act roughly equivalent to bleeding in shark-infested waters.

Joe Wallingford had felt her rising distress. He knew she was foundering; they had both underestimated the media's interest in the assassination reports about Congressman Wilkins. He should stay on the sidelines. She was the Board member; he was only staff. Staff should be seen and not heard. Yet he found himself striding quickly to the microphone without considering the action, moving in front of a startled Susan Kelly and addressing the group.

"I'm Joseph Wallingford, the investigator-in-charge of the NTSB field investigation into this crash, and I'd like to point out something to you. We've only been here a few hours. At this very preliminary stage, I can tell you categorically that there is no evidence whatsoever of any sabotage, and it's ridiculous to keep pursuing the question at this time." He paused again, raising his right index finger to indicate more was coming, his deep voice ringing through the room. "And, as you've heard Dr. Kelly say, at this stage you rule nothing in and nothing out. It is fruitless and perhaps embarrassingly incorrect for anyone to go off chasing the idea of sabotage until we have hard facts."

Joe turned to Susan and leaned close to her ear. "Might be a good time to end this." He blinded himself to the flint-hard look she was directing back at him and turned to resume his position at the side of the room.

Susan Kelly raised her hand for silence, and slowly the audience responded, cameras and tape recorders still rolling. "We're going to end the conference at this point, because, frankly, we don't have enough factual information to say anything more. Please utilize the services of our public-information people, and I'll make myself available to talk with you later today and tomorrow when duties permit."

There was instant movement as the news people rose from the chairs and advanced on Susan Kelly, each of them eager to ask more unanswerable questions. Joe took the opportunity to slip out, confident she could handle things at that point, and was startled when the sound of a ballroom door being slammed open was followed by a sharp command from a female throat not twenty yards behind him.

"Joe!"

He turned, facing an angry scowl of destabilizing intensity as she advanced on him, head down, jaw set, her stride measurable in meters as she pointed to the small conference room they had been briefed in several hours ago. "Inside. Now!"

Joe sheepishly followed her finger through the door as she held it open and turned back to her with the clear and present intent to apologize—a chance she was not going to give him.

"What the hell did you think you were doing in there, *Mister* Wallingford?"

"I . . ."

"Common sense alone would tell you, I would think, that under no circumstances short of nuclear war do you have the right to shove a Board member aside and take over a . . . a . . . meeting, hearing, press conference, or anything else! You made me look like an idiot in there, and I do *not* appreciate it!"

"Susan, I . . ."

"Shut up. Listen to me. I'm as entitled to sweat up there without assistance as any other Board member, male or female."

Joe found his head swimming in complete shock, his mind racing over various options for reply, his instincts for counterattack and defense swallowed by his recognition of her authority so surprisingly expressed, as well as what he had to admit was his attraction to her, and admiration for her. Good Lord, was she a fighter. And without having time to form the ideas as actual words in his mind, he knew she was right. It had been the damsel-in-distress syndrome. He had ridden to her rescue when she didn't want rescue.

"Su . . . ah . . . Doctor, I am most sincerely sorry. I acted on instinct. I didn't mean to undermine you."

"But you sure as hell did."

"I . . . ah . . ."

She had turned away from Joe for a few seconds, walking toward the conference table, leaving him standing by the door, making apologetic, explanatory gestures to her back. She whirled back on him suddenly. "Look, I respect your position, Joe. I expect you to respect mine. I have not succeeded in life by permitting people to rescue me before I've called for help. If I want help, you'll hear the distress call loud and clear, and it won't be in a whining tone of voice."

"Honestly, I'm very sorry."

"Well, you may have created more problems than just that. You told me earlier how politically charged things were, and you just as good as told the media we weren't going to take sabotage seriously. I do know the political world, Joe, even if I am new to the Board. That could cause severe trouble."

"Really?"

"I'm afraid so."

At ten minutes before one, Linda Ellis felt herself begin to move vertically as the sling carefully placed around her was winched up a few inches, her body tightly lashed to the apparatus, her skewered right leg on a splint with the cut ends of the metal rod protruding from the bloodstained wrappings the doctor had fashioned to get her through the ordeal and to the hospital.

Slowly, painfully—every lurch of the cable sending sharp stabbing pains through her—the crane pulled her up.

The air felt good despite the cold, the sky a welcome sight despite the heavy clouds and drizzle. The sound of men shouting orders at each other in a blend of voices formed a background to the sounds of shifting metal debris as rods were bent out of her way, and sheet metal was sent clanging to one side or another, clearing the way to extricate her.

There was applause and cheering again, just as when Jill had been pulled free minutes before.

Suddenly she was on the ground, being transferred to a stretcher, a voice in her ear. "Your parents are on the way, Linda. They've flown in from Texas. We're taking them to the hospital to meet you there."

She had insisted they take Jill first, and they had done so, the doctor joined by a second surgeon, both of them engulfing the little girl in a cocoon of dressings, strapping her to a body board before bringing her out. Linda had wanted the little boy to be taken out then, but they convinced her to go next. They needed her out to get him out, or so they said. She didn't much believe it, but she was too weak to protest any further. Now she saw an ambulance tearing away with lights and siren going, carrying Jill. God go with her, she thought. Even if she lives . . .

Jill's seven-year-old brother Jimmy was pulled out last, emerging into the same glorious daylight Linda had already experienced. He was placed in another ambulance. From where she lay, Linda could still see the wreckage which had held her prisoner for so long, and it started the searing pain all over again. God! How could she have lived through *that*? How could *anyone* have lived through that?

She reached up weakly and grabbed the paramedic's sleeve as the ambulance doors were closed. "How is Jill?"

"Don't know, Linda. You just lie back and relax."

"How is she? Will she make it?"

The man smiled at her, but through her own hazy vision she could see a tear in his eye as he looked at what she couldn't see—the splotchy, red, burned skin that had been her face before the kerosene from the disintegrating 737 wing tanks had splashed like a wave over the open cabin so many hours ago.

'I'm sure she'll make it, Linda. She's safe now, just like you."

Linda Ellis could recognize another well-intentioned lie when she heard one, but she held on to it for all it was worth as sleep overtook her once more.

As the ambulance raced from the taxiway, the rescue team began a final assault on the broken fuselage in an effort to extricate the last survivor. The father of the two mauled children Linda had tried to protect was approaching the end of his endurance.

"My kids. Please tell me. How are they?"

The voice was mere inches from him now. "They're alive, Mr. Manning. They're on their way to the hospital now."

"They wouldn't answer me a while ago."

"We had them heavily medicated. Now, be still, sir. We've got to get this last piece pulled back."

"My wife . . . my wife is gone. She . . ."

"I know, sir. I'm sorry. But let's get you out first."

"You won't leave her?"

"Of course not. But you first. She'd want it that way."

"You don't know what she'd want."

"Maybe not, but you can't help your kids if you don't make it."

For the past thirty minutes Jeff Burnsall had battled the last few pieces of structure holding Jason Manning in his seat. As a paramedic it wasn't his job, but he had insisted on doing the work. The weary fire rescue team had let him continue, since he had some experience in accident rescue procedures, and he was medically attending the victim while he worked to free him. But the last piece of greenish aircraft debris didn't want to budge. He thought he could move it with his hands, but it wouldn't move, and he was getting angry.

Burnsall was lying on his stomach on a thick tarp, which in turn was barely supported by the mass of sharp metal lattice-work. He had just enough leverage to get an IV into Manning's arm while he worked, administering the painkillers the man had needed for fifteen hours.

"Goddammit!"

"What?" Manning's voice was instantly alarmed, and Burnsall was ashamed of himself for crying out. "Nothing. Just a little frustrated here. Hang in there Mr. Manning."

The smell of jet fuel was still heavy in his nostrils. Obviously, the foam had not washed it all away, and just as obviously, Manning's clothes and hair were still soaked. Burnsall knew he would have to be very careful, as he had been warned. The nozzle of the foam truck still hovered mere feet away, but the firemen at the controls had long since decided the threat of fire was significantly diminished. Burnsall finally snuggled his body into a brace position, feeling his support to make sure it would hold, wrapping both gloved hands around the brittle aluminum-alloy rib. If he could pull it back about 12 inches, he could hook it over another protruding member, then get in there and attach the sling to Manning, pulling him directly upward. They could position the hydraulic jaws to do the task, but it would take another hour to get it in position safely. This would be much faster, and his patient needed out of there.

"Now, be absolutely still, sir. Do not move a muscle."

Slowly he applied pressure, feeling the rib give a few millimeters. Bit by bit he increased the pressure, the metal bending farther at his command, coming toward him, the feel of the toes of his boots locking into the shards of metal behind him, absorbing some of the pressure he was using on the rib. The arrangement felt secure, so he kept increasing the pull. Three inches of displacement, 4, then 6, and it seemed to be coming almost smoothly. He still had strength in reserve, plenty of it, but he would need every ounce. The rib would have to come back 6 more inches before he could hook the end of it.

"That's better." Manning was feeling less pressure in his chest with the rib back, but he mustn't move. Burnsall saw the look on the agonized man's face and knew he was beginning to drift with the Demerol in his system. If he kicked . . .

Burnsall reluctantly relaxed his pull, letting the rib slowly return to its previous position, pressing against the metal panel which imprisoned Manning. He let go and closed his eyes, breathing hard, gathering strength for a second. "Mr. Manning, can you hear me?"

"Yeah. Hurry up. It's pressing on me again. Please! I hurt so bad! Please!"

"Hang on, sir. I had to pause a minute. Now, you must promise me not to move, not to talk. Can you do that?"

"What?"

"Can you be absolutely still for me?"

"Yeah. Just hurry. I don't know how much more of this I can take."

Manning was not reliable, but the man was hurting. If Burnsall somehow dislodged his grip, if he let go of that rib, it could slam into Manning's chest and do more damage. Perhaps he should back out of there and let the rescuers take over. The sight of the man's wild-eyed look, though, told him he had to try again.

"How's it going, Jeff?"

The voice behind him was from one of the fire rescue team.

"I'm okay. I've got to move one piece, then I can get the sling in."

Burnsall took a deep breath and grabbed the rib again, straining evenly as he displaced it through 4 inches, then 6, 8, and 10 inches, keeping his grip firm and even, watching the target piece he must hook it to, getting the rib within a few inches. Just . . . a . . . little bit . . . more . . . and . . .

"No! I'm . . ." Jason Manning's voice cut through the tangled space between them, startling Jeff. Manning's sudden attempt to shift his position began with a lurch of his upper body, which moved the debris supporting Burnsall, dislodging his foothold, throwing him to the right. He tried to hang on to the rib in the millisecond of movement, but the distraction was too much, and like a slow-motion sequence the rib slipped from his fingers and slammed back toward Manning, impacting the sheet metal separating Manning from the rib, knocking the breath out of him and sending the one thing they had all feared the most— a shower of tiny sparks—right at the man.

"Fire! Goddammit, fire! Foam. Get the foam in!"

Manning exploded in flames almost instantly, a cry of surprise coming from his throat simultaneously with the impact of the snapping rib and the ignition of the kerosene-soaked clothes and seat.

Burnsall felt himself tumbling off to the side into an unsecured area of sharp metallic debris as he turned to scream at the firemen at the controls of the foam nozzle. It took only seconds, but the firemen had relaxed their vigil, and he heard someone clambering to the controls as voices echoed the yell of fire, the flames now radiating heat at his head and back as he tumbled down uncontrollably, something sharp piercing his back, searing pain accompanying the sensation, his breath coming hard all of a sudden as the sound of a hand-held fire extinguisher being directed helplessly from too far away met his ears along with the screams of Jason Manning, now fully engulfed in flames and literally about to burn to death. Burnsall tried to look up and back, but a wall of flame blocked his view, flame which found more puddles of kerosene beneath where he had fallen, fuel which now began to engulf him as he lost consciousness.

The stream of fire-suppressant foam shot from the end of the nozzle after what seemed like an eternity to the firemen who had heard Burnsall's first call, then seen the flicker of flames. They had foamed the structure repeatedly through the morning, yet within seconds Jason Manning had been horribly burned, and his would-be rescuer lay impaled on a shard of aluminum, also seared with third-degree burns. Two of the firemen jumped into the tangled rubble within seconds of quashing the fire, one grabbing for Burnsall and pulling him up before realizing the extent of his wounds. With help from the crane, they had him lifted free and onto the pavement in minutes, another paramedic tending to his injuries: a collapsed right lung and internal bleeding.

Manning, however, was just as trapped as before. A chain was thrown around the offending rib and attached to the jaws mechanism with great haste, the possibility of creating sparks now a distant concern after what had happened. Once attached, the chain pulled the metal permanently back with an ease that Burnsall couldn't have managed.

Finally they had Manning exposed, and two men struggled to get the sling beneath him, the odor of burned flesh sickeningly pungent in their faces. He was still breathing but blackened and unconscious as they lifted him quickly, swinging him over to a stretcher by the ambulance, where a doctor immediately searched for a heartbeat and heard the faint sounds of a heart entering coronary arrest.

For fifteen minutes they labored, using every means available to keep him alive, but at last the bone-weary doctor looked up and shook his head. It had been just too much.

At 5 P.M. Joe pushed open the door to his room and flung his topcoat on the bed. The organizational meeting had gone on longer than he had wanted, several of the parties wrangling over who should be assigned to what group. He needed sleep, but that would have to wait a few more hours.

Joe flipped on the TV as he ran mentally through the events of the previous hours, searching for anything he'd missed. He knew Airbus would be in complete turmoil, hoping and praying the crash hadn't been caused by any basic design defect in their sophisticated electronic fly-by-wire control system, but if sabotage was a possibility, that too could involve the flight controls.

The item that had him almost scared, however, was the initial search in the Airbus tail section for the black boxes. The flight recorder had been exactly where they expected, but the cockpit voice recorder—the CVR—was nowhere to be found, and even its mounting bracket was missing. They needed that CVR as soon as possible. The solution to the accident could be on that tape. The flight recorder readout would tell them volumes about what the aircraft did, but only a live crew member and the CVR could tell what the pilots did. Barbara Rawlson's group was stepping up its search. Joe wanted to get the cockpit voice recorder on the way to the NTSB lab in Washington on a late-evening flight, if possible.

Connie Chung's face was on the screen now with the CBS Saturday Evening News, and Joe turned up the volume as the scene shifted to a CBS correspondent at the hammerhead of Runway 19 at Kansas City Airport, reporting the latest on the crash and the rescue efforts, which had come to such a tragic end for the father of the little children pulled from the wreckage. Most of the story was on the rescue and the fire. The injured paramedic was in critical condition, as was the little four-year-old. The sabotage story was repeated then, along with a diagram of how the flight-control system worked, and how, presumably, it could be sabotaged.

And without warning, Joe's own face appeared on the screen, a shot from the briefing a few hours ago. Joe, not Susan. The correspondent was talking over the picture, saying that the NTSB was refusing to acknowledge the possibility that the congressman had been assassinated.

". . . I can tell you categorically that there is no evidence whatsoever of any sabotage, and it's ridiculous to keep pursuing the question," Joe heard himself say as he stared at the screen, dumbstruck. The clip had been the sum total of the news conference used, and Joe had just told the world, apparently, that there was no possibility of sabotage. At least, that's how it would appear. Susan was right. This would be a problem.

Within fifteen minutes the phone rang, and the voice of the NTSB's chairman, Dean Farris, was instantly recognizable. Undoubtedly he had seen the newscast.

"Joe, you there?"

"Yes, sir."

"Joe, what the hell are you doing to me out there?"

"I'm trying to conduct an investigation. What do you mean?"

"You see the news?"

"Yes."

"Well, congratulations old dad, you made NBC, ABC, CBS,

and several other newscasts with the same statement, and your face hadn't been off the screen thirty seconds before my phone began to melt down.''

"Look, they took the middle of a statement. What I said . . .''

"Oh, come on, Joe, you've been at this game long enough to expect that. You know they'll take it if you give it to them, and you apparently paused in all the right places.''

"I'm very sorry, but it certainly is not a major problem.''

"Oh no? Hey, I'm the one on the political hot seat, okay? Let me tell you, within ten minutes I had several calls from friends on the Hill who were very concerned that this might really be a political assassination and you might be refusing to consider that possibility.''

"That's ridiculous! All I said was . . .''

"Joe, I *know* what you said, I heard it. The point is, this wild man from Louisiana has a lot of faithful followers and they scare people up on the Hill, and frankly they scare me. Has the FBI shown up?''

"This morning. Of course. An agent was here before we arrived. By the way, I need to talk to you about Caldwell and the FAA airplanes we didn't get to use.''

"Later. What did you tell the FBI?''

"What do you mean, what did I tell them? We compared notes on what we had, which isn't much just out of the starting blocks. They'll stick with us every inch of the way, just as they always do. What are you getting at?''

"Well, it looked on television like you might have told them to go home.''

"You know I wouldn't and couldn't do that. They can do as they please.''

"You should have told the TV cameras the FBI was hard at work on it. Matter of fact, you shouldn't have been on camera at all. Where the hell is Susan Kelly?''

Joe decided to ignore that question and hope it would not be repeated. He did not want Farris knowing he had upstaged and angered Susan.

"Good Lord, Mr. Chairman, all we've got so far is someone making anonymous phone calls with unsubstantiated allegations.''

"Yeah, and an upset Congress, and an upset electorate, and

an upset press. We'll probably be tarred and feathered by every radio evangelist in the country by tomorrow morning. Look, I know *we* tend to look at Wilkins as a racist and white supremacist, but Joe, the man was an elected congressman with a massive constituency which runs far beyond his district. He was powerful, and any hint of an assassination must be taken with stoic seriousness. I don't want to interfere with your investigative prerogatives, Joe, but I can't allow you to get this Board in trouble, however accidentally. You understand me?"

"Yes . . . yes I understand."

"Get this problem fixed, for Christ's sake."

"Okay. First thing in the morning. We'll hold another briefing and trot out the FBI."

"What are you going to tell them?"

Joe hesitated, several ill-advised remarks fluttering across his mind. Susan had been right. Joe's mistake had mushroomed, and he had said too much already. However much he detested this pompous politician, the man was still the boss.

"The truth."

There was a snort from the other end, followed by a dial tone. Joe sat holding the receiver for a few seconds, wondering if it really could have been sabotage. That mystery car, for instance. Was that connected? It seemed very farfetched, but with Farris upset, he'd have to pay it lip service.

"Goddammit!" He slammed the receiver back down. "Here we go again. More political games!"

Yet how abysmally powerless he was to change anything—clearly outmatched and outgunned by Farris. As infuriating, as upsetting as it was, he had to face the reality of the matter: if he wanted to play in Dean Farris's game, he had to play by Dean Farris's rules.

The phone rang again immediately, and Joe ripped it out of the cradle, fully expecting Farris with a postscript. Instead it was Barbara Rawlson.

"Something weird, Joe. That Air Force C-5 trapped at the north end?"

"Yeah?"

"I guess he didn't like our wreckage on Runway one-nine, so he moved it."

"What?" That made no sense, and Joe's tone was impatient.

"About an hour ago. A swarm of Air Force security people

suddenly drove out on Runway one-nine and shoved most of the wreckage to one side; the C-5 taxied by and immediately took off on the other runway. The airport manager finally got around to telling us. He said they didn't even ask him.''

"They can't move that wreckage!"

"I know, but they did, Joe. No apologies, no explanations, and no warning. They even threatened one of the airport cops who tried to stop them. I guess he wasn't going to argue with automatic rifles.''

"Jesus.''

"No harm done, though. We already had the wreckage photographed and located. There wasn't much on the runway, as you know.''

"That's not the point.''

"I know, but at least they didn't monkey with the main wreckage.''

Joe shook his head.

"There is some good news, though," Barbara continued.

"Oh?''

"Yeah. Your bag is on the way up. Our luggage just returned from its unaccompanied holiday in San Francisco.''

6

Saturday, October 13, Salina, Kansas, 5:02 P.M. CST

Kell Martinson was the only one on the planet who knew that Cynthia Elizabeth Collins was dead, and that fact was tearing him up. He had wasted most of Saturday afternoon pacing the floor and wondering what to do when Fred Sneadman called. His young legislative assistant had been working late on what was supposed to be a quiet Saturday afternoon.

"Senator? I'm sorry to bother you at the farm, but the phone hasn't stopped ringing with media calls about Congressman Wilkins, and I can't locate Cynthia Collins."

"The plane crash, you mean?"

"Yes sir. The media is determined to get your reaction. You know, because of your opposition to Wilkins."

"I have no public reaction. Why are they calling me?"

"I think, Senator, that you're pretty well considered Wilkins's number-one detractor inside the Beltway."

"That's bullshit, Fred. The man was an insult to the process and I've said that, but I wasn't out to get him."

"They seem to think so, sir."

"Look . . ." Kell realized his right hand was in the air in a frustrated gesture Fred Sneadman couldn't see. "I'm not interested in dealing with that right now. You say you can't find Cynthia?" Cindy's trips to meet him in Kansas City were always clandestine, so no one in Washington would suspect that she had been on that airliner. Cindy's parents lived in St. Joseph, Missouri, a sleepy, historic town northwest of Kansas City. She had grown up there, so a trip back to St. Joseph had always been the backup excuse she was to use if her flights to meet Kell in Kansas City were ever discovered. Now her folks would have to be told the tragic news, but by whom? He wasn't even sure she had booked the flight under her own name, and there were no passenger lists out as yet. How could he alert Fred innocently?

"No sir. I've tried all afternoon."

"She might have left town for the weekend, Fred. Try her once more, and if you get her on the line, tell her to call me out here immediately. And call me back if you can't locate her."

He replaced the receiver, knowing Sneadman would call within a few minutes to report Cindy still wasn't there. He would mention her parents in St. Jo, then, and the possibility she had flown out to see them.

"Damn!" He sat down hard in the wingback chair in the living room, feeling numb. Cindy had meant far more to him than he had ever really admitted to himself, and now a deep hollowness filled him, as if all the bright promises and dreams that had seemed to be just ahead of him had suddenly been ripped away. Loving her had always been heavenly: the sex, the companionship, and even the feeling of playing out some fantasy role, as though they were clandestine operatives skulking around, beating the system, using code words and phrases, making certain they didn't compromise his political future. He was, after all, a married man. That would come to an end quite soon, but in the meantime, there were vast numbers of loyal voters and political enemies alike in the state of Kansas who would never understand or forgive—not even if they knew the agony he had gone through losing his wife to his career.

Julie had hated political life from the first, and moving to Washington had quickly eclipsed their earlier, happier years when he was a young lawyer in Wichita. She hated the constant public attention, but she claimed it was his priorities that had frozen her out, forcing her into an also-ran position when it came to his time and attention. What Julie and he had felt for each other had died with the second term, and the idea of a quiet divorce became a welcome coup de grace for an empty shell of a marriage. Finding Cindy had helped fill the void, not create it.

With surprise he realized he had a great urge to call Julie. The automatic need to have her hold him and help soothe the pain, as she used to do when the path became rough, was nothing but a learned response—a ghost of a memory of happier times. Yet

Kell was acutely aware of how urgently he needed that sympathy.

"My God, Martinson, you're an idiot." He shook his head in disbelief, sitting back in the chair a little deeper as if to guard against moving toward the phone. "That's right, boy," he said, and snorted, "call your estranged wife for sympathy because you've lost your girlfriend. She'll be touched."

Kell realized he was listening for the phone to ring. Sneadman had the number, and enough time had passed. Why hadn't he called? The waiting was intolerable. He realized he needed someone to grieve with him.

Kell had been ignoring the flashing message light on the phone answering machine since he'd arrived early that morning. It was always blinking when he came home. Absently he pressed the message replay button as he walked past, getting several feet away before the beautiful voice filled the downstairs of the house, the words merely incomprehensible music at first, and a music that filled him with great sadness.

It was Cindy's voice.

He covered the distance to the answering machine before her message had finished. Her voice had startled him, and he couldn't think of a single reason why she would have called the farm on Friday when she knew he would be in Wichita, and then on the road to pick her up in Kansas City. He fumbled for the right control, rewinding the tape and pushing the play button once more, listening intently for the words as her voice began again, quiet and subdued, devoid of her usual flair or enthusiasm.

"Hello there. I know you've just walked in from what was probably an angry trip back from Wichita, and I imagine you've spent the last few hours on the road quite upset over my message about the Kansas City situation, so I figured I'd better explain a bit more. I'm sorry I had to do it that way, leave it on your cellular voice mailbox rather than call you directly, but I guess I didn't want to be second-guessed or talked out of it. I just think things are too complicated with that issue to discuss it over the phone with you. It's confusing me, and I think what this assistant of yours needs is a little time. Therefore, I would appreciate it if you wouldn't do what I know you're thinking of doing—calling me at home the instant you get to the farm. I know you, Senator. Let's please give me enough time to get this issue in hand, and we can discuss it on Tuesday when you get back. Please, I'm just not prepared . . . with this brief, I mean. . . ."

What message? What brief? What on earth had she been talking about?

The answering machine sat with the telephone on a delicate mahogany campaign desk by the stairway. Kell steadied it now against the vibration of the rewinding message tape as he watched the strobe lights of a distant airplane blink across the night sky through the picture windows in the dining room. Focusing his thoughts was suddenly a task. A new possibility had begun fluttering around the edge of his consciousness, but he repressed it. Yet, why had she called Friday to say they would discuss things on Tuesday when they would be together that very evening in Kansas City? The message had to have been left Friday afternoon. And why would she call here to Salina? Their weekend hideaway was to have been in northern Missouri. She knew damn well he wasn't heading for Salina, unless this was some sort of contingency plan or smoke screen. And where was the message she was talking about? The questions cascaded in his mind, but the answers were not following.

There was a rueful irony in her leaving a mystery as a last act in her life. Or perhaps she had left the message to tease him—intending that he find it after their weekend together. That must be it. His cellular telephone number in Wichita had electronic voice mail, which worked like an answering machine. He had listened to his messages before leaving Wichita Friday afternoon, and there was nothing there.

Or was there?

Kell lifted the phone receiver, punching in his cellular phone number in Wichita. Suddenly the memory wouldn't come. Had he, in fact, listened to his messages on Friday? Getting away from the last political function, another rubber chicken dinner meeting in downtown Wichita Friday evening, had amounted to an escape. The people there were supporters as well as constituents, so he'd had to be gracious and feign interest, but all he could think about during the dinner, the rambling introduction, and his own speech, was Cindy and the coming weekend. He had left immediately afterward, heading his car toward Kansas City with just enough time to reach the airport before her flight arrived. Could he have forgotten to check?

On the other end of the line, he heard his own voice begin a familiar litany about being out of range and leaving a message, but he interrupted it summarily with a series of keystrokes, waiting then, impatiently, for the computer to cycle through several mundane calls. With the grandfather clock in the hallway loudly chiming 8 P.M., he had to strain to listen, jamming the receiver tighter against his ear. There were six messages, four of them left Friday during the day. One by one he listened to each recording, but it was the fourth message that contained her voice, and he stiffened with anticipation as it began.

"Senator, this is Cynthia. About the Kansas City project, the one involving North America. I'm sorry to just leave you a message, but I won't be available to discuss the project this evening. I'm going to cancel the planned conference. I'd rather not discuss the reasons over the phone, but I'll be available to meet with you on this subject next Tuesday. I just need some time to . . . work on this. I'm leaving the office now, and I'm, uh, sorry to change plans like this."

Kell stood transfixed for a second before replacing the receiver. She had canceled Kansas City. She had canceled their weekend. That meant . . .

The ringing of the phone startled him, almost as much as the speed with which he grabbed the receiver. He was overreacting.

"Hello?"

"Senator?" The voice was cool and flat, but instantly recognizable, and the sound of it triggered a flood of thoughts and feelings, emotions and realizations crammed into a split second. She couldn't be alive! He had not dared to hope she might be alive. He had given up. But all his life, it seemed, the prerequisite for success was a final acceptance of failure—the price of gain, the realization of loss.

Kell realized he had been holding his breath.

"Cindy? My God, is that really you?" His left hand climbed to his forehead, as if to quiet the high-speed recalculations of his life raging within. "Lord, I don't believe it!"

"Well, you told Fred I was to call you immediately. So here I am. Who else were you expecting?"

"I . . . I didn't expect . . ." Kell fought to gain control. "Cindy, I just now, just this minute, listened to your message."

There was silence from the other end for what seemed a long time before she began again, not seeming to understand.

"I really don't want us to talk right now." Her voice was

suddenly unsteady, shaky. "I need to sort things out . . . the issues, I mean, regarding the, uh, North America matter."

"Screw the issues and screw our code words. You're alive, and I can't quite believe it. I thought I'd seen you die!"

A thousand miles to the east, Cindy Collins pulled the phone from her ear for a second and looked at it, as if her expression could be seen in Salina. It was a useless gesture for an absent audience, but it was cathartic. His words made no sense. He knew she was at home. The soft decor of her carefully furnished living room had been her refuge since she had stumbled into her small apartment near Dupont Circle on Friday night, consumed with uncertainty over whether she should have canceled their rendezvous in Kansas City. Even after her intended flight had crashed—even after she had realized that most of those aboard had died—she still caught herself feeling guilty. She had ignored the ringing phone most of the day, expecting the press reaction connecting her man with Wilkins but not wanting to deal with it and slightly afraid Kell might call before she was ready to talk. But the incessant ringing finally became too much. At last she had yanked the receiver from the hook to find Fred Snead-man on the other end.

"You mean the crash in Kansas City?" she began. "I know . . . I'm still shaking. If I hadn't canceled on you . . ."

"No, no, I don't mean that," he replied hurriedly. "I mean, yes I *do* mean that it scared me to death, but, Cindy, honey . . . I didn't get your message from my phone in Wichita until just seconds before you called. I didn't know you weren't coming last night." Kell paused and, hearing no sound from her end, continued, his heart pounding, breathing as if he had just run a three-minute mile. "Cindy, I went to Kansas City, to the airport, to meet your flight."

The significance of what he was saying finally grabbed her, and Cindy sat forward on her sofa as if convulsed. He hadn't known. He had driven hundreds of miles to meet her for nothing. While she had sat on her overstuffed couch nursing a bottle of white wine and feeling sorry for herself, he was watching a real-life horror.

"Kell, I had no idea."

"I was sitting there by the runway where I shouldn't have been, sitting there in the car waiting for your plane. I saw it crash, saw it torn apart. I thought I had seen you die. I didn't know you weren't on it, but thank God you weren't.''

''But you always check your messages. You never fail to check.''

''I was too eager to get away from Wichita . . . too eager to get to Kansas City to pick you up. I must have forgotten.''

''You were right there?''

''Yeah. I've been in agony. No one knew you were on—or were supposed to be on—that flight. They haven't released a passenger list. I was the only one who knew. That's why I told Fred to call you. I was hoping someone would find out besides me. Lord, I do not believe this!''

''I'm so sorry, Kell.''

''That's all right! I'm just so grateful to find out you're okay. Yes, I would have been upset had I heard your message. I probably would have called you when I got up here. But . . . well, I'm full of so many conflicting feelings right now. You know? Why didn't you come, but then thank God you didn't. Cindy, we have to talk.''

''I know.''

''No, I mean we have to really talk. Now I have a second chance to tell you everything I was wishing all day I had told you, things I had been putting off. I have a chance to tell you I need you, and I love you, and I don't give a damn who knows it.''

She did not answer for a few seconds, and Kell realized he was holding his breath for a second time, listening for any nuance, looking for any window to her feelings.

''I think I love you too,'' she began, sounding more distant than before, ''but I need to be sure. Things are going too fast. That's why I didn't come.''

''I would have lost you—I thought I had. But I guess that proves there was a purpose in all of this.''

''Maybe. But we *do* need to be careful what we say.''

''Not now.'' He was emphatic. The game had changed. There was no longer a game.

''Yes, Senator, now. I'm not going to let you blow this. You are still attached.''

''Not for long.''

''But as long as you are, we stay underground. Especially until we find out if there really is a 'we.' ''

"Don't . . . please. Don't snatch you away from me again."

There was a small laugh on her end. "That statement is a grammatical disaster."

"I mean it."

"I know you do, but I'm not going anywhere. I just want to be sure, and right now I'm very confused."

"I'm coming back tonight."

"No Kell, don't . . ." She felt the tears on her face, and that surprised her, but the image of him all alone at the farm, pacing around like a caged animal, so powerful yet so helpless, tugged at her.

"No, that's okay," Kell was saying, "I won't see you until you're ready, but I'm in no mood to sit out here in a wheat field until Monday evening."

Cindy smiled, unseen, as she ran her hand through her long, blond hair—a mannerism he loved. She knew how impatient he could be.

"I won't batter down your door. But I may sit outside it looking unbearably lonely if you won't let me in."

"Now wouldn't that be a wonderful image for some future confirmation hearing—'Lovesick senator wastes away outside bimbo's boudoir.' The *Miami Herald* could relate to that. They'd figure you were practicing for a presidential run."

"You're no bimbo, honey."

They had slipped back into normal conversation, he realized, normal bantering, her sharp sense of humor teasing and enticing him. Normal, but not completely so. There was still reserve in her voice.

"No, I'm not a bimbo . . . but I'm not your wife, either, Senator Martinson."

He couldn't quite find a reply for that, just a silent promise to change that fact as fast as the law would allow.

"Will you call me when you're ready?" he asked.

"Not until Tuesday, Kell."

"I love you, Cindy."

She heard his voice break as he said the words, yet she choked on her reply. It was the one phrase she had prayed he'd use someday. Why did it scare her so now?

"I know," she said simply, replacing the receiver as gently as if she were caressing his face, personal and professional worries competing furiously in her mind.

She had tried to defuse the controversy a year ago, but Kell had become firmly entrenched as Wilkins's most outspoken critic on the Hill. Wilkins had publicly slandered a valued friend of Kell's in the House—a former Vietnam POW who happened to be black—questioning his patriotism. Not even Cindy could control Kell's outrage at Wilkins's attack, and though his statements on the floor of the Senate had been eloquent and gentlemanly rebukes, one unguarded comment to the media had been the lead story on the national news and had propelled the Martinson camp into an unnecessary battle. "This man is a racist and an insult to the Congress," Kell had said. "While the voters have the right to send anyone they choose to represent them, the Congress has the right to reject those who are unfit to serve, and Mr. Wilkins is morally unfit for any public office. I'm going to do everything I can to get rid of him."

Suddenly the weekend's TV images of burning airplane wreckage and voice-overs regarding Larry Wilkins's extremist positions merged with Cindy's mental picture of Kell sitting mere yards away from the runway as his perceived archenemy had died in a crash that some reports were already claiming was sabotage. The implications were all too clear. There was a disastrous possibility—however remote—that Kell's Friday night whereabouts might somehow become public knowledge, and there was only one word that seemed to sum it up. Cynthia Elizabeth Collins plunked herself into an armchair and addressed the far wall.

"Shit!"

It was 11 A.M. Sunday morning in Washington, yet the chairman of the National Transportation Safety Board had already logged four hours of pacing around his den, keeping an eye on the television coverage from Kansas City. Now the face of a CBS anchor filled the screen before the scene cut to Kansas City International Airport and a brief interview with the NTSB's Joe Wallingford. Dean Farris stopped his pacing to stand in front of the set, quietly studying his subordinate's performance with suspicion. His wife, looking on from the kitchen, had seen him upset over Wallingford before. "A loose cannon on a rolling deck," Dean had called him.

Wilma Farris put down her coffee cup for a moment and watched her husband, concerned as usual at his preoccupation.

They had been in academic heaven just three years ago, he a full, tenured professor of management at the Stanford Business School, and she a contented homemaker happily raising two kids. She had never begrudged his interest in politics, though he had spent far too much time helping the local Republican party for over a decade. But when the Republican occupying the White House had needed a panel of respected and ideologically trustworthy businessmen and academics for a blue-ribbon panel on deregulation and airline safety, Dean Farris had been in the right place at the right time, and a building political debt of many years was partially repaid with the appointment.

She had seen little of him for the next nine months as he took to the project with immense seriousness. It was ironic that he hated to fly, but his theory of management transcended technical knowledge: a good manager could manage anything, including a blue-ribbon panel, or so he believed. With the final report's release, she had prepared herself for a return to California and normalcy. Instead, the White House had called again, flushed with pride over the fact that Farris and his commission had absolved the administration's free-market-at-any-cost policies of any blame for declines in the airline industry's safety margins under deregulation. This time, they said, the President wanted him to move to Washington to take over as chairman of the NTSB. Dean was thrilled, but Wilma had come to regard their new Reston, Virginia, home as a prison, her friends and family three thousand miles away.

What frightened Wilma Farris the most was the change in her husband, and his sudden lust for greater position someday. They had not discussed it, but she knew he was eyeing a cabinet post in a future administration. And whether her energetic fifty-two-year-old spouse could achieve it or not was never a question in her mind.

"No! Goddamn it, Joe, *no*!" Dean Farris's voice echoed off the televised picture of Joe Wallingford and rang through the house, startling their golden retriever, who jumped up from the kitchen floor to stand, quivering, at attention.

"What is it, Dean?"

He turned around to face her, pointing at the offending screen, his bony, angular features screwed up in disgust, an unkempt forelock of dark hair hanging down to his right eyebrow. With a beard, a frock coat, and a stovepipe hat, he could have played

President Lincoln, she thought. Several reporters had made the observation, and it amused him.

"Last night I specifically told Wallingford to make it clear we were investigating sabotage along with everything else, and this morning he makes the statement I told him to make, but then tells the world one more time—as if they hadn't heard it the first time—that there is absolutely no evidence that would lead anyone to believe there was any sabotage."

The dog was standing in the kitchen doorway now, tail wagging furiously, looking mightily confused as he watched his master for the slightest hint of a command. Dean Farris dropped his arm and walked around the sofa toward Wilma, shaking his head, his deep baritone voice tinged with a reminder of his Oklahoma youth.

"Now you just watch, Willie, that phone will ring again within the hour with someone else on the Hill worried that I may be losing control and letting my people play politics with a crash investigation."

"I don't follow you."

"We have to put on a good show. As long as Wilkins's supporters are riled up, we have *got* to look like we're taking sabotage seriously. Wallingford—damn his hide—makes it sound like we're *not*."

"You think it *was* sabotage?"

"It doesn't matter whether it was or wasn't. We've just got to look like we're kicking over all the rocks at the same time. Wilkins's people are repulsive, but they're a powerful group in the South.

"I think I'd better contact Susan Kelly. I trusted her to babysit Wallingford and she isn't doing the job."

Consciousness had come hard for Dick Timson all weekend. He had barely achieved it at all during Saturday, and then only for short periods. Sunday morning was no exception.

He had a memory of banking an airplane into a final turn for an airport runway somewhere, but there was nothing else—until the walls and ceiling of an operating room had come into focus in the dark hours before dawn after the accident. Then the images had dissolved into a fitful sleep of sorts. That was . . . when?

"What day is it?" The husky-voiced words startled Louise Timson, who had been dozing in a chair next to his bed.

"Dick?"

"What . . . where am I again?" He put a tentative hand to his left temple, which was throbbing. This was a hospital, he remembered that. There had been a crash. There were nightmarish scenes he couldn't identify which had passed for dreams, and he had wobbled in and out of semiconsciousness it seemed for an eternity.

"It . . . it's Sunday morning, Dick. You're in a Kansas City hospital—Truman Medical Center." Her voice seemed tremulous, but he hardly noticed. Eyes squinting, head pounding, he lay back into the pillow and tried to focus, realizing it was his wife's face hovering before him, a distraught look in her eyes.

"My God, Louise, what's happened? I . . . I know there . . . there was a crash. You told me. I don't remember . . ."

"Do you recall anything?"

"No." He lied to her on purpose, wanting desperately to know what she knew first. His memories were unreliable.

Louise Timson wiped her eyes and stroked his forehead, being careful not to disturb the white turban of bandages.

"The doctor says you'll be all right. Your hand was hurt, and you have a skull fracture, but you'll be okay."

That explains the headache, he thought, realizing suddenly that his right hand was sheathed in gauze and hurting too.

"But what happened?"

Louise Timson stopped stroking him, her hand dropping, her gaze averted downward. God, he thought, was it that bad?

"You crashed while trying to land in a storm at Kansas City Friday night, Dick. I don't know why. Your plane hit another plane on the ground." The words left a cold, empty feeling in his middle. Crashed. Hit another plane. How on earth . . . ? Oh Lord, and I was captain . . . chief pilot. How on earth did this happen?

He noticed her delivery, then. Her words were slow and metered, as if painful to pronounce, her eyes fixed on her hands as she held them tightly together in her lap, sitting uncomfortably on the edge of the bed. Dick could see she had been at loose ends for some time. Her hair was a stringy mess, she wore no makeup, and the deep bags under her eyes looked awful. She looked like hell warmed over, he concluded.

"A storm?" he managed.

"I was told it was a windshear storm, or something like that," she said slowly.

He remembered the microburst. But that had been their initial approach, hadn't it? Could he have dreamed a second approach?

"How . . . how many were hurt?"

She swallowed again, nodding and shaking her head alternately. "At least a hundred dead. Terrible injuries. Terrible. A little girl . . ." Her hand gestured to one side as she closed her eyes and shook her head slightly before looking at him again. "Oh Dick . . ." Louise sat quietly for a few seconds and he let her alone, confusion filling his drug-numbed mind.

"Are they sure it was windshear? Louise, do you know for sure?" His voice was low and strained. He could manage no more volume, but he had to know what he had done.

She looked up at him then. "No, I'm not sure."

"Why? Wasn't I captain?" Now *his* voice was tremulous, the enormity of the nightmare he had awakened to beginning to overwhelm him.

Dick saw his wife clenching her teeth, her chin trembling. But he had to know.

"You just weren't . . . at fault. I'm sure." She looked at him again then as a soft knock sounded on the door and a nurse stuck her head inside.

"You're awake! Mr. Timson, do you feel up to a visitor for a few moments? He's insisting, and the doctor said it was okay if you agreed."

Dick looked at her in confusion. The nurse had said "mister" not "captain." Had he already been fired? That would be unbearable, the worst blow of all. He was panicking, though. They wouldn't do such a thing. Stop panicking! He issued the order to himself without moving, staring quietly at the nurse as she stood in the doorway.

"Sir? You want to wait?"

Dick recovered some composure finally and shook his head. "It's okay. Send him in."

Louise had already left the bedside, moving behind him, probably sitting in the corner, he figured, his head hurting too bad to risk looking around to be sure. At first Dick didn't recognize the man in a hospital gown who walked slowly into the room, his sad eyes surveying the room with great distrust, as if he were ready to run at the slightest indication the welcome had been withdrawn. He looked familiar, and from somewhere in Dick's mind the image of the big man and the name Pete Kaminsky, one of his pilots and an old acquaintance, came together.

"Pete?"

"Yes. I came to . . . see how you were doing."

"What are you doing here?" There was no rancor behind the question, just puzzlement, but it struck Pete like a challenge, for which he must have a defense.

"Uh, I'm . . . down the hall. My room." He gestured awkwardly over his left shoulder.

"Were you aboard my airplane?" Dick asked quietly.

"No. Uh, the 737 your flight hit? That was mine."

The two men stared at each other for a few seconds while that sank in. "Oh, Lord. You were in a 737? We hit you?"

Pete nodded, slowly, watching his reaction carefully. "You remember I called you on the radio on your first approach?"

So there *had* been a first approach, Dick thought, his mind trying to come up to speed. He raised up slightly from the pillow, a wave of pain in his head limiting the process, his view of Pete wavering for a second as if a TV picture had been disturbed.

"It's all very hazy, Pete," he began. "Could you . . . tell me what happened? Please. I need to fill in the gaps."

Pete Kaminsky pulled up a small, gray metal chair and sat down a foot away from Dick's bedside, saying nothing for awhile as he thought back over the crash sequence and tried to choose his words carefully. Dick Timson listened in horror, remembering almost everything up to his turn to final approach on the second landing attempt. Somewhere in there the memory was erased . . . gone. It had to be the concussion, but it panicked him.

"Pete, you say we stopped turning and started sinking?"

"Yeah." In a halting voice, Pete Kaminsky filled in the details for Timson, looking up finally at the battered chief pilot. "I killed a lot of people trying to move, Dick. I saved myself, but you hit us in the middle. If I'd stayed put, more of my people . . ." He stopped, unable to continue, and Dick Timson wanted to reach out and assure him, but he knew he couldn't do it physically. Every time he moved, his head swam with unbelievable pain. His stomach was a cold block of ice now, hearing the details. Something had happened as they turned the last few degrees. Was it windshear? Had the controls malfunctioned? Something had pitched them down, and he couldn't remember what it had been . . . what it might have been. That wasn't unusual, was it? Loss of memory with a head injury?

"Pete . . . I . . . I don't know what to say. I'm still very fuzzy on the details. But you can't blame yourself. You did what you thought you had to."

Kaminsky just nodded, but he didn't look up.

"Pete, my copilot. Don Leyhe. Did he . . ."

"He's alive, but in a coma. Bad head injuries. You both must have been slammed around horribly in the cockpit when the plane broke up. He had part of the windscreen embedded in his head." Pete had looked up at last, and Dick was startled to see only a vortex of pain and grief in those eyes, which seemed to be looking right through him.

The two pilots stared at each other in silence for a minute before realizing there was nothing left to say. Pete got up as if lifting a block of lead, fatigue and despair intertwining—an inescapable weight pulling him down.

Dick Timson's eyes were misting with tears. He remembered raging at his son that men don't cry, and he tried to turn away, but the movement hurt too much. His carefully structured life, his executive position, his ability to fly as a pilot, his self-respect—everything, gone in a split second he couldn't even remember. And people had lost their lives in his airplane, as well as in Pete's. Why? Not even the NTSB needed to know what had happened as much as Richard Timson needed to know.

Barbara Rawlson's worried expression mirrored Joe Wallingford's as the two of them stood in the Sunday morning sunlight and tried to imagine what could have become of the cockpit voice recorder for Flight 255.

"Joe, we've looked everywhere in and around the tail section. I can't understand it. Is there any chance, do you suppose, someone could have removed it before we got here?"

"Not possible, Barbara." Joe was shaking his head. "Show me where it was mounted," he said, pulling on heavy gloves, a hard hat with the NTSB crest already on his head. Barbara led the way gingerly through a jagged break in the tail section of the Airbus 320 and Joe followed, both of them carefully inching along to a point where the jumble of torn wires and metal bulkheads held a single twisted rectangular bracket partially dislodged from its principal brace. Barbara immersed it in the beam of her flashlight. "There. See that, Joe? That's the digital flight recorder rack. We were able to just pull back the locking arms and pull it out. Now . . . where . . ." She moved the light a foot to the left where nothing but open space and a confused array of broken metal stringers dangled. ". . . here is where the CVR box should be. But there's no box, no bracket, no support brace, no anything. We can't even find the wiring harness. Now, we figured, with the dynamics of the impact, it might have been pulled downward, and that does look to be the case with some of these scratches and gouges along the side. But where the bloody hell *is* the thing?"

"You've . . ."

"Before you ask, yes, we've poked through every scrap of this tail section, and gone back down the taxiway. All I can figure now . . ." She slowly disentangled herself as Joe backed out the opening, helping her down. "All I can figure now is to go through the main section wreckage on the theory that it was flung into there before the empennage broke away."

"Oh, Lord."

"I know. I know. That could take a day or two. But I'm stumped otherwise."

"That's all we can do, Barb. We've got to find that CVR and fast. The speculation is heating up and I'm gambling we can defuse some of it when we know what they said."

"How is the captain? Can you talk to him yet?"

"He's coming around, but Andy was told he didn't want to talk to us before Monday."

"We'll have the flight-recorder data by then, won't we?"

"Maybe. That went back to the lab an hour ago. But we need that CVR. It could conceivably be the key."

"I've got your permission to move the tail now?"

Joe nodded, and Barbara motioned a thumbs-up to the other members of the systems group who were giving orders to a crane operator with a sling already in place. The cable began tensing immediately as they stepped back, watching the section lift clear of the concrete with great protesting sounds of scraping and bending metal, a cascade of small items clanging to the ground.

The contrast was startling, Joe thought. The ugliness of the shattered tail in the grip of a huge crane framed by the beauty of a crisp blue autumn sky. Bit by bit his team was authorizing removal of the wreckage, but days of work remained before they could return to Washington. Joe watched Barbara Rawlson give additional orders to the crane operator as they began swinging the fragmented structure toward a waiting flatbed truck, more pieces of metal and cloth, plastic panels and wiring harnesses dangling and occasionally dropping as they moved it gingerly, a few feet at a time.

Joe knew he was pushing her too hard. Barbara was chairman of the systems investigation, and it had been a trial for her, with the men from Airbus Industrie—the builders of the Airbus 320—hovering over her, hoping their airplane was not at fault.

The crane stopped its movement for a second, the tail section swaying slightly at the end of the thick, steel cable, the sound of diesel engines and a distant jet engine competing with a 10-knot wind blowing past his ears. The smell of burned aircraft material still hung in the air, clinging to the broken airframe and the very concrete on which he was standing. His memory of a very similar scene in Washington after the Air Florida crash of 1982 was equally sharp in his mind, as the shattered blue and white and green tail of that airplane had been lifted from the water of the Potomac River onto an identical flatbed. Ironic, that transition. Like the dust-to-dust incantation humans use for each other at death. A jetliner begins as thousands of parts, many shipped in by truck. And some go out the same way—not many, of course, but for the few that slip through the cracks in the safety system, the flatbed truck becomes their pallbearer.

"Joe, can I see you a minute?"

He hadn't noticed the man's approach, but Gary Seal, heading up the operations group, was standing beside him with a videotape in hand.

"Sure Gary. What've you got?"

"I'm not sure. You remember our mystery car?"

"The one in the cargo area, right?"

"That's right. We got him on tape. A security camera by the gate."

"Wonderful!" Joe brightened. Perhaps they could get to the bottom of this and either get rid of the issue or validate it as a problem.

"Not wonderful. We can't read the license plate."

"Not even close?"

"That's where I had an idea. I ran the master tape back and forth, then recorded this dub, which is even poorer quality. The airport police will lend us the master tape, though, and I was thinking that if we could get that one shot of the rear of the car computer enhanced, it might bring out the license plate number."

"That's a good idea, Gary. I'll call a friend of mine at the bureau tomorrow. Meanwhile, let's get that master tape off to Washington."

"You want this one? It's on VHS."

"Yeah. I'll look at it later. Thanks."

"Uh, Joe? Susan Kelly is looking for you. Is your phone on?" Seal was trying to be discreet about it, but Joe had violated his own maxim to the team: if you've got them, use them. Portable phones on at all times. His was off, bigger than life.

"Damn!"

"She's back at the hotel and wants to see you."

Joe punched the on button on the telephone, listening to the beep that signaled its operation, and shook his head in disgust as he and Seal began walking toward the car he'd left at the edge of the taxiway. Barbara had to run to catch him.

"Joe, one other thing." She was panting, and Joe suppressed a smile. Barbara was always harping on him to keep in shape and work out. She had tried to get him to join her health club—for ulterior motives, Joe had decided. She was divorced and on the prowl, but he wasn't interested in her. Barbara was wiry and small and cute, her dark hair worn short. She was fun to be with but frighteningly aggressive.

"What?"

"If we don't find the CVR quickly in the main wreckage, we'll have to lift the bigger pieces before going deeper, and that may take days."

"Which means keeping the taxiway closed."

"Yeah. After the C-5 bullied its way out of here last night, the airport manager reopened the runway as a taxiway so they can get in and out of the air cargo ramp now. That takes some of the pressure off."

"We're desperate for that CVR, Barbara. Do whatever's necessary, and take however much time you need. And if there's anything near those flight controls that shouldn't be there, you've got to find it.''

"Okay.'' She smiled and departed, dashing back toward the wreckage as Joe made his way to the hotel.

Susan Kelly was waiting for him outside the headquarters room when he walked in, a scowl on her face. Joe approached her with hands out to the side, palms up, and a shy smile.

"I'm sorry, Susan, I screwed up.''

"Human factors and human performance, Joe. You're learning.''

"Yeah. But you see the strange thing is, I never make mistakes.''

She pointed the way to an adjacent meeting room and matched his stride without responding to his attempt at humor.

"We need to talk.''

"I gathered that. Something more than a dead phone, I take it?''

"Yes.'' Her reply was terse as she pushed the door open for him, following him inside and then leaning back against the closed door with her head cocked.

"Joe, we've got a big problem. Or maybe I should say a *tall* problem.''

"We've got a chairman problem, in other words. He called after the interview?''

She looked at him for a moment without blinking. "Within minutes.'' She walked over and sat down in one of the chairs next to Joe. "He griped and bitched at me that you were not following orders. Let's see . . . 'out of control' and 'an insufferable technocrat,' I believe are the terms he used. And I'm not supposed to tell you any of this other than to say you'd better shape up or he'll ship you out.''

"Well, I . . .''

"Now wait a minute.'' Her hand was up for silence, which he provided. "Joe, we've already had it out about the news conference yesterday. That's between you and me and it's a closed issue as far as I'm concerned. But I did warn you what might happen, and it has. Dean is getting pressure from the Hill, and, as I have already learned to expect with him, he's not shy in passing it right back through to us.''

Joe nodded thoughtfully and bit his lip, wondering if he was going to reach the end of his endurance of *her* browbeating as well. She was getting awfully pushy; Board member or not, he was still in charge of the investigation.

"Susan, I'd rather just stay the hell out of the limelight and away from the cameras."

She was chuckling. "You know what you did, Joe. You gave Dean his retraction and then went right back to the truth. In some ways I admire you for that. But if we let you do it again, I'll be working this investigation alone. So yes, let's keep you away from the cameras and keep ourselves quietly in lockstep, okay?"

Joe nodded as Susan Kelly got to her feet, glancing at her watch and motioning to the adjacent room. "We'd better get over there, Joe. But if we see any cameras, you run for your life, and I'll throw myself on the nearest one." Susan watched Joe's response with pleasure as he leaned back slightly and laughed, the tension of the past few hours abating somewhat. "I thank you, noble lady, but I wouldn't hear of such a sacrifice."

She let him open the door for her on the way out, fully realizing that a man like Joe might not recognize it as a concession.

Walter Calley looked behind him once again, convinced he was being followed. It was 2 P.M. Sunday, a perfect time to do what he had to do—which was run. There were two more tasks to perform before he could head south. He was starving, but there was no time to eat, just as there had been no time to sleep in the agonized hours since Friday's crash.

Calley wheeled his cream-colored Camaro into a nondescript shopping center in North Kansas City, scanning in all directions. There was a cash machine at one end of the strip mall, and with only a few cars in the parking lot this Sunday, he could use it in reasonable anonymity, withdrawing five hundred dollars. It would be late Monday before anyone could trace the transaction, and he would be long gone by then.

He had passed the airport an hour back, coming in from the Kansas side, and despite the horror of what had happened, he found himself drawn to return one more time. The parking lot there provided cover for the last item on his list.

With an engineer's meticulous care he found the right target in the long-term parking plaza, a car with a relatively flat rear bumper and a fresh license plate. Waiting for the right moment, he parked behind it, using his car as cover as he unbolted the plate with an electric screwdriver, stowing it under his seat by his .357 magnum. He backed up then, made sure no one was watching, and carefully sideswiped the rear of the same car, crushing the license plate bracket in the process before pulling away at a sedate speed, paying the small toll at the exit, and crossing the interstate, motoring into the farmland near Ferrelview until he found an unobserved spot by the road where he could install the purloined plate on his car. With the evidence of a crushed bumper back at the airport lot, the plate would be deemed an accident victim. He might have a week or so before anyone would list it as stolen. He would leave the front plate alone. For his purposes, it wouldn't matter.

The final task complete, Calley retraced his path to the interstate and headed south toward Louisiana. He would make the call in a hundred miles or so. He had already mailed the cassette tape.

The Go Team—NTSB people only—had quietly assembled in the hotel lobby at Joe's direction at 6 P.M. Sunday evening, all of them in casual clothes. From long experience Joe knew they needed to unwind, but there were victims' families staying at the airport hotel. Smiling, joking NTSB investigators were the last thing a grieving relative needed to see—though that was exactly what the team needed to do. They could only internalize so much.

The group took three of the rented minivans and headed in loose formation several miles south toward downtown Kansas City to a tavern and restaurant one of the team members knew and liked. Within a half hour the grim faces began to soften, the volume of the conversation and the volume of the liquor consumption becoming barometers of the relaxation process. Joe played host as long as he could, then passed the duty to Andy, making sure there were at least two stone-sober people, including Andy, left to drive back to the hotel. They were expected at Captain Timson's bedside for an initial interview at 9 A.M. the following morning.

Joe took one of the vans then and returned to the airport and the flight line, taking a flashlight and a cigar with intentions of walking along the taxiway amidst the wreckage. He needed time to think.

The danger of fire was minimal, so lighting the cigar seemed a reasonable breach of caution. He seldom smoked, but after a good dinner and coffee, a cigar was a luxury he sometimes allowed himself.

Joe found himself moving toward the point where the A320's tail section had been found, the puzzle of the missing CVR box drawing him in, the question of sabotaged flight controls consuming his mental picture of what to look for in the wreckage. The tail itself sat on a flatbed trailer, but the bulk of the shattered fuselage remained on the ground, looking ghostly in the garish glow of the portable spotlights.

Joe had stuffed his portable phone in the pocket of his coat before leaving the hotel, but when it rang suddenly, it took him by surprise. Somehow the solitude of the nighttime airport taxiway seemed safe from telephones. Obviously it was not.

"Joe Wallingford? This is Bill Caldwell, associate administrator, FAA. We've met before."

"Sure, Mr. Caldwell. What can I do for you at this late hour?" Why the hell was he calling so late? The thought that he was going to apologize for the withholding of the FAA's airplane crossed his mind.

The FAA and the NTSB did keep tabs on each other, but this was highly unusual. Caldwell was the number-two man in the FAA.

"I know you're on a portable phone, so I'll keep this brief. We're concerned about the Airbus 320's flight controls, and whether they can resist outside radio interference."

"You mean EMI, electromagnetic interference? Microwave and other shorter-wave radio energy?" Joe was not about to let Caldwell get the upper hand. He knew Caldwell's reputation for digesting one briefing paper and becoming an instant technical "expert."

"Very good, Joe. We've got guidelines published, and so far the 320's had no problem. But I need your help. Unless I can be sure that this accident did *not* involve either EMI vulnerability or some flight-control-system failure, we might have to consider certificate action while waiting for more information."

Joe froze. The sound of jet engines winding down as a flight arrived at one of the terminals in the distance left a void of silence in the air and on the phone. If Airbus representatives could hear this conversation, he thought, they'd have coronaries. Caldwell was hinting at a possible grounding. Good God, just like the DC-10 grounding more than a decade earlier, a move which cost untold losses with questionable results.

"I, ah, would think that this is a grossly premature discussion, Mr. Caldwell. I mean, we haven't even talked to the flight captain yet. We have virtually no evidence or even rumored evidence that this involved the flight-control system."

"Joe, my people out there are telling me it might not have been windshear, and that the airplane nosed down on final, which may be a flight-control problem. Now, regardless of the controversial congressman on board, if it *wasn't* windshear, and if it *did* nose over, we're probably either down to the flight crew screwing up, or a flight-control glitch. If it's the latter, I do *not* want the administrator blindsided. We've got a lot of delicate considerations here you don't normally deal with, Joe, so what I'm asking you, in the interest of good relations, is that you keep this between you and me, and you tell me as soon as you know that this was definitely *not* flight-control trouble."

Joe couldn't find his voice for a second.

"Joe? You still there?"

"Yes sir. I . . . I don't know what to say to you, Mr. Caldwell."

"Joe, it's simple. I'm asking you to call me the minute you're sure one way or the other."

"But if I can't, or don't, tell you it was *not* flight-control failure or radio interference, you'll move? You're going to consider grounding all Airbus 320s nationwide?"

"That's the last resort, Joe, but I can't run any risks if there's even a chance these planes have a flight-control-system weakness. What do you think? Did it go where they aimed it, or did it wander off on its own and crash? That's the question. I just need the earliest possible word."

Joe felt his temperature rising. This had to be a bluff. At this stage of an investigation, it was totally inappropriate for the FAA to leap to unsupported conclusions and act so rashly. If there were a shred of evidence it would be different. But why would Caldwell bluff the NTSB? And how dare he throw such a gauntlet at the Board's feet!

"How much time do I have to do the impossible, Mr. Caldwell?" Joe knew his tone was turning from respectful to acidic, but this request warranted it.

"Well, I would certainly hope to hear from you within a few days."

"And if you don't?"

"I'll have to draw my own conclusions and advise our administrator accordingly. But I know I can count on you, Joe. I know you're shocked, but extraordinary problems demand creative solutions."

"Mr. Caldwell, there is no justification for considering a grounding."

"I'm not saying we're going to ground it. Call me, Joe, when you can tell me there *isn't* a control problem. I know Airbus is a good company with a good product, but unless their A320 meets all our standards, it won't fly within our borders."

"Sir, we've got several large airlines flying scores of these planes."

There was a pause and a chuckle on the other end before Caldwell replied, "Perhaps they should have bought American planes, eh Joe?"

There was no question he should call Dean Farris. Farris had a right to know about Caldwell's intrusive request. But that call could wait for a day or two, he rationalized. At least until they talked to the captain. If he was lucky, perhaps he could tell Caldwell what he wanted to know, and put the issue to bed quietly. Perhaps.

7

Monday, October 15

A sudden gust of cold wind rocked the car as the nighttime thunderstorm broke overhead, and Walter Calley pulled his coat closer to stay warm, momentarily forgetting where he was. The sound of thunder crashed again nearby, drowning out the rumble of heavy truck engines which were droning all around him in the back lot of the truck stop. He had made it as far as Monroe, Louisiana, before sleep became unavoidable, and the crowded anonymity of a truckers' haven had seemed a safe place to hole up for a few hours. So far that premise had been right.

Walter reached out and started the engine again, longing for the heater to kick in and warm the car's freezing interior. Maybe it was just fear causing him to shiver. He'd never felt quite so alone and outcast.

The damn phone call he had made the day before still haunted him. There had been clicks on the line, which made no sense. How could they find him? Even he didn't know which pay phone he was going to use until he pulled up in front of it. He was a sophisticated electronics engineer who understood computers and the technical gadgets professionals used to spy on other people. But for someone to spy on you, they had to know where the hell you were, and half the night he hadn't known himself where he was.

He had stayed on the back roads after the phone call to New Orleans, taking twice as long to work his way south, staying away from towns like Fayetteville and Shreveport, winding through mind-numbing little burgs and endless, unlighted, rain-slicked country curves on nameless two-lane blacktops, almost running out of gas before he found an all-night station in the mountains of Arkansas.

Forrest Rogers had answered his home phone on the fifth ring, absolutely dumbstruck when Walter had snapped out his message.

"Forrest, I'm in bad trouble. I need your help. I need you to come meet me Monday night, eight P.M., at the old place. You know where it is."

"What? What the hell are you talking about, Walter?"

"Doesn't matter. Just don't say anything about where that is over this phone, or to anyone, and don't let yourself be followed. I'll tell you everything when you get there."

"Walter, where are you?"

"I can't tell you, Forrest. Someone might be listening."

Rogers had paused then, the puzzlement obvious at the other end of the phone. "What have you done, Walter? You sound like you're running, and that scares me."

"I *am* running."

"Good God, from who? You running from the law?"

"Forrest, just be there. Please."

"At least give me a goddamn hint!" Forrest sounded half-frantic.

It was Calley's turn to pause. Forrest was right. If the line was tapped, it was too late anyway.

"You know I've been working in Kansas?" Walter said at last.

"Yeah, I heard from our friends in Baton Rouge."

"And you know what just happened at Kansas City Airport Friday night. You have to know. All of Louisiana has to know."

"What are you saying, Walter? What the fuck are you saying? What have you done?"

"It was me, Forrest. I can't tell you any more till I see you. But I sent you a tape to be safe. I put the whole thing on a tape I mailed this morning. If anything happens to me, you'll get the tape at your office. Man, believe it when the TV reports say that crash wasn't an accident. Damn right it wasn't an accident. You're talking to the man responsible."

"Don't . . . for God's sake, Walter, you stay away from me, hear?"

"No, no, Forrest! Whoa, man, you've got to hear me out! It's not what you think. Larry was coming Friday because I called—I set it up. There were good reasons, Forrest, believe me. But I'm the only one who knows what really went down, and I can't tell it if I'm dead. Please be there, man. We've been friends for too many years for you to run out on me now. Be there. Please.''

"What do you mean, if anything happens to you?''

"I can't talk. Gotta go. See you tomorrow.''

He had hated hanging up on Forrest, but an approaching car seemed to be slowing down as it headed for the roadside phone booth, and he had an uncontrollable urge to run.

Some nine hours later the sight of a Louisiana state police patrol car cruising into the truck stop near Monroe brought Walter Calley back to the present. He watched the trooper from his protected vantage point between two giant eighteen-wheelers. The lawman found a parking spot by the restaurant and got out, apparently uninterested in anything but food.

Or was he?

Calley watched the trooper disappear around the front of the truck stop, wondering if there were others quietly searching the lot. Could they have been tipped off he was there? Was there a manhunt going on? The FBI, the CIA, the military police—any of them could be tearing up the landscape and hunting him by now.

One thing's for sure, he thought to himself, if they're smart enough to find me, they won't be wearing uniforms. They'll walk up in civilian clothes and blow me away with an Uzi. There's no way they can let me live. Only hope is to get them first.

He turned off the ignition and listened, cataloging each raindrop as he watched and waited for anything suspicious, letting a half hour pass before he could bring himself to crank the engine again. He put the car in gear then and moved slowly back to the highway, never glancing at the restaurant, but feeling the trooper's eyes following him.

Calley checked his watch, as he headed west on the interstate, squinting to make out the time, which was 6:41 A.M., almost daybreak. He would turn south on U.S. 167. Alexandria was two hours away, and the old fishing camp he hoped Forrest would be heading to was on a lake near Marksville. He wanted to be there before noon to hide the car and dig in. The faceless men with the Uzis couldn't be too far behind now.

* * *

A warning buzzer erupted somewhere nearby as loud as a Klaxon, saturating his brain with overwhelming noise as Joe Wallingford struggled against unseen impediments to find the microphone and radio a warning. They must not take off! The smell of kerosene burned in his nostrils as he saw the airliner getting ready for what he knew would be a fatal attempt to lift off. The sight triggered primal feelings of helplessness and impending disaster, and as always, he could do nothing.

Joe swung himself into a vertical position instinctively, reacting to the buzzer, sitting on the edge of the bed, his mind racing. The fact that he had been having that same recurring nightmare came slowly to his consciousness as the images evaporated from mind and memory. Usually he could not hold on to dreams, to remember them later and study them. They were gone in an instant like a puff of smoke, leaving only a vague feeling that something was unresolved.

The blackout curtains in the pastel-and-oak hotel room held the darkness and night within, masking the first rays of dawn he knew must be visible outside, the rising glow of sunlight streaming over the airport terminal. Inside he could barely see a thing, the bathroom light failing miserably as a night-light. He had learned the hard way about sleeping in total darkness: years before he had chipped a tooth in a pitch-dark hotel room lunging from a bed into a hallway that turned out to be a wall. This morning it also took a few seconds to figure out where he was— a common problem on the road. Once, before they were divorced, he had teased Brenda one morning after returning from a long field investigation by patting her face in the dark and asking, "Where am I, and who are you?" She had not been amused.

As he tried to focus, the distant aroma of aviation kerosene wafted around his head, propelled by the window air-conditioning unit. Most likely the source of the nightmare, he figured, or a contributing factor.

Joe strained to read the offending clock as it continued to buzz, locating the control switch by feel and sliding it into silence as he noticed the digits indicating it was 6:30 A.M. Monday. He had called a meeting of the entire team for 7:45 A.M., and it wouldn't do for the leader to be late. At 9 A.M., they were to interview Captain Timson.

Joe fought his sleepiness with thoughts of relaxing in the shower, snapping lamps on one by one as he headed for the bathroom, wolfing down the piece of hotel chocolate left on his pillow the evening before, and finally resigning himself to sustained consciousness.

The dream might be gone, but the memories of last night were there. Joe began the practiced rituals of morning, thinking about the litany of problems that had kept sleep at bay for hours.

Cobwebs still filled his head as he adjusted the streams of water, letting the stinging sensation reacquaint him with a network of nerve endings numbed by fatigue and inadequate sleep. There had been no alcohol last night—he never drank a drop while on a field investigation—but it felt like a morning after. Moving deliberately with slippery feet, he stepped out of the shower at last, toweling dry as he appraised his browned but slightly shopworn body in the mirror, noting with pleasure the flatness of his stomach. Still a lot of muscle there, he assured himself, though he should get back to regular workouts. Ever since high school football he had been in reasonably good shape. His face bore the signs of weathering, a small network of lines and creases providing character of sorts, the flesh under his eyes beginning to sag a bit. Five foot eleven, one hundred sixty-five pounds, and about 80 percent of the originally issued crop of hair left up top. Not too bad for a guy of forty-five.

Joe threw a towel around his shoulders and padded out to the TV, flipping it on and shoving the movie control box to one side in order to find the listing for the local network stations. It was 7:03 A.M. and the morning shows from New York would be focusing on the crash. He was still rummaging around in his bag for a fresh pair of undershorts when the overly familiar backdrop of the Kansas City Airport appeared on screen, a network aviation correspondent explaining the progress of the investigation. Sabotage was the main and growing theme, and the media was worrying it like a pit bull on a pet chicken.

Joe listened briefly to a report on the Manning children, the four-year-old girl now described as permanently crippled and still in critical condition, the seven-year-old boy physically intact but fighting infection and internal injuries. The two orphaned little children were the focus of an outpouring of sentiment from all over the nation, with funds established and background stories playing on each newscast. The young college student who had helped keep the brother and sister alive was being touted as a heroine.

A new image on the screen caught his attention suddenly, an artist's diagram of the Airbus 320 control system with the outline of a small dish antenna pointed at the cartoonish airplane from one corner of the screen, lines representing radio waves radiating from the antenna to the plane. "What now?" Joe reached across to turn up the volume.

". . . investigative efforts have revealed disturbing information this morning regarding the control system of the foreign-built jetliner. Critics charge that it might be possible to freeze the controls—take control away from the pilots—by using radio waves aimed at the airplane. And indeed, investigative efforts over the weekend have turned up FAA reports which set certain limits on how close this airplane should be allowed to fly to radio transmitters."

Good Lord, Joe thought to himself. This was getting way out of hand. The uninformed speculation he'd just heard from the blow-dried young reporter on the screen could do real damage to Airbus's reputation. Yet what could *he* do about it? The future of the 320 might already hang in the balance, considering Bill Caldwell's attitude.

Joe wished he could get the reporter's nose into a recent report on radio interference, but it would be too technical for him. There were far too few knowledgeable aviation people willing to speak to the cameras, so in their absence, the uninformed and misinformed ended up telling the nation things that were, quite often, simply wrong. The radio limits the reporter was referring to concerned extremely powerful ship-mounted transmitters throwing out thousands and thousands of watts of radio energy, and there were only a few places on earth where such transmitters came anywhere close to airports that the A320 could use. Kansas City was not one of them.

Joe left the room on time, holding the 7:45 A.M. meeting down to thirty minutes as the team compared notes, then motoring toward Truman Medical Center with a sleepy Andy Wallace.

"Joe, I had a visit late last night after we got back—he was waiting in the lobby, a fellow whose wife and two little boys were killed in the 737. He's a clinical psychologist, and someone I've heard of . . . one of the people working on the stress profiles of employees of failing airlines.''

Joe nodded and Andy continued.

"Joe, he's not hysterical, but he's determined.''

"About what?''

"I'm . . . I'm working up to that. This is unprecedented, so I wanted to lay the groundwork for you. He is a pilot and a qualified aviation-oriented psychologist. No, he's not totally objective, but he's determined to help, and I wanted to get your thoughts on a suggestion he had.''

"Which is?''

"He wants to become a formal party to the investigation.''

Joe was startled and showed it. "A what? A party of one? You know we can't do that, Andy, we . . .''

"Yes we can, Joe. We can grant that status legally.''

Joe looked at the crowded roadway ahead, thinking it through.

"My Lord, that poor fellow,'' he said at last.

"There . . . ,'' began Andy, "there could go any of us.''

"That's true, Andy, but we'd never be able to maintain control of someone who's lost so much. We need objectivity, not emotional dedication. I feel terrible for him, but we cannot compromise an investigation to help him stay busy.''

"Joe . . . Joe, believe me, if I'm any judge of character, whether we say yea or nay, this guy's gonna be in there at every turn. He is absolutely determined.''

"What does he think this is, a human-error accident?''

"Aren't most of them?''

Joe looked at Andy Wallace, half-irritated. They had gone through the human-failure–mechanical-failure debate many times, and though Joe was not about to admit it, Andy had opened his eyes to aspects of human failure he had never considered. This request, however, was out of line. Andy saw Joe's head shaking vigorously from side to side.

"No. We can't, even if it is a pilot error . . .''

"Human error, not pilot error,'' Andy said sternly, index finger in the air, eyebrows contracted for emphasis.

"Okay, okay. *Human* error. He's liable to turn into an inquisitor rather than a professional interviewer. We can't do it, Andy. I'm sorry.''

"Get used to him being around, then.''

Joe considered that in silence for a moment as he changed

lanes, appreciating the visibility from the driver's seat of the sleek minivan with its huge windows.

"What's his name?" Joe said at last.

"Dr. Mark Weiss."

"His entire family, Andy?"

Andy Wallace nodded, biting his lower lip. "Yeah. I don't know if I could handle something like that, Joe. He had just put them on the plane. Found them himself in the wreckage."

"Good God."

"Amen to that, sir."

Hospitals unleashed special fears in Joe Wallingford. Perhaps it was memories of his appendicitis as a boy, or perhaps the waiting-room trauma of the car wreck which almost took Brenda from him—before divorce effectively accomplished the same thing. Regardless of the reason, the inner sanctum of Truman Medical Center at 8:50 A.M. triggered all the wrong feelings as Joe flipped his NTSB credentials at a private security guard hired to enforce privacy for the crash victims and watched the man respectfully melt to the sidelines.

Andy Wallace walked silently in tight formation with Joe as they approached Captain Timson's room, well aware of the importance of the mission. What did the pilot remember? What did he know? The stakes were high, which made the presence of an unfamiliar, stern-faced man in a three-piece suit outside Timson's room an instant threat.

"Just a minute." The man moved protectively in front of the door, blocking them, as Joe repeated his artful sweep of the badge wallet, his hand coming to rest in midair twelve inches in front of the man's face, the logo of the NTSB impressively visible.

"Joe Wallingford and Andy Wallace of the NTSB. We had Captain Timson's agreement to a nine A.M. interview."

The man nodded but had barely looked at the identification. He knew who they were. "We need to talk first, Mr. Wallingford. I'm John Walters, vice-president of operations for North America. I want some ground rules here." He did not offer his hand.

Joe fixed Walters with a steady, neutral gaze. Usually they slammed into a protective contingent from ALPA, but in their absence, Timson's boss apparently was going to play the role of protector.

"What, exactly, do you mean, Mr. Walters?"

Walters kept his voice low, as if muttering at a funeral. "What I mean is, our man in there is still in bad shape and under medication. He doesn't remember a great deal at this point. The doctors tell me his memory has been affected by the skull fracture he received, as well as the emotional trauma. I want to make sure you fellows aren't planning on taking a major deposition at this early stage. You know, his memory doesn't click on some point, then you beat us to death with it later on?"

Joe was rapidly developing a distaste for the North America executive, but he had to be evenhanded.

"We do the formal deposition with a court reporter later. All we use here is a tape recorder. There has never been, in my nearly twenty years with the Board, any reason for an honest man to fear correcting the record later if there's something he forgot or misstated in the informal interview, Mr. Walters. But right now we need as much information from him as we can get."

"Well, Dick Timson's an honest man, but an injured one. I'd rather you called this off," Walters said.

"You're joking?"

"No, I'm not. He's in no condition to be interviewed."

Joe shook his head and stared at John Walters. He could feel Andy's temperature rising as well. "You mind telling me why you didn't contact us before with this request? We just drove 12 miles from the airport with important business going begging behind us."

"I just got here late last night."

"It's no mystery where we're staying. . . ."

"Look, it's only been this morning that I've had a chance to talk with Dick myself. I didn't have a chance to call you."

Joe sighed and dropped his head, studying his shoes for a moment, trying to decide between diplomacy and force. He snapped his head back up then, looking Walters in the eye. "We have scores of people dead and injured, two aircraft destroyed, lives ruined, the media in an uproar, the fate of a sophisticated airplane—which, by the way, you people own a lot of—in the balance, the Congress upset, the FAA worried, and a runway at the airport closed, and I need information as fast as I can get it. I don't care if your captain can only hear every third word and communicate in sign language, we're not here to prosecute him or anyone else. We're here to talk to an eyewitness to a major accident, and that is precisely, Mr. Walters, what we intend to do.''

"I'm not going to block you—"

"You couldn't anyway, without a court order.''

"Well, that remains to be seen, Mr. Wallingford. But the fact is, I'm not here to make your life difficult, I just want you gentlemen to realize that whatever Dick says to you may be grossly inaccurate until he's recovered his faculties. I want this kept private.''

"This ends up as public record, you know that,'' Joe said.

"I do, but you don't have to run to the media immediately.''

Temper, Joe, temper, he cautioned himself. The pompous little ass.

"Mr. Wallingford, I must go on record as protesting this interview.''

"So noted,'' Joe said, pushing past Walters, "and so rejected.'' Walters stepped aside reluctantly, then followed them into the room.

Dick Timson was far more conscious and alert than Joe had expected after the exchange with Walters. They spent ten minutes trying to defuse the tension, Mrs. Timson hovering nervously behind her husband's bed, and Walters staying near the door, a position which irritated Joe even more. Timson could see Walters's every expression, Joe and Andy, concentrating on their subject, could not.

"Okay, Captain, I have the tape recorder on so that we can prepare accurate notes of what is said here. Please tell me everything you can remember from the beginning of your first approach to the impact.''

The captain nodded, his expression serious, his face very sad. Joe felt himself softening in spite of the encounter in the hallway, which in any event was quite probably none of the poor captain's doing.

"I don't recall the impact itself,'' Timson began. "I'm having a hard time putting everything in focus, you know?'' He tried then, honestly, it seemed to Joe, to piece together the windshear encounter and the subsequent decision to make a quick visual, closed pattern back to the runway after their go-around. Yes, he admitted, the windshear encounter was very serious. They had been low enough at one point to crash. No, he had

had no indication of windshear, and the tower never used the word. He had no warning.

Finally his narrative reached the fatal turn to the runway.

Timson stared at the wall for a few seconds before beginning, his voice slow and metered. "I was fairly close in, so I rolled into a tight right descending turn, planning to keep the turn going until I rolled back to wings-level on final. I was on the right airspeed. I figured the windshear we had gotten into before was several miles to the north, and moving east. Anyway, everything was fine until about two-thirds, maybe three-quarters of the way around. My . . . my memory's still fuzzy, but I remember trying to keep the nose up and the turn going, and it wasn't working. The nose was dropping and we were sinking fast. I had full power—I was trying to turn and pull up, but it wasn't responding."

Timson's sad eyes fixed Joe's, an almost pleading look on his face, made even more pathetic by the bandages swathing his head. "I tried . . . tried to get her up, but something wasn't working."

"You mean the controls weren't working?" Joe asked, the specter of control failure hovering over Timson's words.

"Well . . . I'm not sure I can say the controls weren't responding, but the plane wasn't responding. She kept sinking, the nose down."

"Could it have been windshear, Captain?"

"Maybe. It kept dropping. I don't know. It's a fuzzy memory, a—I hate to say it—panicked memory, you know? You're trying everything you can, and it's not working. I had the stick controller full back, and the nose wasn't coming up fast enough."

"But it *was* coming up?" Joe asked.

"Well . . . I don't remember how we hit the other airplane, but I seem to recall my nose was up then, so it must have been . . . a question, you know, of how fast she was coming up. I know it wasn't enough."

"Captain, I have to ask you this: Could you have been demanding too much of the airplane in that turn to final?"

"I . . . don't follow you," he said. Joe watched Timson's eyes for defensiveness or a flicker of anything. Someone fabricating a story would look away in response to a question like that. Timson did not.

"If there was no wind and no malfunction of any sort, would the Airbus 320 be able to make the turn to final that you were demanding of it with that airspeed? In other words, are you sure you were within the airplane's performance envelope?"

"Oh." Timson grimaced and nodded, still engaging Joe eye-to-eye. "No question. I've flown turns like that before. She can turn even tighter than that. There was no . . . I mean, yes, she could have done it. I don't know why she didn't."

Andy took over then, taking Timson through it once again.

"To recap, Captain," Joe began at last, "you can't tell us whether the flight controls failed to follow your commands, or the aircraft was affected by windshear, or both?"

"I'm sorry . . . I can't. I only know she wasn't doing what I was telling her to do all the way down. All the way to . . . ah . . . impact." Timson looked down and squinted his eyes closed for a second, shaking his head, his wife moving in to comfort him.

Joe had started to get up, but then sat down again. "One other thing. When you found the aircraft wasn't responding, who was at the controls?"

"I was flying."

"All the way down?"

"Yes."

They left it at that, Andy and Joe adjourning to a nearby family waiting room for a quick discussion.

"He seems to be trying hard to remember, I'll give him that," Andy began. Joe nodded.

"But what does this give us, Andy?"

"Goddamn near nothing. The plane pitched down and started descending, and he doesn't know why. Could be windshear. Could be control malfunction. Could be radio interference."

"How?" Joe's retort was too loud, and a bedraggled young mother holding a dirty two-year-old glanced up from her chair, startled by his voice. Joe apologized with a wave of his hand before continuing, his eyes wide open and flaring at Andy. "You've seen the parameters. You'd need a transmitter the size of a ship!"

"Do we really know how much wattage it would take for such a radio, Joe? Do we really know how big a container it would take? There are a lot of military radars in the world, and many of them are portable."

Joe stared at Andy and shook his head. "I guess I see your point."

"Too soon, Joe. We gotta deal with what we've got."

"Which is nothing."

"Well . . ."

Joe looked up at him suddenly. "I mean it. We've got nothing. Can you rule anything out based on what that poor guy just told us? I mean, not that it's his fault that he can't give us an answer."

"You got your hopes too high, Joe." Andy saw Joe nod finally, as he leaned forward in the chair, elbows on his knees, face cupped in his hands.

"You're right. The pressure is skewing me off center. I know better. What we have is simply preliminary."

"We need the CVR. That's next."

"No, the flight recorder is next. The readout should be in this morning. Maybe that can tell us something about the windshear question. Then if Barbara ever finds that damn CVR box . . ."

The two men stood in silence for a moment, Andy's thoughts drifting to the range of human emotions that went on daily in hospital waiting rooms: life and death and the sudden loneliness—emptiness—that people faced in such a place, the struggles to accept unacceptable realities, the silent screams and quiet desperation. How many times had the selection of dog-eared, ragged magazines been stared at by people who hadn't seen a word or picture? A hospital was where one went to face the realities more easily ignored in other places. And the reality faced by Joe Wallingford and Andy Wallace was that there might be no easy answer to the Kansas City disaster.

What, for God's sake, had happened out there on final approach?

8

Monday, October 15

The sullen, disheveled man who had paid for his sandwich and Coke with a twenty-dollar bill had worried her, even more so when he failed to scoop up the ten-dollar bill that was part of his change. To the 7-Eleven clerk, that was too much money to just forget—especially when she saw Jimmy Lansing, a city policeman she knew, approaching her counter. She liked Jimmy and wanted him to think of her as honest and honorable—as well as sexy.

"Dammit, Jimmy! That fellow left his money." She was holding the bill and looking outside, hoping he'd offer to help.

The policeman glanced at the car pulling out of the lot and smiled at her as he laid down the exact change for a bag of potato chips. "I'll catch him and give it back, darlin'. Probably be a new experience for him—cop stops you to give *you* money. Don't see that every day." He laughed and she looked properly pleased.

It took six blocks of Alexandria's main drag to catch up with the man, but the officer was grinning and looking forward to scaring—then pleasing—the man behind the wheel. He reached over and flipped on his rotating blue-and-white beacons, then hit a burst on the electronic siren just for good measure, his foot poised over the brake for the inevitable shocked slowdown before he pulled over.

Instead, the sound of squealing tires and massive acceleration just ahead caught him by surprise as the cream-colored Camaro burned rubber southbound. Officer Lansing hesitated a second in shock, then fell into established procedure, flooring his patrol

119

cruiser in pursuit and radioing to his dispatcher to report a developing high-speed chase.

"That sumbitch is going to try to outrun me!" he said out loud as the speedometer passed 80, still accelerating. The Camaro was weaving now around slower traffic, and Lansing had to anticipate his car's reaction to do the same. The city limits were coming up fast, and once again he radioed, reporting position, direction, speed, and the request for state help.

A confused county sheriff's car on a different frequency had pulled up to a stop sign leading onto the highway as the Camaro flashed by.

"Thank God he looked left first and saw me coming!" His speed was pushing 100 now. If the sheriff's car had jumped in front, the results would've been fatal. Instead, the deputy pulled in a distant third and slammed *his* pedal to the floor.

"Thirty-four, we've notified the state, they're on the line and relaying. Keep after him and we'll let you know when to break off."

"Thirty-four, ten-four." His voice was an octave higher now, it seemed. Chases were always adrenaline pumpers, though this one was basically straight and level—a speed contest the Camaro seemed to be winning.

Lansing's car was topping out at 120, bouncing and trying to become airborne, the slick road threatening to release the tires to an uncertain, high-speed fate, and he backed off a little. The Camaro was having the same trouble, and Lansing had already watched him fishtail around one tight curve in the distance as he continued to pull away. There was yet another curve coming up, but the brake lights on the Camaro told the story—the driver had seen it in time and was around and off again, still pulling away.

Walter Calley had never taken a high-speed, high-performance driving course, but he knew he had a well-tuned fast car, and he was going to use everything it could give.

So they had found him! How wasn't important. Getting away was. He didn't know police procedure, but there would surely be someone waiting up ahead, a roadblock or whatever. But if he got off on a country road that they knew and he didn't, he'd be fried.

"Lord, Lord, Lord . . . what do I do now?" The words were yelled into the empty interior of his speeding vehicle as he watched the oncoming police car in his rearview mirror. The only answer, he concluded at last, was lying beneath the seat—his .357 magnum.

Calley slammed on the brakes, slowing below 40 before throwing the wheel to the left against an empty two-lane road, reversing course just like a Hollywood stunt driver—and nearly breaking his neck in the process. The Camaro staggered onto the shoulder, threatening to careen off into a deep ditch. Calley fished for the gun as the police car bore down on him. The cop wouldn't be expecting this, he thought, but where was the gun? "*Where the hell is that gun?* Oh God! Oh God, no!"

The police car was less than a quarter mile away now. The cop had spotted him and was braking, fishtailing as he decelerated, trying to figure out what was going on.

He felt the gun's handle, then lost it. Mere seconds left! He had to have time to aim. There wouldn't be a second chance!

Finally! The butt was there, he clawed at it, bending a fingernail back to the quick and not caring, finally grasping the weapon and coming up, opening the door, and leveling the barrel at the oncoming car at the very last minute, sighting through the crack in the door jamb where the oncoming cop couldn't see what he was trying to do.

The front and rear sights aligned with a point in midair in front of the police car as Calley forced himself to wait the few split seconds until the car was in the right position and still going fast enough.

He had already cocked the hammer. All that remained was a steady pull on the trigger, keeping the sights aligned, waiting for the narrow target to come into view.

"There!"

The trigger seemed to travel back for an eternity before the kick of the .357 shoved his hand up, the raised barrel of the lethal gun obscuring the sight of the police car, which was still traveling at over 60, a new squealing noise now betraying the instantaneous loss of the right front tire—which had been his target. As he had figured, the policeman had no time to do more than fight the car for control, fight to keep it out of the ditch, which was a battle he was losing. Calley jammed his accelerator back to the floor and flew past the out-of-control cruiser as it hit the shoulder of the highway, kicking up an enormous cloud of dust and debris as it went over the side and into the ditch. Only then did he see the county sheriff's car also in a four-wheel skid, trying to avoid hitting the police cruiser as he too decelerated.

There had been several crossroads about a mile back. If he could reach one of them before he was spotted again, he had a fighting chance. The road seemed clear behind as his speed shot up to 110 again, his eyes searching the highway back toward Alexandria for oncoming police units and the rearview mirror for signs of the sheriff's car. For some reason it wasn't back there. The deputy must have stopped to help his colleague.

Jamming the brakes to the floor again, he wrestled the car around the 90-degree turn to the side road, almost losing control, hoping against hope he could disappear around a bend and behind a grove of trees before anyone spotted the maneuver.

The road ahead was little more than a country lane, winding among fields and bayous, and he looked frantically for someplace to run, someplace to hide. Down a small draw and across a creek the open entrance to a hay field and a ramshackle barn with its roof half-gone seemed the best hope. He raced through the gate and bounced across a pasture right through the door of the structure, aiming for a compacted haystack in one corner and driving full bore into the middle of it.

Calley wrestled the door open, carrying the gun, and worked against time to finish covering the car with the moldy, rain-soaked hay, climbing then amidst creaking timbers to an upper loft where he could lie on his belly out of sight and watch the road. There were no farmhouses or farmers around he could see. Maybe, just maybe, his wild entrance had gone unobserved.

Thank God he had sent the tape. The old place seemed light years away now. There was little chance he would ever see it again. He knew that instinctively. Whoever was really after him—whoever was determined he wouldn't live to tell what he knew about Friday night, the crash, and what he had seen in his employer's plant in Leavenworth—wouldn't silence him as long as Forrest got the tape.

Unless, of course, Forrest was part of it too.

As officer Jimmy Lansing felt his cracked nose and sloshed from the wreck of his patrol car to the proffered hand of the sheriff's deputy, six hundred miles to the north in Kansas City NTSB investigators Joe Wallingford and Andy Wallace made their way to the parking lot of Truman Medical Center just as

North America vice-president John Walters was leaving room 940-E in a barely contained state of agitation.

Walters was convinced he knew where the investigation was drifting already. Pilot error. Pilot error or mechanical malfunction. The questions those two investigators had asked were obviously designed to build a case. Either the captain negligently flew back into windshear, or their airplane was screwed up, possibly by radio interference. Either conclusion would be a blow to the jugular of North America, and North America was already waging a battle to stay afloat.

Andy was driving when Joe's portable cellular phone rang, which was fortunate as Joe had to struggle to get it out of his overcoat.

"Joe?" The voice belonged to Walt Rogers, power plant group chairman, who was back at the airport.

"Yes."

"We've got a problem." There was fright in Walt's voice. Joe was instantly tensed, sitting up suddenly in the right seat of the minivan.

"What?"

"Barbara . . . uh . . . fell while working in the wreckage. She broke through a floor panel, and she's hurt."

"How bad?"

"She's on her way to the hospital by ambulance right now. She got cut, Joe, right up the chest, by a sharp section of metal. It looked like she'd been in a knife fight. She's in a lot of pain, and I think she's lost a lot of blood."

"Oh Lord. Which hospital?"

"Truman Medical."

"We were just there." Joe saw Andy's questioning look. "Stand by a second." He looked up at Andy. "Barb's been injured, cut badly falling in the wreckage. Turn around. We've gotta get back to Truman."

Joe spoke into the phone again. "Okay, we'll meet her. How long ago did they take her away?"

"Five minutes. She's worried about transfusions, Joe. We all are. You know, whether it's safe blood and all."

"I understand. We're going back."

"Joe?"

"Yeah."

"The flight recorder printout has arrived. I've looked at it. You want me to tell you . . . ?"

"Not right now. Later, when things are calmed down. Keep everyone out of the wreckage until I get back, and get a report started. Call Washington and make a formal accident-injury report, tell them I'll check in from the hospital."

Joe punched the disconnect button as Andy negotiated the off ramp and prepared to swing under an overpass to regain the southbound lanes.

"She got too eager, Joe. Barb does that."

"Yeah. And I pushed her." Joe watched the maneuver in silence, feeling positively ill.

The ambulance was unloading when Andy brought the mini-van to a halt outside the emergency room. Joe jumped out, making his way to the stretcher as the two paramedics rolled her in the door. Barbara's face was very white, he noted, but she was breathing and her eyes were open and moving. Joe paced the group as they showed their federal ID cards and were directed immediately down a hallway and into a trauma operating room, where a doctor and two nurses were waiting—alerted, Joe figured, by radio.

"How is she?" Joe asked one of the departing paramedics as he turned to leave.

"Spunky and conscious. Ask her yourself. She'll survive."

Joe moved to Barbara's side, shocked at the crimson mess her clothes had become, ignoring the sight of her breasts as the nurse pulled away her torn blouse and bra, leaving only the emergency bandages.

"Joe! Sorry about this. I . . ."

"Hey, don't." He held up a hand to stop her apology. "What happened? Walt said you fell through the floor of the wreckage?"

"Stupid mistake. At least I had my hard hat and gloves on." She smiled weakly, looking behind Joe and adding, "Hello, Doctor Kelly."

"Susan." Joe was surprised. He hadn't seen her in the entryway.

"I followed you in, Joe. I had to get Barbara's things from the ambulance."

Joe looked at the doctor as he worked to assess the gash,

which seemed to run from Barbara's navel to a spot between her breasts.

"A clean cut, and no muscle damage, I think," he announced, peering at her. "What'd you do, tangle with a scalpel?"

"Is it that clean?" Barbara asked.

"A nice, clean cut. If you *had* to do it, at least you did it right."

They talked while the physician began his work, Joe trying to keep Barbara's mind off the pain as local anesthetics were injected and stitches begun. There was no need for a transfusion. The blood loss looked worse than it was.

"I still can't find the CVR, Joe. I'm about to the point of figuring . . . ouch . . . ow . . ." She closed her eyes and fought tears of pain with gritted teeth for a second.

"Sorry, Miss Rawlson. That's as bad as it'll get."

Barbara swallowed hard and opened her eyes, taking a tentative breath, eyes roaming to the doctor. "I'm beginning to think someone stole it, Joe. That sounds impossible, but the damn thing's nowhere."

"You completed the search?"

"I was just getting into the last section, so to speak. Guess I did it too literally . . . *ouch!* THAT . . . HURTS!" Her eyes closed again, her hands rolled into fists, and tears streamed down her face.

"Hang in there, Miss Rawlson." The physician hadn't batted an eye as she reacted, looking through his half glasses at the wound as he stitched her up.

"You're lucky, young lady," he said at last. "This is clean enough so that, with a little cosmetic surgery, I don't think the scar'll show. Your cleavage will remain intact." He looked up at her. "In fact, it may end up more pronounced."

Barbara tried to laugh, wincing at the pain. "For a girl with no boobs to speak of, that's reassuring—I think."

Everyone, including Susan Kelly, laughed at that. All except Joe, who cleared his throat at last, aware he was being watched by Susan with some amusement. "I'll have your team continue the search, Barbara, with a little more respect for the wreckage."

"Yes. Please." She rolled her eyes while Joe continued.

"But, if the CVR doesn't show up, I may have to agree with

you and declare it stolen, though I can't figure out who'd want to steal it. God, I'd hate to lose that tape. The captain gave us next to nothing this morning."

Susan elected to stay with her while Joe and Andy headed back to the airport, leaving Barbara to at least a couple of nights in the hospital at government expense, with promises to keep her in the investigatory loop. Susan said she would take a cab back. It was on the way out that Dr. Mark Weiss spotted the two NTSB men, and vice versa.

"You must be Joe Wallingford."

"That's right."

Andy motioned to Weiss. "Joe, this is the man I told you about."

Joe looked at the psychologist with a mixture of sympathy and uneasiness. What do you say to someone who had lost so much? Especially when the only news you could give him was negative. He seemed calm and collected, if somber, but his eyes were flat and lifeless, and though his clothes and hair were neat in appearance, Joe saw his face was rumpled and worn, especially for a man of his age, barely thirty-five.

"Have you had a chance to consider my request, Mr. Wallingford?" His voice was quiet and even.

Joe nodded and glanced down before engaging Weiss eye-to-eye. "Yes, I have, Doctor. I must tell you I sympathize completely, and I recognize your qualifications . . ."

"But you won't do it because I'm too close and too interested."

Joe sighed and bit his lips before nodding. "Not only that. Parties of record in an NTSB investigation are representatives of companies and organizations, not individuals. What you're suggesting would set a very dangerous precedent."

"I knew that'd be your objection. Future crash victims' families would want in. Can't you admit me based on professional expertise?"

Joe shook his head, realizing his hands had gone to his hips out of frustration; he wanted to help but knew this wasn't the way. "Your type of expertise isn't involved here, Doctor. This will most likely be a very complicated accident involving systems failures and perhaps procedure problems, and yes, as Andy reminds me, perhaps some human failure. I know you've been working with an airline that has badly impacted the psychological balance of its pilots, but that airline isn't involved here.''

"You don't know that yet.''

"Well, we've already met with the captain,'' Joe began, slightly upset with himself for gearing up to throw a half truth at Weiss but intending to hint they had the cause somewhat narrowed down, "and he gave us indications we could be dealing with weather or system failure.''

"I know, I saw him, too,'' Weiss replied. Joe must have looked startled, because Mark Weiss raised his hand to allay Joe's concern. "I just dropped in on him a while ago. I . . . needed to hear it for myself. What he remembered, I mean.''

Weiss's voice caught on the last word, and he looked away for a few seconds, taking a deep breath and trying to stay in control.

"What did he tell *you*, Doctor?''

Weiss looked back at Joe suddenly. "That he flew it right, but it didn't go where he aimed it.''

"Well, that's what I mean.''

Weiss shook his head. "But it's too early for what he says to be reliable. This is a complicated man who's scared stiff.''

"Scared?''

"Of course. He's a tough administrator and pilot. He's obviously worried about losing his job. I deal with men like this all the time. They're very complicated and need professional evaluation.''

Joe saw Andy's head nodding to one side and gestured to him. "That is Andy's field, human factors. I just don't see it here as anything but an interesting sidelight.''

"So far, Joe,'' Andy reminded him.

"Yeah. So far.''

"I could help with that,'' Weiss said.

Joe shook his head again, looking Weiss in the eye and placing his right hand on the younger man's shoulder. "Doctor, I can't know all you're feeling. I grieve with you for your loss, and you're showing remarkable restraint and composure to even be discussing this. But I cannot do it. I have more than your feelings to deal with. I have to get to the bottom of a technological mystery. If there's a hidden technical flaw, we have to find it rapidly. I can't afford distractions.''

Weiss looked back impassively, finally nodding. Joe offered

his hand and Mark took it warmly, which was a surprise. Joe
had expected hostility. "I'd like to stay in close touch. I'd like
to see you in Washington later," Mark said.

"Any time, Doctor."

Mark Weiss shook Andy's hand as well and walked away,
thoroughly undeterred. If he couldn't go in the front door of the
investigation, he'd go in the back door. Or maybe he'd create
his own door. It wasn't just the pain of losing Kim and the boys
driving him to some vengeful attempt to find someone to blame.
That was there too, he had to admit. But the only way he felt he
could accept their loss was knowing it had served some purpose
other than just causing the mindless agony of those left behind.
For their sake—for his sake—he had to know that whatever killed
his family was identified and corrected, if possible. He had to
be useful. He couldn't just sit around and grieve.

Mark thought of Timson and his wife, and the empty look in
her eyes. He had recognized the captain's fears immediately,
but he couldn't quite read his wife, and the visit had been too
brief, and too difficult, to learn more. But Mark had an intuitive
sense that Timson's ability to live with what had happened was
somehow tied to his wife's reaction.

Walt Rogers was waiting for them when Joe and Andy returned to the ballroom at the airport Marriott.

"You gotta see this readout." Walt ushered them into the
small conference room and began spreading the 8½-by-11-inch
sheets of paper on the table, multitudes of numbers in seemingly
endless columns representing the readout of different flight parameters sampled and recorded digitally every few seconds.

"Thank God this was a digital recorder," Joe said as he leaned
over the sheets.

"Tell me about it. I felt like throwing a party when the last
of the foil-tape stylus boxes was removed. Eighty percent of our
efforts used to go into deciphering the readings themselves. It
was hard to get to the questions of what the data meant."

Joe looked at Walt. "You've been going over these, give me
a clue."

Rogers smiled and shuffled through the papers until he found
the sheets representing the last minute of flight for the Airbus.
The columns of numbers held engine-power settings, flight-

control positions, the speed, altitude, attitude, and several other key readings.

"In a nutshell, Joe, the speed never dropped."

"Really?"

"Never. It increased in the last twenty seconds. The aircraft did pitch down, the G forces lightened, meaning he unloaded the back pressure, and then suddenly you see in these numbers that the elevator moved back to the nose-up position, the engines started accelerating, the bank shallowed and they tried to roll wings level, and they started trying to pull up. I'm not sure whether the flight recorder captured any data past the moment of first impact or not, but the last pass of figures shows that the engines are almost at full power and the aircraft is level at an altitude of about fifteen feet."

Joe said nothing for a while as he followed Andy and Walt through the columns, muttering occasionally and constructing a three-dimensional picture in his mind of the last seconds of the Airbus 320's flight. Finally he straightened up and looked at his two colleagues. "Okay, check this logic, and my conclusion. If this had been windshear, whether a headwind shearing to a tailwind suddenly, or even a major downdraft, we could see it in the airspeed, which would drop, and even though they'd be losing altitude, the airspeed would not increase."

Walt Rogers, an experienced pilot, nodded. "That's correct."

"How about a catastrophic downdraft?" Joe asked. "One that doesn't change the airspeed, but simply gives them a high sink rate?"

Walt sat on the edge of the table and sighed as he thought that over. "I can't say it's impossible, Joe, but we should have some other indication. This is awfully low to the ground—less than 300 feet—for that sort of phenomenon. Any major downburst should have spread out laterally by this point. But I can't say it's impossible."

"Look here, though. You're missing the key element." Andy was pointing to the figures and Joe followed his finger. "Look at the position of the elevator just as the rate of descent begins to increase. It's negative. It's moving to nose down. He had positive elevator, nose up all through the turn here . . . and here . . . see?"

"Yeah . . . right there."

". . . and then it suddenly moves down from plus three to minus values, and the descent starts. All that time the airspeed is steady."

Joe was nodding. "He pushed the nose over."

"Or," Andy corrected, "the airplane itself nosed over despite controls positioned to the contrary."

Joe Wallingford looked up at Andy and smiled, glancing at Walt Rogers for support. "Walt, you're a witness to this. Andy, my human-factors guru, is arguing nuts-and-bolts failure versus human failure."

"Hey," Andy said, trying to look offended and not succeeding, "call a spade a spade. Even I will acknowledge it when a wing comes off." He grinned at last, and Joe shook his head in mock disgust.

"Check this logic," Joe began again. "In order for windshear to have contributed, it would be merely coincidental to the fact that the airplane got a nose-down command and followed it. The main failure point is the nose-down command, right?"

Andy and Walt both were nodding guardedly. "Yeah."

"That's what I see, Joe."

Joe took off his reading glasses and looked at them both. "Then, subject to a careful, in-depth reading of these numbers, we can rule out weather and windshear, microbursts and down-bursts on the final approach as the singular cause, if not as a cause?"

"Tentatively," Andy confirmed.

"Of course. Tentatively. At least that's one down," Joe said.

"Two down. The engines were running," Walt said.

"We never doubted that, though."

"*We* didn't, but remember the witness who swore the engines were on fire before impact." Walt raised his hand and closed his eyes. "I know, I know, there's a witness like him in every accident."

"But Joe," Andy said, "the evidence of a massive windshear on the first approach is in these figures, too. They could have crashed there as well. I don't think we can ignore the poorly handled weather aspect of this just because they pulled it out on the first approach. Hell, it could've been that their adrenaline levels after that first approach led them to do something stupid and crash on the second approach."

Joe bit his lower lip and looked at Andy. "You're right, and we won't ignore it. But why did they pitch down? Now that we can see they did, why? That's the question. The captain said the airplane wasn't following his commands.''

Walt Rogers tapped a finger on the table. ''Any chance of talking to the first officer?''

Andy shook his head. ''Still in a coma, in critical condition.''

''So where does that leave us?'' Walt asked.

Joe got up and wandered toward the back of the room, hands stuck in his pants pockets, deep in thought. The other two watched him for a moment. Joe was given to wandering like that in the middle of a conversation, but the thoughtful statements which usually resulted were worth waiting for. He turned suddenly and sighed. ''All we know is the plane pitched down and the only pilot who can talk says he didn't do it, which leaves a control failure of some sort or electronic interference, which means this airplane may well be in deep trouble.''

''Don't forget sabotage, electronic or mechanical,'' Andy added.

''And if we can't find the exact cause?'' Walt asked, watching Joe's perplexed expression deepen.

''Then we're all in trouble,'' Joe replied at last. ''The pressure will be unbelievable.''

9

The White House loomed in the distance, framed by an urban forest of trees and fully noticed by Senator Kell Martinson as he stood on the north side of Lafayette Square and adjusted his topcoat.

Where was she? Kell looked the park over carefully, the rustling rainbow of fallen leaves carpeting the ground beneath the grand old deciduous trees that filled a living picture postcard, a scene almost too perfect to exist. The brisk autumn wind rumbled in his ear, blowing his hair and whipping the lower flaps of his coat as the senator turned to look again at his license plate.

This time it was a different plate on a different car that met his vision. The Riviera was safely parked back in Wichita, where he usually kept it. His "Beltway bomb" was a three-year-old Ford Taurus, a balance between conservative and flashy, the increasingly ubiquitous cellular antenna visible on the back window. But it was the Riviera's Kansas license plate that kept haunting him. The press, the NTSB, and perhaps the FBI were hunting that plate, that car, and though they didn't know it yet, hunting him. There was a very tough decision ahead, Kell knew. Should he go to the authorities and try to explain it? Or hunker down and hope no one had copied it? If he chose wrong, his career could go up in smoke, rendering any thoughts about future occupancy of the white building on Pennsylvania Avenue a moot exercise in fantasy.

A stylish young woman with flowing blond hair and a brisk stride caught his eye to the left, but it was not Cindy. Kell checked his watch and read 10:04 A.M. She had called less than an hour ago, knowing instinctively that he would be in his Senate office early. He did not tell her the couch had been home for yet another night—she and the staff always worried about his sleeping in the office. That was okay for a slightly bohemian congressman, they felt, but not for a senator. Ten A.M., she had said, but not at her home. It was too soon, and that would be too much pressure.

"Where, then, Cindy?" He had felt a great letdown at that, even a tinge of panic, as if the neutral ground of the park she suggested was to be a point of departure, a "safe" location from which she could relegate him to her past and move on. But that couldn't be what she had in mind! It made no sense. Yet the possibility had unhinged his concentration.

Part of his mind also kept chewing over the early-morning call from Senator Lew Whitney, his favorite deep South Democrat from Georgia, who was obviously madder than hell the moment he roused Kell from the couch at 7:30 with the incessant ringing of his private line.

"Kell, you snake! You got us to hold off testing our key components, and now your people are sneaking around getting ready to test yours. Aside from treaty violations, Senator, you've broken our agreement. Does the allegedly honorable gentleman have anything to say?"

"Yeah, Lew," he had replied, rubbing his eyes. "What the bloody hell are you talking about?"

"Star Wars, Kell, SDI. Remember? Our agreement? The one you promised to enforce when we were at each others' throats two years ago and you begged and pleaded with us to trust your side not to trash our approach. I remember the junior senator from Kansas telling me that both the correct program—*my* program—and your K Mart concept, "Brilliant Pebbles," could coexist if we trusted each other not to go off and secretly test. Well, bub, I've got a rumor here that your side's been doing exactly that."

"Not as far as I know, Lew. What are you hearing?" He had come wide awake with that news.

"Some scientist saw a tracking test module outside the factory over the weekend gettin' ready to be hauled away somewhere. It shouldn't even *be* outside the factory, Kell, let alone be moved somewhere. That can mean only one thing: testing. And, of course, if it's outside, the Soviets will have already photographed the hell out of it from space."

"I'll get on it, Lew. But I need to know a few more details, like where it was seen, what, exactly, it looked like, et cetera."

"I'll have one of my people call you, the man who got the call in the first place."

Cindy had called at that point and his concentration had jumped the track, but a quick and angry trip to the Pentagon would be a necessity within the next few hours. He wanted to think only of her, but duty called as well.

The 50-degree temperatures were low enough to be bracing, but sufficiently warm to be pleasant. Kell wished he could enjoy it, but foreboding stood in the way. He had never handled suspense very well. He wanted answers and solutions as fast as possible, and dangling human relationships were the worst trial of all—especially involving someone he loved. Political life demanded a tough facade and a tough-minded interior, and he could meet that challenge on most things. But in matters of the heart, Kell Martinson was vulnerable and he knew it.

Her form caught his eye first, walking with a familiar, energetic gait from the east end of the park, her hands thrust deeply into the pockets of her contoured, full-length leather coat, her beautiful hair tousled by the breeze. He watched her carefully as she approached, as if he might spot the telltale evidence of what was bothering her and what might be imperiling their relationship. But when she looked up at him, the smile that broadened her mouth was anything but a threat, and instinctively he moved toward her. Her smoky blue eyes looked directly at him, boring in for endless seconds before she spoke.

"Why were you in Salina?"

For a moment Kell didn't comprehend the unexpected question.

"What?"

"Salina. You called me from Salina. Why were you there?"

"That's . . . where else would I go?"

Cindy gently pulled her hands away and turned. They began walking, slowly, as she continued. "Kell, you thought I was dead . . . killed in the crash. The crash was in Kansas City. Why did you go to Salina?"

He shrugged and held out his hands, palms up, nonplussed by her intensity. "I don't understand what you're getting at. I . . ."

She stopped and turned toward him, a flash visible in her eyes.

"My body, or what would have been left of it, would have been in Kansas City. My parents are north of there in St. Jo. There would have been arrangements to make, people to notify, remains to identify. You say you love me, and I want to believe the type of love you're talking about is what I want and need, but why did you leave? Politics?"

Kell realized the question had frozen him in place, his subconscious plan to suppress the reality of what had driven him from the horror of the Kansas City flight line now in shambles. He looked away and found himself examining the cracks in the sidewalk, unable to meet her eyes.

"You've always had amazing insight, Cindy. I ran. Plain and simple. What I saw scared me to death, and like a whimpering coward, I jumped on my horse and rode. I sped through that gate and drove straight west, and I couldn't get myself to stop for an hour."

She was silent for the longest time, then nodded slightly and began to walk again, Kell instantly falling into step beside her.

"Then what?"

"I stopped at a roadside park, a rest area, and got on the phone. I must have called every hospital in Kansas City, hoping you might still be alive. When I saw it crash, I didn't think anyone survived in your airplane. But then there was this radio report about survivors from the flight. That's why I called . . . I would have gone back in a second if there had been any hope. I just figured . . ."

"You just figured," she continued for him, "that your cookie was dead, and yes, you did love her, but now she was gone, and getting caught in Kansas City would be a career threat. That was more important."

Kell didn't answer. He couldn't answer. The lie that had formed in his mind could not be spoken. She knew him, it seemed, far too well.

"I ran at first because it frightened me. As I ran, as I left, the thought kept crossing my mind, hell, it kept inundating my mind, that if you were gone, it would do me no good to ruin my career too. I didn't know whether it could hurt my career, but it didn't seem a reasonable risk. I told myself you would have wanted me to go."

She was silent, head down, watching the sidewalk as they

moved along, turning slowly at each corner of the park to stay within its borders.

"And there's more, Cindy. Something I'm . . . well." Kell stopped and gently reached for her, gingerly swiveling her around to face him lest she resist, which she did not. Her lips were lightly brushed by a pale lipstick and firmly closed, and a wisp of hair was dancing back and forth across her eyes, which were boring into him again. The story tumbled out, the approach, the collision, the tumbling wreckage flashing past, and his inability to move from the car. He decided not to mention the fact that his car had been seen. At least not yet.

They were in public, in the open, within view of the street and the White House guard stations and the U.S. Chamber of Commerce building to the north, yet she came to him suddenly, her head on his chest, his arms instantly around her. She said nothing as he held her, feeling her breathing, wanting her physically and emotionally to the exclusion of caution. And when she pulled away, her eyes met his again, accompanied by a warmer smile than he had expected.

"I thought I knew what was bothering me, and now I'm sure of it. I want . . . I *need* to be sure, before we take this any further, who comes first. Lady politics or me. I can be happy with such a ménage à trois, as long as I know, really know, that if one of us has to vanish from your life, it will not be me."

He began to answer, a hundred well-phrased arguments rushing forward at once, but she raised her hand and gently put a finger on his mouth.

"No, don't. Not words. It's something I have to see, and decide. This is not something you can lobby. I need time."

"I've changed, Cindy. Friday night's reaction was not me to begin with, but if my priorities were screwed up, they aren't now. Not after that—after this weekend, after a taste of what losing you would mean."

"Those are pretty words, Kell, and you're good with pretty words. I need to watch you for a while . . ."

"And I need to marry you."

"Which is a strange way to ask a girl." She glanced at him, half-amused.

"Okay. *Will* you marry me?" he corrected.

"I probably will, when marrying you will not result in charges of bigamy."

"Cindy, the marriage is over. You know that! Julie and I don't even talk anymore."

"She came by last month. To the office, to see you. It broke my heart, she looked so miserable."

He looked at her quietly for a moment. "It was Julie's idea, Cindy. She wanted the divorce, and it'll be final in January. In practical terms it's final now! I'll always care for her, but I'm not constrained anymore. I am out of her life." He hesitated, looking uncomfortable.

"When it's final, we'll talk." Her look was unyielding, and that scared him.

"Can we still . . . I mean . . ."

Cindy looked up and smiled slightly. "Meaningless sex, you mean?"

"Well, that's not—"

"You don't handle celibacy well, do you, Senator? Tell you what. I'll be back in the office tomorrow, and . . ."

"In the office? Won't that be indiscreet?"

"Cut it out. As I said, I'll be back tomorrow, and tomorrow night, if you want, you can come to my place."

She looked away with a sly smile, but Kell saw it and it buoyed him, wiping away for the moment the apprehension that she might exit stage left from his life, but leaving the spotlight on the more pressing problem.

Just as quickly her expression changed. "I've got to put on my administrative assistant hat now, Kell. We're in big trouble."

"What do you mean?" How had she found out about the license? he wondered. That had to be it.

"You know Larry Wilkins died right in front of you, right?"

"Yes, but that has nothing to do with me."

"Who comes to everyone's mind around here when the 'Most Opposed to Congressman Wilkins' category comes up?"

So that was it. The Wilkins thing had spooked her. "Okay, me. But I still don't . . ."

"You also know, don't you, that there's a serious possibility that the flight was sabotaged?"

"I heard, but I don't know that it's a credible rumor."

"And who just happens to be sitting there waiting for it but Wilkins's archenemy! How is that going to look? Waiting for your bimbo is one thing, a whiff of assassination is entirely different.''

Kell looked like he'd been scalded. *''Assassination?''*

''Kell, I'm not kidding, we need to figure out what to do and say if somehow it's discovered you were there. Does anyone know?''

He all but hung his head with a sigh, and her heart sank.

''Oh God. How?''

Kell told her the details, and the news reports of a videotape showing a luxury car with blurred plates. ''I don't have any reason to believe they can get the license number.''

''You don't have any reason to believe they won't, either. Kell, *we* know the mystery car is yours. If people find out before you tell them voluntarily, it could be a disaster. It may be anyway. Let's figure out what you should say, but we've got to get to it before they do.''

''I can't call a press conference on this!''

She fell silent, watching the worried look on his face. ''Okay, Kell. Let's think about it the rest of today and be ready to formulate a plan tomorrow. We can't hide from this.''

They said good-bye quickly and Kell headed for the Pentagon, negotiating his way through the military labyrinth like a veteran to the office of Air Force Lieutenant General Frank Roach, who was spearheading the ''Brilliant Pebbles'' research effort. The three-star was in, surprised and off balance as Kell pulled senatorial rank to sail past the secretary, angrily relating the essence of Senator Whitney's complaint.

''Senator, that's not true.'' General Roach sat back slightly in his chair, still off guard and wary, unprepared for a broadside from one of his program's staunchest supporters on the Hill. Kell watched his eyes as he spoke, noting with alarm that the general was not looking at him.

''I want to hear this from you, eyeball to eyeball, Frank. Are you or are you not attempting to sneak around the agreement?''

The general fixed Kell with a steady look, straight in the eye at last. ''You have my word, Senator, that we are neither testing, nor preparing to test. If anything was really moved outside the area, Senator Whitney's sources are misinterpreting the reason.''

''I need to know, fast. I can't hold this together, safeguard your funding without a major floor fight, or keep this off the Security Council agenda if I don't have immediate, reliable information.''

"I know that, Senator. You'll have it in a few hours. You may be sure I'm about to pull the fire alarm."

Kell got up to leave, shaking the general's hand, then hesitating in the doorway. "Frank, just moving some key piece of equipment could already have destabilized everything. You know that, don't you?"

The Air Force general drummed his fingers on his blotter and nodded his head, silently. "We're not testing, sir. That I can tell you. If anything was moved, it was for an honest purpose."

Kell returned to his office in a heightened state of agitation, convinced he was being misled. The drive back from the western side of the Potomac was barely remembered. He had spent the entire trip trying to think of ways to defuse the explosion of indignation Lew Whitney would unleash if Kell couldn't hand him a compartmentalized explanation, and fast. The incoming call from Whitney's administrative assistant, Hugh Walton, came at exactly the right moment, as Kell sat down at his desk.

"This guy got me out of bed, Senator, on Saturday. I promised to keep his name out of it, but he's one of the project directors for the particle-beam research going on at Lawrence Livermore in California. The man has toured most of the Pebbles installations, and he knows the hardware. He agrees with us that at best your system is a stepping-stone to ours, but the point is this: he was flying home from a conference, and at an intermediate stop on Friday he looks out the window of the airplane and sees the Air Force loading this mammoth self-propelled machine into a MAC transport."

"Do you know what it looks like, Hugh?"

"If I understood him right, it's like one of those big missile carriers, with a driver's compartment up front and a huge, rectangular body behind. You can get it down the highway, but only with pilot cars. You move something like that straight from the factor to the nearest airport in late evening or overnight."

"Sounds like the transporter for the Midgetman missile."

"Yeah, it does, a bit."

"What's in it? Any idea? Or can we talk about that?"

"Tracking test equipment. Acquisition and targeting and command-tracking stuff—very powerful, very secret technology."

"Hugh, are you sure the man saw what he thought he saw? I mean, at night, across an airport, and through the window of a commercial airplane, how'd he know what he was looking at?"

"Three reasons, Senator, and they're good ones. First, the size and shape are unique. He made a point of that. Second, it's from the Leavenworth, Kansas, facility. Third, the guy who saw it and reported it is a former member of the team that designed it several years back."

"Pretty convincing." Kell's pen had been scribbling a steady stream of notes onto the yellow paper of his legal pad as the man talked. He added the location of Leavenworth, Kansas, then stopped, inscribing a small question mark.

"Wait a minute." Kell Martinson sat up in his chair, the sudden image of an Air Force C-5B in the process of loading a large container triggering in his memory, the plane surrounded by security men he hoped had not observed his presence. "Where was he, Hugh, when he saw the container? Which airport?"

"I didn't tell you? That was the topper, why there was no doubt it came from the Leavenworth facility. They brought it to the closest airport that can handle a big MAC transport, Kansas City International Airport, last Friday night. You know, Senator, the night of that terrible airline crash."

The office of the chairman of the National Transportation Safety Board contained a desk, a rug, a set of leather chairs, a couch, and several windows overlooking Independence Avenue, and by 2 P.M. Monday afternoon it also contained an agitated chairman pacing around with a telephone receiver that had been on hold for nearly ten minutes. On the other end of the line was the office of the White House chief of staff.

"Goddamn it!" Dean Farris's upset voice boomed through the door to the ears of his secretary, who ignored it. Farris was easily frustrated.

The assistant to the chief of staff had gone off somewhere to check on just what the common wisdom of the administration was regarding the Larry Wilkins affair. Farris had worried his way through the weekend over how to play it. Should anything more be done by Joe Wallingford to counter the media impression that the NTSB was not paying serious attention to the possibility of sabotage? Was the President concerned about a political backlash? He knew very well that such concerns were not binding on the independent board or its chairman, but he also knew this was sensitive, and intergovernmental cooperation seemed important at such a moment.

Suddenly the man was back. "Uh, Dean? You there?"

Farris pressed the phone back to his ear. "Yes."

"I think the general wisdom here is that whatever happened—
and of course the determination of cause is entirely your bailiwick—we wouldn't want anyone thinking we were a party to
some sort of celebration of Congressman Wilkins's demise. We
also wouldn't want anyone thinking we are interfering with your
investigation of sabotage. By the same token, this isn't exactly
the death of a President. No one here is terribly broken up."

"If we find it's *not* sabotage, and there was something badly
wrong with the aircraft's design or black boxes, does anyone there
have any concerns that I ought to keep in mind about Airbus?"

The reply carried a puzzled tone. "Why?"

"Well, I mean, that plane is the pride of France. Should I
check with someone at State?"

There was a long pause at the other end as the assistant chief
of staff thought out his response and phrased it with extraordinary care. "Dean, the only concern for any of us in the executive
branch, or in an independent agency such as yours, should be
normal diplomacy. Even if the Airbus is a problem, no one here
is going to suggest you pull whatever punches you think appropriate. I would say, however, that it might raise more questions
and problems to go phoning around State asking how they feel
than by just playing it the way you see it. As long as you don't
announce that the Airbus is a dangerous flop, and the French
are homicidal maniacs for building it, or some such nonsense, I
can't imagine how you could create a diplomatic incident."

"Okay. I understand you. I just wanted to make sure I understood all the balance points."

"No problem."

"Tell the President we'll handle it."

"You bet," the man said, pleasantly, as he hung up the phone
and stared at it, shaking his head. Tell the President indeed.
What else was the NTSB supposed to do but handle it?

Dean Farris had often thought about getting a lightweight
telephone headset since he spent so much time on the phone,
but it seemed unchairmanlike. Instead, he contented himself with
a practiced balancing act, the telephone handset rocking precariously on his bony shoulder as he punched up another line and
entered the number of Susan Kelly's hand-held phone in Kansas

City. A series of clicks and the sound of electronic ringing preceded Susan's voice.

"Hello?"

"Susan? Dean back in D.C. What's the status this morning?"

"Hello Dean." Her voice was flat and unenthusiastic, but Farris did not notice. "Well, where do I start. Barbara Rawlson will be out of the hospital on Thursday, and she should have no permanent damage. We still have no clue where the cockpit voice recorder is, and Joe Wallingford tells me he's on the verge of concluding it was stolen. It's driving the systems group crazy."

"What do you think of the flight-recorder data?"

Susan hesitated, figuring out his meaning. "Is it out here yet? I haven't seen it, Dean."

"Ah. Well, get Joe to go over it with you. I have a copy but haven't studied it yet."

And neither of us could probably interpret it by ourselves, she thought to herself.

"Are you keeping Joe out of trouble?" Farris asked.

There was a pause on the Kansas City end. "Is that what this call is about? Dean, please remember what I told you Saturday. I'm not here to baby-sit the staff, and I'm certainly not going to try to ride herd on Joe Wallingford. If you have a problem with what he's doing, *you* call him. I think he's doing just fine."

"Well, at least keep me informed of anything startling."

Dean Farris ended the conversation with a few empty pleasantries, and immediately punched in the number of Gary Seal, the investigator heading the operations group. Farris had no way of knowing where Seal was at the moment his portable telephone began chirping in the hallway of the hotel, nor could he see Susan's expression of disgust as she heard it several steps behind her. There was no question in Susan Kelly's mind, however, who was on the other end.

"Gary? This is Dean Farris. I hadn't heard from you."

"There's been no time, and nothing to report."

"You keeping an independent eye on things?"

"Yes sir."

"Well, now don't think I don't trust Joe. I just want to make certain I have a balanced view of all that's happening out there."

"No problem."

"I got you . . . you can't talk right now. Right?"

"Uh . . . right."

"Call me later when you're in private if you've got anything interesting to tell me, and I guess, having said that, I should ask whether to expect a call from you?"

"You should, yes."

"Okay. Later, then." Farris recycled the phone once more, entering a sequence of numbers leading through the federal telephone system to an office one floor above his in the FAA's section of the FAA building. The voice of Associate Administrator Bill Caldwell came on the line. In the past few years Farris had come to regard Caldwell as an ally and confidant, even when they squared off agency to agency over issues of safety.

It was difficult for the NTSB. Whenever they determined a change was needed in the regulations, they could only ask the FAA to make the change; there was no way for the Board to force anyone to do anything.

The two men exchanged pleasantries before Farris jumped to the warning he had been eager to pass on.

"Bill, my people tell me your control tower in Kansas City may have screwed up Friday night. I wanted to give you a heads-up warning."

Bill Caldwell's mind raced ahead, reviewing the previous evening's telephone conference with the FAA members assigned to the NTSB team in Kansas City. He was acutely aware of the problems and the threat to the FAA. The shift supervisor, one Carl Sellers, had already been questioned extensively and copies of the tower tapes had been sent to Caldwell on Saturday. The apparent failure of the tower personnel to give out the proper windshear information might add up to a damage containment problem for the agency, and he damn sure wasn't going to discuss such sensitive information with an unprofessional politician like Dean Farris. Farris had cozied up to him over the past few years and Caldwell had encouraged the apparent friendship, not necessarily for purposes of expediency. Farris was indeed an interesting fellow, with wide-ranging interests and an analytical mind. But as a politician he was a rank amateur who didn't realize it. That, coupled with his big mouth, was a potentially disastrous combination within the Beltway. Farris, however, had also been a wonderful source of advance information into NTSB activities. Caldwell had been able to maneuver the FAA out of several potentially embarrassing problems because Farris leaked confidential details in the early stages of several crash investigations.

"Yeah, we're aware of the initial details, and I'm watching it. Any feelings on how the overall investigation is leaning, not that they lean, of course?"

"Of course." Dean Farris laughed easily at the shared inside joke and filled him in.

Caldwell listened carefully as he checked his desk calendar. "Dean, join me for dinner tomorrow? Your wife mind?"

"I'll tell her it's necessary."

"Good. I want to get your ideas on several of the upcoming airworthiness directives we're considering for the DC-8 aging-fleet program." Caldwell knew the ADs he was mentioning were set in concrete, but Farris loved to feel included. He'd throw Farris a dry bone, and Farris might reciprocate by innocently tossing him a live bomb with enough time left to defuse it. Such were the methods of protecting his boss, the FAA administrator, as well as his own tail.

Bill Caldwell shook his head as he hung up the phone, glancing at an aide who had been listening on an extension.

"Not a word of this to the administrator yet, but I think we're going to have problems in Kansas City. I feel it. Get hold of our people out there, figure out who is closest to the NTSB's IIC, and make a spy out of him. If we're going to get broadsided, I want early warning."

The aide nodded and left as Bill Caldwell let his mind dart up and down the different corridors of possibility, peeking behind all the doors. He had always survived as a nonaeronautical bureaucrat in an aeronautical agency by playing it like a giant chess game. You either schemed and plotted several moves ahead of your opponent in order to put him in check, or he would blindside you and put *you* in check, or worse: checkmate. He looked at everyone that way. There were the kings, such as the administrator, who were to be carefully moved around and told what they needed to know, but no more. There were queens in the agency as well, he chuckled to himself, but that was another story. The department heads, one rank beneath, Caldwell regarded as knights and bishops. Strong but expendable. He could throw them judiciously into battle and sacrifice one every now and then to a congressional broadside, yet survive unscathed himself.

And then there were the pawns. Thank God for pawns. He enjoyed relegating people to the status of pawns, even those who were technically of higher rank. There were thousands of them, all available to do his bidding if properly moved around the chessboard of the FAA: air-carrier inspectors, air-traffic-control managers, engineers, and more. Even Dean Farris had let himself become a pawn in Caldwell's game, though he would never know it.

He loved the chess analogy. It had kept professional life in perspective during some dark days, when miscalculation born of not being from the world of aviation had nearly trapped him.

There were dangers, though. Even pawns like Farris could turn on you if you let them. The very move you fail to consider will always be the one that gets you. Chess was like that, and so was the job of associate administrator, and he was a master at both.

Bill Caldwell realized he had been drumming his fingers loudly on his rather plain desktop and willed himself to stop, getting up suddenly and aiming his athletic body toward the door as he double-checked his watch. He had a meeting in ten minutes four floors below, and as usual, he wanted to time it to the second. He liked the fact that people around 800 Independence could set their watches by his precise movements. If Bill Caldwell said he'd arrive at a given time, you could bank on it, and that slightly unnerved everyone, giving him the upper hand—keeping him one move ahead.

As Caldwell walked out of his office on the ninth floor, Beverly Bronson walked into Dean Farris's office one floor below, her teased auburn hair cascading over broad shoulders draped by a soft chiffon blouse which clung to and emphasized what the males in the NTSB were sure was the most magnificent female figure in U.S. government service. Miss Bronson had been appointed by parties unknown on the Hill to a job in NTSB public and governmental affairs, and had proven good at congressional liaison. It was her job to protect the image of the Board, especially in front of the congressional committees that controlled its budget. She was also amazingly adept at keeping track of NTSB gossip: what the troops were doing, who was sleeping with whom, and who might be secretly talking to the outside world about NTSB internal business. Her success in that area had earned her the suspicion of nearly everyone on the eighth floor—except Dean Farris.

10

The group of worried men in the boardroom of Rogers Drilling in downtown New Orleans had been filling the air with tobacco smoke and nervous profanity for the past hour. Now they were listening in silence as Forrest Rogers called the fishing camp one more time, the clock now showing 8 A.M. The weary voice on the other end came through the speakerphone tinged with a Cajun accent and the distinctive rhythm of bayou country. The man assured them that Walter Calley had not show up, and yes, as he had already promised them, he would call the moment the errant electronics engineer arrived—if he did.

Rogers launched a felt-tip pen at the far wall. "Goddammit! Where the hell *is* he?"

"Forrest, that tape'll be here in a few hours, I suspect. You said he sent it Sunday?"

"Said he did."

"Okay. Let's all calm down. We don't know what Walter has or hasn't done."

Rogers whirled on him. "What he's apparently done somehow, Edward, is murder the man it took us damn near two decades to get into the U.S. Congress, and by the by, he killed about a hundred other folks at the same time! I don't know how, but the son of a bitch killed Larry Wilkins, the white man's one true hope in this screwed up country! That good enough for you? I still say we call the FBI."

"Hold on, damn it!" A meticulously groomed man in the far corner of the room held up his hand, and the others listened respectfully. "The last *gawdammed* thing we're going to do is call the very bunch of mindless hounds who've been trackin' and doggin' every move of every conservative organization since Bobby Kennedy declared war on the South . . . since before most of you boys were shavin' age. Now, maybe Mr. Calley's gone and lost his mind and become a mass murderer, and maybe he hasn't. Maybe he knows something. He told you—you said it Forrest, I didn't—that he had good reason for what he did, and he wanted to explain, right?''

"Yeah," Rogers said, "yeah, Bill, and he also admitted he persuaded Larry to fly to Kansas City."

"But we don't know *why*, now do we? Until we hear his tape, or hear him explain, we don't know why. Could be someone else killed Larry and they're after Calley to shut him up."

Forrest Rogers paused, then looked the man in the eye. "I figure at least that's what Walter thinks, the way he sounded. But what we *do* know, Bill, is this: Larry Wilkins was murdered, if not by Walter, then by somebody else. Walter told me that himself."

"Okay." Bill nodded and smiled. "Okay, so that's what we do in the meantime." He turned to a sandy-haired young man sitting at the long table. "Jess? You arrange to have Larry's office issue a press release or hold a press conference *this afternoon*, an' announce that they've got proof positive it was an assassination. Get all the networks and news people in a frenzy. Have 'em say the details will be revealed in a couple of days, and then either we'll turn over the idiot himself if he did it, or relay what he knows to the world. Hell, we may just have us a martyr here, and I think Larry would have wanted it that way— if he had to go in the first place, of course. He's not the first one gave his life to get this country back in control." Bill sat down heavily and looked at the group. "An' boys . . . he won't be the last either."

Forrest Rogers looked startled. "We can't turn him over to the FBI!"

"What do you mean, Forrest?"

"With what he knows about all of us, Larry's promises and agenda, and who supports us around this town. Walter, remember, was an important part of the campaign team. He was up there at that factory because Larry asked him to be there. You told me that. I didn't know he was spying. Anyway, if he got really scared and was facing murder charges, he'd probably start talking, and the public—they'd be so infuriated we'd never get anyone else elected.''

Bill stayed silent for a few seconds, looking straight at Forrest Rogers without changing expression. ''What are you recommending?''

''Christ, I don't know. But we can't just throw him to the wolves, can we?''

Walter Calley punched the small light on his digital watch and read 8:05 A.M. The air in the Camaro was stale, covered as it was with hay, but worming his way back inside had been the only method he had of staying warm. There were extra clothes in the trunk, but no blankets.

He had stayed flat on his belly in the open loft of the barn until sundown, silently watching through the open doors, noting the helicopter that flew back and forth over the area for several hours before noon and the police cars that roared up the road and then back again, none of them spotting the telltale tire tracks leading into the pasture.

In midafternoon a sheriff's deputy had turned into the field. Walter had quietly cocked his gun as the young man got out and walked to the barn to look in. He had prayed the deputy would see nothing, hear nothing, *feel* nothing, and his prayer was answered. The thought of having to actually shoot someone was horrifying, but he could not let himself be captured. The lawman had returned to his car and motored off to the west, oblivious of the firepower that had followed his every move near the barn. Walter saw him stop and approach another barnlike structure in another field, moving with equal disinterest and lack of caution. After sundown Walter had returned to the car for a fitful night.

If I'm not found before tomorrow, he had decided, I'll take off cross-country on foot. He had been trained well in the Army how to ''E and E''—escape and evade. This was his neck of the woods after all, and the fishing camp couldn't be more than 40 miles.

Carefully and slowly he rolled down the driver's window and hauled himself through the hay to the surface, stopping and listening at intervals, expecting to hear the collective click of a dozen revolver hammers as his head came into filtered daylight in the ruined old barn.

Instead, the sedate sounds of distant birdcalls on a frosty

morning meadow greeted him, shafts of sunlight slicing through the musty interior. After pulling what he needed from the trunk, he covered the car completely once more with hay and took up his position in the loft again to wait out the daylight, taking stock of his meager supplies. Fortunately he'd brought some water and snack foods—an old habit. He could last several days on those alone, and by wearing several layers of clothes for warmth and using the stars for navigation, he should be able to make ten miles or so a night. The police and FBI would be looking for a Camaro, not a midnight evader: one man traveling by foot in the darkness. He had a fighting chance.

At the same moment, 600 miles to the north in Kansas City, NTSB investigator Nick Gardner smiled a slightly perverse smile as he snapped off the small, plastic radio in his hotel room, having just heard a local news station play the Kansas City control-tower recording from Friday night. The FAA and NTSB would go crazy looking for the source of the leak, and he was it.

The original audio tape—a reel from a machine in the tower which slowly recorded all radio activity to and from the tower's radios—was still in the possession of the control-tower chief, who would undoubtedly appear before his scandalized superiors shortly clutching that tape to show it had not been stolen. That would confuse FAA headquarters for at least a few hours. But the tower chief had made an official duplicate for the NTSB investigators to examine, and Nick, as chairman of the air-traffic-control group, had surreptitiously copied that one, slipping the cassette to a local radio news reporter Monday night in the airport hotel parking lot. There would be no way to prove which dub had been copied, and Nick was counting on that uncertainty to keep himself employed.

"I want the world to hear for themselves that the controller never mentioned—*never mentioned*, mind you—the possibility of windshear while the Airbus was on its first approach," he had told the reporter, who promised to give the tape to the national media as well. He would have liked to explain why he knew the FAA so very well, but the explanation would have make him seem biased and unreliable as a source.

I *am* biased, he thought, but not unreliable. But if I tell the reporter I'm a former traffic controller myself, he won't trust me. For over a decade he had worked the scopes, almost destroying his life, the lousy excuse for FAA management making the high-pressure job impossibly stressful. In the face of failing health, chain-smoking, chronic migraine headaches, and dangerous blood-pressure levels, he had been granted medical retirement just two months before the illegal PATCO controllers strike—which was the only reason he had been employable by the NTSB, all the PATCO strikers having been barred from other government positions. Nick's great escape had proven a perfect solution, but he couldn't forget his past, or the things within the air-traffic-control system that still cried out for change.

By 10 A.M. in Washington, all three television networks and a host of radio networks had played the tape, and by 11 A.M.— as Gardner knew would happen—accusations, recriminations, and frantic phone calls were erupting in reaction. Once again, an FAA-controlled tape had found its way into the public domain.

By 11:20 A.M. in his Washington office, NTSB Chairman Dean Farris had replaced the receiver with his ears red and his blood pressure rising. FAA Associate Administrator Bill Caldwell's accusations were infuriating. How the hell could Caldwell be sure it wasn't his own FAA people in Kansas City who released the tower tape? There was no justification, he had sputtered at Caldwell, for concluding that the NTSB team had leaked the tape to the media. And in any event, it probably didn't matter.

Farris had punched Wallingford's cellular phone number with poorly contained fury, calculating a high probability that he was responsible and jumping at the chance to ream him out.

"Joe? What do you know about the leak of the tower tapes?"

There was momentary silence on the other end, and Farris interpreted it darkly.

"Nothing. I just heard about it a few minutes ago."

"You know that came from our people, don't you? That was the NTSB's copy they played." Farris tossed it out as a statement of fact, listening carefully for the tone of the reply, which was that of an offended man.

"*What?* Where did you get *that* idea, Mr. Chairman?"

"The FAA accounted for their tape. Have you accounted for yours?"

"Nick Gardner is in charge of the ATC group. I'm looking for him now, but he wouldn't—"

"Bullshit, Joe. Under your loose control, I'm surprised you haven't asked the media in as a formal party to the investigation."

There was silence, and with perverse satisfaction, Farris could imagine Joe Wallingford counting to ten—which, in effect, he was.

"Mr. Chairman, that was uncalled for . . . not to mention an insult."

"If the shoe fits, Joe."

"It does not." Joe realized he was squeezing the phone in anger.

"Perhaps. In the meantime, the FAA is convinced we did it, and they're madder than hell. On top of that, the media is hammering away at sabotage on every network. They're convinced someone murdered Larry Wilkins and took all those passengers with him, and Caldwell is saying he's all but convinced the flight-control system of the A320 was sabotaged by radio waves from the ground! I'm sitting in the middle of mass hysteria. I need you back here now."

Joe thought he'd misunderstood. Farris couldn't be ordering him to fly home. "What?"

"I want you to head back here this afternoon."

"I'm in the middle of the *field* investigation." This is unbelievable, Joe thought. The man has no concept of what we do out here.

"Joe, follow orders, for Christ's sake. Get back here. Leave Andy Wallace in charge. He can handle it. First thing when you get back, I want you to go up to Caldwell and explain what happened with the tower tape—if you can, that is. You say Nick's people didn't do it?"

"That's my assumption."

"Good. You go tell Caldwell."

Joe punched the disconnect button on his phone as he fumbled for the list of phone numbers to the cellular phones carried by the rest of his team. He located Nick's at last, punching in the numbers and waiting for his voice, which came on line with the first ring.

The conversation was quick. Yes, he had heard the broadcast. No, he hadn't leaked the tape, and for that matter, no one had ever had unsupervised control of the NTSB's tape. In short, the tower had to be responsible. The tower personnel were lying.

"Nick, you are certain? I'm going to be defending us to Farris and to the FAA."

"I'm certain," he replied.

There was a 3 P.M. departure to Washington, and Joe reluctantly booked himself on the flight before beginning the process of turning the reins over to Andy. There were too many things to do—too many loose ends. Talk to all the group chairmen, check the progress of wreckage removal and the search for the CVR, review the witness interview progress, check in with Barbara, and then worry through two more pages of "to do" items on his legal pad. He had rushed out of his room mentally going over it all when two men from Airbus caught him in the hotel foyer, their faces gray and serious, their mood funereal.

"We would have gone to Ms. Rawlson, but since she's in the hospital . . ."

"I understand."

André Charat from Airbus had been assigned to Barbara's systems group, and the other man, Robert d'Angosta, was an Airbus technical support representative from Toulouse, France. Joe directed them to the conference room, mildly apprehensive and on guard.

Charat began, clearing his throat and talking to his shoes. "We are very concerned, Mr. Wallingford, that the technical realities of the 320's flight-control system be clearly understood."

"By the entire team, I assume?"

"Yes, and most importantly, by you. You are the decision maker."

"Hey, now, I'm only in charge of the field investigation," he began. Charat raised his hand and waved Joe to a verbal halt.

"You set the pace, Mr. Wallingford. You need to know."

Joe had noticed d'Angosta holding a leather portfolio. He opened it at Charat's nod and began spreading electrical-system diagrams on the table as Charat launched into an abbreviated but precise explanation of the flight-control computers in the A320 and why the probability that all of them could fail simultaneously so as to cause an uncommanded pitch down was almost to the threshold of impossible.

"You would stand a better chance of winning the lottery,"

he said at last, watching Joe for a reaction and looking him in the eye for the first time.

"How about EMI? Electromagnetic interference? Possible?"

"Yes . . . ," Charat began slowly, shifting his gaze to the table, remembering the thousands of hours of discussions with FAA people, airline executives, and even French aviation authorities, all nervous over a new technology, "but it's only possible if you have a monstrously powerful transmitter very, very close, as close as 300 feet, and even then the worst that could happen is some sort of momentary instability. Since there are no such powerful radar or radio sources anywhere close to Kansas City Airport, that means this simply *isn't* a valid possibility."

"Have you seen the flight-data-recorder readouts?"

"Yes. Your Walt Rogers provided those a few hours ago. Mr. Wallingford, those readouts prove our point, don't you see?"

Joe was surprised, and Charat noticed, nodding before the word was out of Joe's mouth: "Why?"

Charat shifted in his chair, his right hand gesturing in an intricate pattern as if grasping an invisible control stick, an accomplished mime describing the control inputs while his left hand simulated the airplane responding to those commands. "Because, the readout shows that the flight controls—in this case the elevator—were operating in a positive manner. First nose down, then a steady nose up. No transient computer failure, electrical short, or stray radio-induced signal would have let the elevator operate in such middle ranges. If there had been a control failure to the down position, the elevator surface would have slammed to full nose-down deflection and stayed there. Since here it was operating short of that—as we can see from that readout—that proves that only one thing could have caused this accident."

Charat stopped and his hands descended slowly to his lap as his eyes fixed on Joe, who was holding his breath.

"Yes?" Joe asked it at last, seeing that the Airbus representative was waiting for an invitation to present his coup de grace.

"The pilots commanded those changes. Whoever was flying pushed the nose over and failed to pull it back until too late. Our airplane only did what it was told. Nothing more, nothing less."

Joe caught himself sighing, his right palm held up in the air as an unconscious gesture of frustration. These men were sincere, surely. But they were anything but neutral. They had an airplane to protect, and their conclusion was suspect. "The captain says he never pushed forward."

"The captain, sir, is either lying or deluded."

"That's quite a statement, Mr. Charat."

"And these fanciful and uninformed statements we are hearing, making electronically impossible accusations against our flight-control system, are they not inflammatory too? I tell you, we have information that there are some in the FAA who want to ground the airplanes."

Joe knew his face was being studied for the slightest flicker of a muscle. Charat must know something of Caldwell's attitude, he decided. Or he's a skillful fisherman, casting out his worst nightmare, looking for a ripple on the water of official normalcy. When Joe could stand the impasse no longer, he shook his head. "No one's going to ground your airplane unless there's a clear and certain reason."

"Oh?" Charat sat back, a scowl crossing his features. A Gallic scowl, Joe thought. The French were so good at acting as if they'd been mortally insulted, or was that an unfair, almost bigoted impression? The French executive leaned forward again. "And you are not aware, Mr. Wallingford, that certain people within the FAA have already started threatening the A320 with grounding if it cannot be proven to *their* satisfaction that no control problems could possibly be involved? Is that not an impossible standard?"

"What, exactly, are you referring to?" Joe asked, having just barely stopped himself from asking, "What, exactly, do you know?"

"We have our sources. And we know of certain FAA officials with ties to American manufacturers who would love to ground the 320 for months. We . . . I . . . hope that you, as an investigator with an impeccable record for balance and honesty, will not permit that to happen."

They parted amicably, but Joe was deeply worried. The only explanation that made any sense was a system failure, either internally or induced by radio interference, and yet they had made a convincing case against it. But the hints about Bill Caldwell and his stand on the 320—as well as his intentions—had unnerved Joe. As Charat was leaving, he half mumbled something Joe did not quite understand. Now the words coalesced, as if his mental computer had needed time to decipher a coded message. "Check," Charat had said under his breath, "who owns stock in which aircraft builders before deciding who to believe at FAA." It was most likely a desperate gambit, a scandalous sidelong accusation against anyone in government who opposed their airplane. But like a multipronged fishhook snagged in the skin, it was going to be hard to dislodge.

If the men from Airbus were right that their flight controls were blameless, then Joe would have to accept the idea that Dick Timson, chief pilot, highly experienced captain, and a company vice-president, purposefully or negligently pushed the nose of his aircraft into a shallow dive at a point in time when such a thing would be, in effect, an act of suicidal stupidity, and of all the possibilities, that made the least sense. In fact, it gave more credence to the theory of electronic interference.

Joe found a phone at the back of the ballroom and called Barbara's hospital room. She was supposed to be released on Thursday in time to go home with the team, but she was under everyone's orders to rest in the meantime. Instead, she had spent almost every hour on the phone with members of her systems group, directing the various probes and trying to figure out the location of Flight 255's elusive cockpit voice recorder.

"Farris wants me back early, Barbara." Joe decided not to reveal his fury or the stupidity involved in Farris's order. "I'll leave Andy in charge, and he'll make arrangements to get you to the airport Thursday."

"I'm fine, Joe, and we'll work it out," she told him, still wincing with pain every time she drew a deep breath. "Joe, I talked with my team a while ago, and I'm sorry to report no progress on the CVR. They're sifting through the last portion of the rear fuselage, but I don't expect to find it there. It was stolen, Joe, or it wasn't on the airplane."

"Not installed, you mean? Hmmm. I hadn't considered that."

"Well, it's possible. Either that, or, as I say, it was stolen just after the accident."

"But, by whom, Barb? And how? That's never happened before."

"I know, but what if, for instance, sabotage was the cause, and whoever brought them down also slipped in and took the evidence."

"That's pretty far out, Barbara."

"Well, all I know, Mister IIC, sir, is that we can't find the damn cockpit voice recorder."

Joe told Barbara to relax as he said good-bye, then punched in the number of Susan Kelly's phone, reaching her just before the hotel shuttle was ready to load for the short trip to the terminal.

"I've been recalled," he explained.

"I was afraid of that, Joe."

"You mean Farris has already discussed this with you?"

"Not this, not the FAA's anger over the leak of the tower tape. But I told you what he said to me before, on Saturday. He's not happy with you, Joe. I'm not surprised he wants you out of here."

Joe looked up at the hotel's airport shuttle, which was still loading. "Where are you, Susan?"

"At the terminal." They agreed to meet in ten minutes at Joe's outbound gate, and Joe punched the phone off as he ran for the shuttle. Susan was waiting when he arrived to check in for the flight. They sat on a bench out of earshot of the milling passengers. "Look, Joe, I haven't worked with Dean long enough to know all I need to know about what makes the man tick, but I do know that beneath that excellent intellect and that facade of polished control, there beats the heart of a political animal on the prowl for bigger political game. I should not be telling you this, and I hope you won't repeat it, but Dean regards the NTSB as a refueling stop and not a destination. The problem, of course, is that Dean isn't controllable, and he can ruin you professionally, Joe. You've got to be careful handling him."

Joe was studying his hands and nodding, the mere suggestion of having his cherished position with the NTSB imperiled sending cold chills through the corridors of his mind. "I know that. Look, I love what I do." He looked up at her, letting his eyes get lost in hers for a second. "I would never want to be prevented from serving the Board as an investigator. This is my home."

"Then you've got to outlast him."

"Yeah, but I can't pull my punches when he's dead wrong."

"Diplomacy, Joe. A good diplomat can tell you to go straight to hell with such eloquence you find yourself thanking him for providing directions. Work on that art with Farris. For your sake, and for ours.''

They said good-bye with a brief handshake, and Joe turned for the jetway, the warmth of her hand radiating in his. Some of the cold edge, it seemed, had thawed.

The flight attendants were serving dinner at 35,000 feet by the time Joe realized the man next to him was writing on stationary emblazoned with North America's logo, his expressions and demeanor that of an angry, upset executive. Joe decided to leave him alone, eating dinner in silence, thinking how effectively both of them could pretend the other didn't exist while sitting mere inches apart. But somewhere over Kentucky, Joe's seatmate lost control of his pen and Joe reached to the floor to pick it up—an act requiring eye contact and a thank-you, which slowly led to a reluctant conversation.

The man finally extended his right hand, no hint of a smile on his face. ''I'm Craig Lewiston. And you're . . . ?''

''Joe Wallingford with the NTSB.''

''Interesting,'' he said. ''I was vice-president/maintenance for North America until about five P.M. yesterday, when I reached the breaking point and resigned.'' He held up his right hand again, palm out. ''Nothing to do with the crash, I assure you.''

Lewiston went back to his writing for a few minutes, trying to avoid noticing that the NTSB man was waiting for him to continue.

Joe looked at Lewiston as well as you can look at a seatmate in the crowded coach section of an airliner. He was very tall, perhaps six foot four, a gaunt face framing a large mouth permanently turned at the edges into a slightly amused expression, which stood in contrast to his obvious upset. His huge eyebrows constantly fluttered when he talked and were so prominent Joe could see them in his peripheral vision.

Finally, reluctantly, he sighed and pocketed his pen, speaking with a pronounced Texas drawl. ''As of today it isn't my concern, but what are you finding in the investigation?''

Joe gave him a synopsis, noting the media had settled on sabotage.

''Damned unlikely,'' Lewiston confirmed. ''That airplane's a marvel. I know the system—I worked with it and took the mechanics course myself. I'm a certified mechanic by original trade.''

"Really? A vice-president with greasy fingernails?''

Lewiston smiled thinly. "For all the good that does an executive these days.''

"May I ask why you're leaving?''

"You may. I'm not sure I want to tell the NTSB, though. I'm headed to Washington to interview with USAir and the Air Transport Association, and possibly some others. I have no intention of leaving this business, just the North America war zone.''

He fell silent again, and Joe dove into the void. "Why is it a war zone? You said it wasn't the crash?''

Lewiston snorted as if asked to recount something terribly obvious. "We've—I mean they've—been fighting an impossible financial battle for the last decade, and they're almost out of assets to sell to keep them in the air. The people—including those of us in the executive corps—have taken a series of pay and benefit cuts that really hurt, and now we're in play, a take-over target.''

"I hadn't heard,'' Joe told him.

"It came out just this morning. Fortunately I haven't sold my stock. It immediately shot to thirteen.''

Lewiston checked his watch, knowing their descent into Washington would begin shortly and wanting privacy. Joe caught himself feeling guilty and rude, but the opportunity to probe was too golden to ignore.

"There's something I'd like to ask, which no current maintenance chief could ever answer without toting the company line. But—''

"But since I'm a renegade now, will I tell it like it is, right?''

"Something like that.''

Lewiston nodded his head yes. "What?''

"Have you had trouble keeping your maintenance standards up during the past few years? You remember the fines against Eastern and so many others, and all the arguments that they had let things slip because of deregulation? Did you feel pressure like that?''

"Hell yes. Systemwide.'' He shifted his large frame in the aisle seat for a moment. "You're in the government. You remember when Mrs. Dole and Jim Burnley and all the others at the Department of Transportation came out like good little Reagan soldiers and toed the administration's hard line: ain't no problems in our pea patch, folks! Deregulation's peachy keen wonderful! No one's cut anything. Safety is perfect." Lewiston shook his head again. "And the emperor is fully clothed. Trouble is, I can't accuse them of lying because they were all too goddammed ignorant of the details of aviation safety to be able to lie. They thought all that garbage was the truth, but good Lord, people like me were facing angry leaders like Dave Bayne day in and day out and trying unsuccessfully to justify each overhaul and every part and every salary, and having the heart cut out of our maintenance budget."

Joe nodded. "Many times we saw problems but couldn't document them."

"Of course. Because we didn't kill any more people per year than the number the DOT had decreed was an acceptable slaughter rate. That's why you couldn't document it. The only figures they wanted at DOT were death and accident, death and accident. If those figures didn't go up, it was 'bidness' as usual. We didn't have any way to measure the deteriorating safety *margins* and plummeting standards unless we started killing thousands of passengers. The big lie, Joe, the big lie. Joseph Goebbels would have been proud of them."

The voice of the captain came over the PA giving weather and arrival details for Washington National Airport, and Lewiston fell silent, waiting for the announcement to end. "You got me worked up at a time when I'm disgusted and madder than hell. I'm sorry."

"Hey, don't apologize. This helps me understand."

Lewiston thought for a moment.

"Let me give you a tip for your accident probe. If it looks like a flight-control problem, cut through all the bullshit and look for electronic interference. It's a good system. If it screwed up, something got it from outside. But if there's human failure in the cockpit, look closely at who hired the chief pilot and whether he knew what he was doing."

"What do you mean about the chief pilot?"

"Just a hint, okay? Dave Bayne's a great guy, but he's set a management style that trusts subordinate executives to perform, without following up to see that they do. Dave doesn't find out someone's screwing up until we're in a real mess."

"How could that—?"

"I don't know. That's just a tip. I don't know if it has any application here. But if you start seeing strange executive performance, look beyond that level. You'll find we didn't communicate vertically worth a tinker's damn at North America. Take my position, for instance. No one seemed to ever tell me a damn thing."

There was a pause as Joe struggled with a question he dearly wanted to ask. "Did you quit because of the pressure, or because North America's maintenance standards had finally been pushed too low?"

Lewiston sat in utter silence for more than a minute looking Joe in the eye before responding.

"I shouldn't answer that, you know," he said at last.

"But you will, won't you?"

Craig Lewiston sighed and nodded. "Answer B," he said simply.

Joe sat back, his mind applying Lewiston's warnings as they banked to the left momentarily, weaving down the Potomac for a landing to the south under a high overcast sky at National Airport.

There was an airline agent waiting for Joe when he entered the terminal dutifully holding a cardboard sign with the name WALLINGFORD in view of the deplaning passengers. He had an urgent phone call.

Joe found a pay phone and dialed Andy's number in Kansas City.

"We've found something, Joe, in the rear of the 320. It was tangled up in the pieces of the elevator controls—an electronic box of some sort. Joe, the point is, as far as the Airbus guys can tell, it didn't come with their airplane. In other words, it may have been sabotage after all!"

11

David Bayne was out of the elevator before it fully opened, moving with characteristic dispatch down the long carpeted hallway of the North America executive floor. The meticulously groomed chairman and CEO of North America Airlines had been a star running back in his collegiate days at Southern Methodist in Dallas, and his athletic training still showed in broad shoulders and a six-foot-three-inch frame.

Bayne was a study in Dallas-style corporate chic, a starched white shirt and well-tailored Italian suit complementing his sharp, angular face. His dark hair was combed back and slicked down slightly, a style popular among Wall Street climbers half his age. Forty-eight years old, intense, rich, powerful, and darkly handsome in a manner usually not associated with Texans, Bayne turned female heads wherever he went—an ability that had served him well over the years, compensating somewhat for his pragmatic, humorless personality.

He brushed swiftly past the reception area with its photo-realist oil paintings of various airplanes in North America livery and pushed open the heavy double doors to his suite.

"Good morning, Mr. Bayne. They're all inside, sir." His elegantly dressed secretary had already alerted the executives within his office that the boss was on the floor—a small but vital courtesy that kept him from walking in on an unguarded conversation and embarrassing everyone.

She smiled at him as he flashed past her contemporary desk of plate glass and polished chrome and noted with approval the spotless surface which, as per his orders, supported only a sophisticated telephone console and a small crystal vase containing

161

one long-stemmed red rose—delivered fresh every morning before his arrival. A smaller glass surface to one side held her computer terminal and a few working papers.

"Thanks Connie." He walked briskly into his office, tossing a cursory nod at the four senior vice-presidents who had been waiting for the past ten minutes: Ron Putnam, the operations chief; Holman Spradley, general counsel of the corporation; Lillian Buckman, in charge of corporate communications; and Mark Rogers, in charge of legislative and governmental affairs.

As a master of corporate nuance, David Bayne had trained himself for years to assert primacy by little more than body language and timing, and he began playing this assemblage with typical, if subconscious, ease, moving quickly behind the massive antique desk which had once belonged to Argentine dictator Juan Perón. The interior of his office was a traditional rectangle, with floor-to-ceiling windows forming the wall opposite the desk, framing a magnificent view of North Dallas and the city's original airport, Love Field.

Bayne sat down, aware of the four highly paid people on guard and watching his every move, taking time to place his leather briefcase on the credenza with precision before picking up his telephone to pass a few assignments to his secretary, carefully avoiding for a moment any further acknowledgment of their presence. Swiveling around at last, he removed a yellow legal pad from the top drawer of the desk and unscrewed his fountain pen, placing an elegant pair of half-frame reading glasses on his nose before looking up. "As you know, yesterday we came under takeover attack. We'll get to that in a minute. First, I want us to get completely up to speed on the Kansas City accident. Proceed, Ron."

As senior vice-president/operations, Ronald Putnam had no illusions about David Bayne. They had been professional and personal friends for years, but only Bayne was in charge at North America. In his presence, high corporate titles and six-figure salaries were golden shackles binding one to David Bayne's will, and since Friday's crash in Kansas City, his will had concerned damage control.

"In a nutshell," began Putnam, looking intently at his notes, "it looks like either direct sabotage, or some sort of accidental radio interference with the flight controls. Internal flight-control failure or pilot error are a distant third and fourth."

"Based on?"

"Based on the latest information from our people participating in the investigation on the NTSB team." Ron Putnam related the news of the electronic device found on the remains of the Airbus's flight controls the previous evening, and the impassioned claims of Wilkins's supporters to produce proof of sabotage in two days.

Bayne sat back for a second, digesting the information. "I had already twisted some tails in Washington to get them moving on the sabotage theory when it looked like the NTSB wasn't taking it seriously over the weekend, but I can't say even I really believed it. Now you're telling me this does seem to be a reality. Sabotage?"

Ron Putnam shifted uneasily in his chair and nodded as Bayne drummed his fingers on the desk, looking at the eastern end of the room at an original Alexander Calder painting on the wall—one he had acquired for a fraction of its value from the bankrupt Braniff International headquarters before anyone started keeping close track of the hapless airline's assets. North America had shed no tears for Braniff; its 1982 demise simply boosted their business. And bringing that artifact of fabled Braniff chairman Harding Lawrence into the First International Bancshares Building was a deeply satisfying move for Bayne. Two hundred years ago on this spot, he thought, any fierce Comanche warrior would have had the same sense of pride and accomplishment displaying the scalp of an enemy on his tent pole.

"Okay," Bayne said suddenly, "sabotage, radio interference, or pilot error. Any more?"

"We've also got to consider equipment failure. You know, the flight controls suddenly failed, that sort of thing."

"I could live with sabotage, and even equipment failure," Bayne said, "as long as it was design failure and not our maintenance that's at fault. But we sure don't want radio vulnerability or pilot error."

"We don't want any of it! David, we have eighteen other A320s and more on order," Putnam pointed out. "If we start indicating that the electronic flight-control system is unreliable and prone to failures, whether by design or due to ground interference, we might end up with a mass grounding, not to mention a battle royal with Airbus."

"Good point. What's the story on the pilots? What could they have screwed up?"

"Dick Timson, according to John Walters, is adamant that he did not fly the airplane into the ground, into windshear, or do anything else wrong. Timson says the aircraft pitched over as he approached the runway, despite his inputs. That's all anyone has to go on right now since our copilot, Don Leyhe, is in a coma, and the NTSB team cannot locate the cockpit voice recorder."

"What? Why not?" Bayne had moved forward in his chair.

"It just doesn't seem to be there. They're still looking. Until they find it, all we have is Timson's word and memory."

Bayne fixed him with an inquisitive gaze. "What's wrong with that? Isn't he trustworthy?"

"Far as I know, David. But memories can be rearranged by concussions, and Timson has a skull fracture. The only worry is this: the flight recorder seems to indicate—according to John Walters—that the controls could have been pushed forward, then pulled back before impact. Dick Timson's memory doesn't click with that, though, and no one can figure out why a sane man would do such a thing."

"I remember Timson," Bayne said somewhat absently. "Tough old bird, as I recall."

"Yes sir, he is. Ex-Marine, all business, stern disciplinarian, and the best contract dismissal record in the business. If Dick fires someone, they stayed fired. He's been good for the pilots—keeps them in line, despite the constant grumbling from the pilots' union."

"He was qualified, wasn't he? Timson, I mean."

"Yes . . ."

"I hear hesitation. Why?"

"Well, on his first approach to the airport, Timson flew into windshear and almost hit the ground. They got as low as forty feet."

David Bayne's fingers began drumming his desk. "How do you recommend we play this? Can we save face for public consumption?"

"Okay, one possibility, but any friends we have in Washington are not going to like it. You all heard that the control-tower tape was leaked and played nationwide yesterday? Okay, it shows the controller did *not* warn our crew about windshear. He used the word *gusty*, but that's it. We could try to pin this on the FAA as a major contributing cause for failing to give them adequate weather information. In fact, the flight recorder readings probably rule out windshear . . . but we're sandbagged in any other way. If it's a problem with the flight-control system, what do we do with our other 320s? They could end up grounded for an extended period. But if it's pilot error or negligence—for instance, if Timson overbanked the airplane or somehow flew it wrong—then we're in big trouble because *he* is *us*. Even if it's simple sabotage, we look weak and ineffectual in security. If we can at least dilute the blame by pulling the FAA into this, barring any sudden revelation we haven't considered, I think it's our best course of action.''

Bayne was looking toward the far wall and thinking it over. Putnam decided to push a bit harder. ''The point is this: if we sit around here and don't aggressively sell our view that ATC is responsible or that they are contributorily negligent, we'll end up holding the bag all alone. Especially with this NTSB chairman, who is well known for blowing with the prevailing wind, and who's not terribly interested in attacking the FAA, which is a finger, so to speak, of the political hand that feeds him in this administration.''

''Okay,'' Bayne began, ''I agree we should try to get the FAA in the barrel with us if we can. Anyone violently object?''

No one objected.

Bayne shifted in his chair, preparing to get to his feet. ''All of you, keep me informed constantly on this. I'll think about what we should do on the Hill, if anything. Mark, you want to stay a few minutes? Let's go over some options. There are at least a few arms I haven't twisted lately. The rest of you, general corporate staff meeting in the boardroom at ten A.M. Come prepared for battle. We lose this one, we're all out of a job.''

For David Bayne the day progressed in a whirlwind of calls and planning meetings, the time slipping by until Connie reminded the chairman that it was 4 P.M., and he was expected elsewhere. He responded by abruptly ending a meeting to exit for the elevators and the garage below, wheeling his Mercedes into downtown Dallas traffic a few minutes later under stormy gray skies and surprisingly mild temperatures, which had hovered in the sixties all day.

He was northbound through the toll plaza on the Dallas North

Tollway almost before realizing it, his mind absorbed by planning strategy for the battle to come, but slowly shifting to more important things. There were, in fact, more important aspects of life than staying at the office, even in a crisis, and it had taken him most of his forty-eight years to realize that. But family matters and family meetings had now become the dominant priority on his calendar.

The next few weeks were likely to be hell. His airline was in deep trouble as an independent company, and he was going to have to maneuver and wheedle and scheme his way out of it if he wanted to stay in command. The investment bankers in New York who had placed him in control of North America were gathering like a war council in Manhattan even as he drove away from the office. He would join them there in the morning, leaving on the 6 A.M. flight to Kennedy, and helicoptering to downtown New York City.

It was a shame he couldn't have positioned the company to avoid this, but the crash had triggered it, dropping the stock price at a delicate moment. David Bayne knew why North America could be an attractive takeover, even if they weren't rich. Like the callous dismemberment of Eastern Airlines by Frank Lorenzo's Texas Air, North America could be broken up into profitable little airline operations and sold off. That—and the coveted order positions on new aircraft coming off the production line at Boeing, Airbus, and McDonnell Douglas years before they could be obtained otherwise—made North America a target.

He took the Royal Lane exit in far North Dallas, noticing for the first time that the cracked concrete walls and uncut grass of the exit were getting a bit seedy.

Once a railroad track had stretched along the same path. It was a branch line of the Cotton Belt, its engines filling the heavy air of Texas summer evenings with the mournful horns of half-empty passenger trains and the clatter of unused boxcars, the wheels of which used to crush pennies for him late at night. The ghostly procession still ran in his memory, rumbling endlessly through his childhood a few blocks from his family home, rattling and wailing south toward downtown Dallas, or north toward the switch with the main line at Addison.

David traveled south a few blocks on Preston to St. Mark's, the tough college prep school from which he had graduated with honors in 1960. His son, Sean, would already be battling his teammates in a football scrimmage his father had solemnly promised to watch.

There had been a time, he remembered with bitterness, when he hardly knew he even had kids. His daughter—now twenty-six, married, and gone—had slipped through his fingers, her life a mystery to him; his life, to her, a classic story of absentee parenting. David was determined not to make the same mistake with Sean.

He parked and walked to the edge of the field in a light rain-coat, spotting the blond mop of hair as the boy took his helmet off for a second to adjust something.

"Dad! Hi!" Sean waved at him, his voice barely audible across the field, smiling as his father waved back.

David glanced back at the campus as the scrimmage resumed, letting his mind's eye see it as it had been when he wore the school uniform. He had enrolled his son two years ago when he was beginning the eighth grade. David, however, had entered from public school in the tenth grade—a scrappy kid of sixteen trailing a record of disciplinary trouble behind him from nearby Thomas Jefferson High School. He had been bored in public school, though he didn't know it at the time. His parents were neither particularly rich nor particularly brilliant, but they knew they had a problem with David, and someone suggested St. Mark's could straighten him out if they could afford it—which they managed somehow to do.

The memories always flooded back when he came to pick up Sean. Memories of taunting from the other boys, memories of instructors tougher and more demanding—and even abusive in their intellectual avarice—than most of the professors he'd encountered in college. Yet the institution had challenged him to a do-or-die contest of wills, the English-accented headmaster predicting quick failure. David had proven him wrong, improving steadily as he learned how to manipulate the school and best his tormentors—a collection of self-assured, snotty rich boys who sailed to classes each day in their Corvettes and Chevy 409s, exuding money and confidence, breezing through courses that cost David sleepless nights and endless weekends in the library. He had emerged determined to become rich and secure as fast as possible, with the resolve that he would never subject a child of his own to such a vicious environment of brutal competition. The first was achieved within a decade. The second crumbled to dust the day he was elected to his first corporate chairmanship and realized why he had been able to get there in the first place: the tempering St. Mark's had provided.

Few solid friendships had developed among his classmates. Instead, lasting alliances arose between strong competitors who had come to respect, though never quite trust, one another. They worked together in business, in civic affairs, and alumni activities, a type of elite among young Dallas business mavens—the second generation of homegrown successful businessmen where wildcatter oilmen had gone before.

"You see that tackle, Dad?" Sean had materialized by his side, and they talked over football techniques as they walked toward the car.

David headed the Mercedes toward Northwood Country Club, where they planned to work on Sean's golf swing.

"One of the guys told me the airline is under takeover attack, Dad."

"He was right."

"He claimed you'd be unemployed by the end of the week. Told me I'd be riding a bike to school and asking for a scholarship."

"It's not that bad." David chuckled. "I negotiated a large golden parachute when I came to North America. If a new owner throws me out, I could take at least four years to cry about it before even looking for a new position. And, with a takeover, the stock options alone could pay us several million. Don't lose any sleep over it."

"I won't. I told him he was insufficiently informed of the realities of corporate finance."

"Wow. I'm impressed."

Sean fell silent for a few minutes, watching the glut of tall buildings as they passed the LBJ Freeway.

"Dad? Could I ask you a . . . a question you may not like?"

David looked at his son, evaluating the determined expression on his face, amazed to find his own defense responses activating. This was his boy. He didn't need defenses.

"Sure. What?"

"Don't leaders of big companies have to consider the welfare of those who work for them? Or are they only required to make money for themselves and the stockholders, whoever the stock-holders are?''

"That's not a simple question to answer, Sean.''

"Well, do you care, Dad, about North America's employees?''

"Of course I do!'' David kept his eyes on the road as he thought through the question, the motivation, and the response. "Son, these are complex matters. As head of the corporation, my first responsibility is to the stockholders who have invested their money in our company.''

"Okay, but say the airline *is* making money and it's got a bunch of very experienced people who've been there many years, and some new group buys all the stock and decides it could make even more money if it didn't have to pay so much in salaries. Let's say it's someone like Frank Lorenzo, and he comes in one day and says''—Sean adopted a gruff voice—" 'Okay, you jerks, you're making too much, so we're going to cut your salary and take away your health insurance and your retirement. That way, we'll make a lot more money, and if you don't like it, we'll just replace you.' Now, this leader doesn't cut *his* salary, he just says *I* make too much, even though maybe I can just barely pay my bills. I'm a little guy with no protection. Isn't there a rule or a law which forces that leader to be concerned about me?''

"In a word, no.''

David looked at his son, half in admiration, half in conster-nation for the grilling. "Sean, look at my situation. I don't own North America, I merely run it. It's my job to keep it in business and out of bankruptcy. I have to answer to a board of directors, and if they decide I'm not running things right or I'm making the company too little money because, for instance, I'm being too generous with our employees, they'll just fire me and hire another chairman and president who will do what they want.''

"Really?''

"Really. In addition, if I give the employees the majority of the profits and then we can't pay decent dividends to our stock-holders, our stock price goes down and our ability to issue bonds and raise funds declines, and our overall ability to command good financing rates and terms is imperiled even when we issue new stock.''

"You're saying you can't care about the people?''

"No!'' David realized his tone was growing irritated, and he softened it. "What I'm saying is that I have to juggle hundreds of conflicting interests, and I can't give everyone everything they want. For instance, I want the best safety system for our airline, but if I go overboard and let our maintenance people spend double the industry average while not being able to increase our fares, or if I fail to cut costs when everyone else has cut theirs, we'll eventually go bankrupt. That's the battle I've been fighting for the last few years, keeping our costs down to keep us alive. Same thing with labor costs—salaries. If our competition can get more work for less money, they can charge less for a ticket and make more profit, so I have to get our people to accept less money, even though it hurts them and makes them mad. I'm sorry if they're upset, but I'm paid not to care so much about their feelings that I hurt the profitability of the company. See, if I don't force them to accept such realities and we go out of business, no one will have a job, so we all lose. You've got to understand that I'm simply the ringmaster trying to keep things in balance. But I don't make the laws of gravity."

David glanced at Sean, half expecting boredom. Instead he found two eyes watching him intently, hanging on every word.

"Your hands are tied, huh, Dad?"

"In many cases, yes. But if I keep the company making money for the stockholders, the employees always benefit. I care how they're treated, but for the day-to-day, hands-on management of them I have to rely on my junior executives and managers. I don't get involved because the chairman doesn't have time. It's a very complex structure operated under complex rules. There's no law that forces the president of a public corporation to check on whether a decision will or won't have an economic impact on his people. He either has a conscience about it or he doesn't. And there's only so much he can do. That's the system."

"Then the system has to change, Dad, because that's dumb."

Walter Calley had been shocked to the depth of his being that moving across Louisiana farmland at night in mid-October could be so damned difficult. He had left the old barn after sundown Tuesday evening, confident his Army survival training was enough. But by midnight he was ready to give up the trek and look for a car to steal.

He must survive, he knew that. The knowledge he had in his head about Congressman Larry Wilkins, his friend and surreptitious employer, must survive. It would scandalize the nation and probably make their dream of becoming a true force in American politics come true. As Senator Joe McCarthy had accidentally done for communism by making commie hunting unfashionable for twenty years, the assassination of Larry Wilkins might make white supremacist bashing unacceptable for a decade. He had a mission, perhaps a historic mission, and he would carry it out. Important thoughts like that had kept him going, but at 12:25 A.M. Wednesday morning, the sight of an old Ford pickup parked at the top of a sloping driveway by a remote farmhouse was too much to resist.

Walter watched the farmhouse for a half hour before slipping slowly into the yard, carefully getting in the truck by slithering through the open passenger window. There was no key in the ignition, but he could feel the wires behind the dash. If he could locate the right ones . . .

The bright light that exploded in his face caught him totally off guard. He had heard no one approaching.

"Freeze, bub! What the hell are you doin' with my truck?"

The owner of the farm had a 12-gauge leveled at him. You don't argue successfully with a 12-gauge, Walter reminded himself, carefully opening the door with his hands in view. "Don't shoot, I can explain."

He began to do so and the farmer, having no love for official Washington, listened, almost believing the filthy, mud-caked man before him was running from injustice, rather than escaping the law. The offer of money, however, was what got his full attention at last.

"Look, I was going to leave you several hundred dollars just to borrow the truck. I'll give you four hundred dollars if you'll let me use it." Calley saw the man relax a bit. "Let me carefully reach in my satchel here—I've been carrying my things in this fish creel, hold on." He diverted his eyes down to the bag, searching with his right hand and watching to make sure he had what he was reaching for. In his peripheral vision, Calley saw the barrel of the shotgun slowly drop toward the ground, the farmer at last removing his finger from the trigger guard, shifting the gun to rest position. Walter Calley had been hoping for exactly that reaction, and as he looked up and smiled at the man, he lashed out with his right foot, catching the stock of the shotgun and flinging it harmlessly off into the dirt several yards away as his right hand pulled the .357 magnum from the bag in one fluid motion, leveling it in the old man's face before he had a chance to react. "Don't!" Calley told him.

The farmer saw he'd been tricked and froze, waiting for the click of a hammer. The man's son, standing silently in the shadows of the porch some 10 yards away, saw only the glint of a lethal gun barrel aimed at his father's head. His Winchester 30-30 had already been cocked, and a bead drawn on the thief's head minutes before as his father had crept forward to surprise the intruder. There was no hesitation now, and no contest as a single shot rang out, the bullet finding its mark just forward of Walter Calley's left ear, destroying his brain and removing most of the right side of his head instantly.

Nearly a half hour passed before the farmer and his son recovered enough from the shock to call the sheriff.

By noon Wednesday, Forrest Rogers and the members of what had been Larry Wilkins's inner circle of advisors, friends, and supporters had heard the details of Calley's death. It had taken only an hour to identify the body—Calley's driver's license was stuffed in his undershorts—but the story didn't hit the state news wires until midmorning. By 10 A.M. someone in the state patrol had backtracked and found the Camaro, partially explaining the mystery police-car-tire shooting of Monday morning. What the county and state police couldn't figure out, however, was why the man was running in the first place. There were no wants or warrants in the computer, the FBI had no knowledge of him, and other than the shot-out tire and what appeared to be a stolen license plate, his actions were a mystery.

"An obscure electronics engineer from a defense contractor in Kansas" had been the line used on New Orleans stations all afternoon.

At 12:45 the tape had arrived at Forrest Rogers's home, a routine delivery with the bills and the rest of his mail. He had summoned the others immediately. Forrest refrained from opening it until they had come. With Walter dead, only the tape would tell the tale.

The weather had clouded over and cooled down, so his wife had started a fire in the den fireplace, and Forrest had perched himself in front of it to wait for the others—who arrived just before 2 P.M.

He shooed his wife out then and closed off the room as the six men settled into sofas and chairs. Forrest pulled the tape from the brown padded mailer and put it in the recorder. There was no note.

He had, Walter Calley's voice told them, called Larry Wilkins on Friday afternoon when he had seen what was going on at the plant near Leavenworth. The main tracking test module, a huge container, had been put on an oversize flatbed. He wasn't supposed to know, but a fellow worker had confirmed it was to be flown to somewhere in the Pacific from Kansas City Airport that night for operational testing.

Wilkins had been ecstatic, Calley said. He had suspected the Brilliant Pebbles people all along of trying to destroy the main Star Wars program for un-American reasons. They had forged a bipartisan agreement not to test components of either system, and here was apparent proof the agreement was being broken— and flagrantly at that! They would never risk moving the thing if they weren't going to test it, Wilkins had told Calley, deciding at the same moment to fly to Kansas City to see for himself. "He was going to get a cab," Calley's voice continued, "go close enough to see, and if it was what I said it was, he was going to take pictures and call the national media right from there and embarrass the hell out of them. But then the plane crashed and killed him, and the second I heard—I stayed at home in Leavenworth—I knew our call had been tapped. I had made the horrible mistake, you see, of calling Larry from my office at the factory, 'cause I was so excited. So someone obviously overheard and knew they couldn't allow Larry to catch them, so they ordered him dead. There's no question. It was an assassination."

Calley had paused in making the tape, and he could be heard clearing his throat and focusing on the next step. "Now, if anything happens to me before I get there, you've got to expose all this. Please. For Larry's sake, for the movement, for the country."

The tape ended and the group sat staring at each other before Bill Hawkins broke the silence.

"What have we got here?"

Ed Trelonas shook his head in disbelief. "We ain't got shit."

There was a collective sigh of astonishment as Hawkins spoke up again. "That little idiot! We've told the whole country we had proof. Hell, if anyone had overhead his call to Larry, it would've been a damn sight simpler to just cancel the shipment than kill an airplane full of people! I agree, we ain't got shit, but we do have a hell of a problem now. What do we tell the press and the feds?''

All six men exploded into simultaneous, animated, urgent discussion, the future of their political influence, the credibility of their public announcements—everything—hanging in the balance.

''They'll think we're neo-Nazi freaks and loonies, seeing ghosts in the woodwork. There's no damn conspiracy here, except what we jumped to ourselves, thanks to that dead idiot Calley.''

''Hey,'' Forrest Rogers said, ''at least let's mourn the poor guy. I've known him for years. Walter was a good man. Too intense, maybe, but will someone here please remember he got his head blowed off trying to bring us a warning, as crazy as it was?''

Several of the men looked at Rogers, remembering his willingness to abandon Calley—or worse—the day before.

All but one of them settled back into various chairs, leaving Bill Hawkins warming himself in front of the open fireplace. ''Well,'' he said at last, ''we're looking at this all wrong. Who knows Calley had no evidence? Calley's dead. We don't know that he put everything he knew on that tape, now do we? Maybe there was more. I mean, either he really had something more or he was a raging paranoid, and I don't think the guy was a paranoid. So, what we do is publicize the truth as we think we see it. We publicize his death. This man Calley had the key to this assassination, we say, but he got killed before he could tell what he knew. He knew it was an assassination, but *he* got assassinated himself.''

''You do that, someone may go after that farmer and his kid.''

''No,'' Hawkins continued, ''we don't blame it on them. Poor old Walter was running from his pursuers, and he made a fatal mistake. It was the people that were chasing him caused him to try to steal that man's truck. Wasn't the farmer's fault. But the FBI or whoever—we can pin this on the FBI and the CIA if we do it right—they pushed him and chased him. Same boys that got Larry were after Walter, right?''

Rogers was nodding. ''I guess. But Bill, what about the tape?''

Bill Hawkins reached over and took the cassette out of the recorder, looked it over carefully, and tossed it into the fire, turning back to Rogers with a puzzled expression.

"What tape was that, Forrest?"

As the word of the strange shooting in a farm driveway in Louisiana was slowly spreading toward New Orleans on Wednesday morning, Joe Wallingford was leaving the elevators on the eighth floor of the FAA building in Washington, headed for his office.

"Joe . . . wait a minute." The voice came from behind him and Joe turned, recognizing the pleasing form of Beverly Bronson as she ran toward him down the central corridor which bisected the NTSB's floor.

"Have . . . whew, I'm out of shape . . . have you seen this?" Beverly thrust a sheet of paper with the FAA logo at the top into his hands. It was a press release, dated Wednesday morning and cranked out by someone a few floors distant in the same building, announcing that the FAA was asking the FBI to investigate the apparent theft of the cockpit voice recorder in Kansas City and the separate theft of the tower tape. In addition, it said, the possibility that the North America crash had been caused by purposeful radio interference was to be probed by a joint FAA-FBI task force.

"Jesus Christ! What is he *doing*?" Joe shook the release in Beverly's general direction.

"Who?"

"Caldwell. This bears the fingerprints of Bill Caldwell."

"What, exactly, is going on, Joe?"

"Later, Bev." Joe thanked her and stormed off to his office to dial Caldwell's number. According to his secretary, he was out until late afternoon, and no, she was not authorized to communicate his whereabouts, even to the NTSB. He slammed the receiver down then and headed for Dean Farris's office instead, finding the NTSB chairman in a grand state of excitement, a copy of the same press release in his hand.

"Joe, what do *you* know about this?"

"Mr. Chairman, we've never formally told Bill Caldwell a thing about the missing CVR—I'm assuming this came from him—but everybody on the investigation team knows the CVR is missing, and that certainly includes the FAA members. And,

David Bayne and his people know. Theft *is* a dim possibility, but none of us can see how or why it could have been done. And, dammit, there's no way the FBI needs to be publicly dragged into that particular question at this point. We could use them on the other item, though.''

"He's trying to get our goat, of course," Farris said, slamming his copy of the release on his desk. "Trying to picture us as incompetent . . . make an end run around us and get the FBI to do his dirty work in finding whether one of our people leaked that tape. What he's trying to do most of all, though, is protect his control-tower people by creating a diversion.''

Farris looked up suddenly, a mental tumbler finally falling into place. "What other item?''

"The electronic box in the 320 wreckage. Barbara Rawlson's team found a small electronic device of some sort, radio-related, in the flight-control wreckage of the 320. Airbus says it isn't supposed to be there. Might be a smoking gun, might not.''

"I hadn't heard. Does the media know?''

"Not yet. I told Andy to keep it very quiet. They were working on it last night. Apparently it's pretty smashed up.''

"I want to know the second you figure out what it is. Now, how about the tower tape?''

"I talked to Nick Gardner," Joe began, "and he assured me the tape wasn't out of his possession and he knows nothing about it.''

"You believe him?''

Joe shrugged. "I have to.''

"Convince Caldwell he's innocent, then," Farris said, pacing.

"I've already tried to get an appointment with him as you asked. He's out, though, or hiding behind his secretary.'' Joe sat down in one of the large, leather wing chairs placed before Dean Farris's desk, but Farris kept prowling the office.

"Wonderful.'' Farris mumbled the words as he faced the picture window and looked out across the Mall.

"There is," Joe began, "something I probably should have told you involving Caldwell.''

Farris whirled, his face a picture of interest. "Oh?''

He related the Sunday phone call from Caldwell pressuring Joe to assure him flight-control failure wasn't involved in the crash, as well as the fact that he had not called the FAA associate administrator back as yet. "I was waiting to see if the issue resolved itself, and if not, I was going to talk to you first."

"*Were* you, now? And just when would *that* have been?" The sarcasm dripped from his words, and Joe knew he was defenseless.

"I promise you I was not about to give him anything until we talked. I, uh, figured it was a ploy to put pressure on us—and on me—to make a critical decision he could blame on us in the event it was wrong."

"Did he tell you to keep the call confidential, Joe?"

"Yes."

"And you complied, of course!" Farris had gone from upset to anger, and it was directed squarely at Joe Wallingford.

"No . . . look, that was Sunday," Joe explained hurriedly. "Monday we were going to talk to the captain. I figured the interview might clear up what happened enough so that I could tell you about the call, and then, with your approval, tell Caldwell to back off, that the idea of grounding this plane was ridiculous. I was not going to call him back without talking to you. I hadn't even seen the data recorder results at that time, and . . ."

The chairman glared at Joe as he made a fist of his right hand and pounded it into his left palm. "Goddammit, Wallingford, you work for the NTSB, not the FAA. Any extracurricular contacts from other high government officials you will relay to me immediately, is that clear? *Damn* you! You let me get blindsided!"

"I don't understand. How could you have been blindside—"

"When Caldwell called me after the tower tape was leaked—before I called you—he was in a monumental rage, but he didn't say anything about the CVR, or about messing around in our investigation with talk of grounding the A320, or about his surreptitious call to you. Since I didn't know any of that—since you left me up here in the dark—I had to sit here and let him yell at me. I would have had some things to chew on *him* about if you'd filled me in. *Damn!*"

"His call had nothing to do with the tower tapes. That was Sunday."

Farris had paced behind his desk again. Now he turned to Joe, his hands clasped behind him in professorial fashion, his head down and shaking from side to side as if dealing with a hopeless idiot. "Joe, Joe, Joe." He looked up with an exasperated expression. "You're way out of your league with someone like Caldwell."

"Hey, I didn't call the man." Joe was struggling to control rising anger mixed with apprehension.

"You're a technician, Joe. Caldwell's a politician and a Machiavellian administrator. You're no match for him."

"God knows I'm not trying to be. I know I'm a technician. That's all I've ever wanted to be." That was more emphasis than he intended, but it didn't matter. Farris was ignoring his answers anyway.

"Whenever Bill Caldwell interferes down here, he's up to something. There are always hidden meanings. For one thing"— Farris waved the press release at Joe—"he's trying to control events here and show everyone on the Hill that the FAA under Bill Caldwell is not going to be slow in properly investigating a possible assassination. He's trying to outflank us at every turn, and when he hears about that device you found . . ." Farris sighed disgustedly. "That's why I've got to stay on top of the political climate around this town, to keep us protected as a board—to keep you innocent little technocrats protected from the real world so you can do your work. If I don't see which way the wind is blowing, we'll all get blown away by it."

Joe looked at Dean Farris with amazement. He really did believe his was a political position. Susan was right. But he was also, as she had pointed out, the boss. And Joe's professional life was in his hands. "Mr. Chairman, I apologize if I should have told you about his call immediately—"

"Damn right you should have."

"Do you still want me to go talk to him, when I can catch him in, that is?" Joe asked the question hoping the answer would be no, but Farris surprised him.

"Yes, Joe, I do. Tell him to back off on the threats regarding the 320's flight-control system, that he doesn't understand how delicate things are at the moment and he's going way out on a limb. Don't, for God's sake, tell him about the new find."

"He may already know," Joe replied.

Dean Farris stopped, his long arm and bony finger still aimed at Joe. "You do agree there's no justification for grounding, don't you?"

"Not at this moment, though that could change. I mean, if it's sabotage, why ground it?"

"Well, until we know more, tell him to back off, that no grounds exist. And when you do, you tell him—if he asks—that you and I have not discussed this. Make him believe that his little extracurricular contact is safe."

"I can't—"

"What, lie? You can't tell him that?"

"I'd prefer not to."

Farris looked Joe in the eye for perhaps the first time in their conversation. "I'm not going to order you to lie, Joe. But try not to let on that I know he called you."

"Why?"

"Intelligence, man. Draw him out. What the hell is he up to? Is it what I think? Is he trying to draw a smoke screen around the FAA's role in all this? And if so, why is he so frantic? I've got to know—fast—and you're the guy who can find out."

Bill Caldwell took the phone call in the den, at his wife's small Chippendale desk. She had answered the call, a surprised looked crossing her face as she informed him that North America's CEO wanted to talk with him immediately and sounded upset.

"Hello."

"Bill Caldwell?"

"Yes."

"David Bayne. Sorry to call you at home, but I've had a disturbing phone call from one of my vice-presidents in Kansas City."

"Oh?"

"Look, I'll be brutally frank with you, Bill." The uninvited use of his first name put Caldwell instantly on guard as Bayne continued. "My man overheard one of your FAA people in a restaurant booth behind him this evening talking about his orders from Washington, supposedly from your office, and that they were to take the position that North America was at fault in this crash because our pilots knowingly flew into windshear. He also said you've issued a press release announcing that you've asked the FBI to investigate several things, including the possibility of radio sabotage, even though no one has any evidence of sabotage, including Congressman Wilkins's staff."

Bill Caldwell could feel his temperature rising and cautioned himself to tread with care.

Bayne continued, his voice betraying anger. "Now, because I believe neither you nor the administrator would ever tilt an investigation, I discounted it. I still discount it, though you have some personnel in Kansas City who need straightening out. I'd appreciate some assurance from you, and I ask this apologetically, but also as the man responsible for the welfare of this company, for your personal assurance that the FAA is not in any way trying to push or shove the NTSB to prejudge this accident against our people just to protect the FAA's interests."

Bill Caldwell mentally counted to ten, absolutely enraged at the gall of Bayne to make such an accusation, directly or obliquely. "David, in no way do you need such assurance, because you already have it. You know, someone leaked that control-tower tape yesterday, and we were mightily embarrassed about that. Naturally, we can't help but wonder. I have to assume that whoever did that was trying to put our people in a bad light with technical conversations the public will misinterpret. You see, I could ask you similar questions about that one, considering it's no secret North America would be well served by a finding of air-traffic-control error—which we do not think occurred."

"Now you're accusing my people, Bill? Hah." There was a brief pause before Bayne continued. "Well, actually, I suppose that's fair, considering I suspect your people."

"Nice of you to recognize the mutual problem," Caldwell said acidly, "but what do you propose we do about it?"

There was a protracted silence from Dallas before Bayne replied, "I just want to make sure we leave this investigating team alone to make their own decisions without pressure. Your people start coming to windshear conclusions, it's going to beg the question of who did or did not tell our crew about the presence of windshear, okay? Nothing will be accomplished by that type of fight." Clever, Caldwell thought, very clever. Bayne obviously wanted to start a public fight over exactly that: windshear. Which meant he already knew windshear wasn't the cause. It was a classic diversionary tactic, but this time the FAA wasn't going to fall for it. "David, let's both look into this and keep in touch."

"Fair enough." They ended the call with the same correct and feigned friendliness. Bill Caldwell hesitated less than a second before raising the phone again and punching in the number of his lieutenant in Kansas City, instinctively aware that from Dallas, David Bayne was doing the same thing with his people—the opening shots of what could become a war between the airline and the Agency.

"Johnson? This is Bill Caldwell. I want you to get the entire FAA team together, and also the tower chief, and tell them from here out to keep their damn mouths shut and understand that North America is going to do everything they can to argue about windshear in the media, so they can then pin this crash on us for not giving them enough information. I want everyone on their guard, you understand? And I want to know by sundown who leaked that fucking tape!"

It was a very sheepish and embarrassed Andy Wallace who relayed the news to Joe Wallingford around 5:30 P.M. Washington time on Wednesday. They had been right on one count: the mystery box they had found was definitely not from the A320. But it wasn't the tool of any saboteur, either. It was, instead, a garden variety antenna coupler from the upper fuselage of the Boeing 737 which had been smashed and mixed with other stray wires as the A320 plowed through the 737's fuselage, dragging the little box along and depositing it in the tangled remains of the Airbus's flight controls. "We saw it and pounced on it at once, Joe. We didn't think it through. There's so much pressure on sabotage with this one, it seemed like an answer. None of us thought it might have come from the Boeing."

"Andy, it's okay. I've been pushing all of you too hard."

"Joe, one other problem. So many of the non-NTSB members know about the box by now, the media may seize on it as the cause of the crash. Someone's bound to leak it."

12

Thursday, October 18

Senator Kell Martinson had slept poorly Wednesday night, his mind occupied with Cindy's warnings that he had to defuse the search for his car, and fast.

Kell got up at 5 A.M. and stood in the shower for nearly thirty minutes, unable to decide what to do, a dilemma finally resolved by the *Washington Post*'s Thursday installment of the Larry Wilkins saga. The NTSB, it reported, had asked the FBI for help, admitting that the possibility of sabotage was real. Kell assumed the "mystery car" was the only thing keeping the sabotage theory alive. That meant he had to confess. There seemed no alternative.

Kell got off the elevators on the eighth floor of the FAA building at 8 A.M. and headed straight for Joe Wallingford's office.

Joe Wallingford, meanwhile, had plopped his overstuffed briefcase behind his desk as he came through the door at 7:30, eyeing his desk chair like a long-lost friend. That was a satisfying habit, tossing his briefcase down with feigned resignation and disgust, registering a resounding start to each day (though the habit had taken a toll on his overused brown leather case).

His office was a refuge of sorts, and he sorely needed it. The circus of confusion and upset and professional peril that had characterized the last few days had followed him back from Kansas City, tumbling along at his heels like an overly exuberant, homeless mutt, eager to come in and muddy up the carpets. At least his office was familiar territory, and he would need that touchstone in the next few weeks.

Wallingford leaned back in the chair, hands behind his head, regarding the government-issue office with the critical eye of a neutral observer. His standard-issue bookshelves lined the exterior wall to the left of the door, stuffed with folders and books and cardboard file boxes. It was all organized and neat, yet it gave the impression of frantic overburdening of mind and matter with an avalanche of details carried on a snowstorm of paper.

"Joe Wallingford?"

The sharply dressed man had materialized in the doorway. Joe hadn't heard him approaching.

"Yes?" The man seemed vaguely familiar as he entered with his hand outstretched, wearing a serious expression. Joe almost missed the little pin in his lapel—the identifying symbol of a member of Congress.

"I'm Senator Kell Martinson of Kansas. Wonder if we could talk in private a few minutes."

"Of course. Come in." Joe left his chair and walked around his desk toward Kell with his hand extended. "Sit down, please. What on earth brings the chairman of the aviation subcommittee of the Committee on Commerce, Science, and Transportation to my humble abode?"

Martinson was smiling at the recognition, Joe noticed, but it was a strained smile. Something was really bothering the man. Kell Martinson quietly closed the door as Joe walked back around the desk to sit down.

"Joe, what I'm going to discuss with you could end my political career. I'm asking for no special favors, and there are no restrictions on what I'm about to say. But I am going to ask something of you when I'm finished." Martinson sat down carefully, resting his arm on the desk.

Joe Wallingford looked the senator straight in the eye. "Go on, please," he said.

"The so-called mystery car in Kansas City was mine." Martinson let that sink in for a second before continuing. "I was driving it. That was me who sped out of the cargo area after the crash last Friday."

He said nothing else for a few seconds, watching Joe's face before continuing. Joe was working hard to show no reaction, though he was profoundly startled. "I was there on purely personal business. Nothing illegal or unethical, just there to meet a particular individual at a point in time when I was supposed to be in Wichita, three hundred miles away. I got there early; my friend was coming in on Flight 255; I'm a pilot, so I decided to get close to the runway and watch them land.''

"That's a restricted area, you know."

"They need to tighten their security, Joe. I just killed my headlights and rolled through the security gate behind a crew bus. No trouble at all. I knew the gate opens automatically on the way out."

"But, why, uh . . ."

"Why come tell you this? Why now?"

"I guess that was what I was trying to ask."

"Okay. I had no way of knowing there had been a missed flight in Washington. I thought my friend had been killed. I mean, I saw the damn thing crash right in front of me. I was convinced no one could have come out of that Airbus alive. I was wrong on that score, of course. But out of sheer panic I decided to get the hell out of there. I was in a very agitated state, and I knew I'd be identified and politically embarrassed if I stayed—I had no idea how much. It wasn't until Saturday that I heard the media getting excited about this so-called mystery car, which was my Riviera."

"A maintenance worker claims you nearly ran him down."

"It wasn't that close, but I scared both of us, yeah." Martinson dropped his gaze for a moment, examining the edge of the desk as he shifted slightly in his chair and thought for a second about how to phrase the rest of it. The man has an intense way of looking you in the eye, Joe thought to himself. Direct, firm, giving the impression of sincerity.

Martinson's head came up again, his eyes locking onto Joe once more. "Point one, I should not have been in the restricted area. Point two, I was not there for any nefarious purpose, and I certainly had nothing to do with the crash, or any radio gear, or any of the other nonsense the press has been putting out. Point three, I should have come to you or called you on Saturday, or sometime before now. I have no good excuse for waiting. Frankly, like anyone in political life, whenever I focused on it, it became a political problem. It was a Nixonian response, of course, but I fell into it. No one saw the license plate or the driver, so that was that. Monday I did some probing. I've got some friends at the FBI, and one of them reported that the lab had failed in its attempt to read the license on that videotape,

and that meant I was safe. So I decided I'd let it blow over."
He paused again, still looking Joe in the eye.

"Why are you here, then, Senator?"

"Because it isn't blowing over, and I have to assume you and the FBI and God knows who else are wasting a lot of valuable time looking for a car and driver that had virtually nothing to do with bringing those two airliners together."

"What are you asking, Senator? You know I have to act on this."

"Joe, this is going to be difficult, and frankly I can't think of a single reason why you should do it for me. I have no political favors I can grant you, and it would be inappropriate to dangle such a carrot anyway. But I must ask you if you could see your way clear to keeping my name out of this. I ask this because my presence there really was a fluke, and my career stands in the balance."

Joe sat back in his chair and looked at Martinson. The request was nothing if not direct. No strings, no blustering, just a plea for help from a rather powerful fellow whose career, according to him, had just been placed in Joe Wallingford's care. A powerful fellow, he reminded himself, who was also on the subcommittee that controlled NTSB funding and oversight.

"One question, sir."

"Kell."

"Okay, Kell. One question. Why would your presence in Kansas City be politically fatal?"

Kell looked at him for the longest time before answering. "Are you married, Joe?"

"Uh, yes. I mean, I was. I'm divorced now."

"Well, I'm about 95 percent there, Joe. I'm in the process of getting divorced. My wife hated being a senator's wife and hates Washington. It's been hopeless for some time."

"So your friend in Kansas City was an inbound lady love."

"That is correct. And I'm not single as yet, and my state can be devastatingly straitlaced. But now, after my waiting around like a coward, it would all blow up in my face."

"Is that it?"

"Well, that's point one." Kell hesitated, wondering how much to tell.

"And point two?" Joe prompted.

"Did you know I'm considered Larry Wilkins's number-one

enemy in Washington? And there I sat, watching him die. His people are already claiming foul play.''

"Oh boy.''

"Right. You can imagine what his fanatical mob would make of it if they knew I had been right there, even though I hadn't the slightest idea Wilkins would be on that plane.'' Kell filled him in on the background of his opposition to Wilkins, but stopped short of bringing in the Star Wars problem. There was too much classified information involved.

Joe nodded and drummed his fingers lightly on the arm of his chair.

"Senator, the FBI and the FAA are involved, and under pressure. Congressman Wilkins's people *are* calling this an assassination. I can't just say, 'Hey! We found the mystery car, and don't worry about a thing, the driver didn't do it.' ''

Kell was nodding resolutely. "I understand, Joe. My telling you was *not* predicated, by the way, on your helping keep this quiet. I can't in good conscience let this mystery continue, whatever happens to me.''

Joe came forward in his chair, a pained expression on his face. "Dammit, Senator, if you just hadn't been in the restricted area . . .''

"I know. I know. Hindsight, Joe. I was feeling cocky and bold. Senators should never feel cocky and bold, I guess.''

Both men sat in silence for twenty seconds or so before trying to talk at once.

"No, go ahead Joe.''

"Look, you . . . you need to get over to the FBI quickly. Right now, in fact. I can tell you who to see, and I'll call him— tell him we're satisfied. But they're controlling the criminal side of this investigation, and it is top priority.''

Kell nodded again. "Okay, I guess they need to know. I had heard they couldn't read the license plate.'' Kell said it again, hopefully, knowing it was immaterial now. He saw Joe lean over and open his briefcase in response, pull out a manila envelope with a NASA logo in the upper left-hand corner, place it on the desk and slide something out from within, turning it around and pushing it across the desktop toward him. It was a black-and-white photograph done by some sort of computer scanner, a side-view shot of the left front bumper of a late-model car, the license plate hidden behind something in the foreground. But clearly visible was the sticker on the edge of the bumper, a monthly parking sticker with a registration number and the name of the city: Wichita.

"You're right. The FBI lab couldn't read the license plate. But they didn't look any further. After the FBI returned the tape, I decided to look at it myself, and I saw something on the left side of the bumper. A friend of mine at NASA computer enhanced it for me. He brought this by the house last night after I returned from Kansas City."

"And," Kell finished the thought, "you were going to call the garage in Wichita this morning to find who spot 344 was registered to."

"You bet I was! I couldn't quite believe I'd found something the mighty FBI couldn't find, but there it is."

Kell studied the photograph, then sat back. "If you'll give me the agent's name, I'll go right over there."

Joe pulled the FBI card from his pocket and called the man's office, setting up an appointment for the senator within the hour without explaining why.

"Senator, I can't guarantee anything, but I'll talk to him by phone later and let him know we're satisfied. I'm just glad you didn't wait any longer to come in. If you'd waited until I handed them this . . ." He gestured to the NASA photo.

"Joe, what do you think caused the crash? Is sabotage really a viable possibility? Or is that just Wilkins's people spinning paranoid conspiracy stories?"

"Two nights ago I thought we had ironclad evidence of sabotage. My people found an electronic box in the wreckage we thought might have manipulated the controls on the Airbus, but it turned out to be nothing. Now the only remaining possibility, I'm told, is if some extremely powerful microwave or radar source was very close to the airplane. If someone used a transmitter like that—either on purpose or accidentally—it's theoretically possible it could have interfered with the electronic flight controls. It's happened before, to the Army's Blackhawk helicopter. The damn things would fly by a microwave transmission tower and the fly-by-wire controls would go full nose down, diving them into the ground. It took several losses before anyone figured out what was happening. But, you see, here that's just not possible. There's no transmitter that powerful anywhere close to Kansas City."

Kell Martinson felt very cold inside all of a sudden.

"Would it have to be that close?" he asked Joe.

"Who knows. If it were powerful enough, maybe a half mile would do. We just don't know, but as I say, we *do* know it's a moot point. There *was* no transmitter near the aircraft."

Kell sighed, trying not to change expressions. "Well, I'd better get going." He stood up and shook Joe's hand.

"Senator, I hope this works out for you. I'm sorry I can't do any more."

"You've been very kind, Joe. More so than I would have expected."

He turned toward the door, a high-pitched roar of decisional crisis in his ears, the truth of what the C-5 had been loading as the Airbus made its final turn Friday night filling his mind, the realization that much of it was classified national defense information bubbling up as a justification for saying nothing. Kell fumbled with the doorknob and made an uncoordinated departure, passing John Phelps, another NTSB investigator, who suddenly appeared in Joe's doorway.

"Joe. I need your copy of the Aging Aircraft Task Force Report issued a few years back by the Air Transport Association." Joe focused on Phelps as his mind changed gears, recalling the report and the FAA involvement during a frantic period when fatigue-related accidents in the airline industry revealed a major flaw no one had considered: the inspection procedures relied on to keep older airliners safe were largely inadequate.

"Say, wasn't that Senator Martinson?"

"Yes it was. You need the file of airworthiness directives too, John?"

"All of it, please. What was he doing here?"

For a moment Joe thought of telling John about finding the driver of the mystery car, then rejected the idea. Not that Phelps wasn't reliable. He just didn't have an immediate need to know a bit of inflammatory information that could cost a senator his seat.

"Just getting some information on the Kansas City crash, John. It affected some friends of his."

"That brings me to my next question, Joe. How was it in Kansas City? The crash involve anything in my expertise?"

When the NTSB had needed an aeronautical structures expert

in 1985, Phelps had been the man, coming on board just as the average age of airliners began to climb to worrisome levels. Joe filled him in on the North America investigation as he fumbled around on the cluttered top shelf of one of the bookcases, drawing down a cardboard magazine file and looseleaf notebook. "What are you working on?"

John Phelps cocked his head and looked at Joe, then glanced at the door as he pulled up a chair.

"I was going to ask if you had a minute, but since you put it that way."

"For you, John, always."

"Remember last week when the Miami Air 737 had a rapid decompression south of the Keys, over water, and found he'd lost a one-by-two foot piece of skin just about over the wing?"

"Yeah. No one hurt as I recall."

"That's right. The Miami field office asked us to send the Go Team, but Dean Farris decided not to because it was just cargo and the crew landed the airplane with no trouble."

"I would have gone to that one instead of to Kansas City if we *had* deployed," Joe added.

"Anyway, they sent me down to their headquarters in Miami, since the field investigator needed some metallurgical help. This was one of the first three hundred 737s."

"Same pedigree as Aloha's convertible in 1988?"

"The same, and almost as experienced in flight hours. Naturally we'd find it flying out of Cockroach Corner in South Florida. Anyway, the piece of skin that gave way had been repaired by what had to be a drunk gorilla. I've never seen such sloppy riveting. He'd cracked the new piece so badly in putting it in, failure was a foregone conclusion, and God knows who with an FAA license ever signed off on it. Anyway, that's not what I'm researching. What's got me curious is some of the repair and rebuilding work this little charter airline did on this airplane after the FAA started issuing all the mandatory repair orders in 1989. With that skin repair done as badly as it was, I wanted to see their other repair records for the forward sections they've had to rebuild. Now I'm having to wait for the FAA down there to help me, 'cause the airline told me to buzz off. In the meantime, I need to study up so's I'll have some idea what I'm talking about."

"You need help? We could go to the Board."

"I'm sure it's not that serious, I just don't like being treated like an irritant and refused access." John got to his feet, gathering up the box of materials Joe had handed him.

"Even when you *are* being an irritant, huh?" Joe laughed.

"I swear, Joe, put you guys in a position of authority and you develop an abusive sense of humor. Hey, thanks for the material. It'll be in my office for several days."

"Take your time. Ah . . . John?"

"Yes?"

"I thought the accepted term for the aging aircraft and shady air operations capital of the Western Hemisphere was *Corrosion* Corner, not Cockroach Corner."

"Naw, Corrosion Corner is too limited a term, Joe," Phelps chuckled. "It leaves out the generous supply of cracks, crackpots, pot, and bug-infested cockpits."

John Phelps departed, and when his footsteps had faded, Kell Martinson suddenly reappeared in the doorway, startling Joe.

"Senator?"

Martinson came in and closed the door behind him again, motioning Joe to sit down, this time in command and with calm authority. Joe complied, totally perplexed.

"Joe, it's not a moot point."

"What isn't, Senator?"

"Were you a military man?"

"Yes. Navy pilot. Why?"

"You had a security clearance then?"

"Yes. Secret. It's long since expired, but why . . . ?"

Kell held his hand out, palm up. "Wait. What I'm going to tell you touches on classified military information, and I may or may not have the right to do so. In any event, it has a direct bearing on your investigation of the Kansas City crash. Joe, you said it would take a very powerful transmitter within a half mile of the airport to cause trouble with that airplane's flight controls?"

"Yeah. Why?"

"And you said there wasn't one there."

"Right."

"Wrong. There was. Right alongside the runway, being loaded onto a C-5B on the cargo ramp at the very moment the planes hit. It's a highly classified self-contained tracking test unit associated with the SDI Brilliant Pebbles program, and it's one of the most powerful radars on the planet.''

Joe sat back, stunned. ''Was it operating?''

''I don't know. And the hell of it is, being a highly classified program, neither of us may ever be able to find out.''

One floor above Joe Wallingford's office, FAA Associate Administrator Bill Caldwell had begun the day leaning back in his office chair with his ear to a telephone receiver and his office cleared of visitors and staff alike. The call was necessary in his estimation, but it was dangerous. The information he was about to leak could backfire, but the way things were going, he had to launch a preemptive strike for the agency through a seldom-used channel. On the other end of the line was a well-known reporter for the *Washington Post*, Fred Russell, whom Bill had come to know over the years as careful and trustworthy. Occasionally he fed Russell stories and insights, acting as a deep background source when it served his purposes. The reporter was no fool— he knew he was being used by Caldwell—but he was equally capable of reading between the lines and independently verifying what Caldwell said.

''Bill, let me make sure I understand this. You're saying the FAA is unwilling to wait for the NTSB to make a recommendation on the Airbus flight-control system, that the situation may be too threatening, and you're considering whether to issue an inspection order in the form of an airworthiness directive?''

''Essentially, yes. We could order immediate inspections of the flight-control computers in each operational A320 in use in the U.S., though we could also suspend the certificate if we found a serious problem—ground the airplane, in other words. But only the Airbus A320 is affected, because it has the fly-by-wire system. There aren't that many A320s in the U.S.''

''Good grief, Bill, what are you looking for? My NTSB contacts tell me that nothing's been found, no sufficiently powerful radio transmitters were anywhere close, there's no reason to suspect a flight-control malfunction, and no one knows at this point exactly *what* to inspect for even if you *did* enter an inspection order.''

''I'm not confirming we're going to do it, but I wanted to alert you that we're considering it.''

''And,'' the reporter interjected, ''you want to make sure

someone gets this in print so you can watch your trial balloon and see who shotguns it.''

"Fred, if trial balloons weren't valuable, would you get any calls from official Washington?''

"Yeah, if not for this sort of thing, then for some other nefarious purpose. Okay Bill, now you're also telling me about all the FAA enforcement actions against North America in the past few years regarding the maintenance department? And you mentioned looking into their training program, which implies pilot error. Are you talking about human-performance stuff?''

"We're trying to be proactive, Fred, not reactive. We're not going to sit around and wait for the NTSB to make a recommendation to us if we can plainly see something needs to be changed in the meantime.''

"And North America has problems?''

"North America has been cited on twenty-eight occasions during the past three years for cockpit procedures violations, many of them involving checklists. That's because they continue to run a captain-oriented airline, and captains get tired of answering copilots and checklists.''

"Why haven't you guys made them change? Aren't you the FAA?''

"We can cite them for the violations, but that's only treating the symptoms. To treat the disease we have to force a change in philosophy, and that's where we're still struggling, trying to figure out how to write a rule to govern a new type of training course called CRM, cockpit resource management—teaching flight crews how to cooperate with each other and communicate effectively while running a disciplined, checklist-oriented cockpit.''

Fred Russell sighed and shook his head. "I know all about CRM. I just don't believe I'm hearing this from the guy who told me three years ago that human-performance people were nothing but professional apologists employed for the sole purpose of excusing negligent pilots. Suddenly you're a convert to human-performance disciplines? How come? You figure this crash was pilot error?''

"I didn't say that. We're simply looking at all the angles.''

"Come on, Bill. Do you have any evidence the crew did anything wrong or not?''

"Nope, absolutely not. And the NTSB is miles away from cause determination."

"Yeah, I know. Anyone else you want to firebomb, Bill?"

"Such cynicism. Should I call someone else?"

"No, of course not, but I'm allowed to be cynical, and in that vein, Mr. Associate Administrator, what's going on here? Don't get me wrong, I'm glad as hell you called me before the competition in New York, but this is a twenty-one-gun broadside at North America. Why? What'd they do, bump you off a flight?"

Bill Caldwell smiled to himself, but kept his voice steady, adding a slightly puzzled tone. "I'm just worried that people not get stampeded in the wrong direction, Fred. That's all."

By the time she walked into the office Thursday morning, Cynthia Collins had heard about the press conference called by Wilkins's people. What they were going to talk about now was anyone's guess, but she dispatched Fred Sneadman to listen and take notes. Fred was on the phone as soon as the conference ended, excited and almost breathless, which was unusual.

"Cynthia, this was weird, and I'm not sure I've followed it all. Same as on Tuesday, they say that one of their people—a long-time Wilkins friend and campaign worker—had proof that the Kansas City crash was an assassination, and that it was carried out by agents of the U.S. government. Here's the crazy part: now they say the same people who ordered Wilkins's death had this campaign worker, a Walter Calley, killed down in Louisiana before he could reveal what he knew. They're trying to blame this on the FBI or CIA, or possibly even the military."

"No one's taking that stupidity seriously, I hope?"

"Wait. There's more." Fred related the details, the pictures of Calley they had shown, and their call for national protests against what was being called an official cover-up that reached all the way to the White House. "It's like they're trying to fabricate another Watergate," Fred told her, "but then they got on the Star Wars project."

Less than a mile away, Cynthia stiffened. "What, *exactly*, did they say, Fred?"

The scientist who had called Senator Whitney had called the Wilkins camp as well, he told her. They called Brilliant Pebbles a fraud and showed a sketch of the Air Force radar tracking unit.

"Oh Lord!" she said.

"There's still more, Cynthia. Their major allegation is that Wilkins found out that radar tracking unit was going to be shipped for testing, which was not supposed to be done, and he jumped on that airplane last Friday night to fly to Kansas City and personally expose the operation. Someone found out what was going to happen, they say, and as the airplane was approaching the field, whoever was pulling the strings ordered the Air Force to turn on the radar unit and aim it at the airliner, knowing it would crash. Isn't that ridiculous?"

"They said that?"

"I've got it on tape, Cynthia. I know where we stand on Brilliant Pebbles, and I knew you'd be interested."

"Interested? Fred, I'm speechless."

Cindy hung up with one hand rubbing her forehead, visions of Kell's name in unflattering headlines on newspapers and TelePrompTers all over the world: senator and U.S. military accused by right-wing group in assassination of congressman.

Mustn't panic, she told herself. Remember, girl, these are fanatics. No one believes fanatics when responsible, believable people are around to set the record straight.

At the moment the Larry Wilkins press conference was ending a mile away on Capitol Hill, an FAA public information officer was talking in low tones to two foreign dignitaries as the three of them stood outside the main NTSB hearing room. "Now, what's in progress here is what we call a 'sunshine hearing,' about a railroad accident. The NTSB has investigated all rail, water, air, highway, and even pipeline accidents since 1974, when their functions were expanded from just aviation."

Joe stood nearby in a quandary, mental images of military radars and North America's A320 richocheting around his head, completely changing the possibilities—and the priorities—of the investigation. He was half listening to the guide's statements about the NTSB, and wondered if the man had any inkling how much the expansion of the Board's responsibilities in 1974 had damaged its ability to do the job in aviation. Rails were as foreign to Joe Wallingford's discipline as aviation had originally been to Dean Farris, and he kept as far away from nonaviation matters as he could.

Joe had been looking for Farris, forgetting about the hearing. He paused at the entrance to the hearing room, listening to Farris verbally dismembering one of the rail investigators. It was the professor in Farris coming out at such times, and he could be witheringly arrogant to his own people.

Susan Kelly sat two places to Farris's right. She had returned to Washington a few hours before. He watched her now for a second, noting with masculine pleasure how feminine and yet in command and self-assured she looked sitting there, peering at the staff over half-lens reading glasses. Joe was well aware of how much she had helped him personally in Kansas City, and he was mightily impressed by her sophistication and intellect— as well as respectful of her temper.

She caught sight of Joe finally, her mouth brightening into a small smile of recognition targeted just at him, and he responded, somewhat embarrassed, feeling like a schoolboy caught ogling the disturbingly attractive schoolmarm.

Someone else had spotted the IIC of the Kansas City crash as well. Joe had not seen the reporter as he approached and did not recognize him, but suddenly the journalist was standing in the hall beside him, speaking in a very low voice. "Mr. Wallingford, I'd like to ask you a few things about the progress of the Kansas City investigation, if I could?"

Joe Wallingford looked toward the doorway of the hearing room and realized the TV reporter had called his cameraman to bring the camera equipment and follow him out. Quietly but rapidly, the word was passing at the media table that Wallingford was within camera range, and the room was emptying of media, all stampeding toward Joe.

"No comment. Take it up with the public information people."

Joe retreated down the hallway with the reporter trailing, a procession of other newsmen and cameramen trundling after him.

"This crash was radio sabotage, wasn't it, Mr. Wallingford?"

Joe looked over his shoulder at the man with an overly startled expression, wondering what he knew. I'm getting spooked, he thought. "We're looking at every aspect of it . . . uh . . . excuse me . . ."

Joe continued walking as the reporter made one last attempt, motioning to his portable phone to explain his next question. "Mr. Wallingford, did you know Wilkins's people have just accused the Air Force of murdering their man and crashing the airplane last Friday?''

Joe stopped and turned toward the reporter with a startled expression. Kell Martinson's galvanizing revelation about the radar tracking unit had come only twenty minutes ago. Was this the same thing? ''What,'' Joe began, as calmly and condescendingly as he could manage, ''are you talking about?''

The reporter relayed the conclusions from the Wilkins news conference. ''Did you know there was radar equipment aimed at that airplane? Could that cause it to crash?''

That did it. Joe held up his hand and began retreating. ''I'm making no statements until we have some idea what's being said.'' He pushed past them, rounding the corner and disappearing at flank speed down the hallway toward his office, the sound of disgusted voices behind him, the reflection of bright TV lights dimming as the crews turned them off one at a time—momentarily absent anyone to interview.

Dean Farris had ignored the first camera crew to leave the hearing room. A bit of coming and going by the media in the midst of a sunshine hearing was quite typical, but when the entire group began stampeding out the door, Farris had looked at the staff, who were looking right back at him with equal puzzlement. Susan Kelly had seen them take off after Joe, and she was working hard to keep from laughing at Farris and his increasingly desperate glances around the room. When the last TV crew had left the hearing, Farris called a recess. Dean Farris didn't exactly live for the media, but he looked forward to open hearings where he could look chairmanlike and build his face-recognition factor with the American electorate.

Joe had already rounded the corner, heading for his own office, when he heard the chairman bustle down the hall behind him and accost the few cameramen who were moving their equipment, asking what had been going on and who had they been talking to. Joe knew the chairman would be pounced on by questions arising from the Wilkins media show down the street, and he'd probably wade right into them, after which he'd be looking for his IIC.

Susan Kelly found Joe first, calculating that he might have headed back down to his office. She was still suppressing giggles when she appeared suddenly in his path.

"You're a bad boy, Joseph Wallingford. You took the media toy away from the chairman, didn't you?"

"I didn't intend to . . . you noticed, huh?"

"Noticed? The American departure from Saigon was more subtle. What are you up to?"

"That's not my fault, Susan. I just looked in and they followed me. But . . . they . . . this thing is coming apart, Susan. We need to talk—quickly."

She fell in step and they walked briskly toward Farris's office, Joe relating Martinson's visit, the presence of the radar unit, and the little he knew of the Wilkins news conference. He was glad of her company, and increasingly worried about Farris's reaction.

She stopped Joe suddenly, pausing for a second while looking at him full in the face, surprised at her own reaction—at how good it felt to be around him. "Joe, remember what I said about Dean, how political he is? We can't react to this like we're prejudging the accident. Remember, he doesn't understand the technology, so he'll take his cues from you—and he'll try hard not to let you know it."

"I'll be careful, Susan. But, I really don't know *what* the hell we've got here. The radar thing is suddenly a very real possibility. Too real. It would answer a lot of questions."

"True," she replied, "but in the meantime, can we avoid being shoved into conclusions? The pressure is going to get unbelievable now, Joe. The entire U.S. government will become involved, including the White House, and they'll all be looking to us as the technology experts to make a decision on who did what to whom. They'll need to counter Wilkins's mob."

"Well, the FBI is involved also," Joe reminded her.

"Right. But ask yourself: are they competent to analyze the flight-control-system interference potential from a Department of Defense radar?"

"I see your point."

"Joe, this is going to be an acid test of the NTSB in every way."

13

The endless electronic beeps which had marked each heavily monitored heartbeat for nearly a week changed without warning to a steady tone—an alteration in the routine which brought sudden sound and motion to the quiet corridors of Truman Hospital as nurses and an on-duty physician materialized from nowhere, rushing into the room. The first officer of North America Airlines Flight 255, Don Leyhe, had entered the twilight zone of coronary arrest.

With the urgent efficiency of a well-choreographed dance routine at twice the speed, the medical people arrayed themselves on both sides of the bed, taking the proper precautions and pushing the proper voltages into the quiet chest, trying to coax his heart back into motion. As they worked, the copilot's wife—numb with fatigue and grief and uncertainty—was summoned from a nearby family room. She entered within a minute, watching in detached fashion as they labored over her husband.

But Don Leyhe was not there and would not return, and after twenty minutes of intense effort, the formal pronouncement was made. Mrs. Leyhe turned and walked slowly to the corridor, a widow now, followed by a concerned nurse. There were no tears—she had cried more than her quota in the previous days and nights. But there was an extreme sadness, principally for him. Whatever had happened out there the previous Friday night, she knew the system he had trusted so implicitly had failed him, just as North America had failed to be the secure, happy, professional home for which he had left the Navy. Whatever had happened, North America had betrayed their trust.

* * *

Kell Martinson awoke with a start in the darkness of Cindy's bedroom, the fact that it was her bedroom evident from the familiar scent of her perfume and the luxurious feel of her warm and silky body molded to the contours of his as they lay beneath the covers, his arm around her as she slept. Small sounds of contentment marked her breathing—small movements betraying her dream state. Their lovemaking was usually the best sleeping medicine, and it had worked well for her.

But not for him. He had tried to concentrate on the fullness of satisfying her and on losing himself in the quest, hoping she wouldn't notice his preoccupation with other matters. But the kaleidoscope of his problems distracted him, and the two of them had been slightly out of phase.

The FBI agent had listened very carefully during their brief meeting at 9:00 A.M. Thursday. But then the agent had taken on the role of prosecutor, doing as so many prosecutors seemed to love to do in such a case: scare a potential defendant half to death. No, the agent had said, he would not guarantee that the investigation would be wrapped up with what amounted to Kell's "confession." Yes, he would promise not to call in the media, but he would make no special efforts on behalf of a U.S. senator. After all, the man had said with a tinge too much sanctimony, a public official must be treated like any other citizen. What next? Kell had asked, and the agent was noncommittal. There were "other aspects" he wanted to investigate before they decided that Kell's presence in a restricted area at Kansas City Airport did not warrant some sort of prosecution. "Prosecution for what?" Kell had asked, and the answer had been vague, though he knew that the only real potential liability was a state charge for breaching the security area. A possible misdemeanor charge, however, was the least of his concerns.

Kell had entered the FBI building at the same moment the incendiary Wilkins press conference was breaking up in the Longworth House Office Building, with no inkling that the Wilkins staff had picked that moment to declare war on the United States government.

But Cindy had heard and was waiting for him in an advanced state of agitation when he returned to the office, and within minutes they were calling their own war council, Cindy pushing hard for a press conference of their own. He agreed only to call a quick meeting of the other Pebbles supporters on the Armed

Services Committee. They would have to answer the Wilkins charges on behalf of the Air Force.

Kell closed the door to his office to return a missed call from General Roach. The head of the Brilliant Pebbles program had called back Monday as promised after their meeting that morning, but he had relayed only more assurances that there had been no attempt to test the radar unit without explaining why it was being moved. Kell had made no secret of his dissatisfaction, and the general promised to seek approval to tell him more, then call later in the week. Apparently he was keeping the promise. General Roach came on the line abruptly.

"Okay Senator, I am now authorized to tell you that MAC was flying it to a more secure location than the factory where it was built. The factory is full of civilians. The unit was vulnerable. There was no testing involved."

"You weren't shipping it to the Pacific test range, were you?"

There was a lengthy silence before the general answered. "Where it was going is classified. *Why* it was going isn't. Testing wasn't involved."

"But why the Kansas City Airport, General? You might as well have entered it in the Rose Bowl parade. That's hardly secure."

"It's the closest airport to the factory that can handle a C-5B. Simple as that."

"I sure as hell hope that's the straight story."

A tired sigh was audible over the line. "Senator, everything I have told you is true."

By noon eleven angry committeemen and -women sat in Kell's office, listening to his paraphrase of the general's explanation and considering a political counterattack on Wilkins's people. In the midst of it, Kell briefly considered confessing his presence at the airport. But they had staff members, and if just one leaked to the Wilkins camp, it would blow up in all their faces.

Kell caught Cindy's eye at one point and shook his head ever so slightly. Now was not the time to tell them. She understood his message, but scowled at him in return.

When his office had emptied, they argued—professionally at first, then somewhat personally. She thought silence was a great mistake, a ticking bomb wired to his career. He was convinced they needed to choose the right moment, and that perhaps it wouldn't come.

"You're trying a cover-up, Kell. That always backfires."

"No, I'm not. I'm thinking politically."

"*I'm* the one who's thinking politically," she snapped as she hesitated on the way out the door. "I'm also thinking about what's honorable and what's not."

Kell left the Hart Building in deep despair. He had stolen no money, nor violated any congressional ethics nor taken any bribes, but he was apprehensive that Cindy was right, and that his career—which had been without blemish—was about to unravel. More important at that moment was the fact that she wasn't happy with him. Running back to her clandestinely after hours, then, had been an instinctive reaction, though they had made no arrangements for the evening. If nothing else, he owed her an apology. Their professional arguments were never supposed to spill over to the personal.

She had returned to the office on Tuesday playing her same cheerful and efficient role for public consumption, and then Tuesday night—and Wednesday night—she had wrapped herself around him, closing out the real world, and taking perhaps too much of a chance of discovery in the process. Though he had parked each of those nights a discreet distance away, he was becoming progressively bolder, parking closer and closer to her apartment.

Thursday evening, however, Kell had been anxious to make amends. He purchased a dozen roses and parked in front of her apartment in broad daylight, waiting for her when she drove up, hoping they could shut out the worries together again, though he knew instinctively it would be another fitful night for him. Now, in the predawn darkness of Friday morning, with Cindy blissfully asleep beside him, it seemed ridiculous that he couldn't sleep as well. He certainly needed it.

Kell pulled his arm away from Cindy carefully, trying not to wake her, punching the button on his digital watch to activate a tiny light. The display showed 4:01 A.M.

At exactly 4:02 A.M. some 14 miles to the south, on the far side of Andrews Air Force Base, Joe Wallingford had snapped wide awake from a deep sleep. His subconscious mind had been searching for the missing voice recorder like a computer dutifully churning through mountains of data looking for a single fact.

He got up immediately and padded into his den, turning on the ceiling light and retrieving small plastic models of the Boeing 757 and 737 aircraft. He sat at the kitchen table then and began flying one at the other, checking the theory that had popped into his head.

What had eluded them was how the force of the collision could have propelled the A320's voice recorder into some netherworld where none of his people could find it. It was too strong to be pulverized. Such high-impact boxes were designed to hit a mountain at cruise airspeed and still be identifiable and recoverable. So it had to have survived the crash and been thrown *somewhere* they hadn't considered.

"The voice recorder simply isn't there," Barbara had said. "We sifted every molecule of the A320 wreckage."

Joe pulled the 757 model to eye level and looked at the tail. The 757 was somewhat similar in appearance to the Airbus A320, but what caught his attention was the angle of the tail cone at impact, together with a mental image of the place where the CVR should have been in the ruined tail section, a missing, gouged area Barbara had pointed to last Saturday with consternation.

The memory of twisted aerospace rubble departing the Kansas City Airport on the back of several flatbed trucks played in his mind's eye.

That was *it*! They couldn't find the damn cockpit voice recorder because they had indeed spent all their time looking in the wrong place.

Joe noticed the time was 4:20 A.M. as he moved to the phone, grabbing his list of NTSB numbers and dialing Barbara's home in Silver Springs, Maryland. She took five rings to answer, her sleepy voice asking who it was twice. But suddenly she too came awake.

"Barbara, if you feel up to it, get packed. I want you to take one of your people and get back to Kansas City this morning. I know where the cockpit voice recorder is."

It was Friday afternoon in Dallas, and Jerry Harris was glancing at his rearview mirror for the umpteenth time, fully expecting a Dallas police cruiser to be on his tail. The light at Northwest Highway and Hillcrest obliged with a solid green, and he sped through, the spray of flowers on the right seat falling over again through the bumpy intersection. He knew his watch was showing ten minutes past two. He'd been checking that constantly as well. Going to funerals was not his style, but when senior management parcels out an assignment—even at the last minute—management trainees hesitate at their peril.

"How the hell did I end up doing this?" he muttered out loud as the entrance to Hillcrest Memorial Park came into view on his left. "Weiss. Weiss. Must remember the name." North America had been dispatching its employees to attend the funerals of victims killed in the Kansas City crash which had occurred nine days before, and this was yet another. Having him buy and carry flowers that should have been sent ahead of time was a bit tawdry, though. He dreaded carrying them in.

Jerry pulled open the chapel door just as one of the funeral directors stepped out. "The Weiss funeral?"

The man looked surprised. "You've missed it. It was at one."

"They told me two, they . . ."

"I'm sorry. You might catch them at the grave site, though. Far western end of the park. Only service in progress. Down at the Temple Emanuel end of the park."

"Is this—was this—a Jewish service?"

"No sir. Methodist." He thanked the man and dashed back to the car, shivering in the chilly breeze on what had become a clear, cold north Texas Friday. "Wonderful! They couldn't even give me the goddamn time correctly." He was muttering again and he knew it, but the tension was getting to him. Good grief, what a way to express condolences. Here, have some flowers, and sorry we killed your wife or husband. Next time we'll show up for the funeral.

The black limousine was visible ahead amidst a sea of cars, and he parked as quickly and unobtrusively as possible, gripping the flowers and walking quickly toward the tent, noticing with a sinking feeling that it was over—everyone was standing and talking quietly, several people holding on to a man standing beside what appeared to be three graves. No one had told him this was a triple funeral.

Jerry Harris squared his shoulders and moved toward the man, facing him finally, pressing the flowers forward with the words he had practiced. "Sir, North America Airlines would like you to know how deeply sorry we all are for your loss."

The man looked him straight in the eye, his face motionless.

Jerry could hear the leaves on the adjacent trees rustling in the teeth of a sudden wind gust. All activity on either side seemed to stop as what he feared most happened: he had become the instant focus of everyone's attention as they watched Weiss for a reaction.

Finally Weiss moved, his face softening just a bit, but his hand did not reach for the flowers, and Jerry wondered what to do.

The voice was soft and low and very controlled, and for a split second, Jerry didn't realize who was speaking. "How old are you?"

"Uh, twenty-five, sir."

"I know you mean no harm, but I don't want your flowers."

Jerry didn't mean to stutter or stumble, but he couldn't help it. "I . . . ah . . ."

"I saw you coming rushing up here at the last second. Too little too late, just like your airline's management. Too little, too late."

"Well, sir . . . ," he began, trying to keep a steady tone.

Weiss's right hand found his shoulder, his eyes boring into Jerry's. "I don't want your meaningless tribute. I want answers. Do you know what I've lost here?"

Jerry glanced to his right at the graves.

"That's right, take a look, you didn't even know, did you?" Weiss shook him slightly. "*DID* you?"

"No sir."

"My wife Kim, my son Aaron and my son Greg. That's what I've lost . . . because I trusted your airline with their lives."

"I'm very sorry, sir. I'm . . ."

Weiss dropped his hand. "Please go. Please get out of here."

Jerry began to turn, but Weiss caught him by the shoulder again.

"Tell your bosses I will remember their display of concern. I will remember. . . ." He dropped his arm.

Weiss dropped his eyes to the ground, and Jerry turned with a crimson face and beat a hasty retreat, his stomach knotted and a lump in his throat, tossing the flowers in the backseat as he got behind the wheel in utter dismay.

Mark Weiss watched the young man go as his mother-in-law clung to him, sobbing softly. Kim's father was recovering from his heart attack, but the shock of his daughter's and grandsons' deaths had been too great, and his doctors refused to let him leave the hospital.

The tears and pain of friends and relatives, the human togetherness in grief, was what they all needed now. Since Mark and Kim had come from Dallas—grown up in Dallas—there had been no hesitation regarding the burial site. Missouri had been their home for only a few years, and there were few attachments there, except for the house. The bitter loneliness of facing that empty dwelling lay ahead, and it was something Mark dreaded. It had been a home. Now it was just a house, and one he could never live in again without them. He would have to pack and store their possessions and put the house on the market as soon as possible. Exactly where he would go was an open question, but in the meantime, he intended to use the time in Dallas to advantage to look into North America's operations and its people, starting with the captain.

A large man at the back of the crowd suddenly caught his eye as the fellow turned to move away, apparently trying to be unobtrusive. Mark was startled, but recognized him instantly, and gently handed over his mother-in-law to a friend as he moved toward the departing figure, catching up with him at the curb.

"Captain Kaminsky?"

Pete Kaminsky turned slowly, embarrassed, his head bowed and his face glistening.

"I . . . didn't want you to see me," he said slowly, "I just needed to come. To be with you folks." With his shoulders hunched over and a pair of worn leather gloves kneaded slowly by his fingers, Mark thought him the saddest man he had ever seen. As deeply in pain as he.

"You didn't need to come, Captain, but I appreciate it more than you know." Mark spoke the words softly, matching Kaminsky's tones. "How are *you*? How are *you* doing?"

Pete looked up, a hollowness to his eyes that Mark understood all too well. "Doesn't matter."

"Yes it does."

"No!" The word was a sharp report, his head shaking from side to side emphatically. "I've tried to go to as many as I could. All my passengers . . . their funerals. I owe everyone at least that." He grimaced and shut his eyes, his teeth showing through drawn lips. "Although a lot of good that does them now."

There was a cold, concrete bench a few feet away, and Mark guided Kaminsky to it, forcing him to sit.

"This was not your fault. My family's death was not *your* fault in any way. Don't you understand that?"

Those haunted eyes again. "I was in command, Dr. Weiss. I was responsible. I . . ." Pete dropped his head again, a grimace on his face, his eyes squinted shut, fighting for control, and finally looking up again.

Lord, Mark thought, the man is in real agony—and in need of help.

"I should be over there. Not them. I promised you," Pete said. "I sat there, I sat there and said . . ." He waved his arm off toward the north, " 'Don't worry,' I said. 'We'll take . . . very good care of them,' I said. I can't forget that."

"Pete, are you married?"

He was looking down again. "I lost my wife to cancer over ten years ago. We never had kids."

"Where is home?"

"Kansas City."

"And you're all alone up there?"

Pete Kaminsky looked up at Mark Weiss and tried to smile. "Dr. Weiss, please don't worry about me. Please." He got to his feet suddenly, readjusting his overcoat and hesitating for a second as Mark extended his hand, taking it finally, his handshake uncertain. "I've got to go. If there's anything I can do . . ." Pete's voice trailed off, and Mark filled the void.

"I'll be back up there next week. I'd like to get together."

"That's all right, I . . ."

"No, I'm serious." Mark handed him a piece of notepaper and a pen. "For your phone number."

Pete Kaminsky hesitated, then took the paper and quickly wrote down the number before handing it back without a word.

"Pete, you mustn't take this on yourself."

He nodded unconvincingly, turned, and left, making his way to what had to be a rental car as Mark moved back toward the graves and the family members. Kim and the boys had been in such a hurry to get to Dallas. And in the end, Dallas was where they would stay.

As he walked back toward the group, a sleek Boeing 737 soared overhead, climbing out of Love Field into the cold, blue Texas sky bound for some distant destination, filled with trusting passengers. But for the first time in years, Mark Weiss refused to notice.

14

Dr. Mark Weiss sat fulminating in a window seat aboard the 6 A.M. nonstop from Dallas to Washington National, his eyes narrowed and hard, his attention riveted on two passengers in the first-class cabin ahead whose conversation he had overheard in the boarding lounge. He didn't know their names, but their words had told the story: they were defense attorneys for North America's insurance carrier, carelessly discussing their efforts to fight the growing number of damage suits being filed against North America, efforts that would involve investigations into the lives of any surviving family who became a plaintiff. Mark had not thought of filing a lawsuit as yet. It had seemed obscene. But ten minutes of listening to the two lawyers changed his mind.

The weekend had been an exercise in stress and emotional upheaval following the Friday funeral. Friday night the enormity of losing his family had crashed in on him, leaving him in the deepest well of gloom and despair of his life, and only the need to know what had killed them seemed to justify going on. The night had crawled by, a slow-motion agony.

Saturday morning he pulled himself together and headed toward North America's terminal at DFW Airport, intent on asking quiet questions about Captain Timson. He was within a mile of the terminal when he heard a radio report of the Wilkins news conference and the charges of military sabotage by electronic interference. Mark pulled to the side of the road in deep thought, the idea of questioning pilots about Timson suddenly pointless. If radio interference had killed Kim and the boys, what was the point of digging into Dick Timson's background?

Yet, those were only allegations, and he needed to keep busy. Mark put the car back in gear and continued toward the airport.

As a psychologist and a skilled interviewer, he gained the confidence of four separate pilots during the day, one a personal friend of Timson's, another a former copilot. By midafternoon he had an emerging portrait of the captain as a hunted, frightened personality masquerading as a firm disciplinarian in full and confident control, though he was a skillful pilot in the cockpit. From his work with other airlines, Mark knew the danger signals which prefaced human error in the cockpit, and Timson was beginning to fit the profile.

Mark spent Sunday with Kim's family, a desultory day of quiet talks and occasional tears. He had already made his reservation to fly to Washington on Monday morning, determined to press Joe Wallingford of the NTSB to let him get closer to the investigation. With what he had learned Saturday, there were things Wallingford needed to know—even if it turned out the Air Force *had* caused the crash.

Barbara Rawlson had made the long-awaited call from Kansas City to Joe's home late Saturday morning. "Joe, you were right. We found it!"

"Where I figured?"

"Just about. It took a lot of digging around in the junkyard to find where the burned luggage had been dumped. They'd already piled a lot of other garbage over it, but when we finally started sifting through the charred bags, there it was, *inside* the remains of someone's suitcase, with a piece of the rib that apparently snagged it still jammed into the mounting bracket. How on earth did you know?"

"The idea literally woke me up, Barb. Remember the antenna coupler we thought was a smoking gun? I suddenly realized that if it could be dragged out of the 737 and deposited in the wreckage of the Airbus, the cockpit voice recorder could have been dragged out of the Airbus the same way and left with the 737 wreckage. I knew you'd looked at everything in the structural wreckage, though, so the idea didn't make much sense until I remembered the bags, and how we usually cart them off as quickly as possible. When I started looking at the way the planes hit—and remembered the missing bracket and the scars in the A320's tail you showed me—I was almost certain."

"Well, you nailed it, Joe! That's where it was."

"Wonderful. Come home. Bring the box."

"On my way," she replied, in a stronger voice than she'd used in a week. Joe was pleased with the strength, and her recovery.

Barbara and the two staff members she had taken with her arrived back at NTSB headquarters Saturday night, delivering the CVR box to the chief lab technician, who spent all day Sunday digging out the tape, checking it, and copying certain channels of it onto backup reels and cassettes. By 11 A.M. Monday the first copy was placed on Joe's desk just as Dr. Mark Weiss arrived outside his open door. Mark stayed out of view, respectfully at first, waiting for the lab chief to finish briefing Wallingford and trying not to eavesdrop, but in the carpetless hallway, he couldn't help but overhear the conversation within. When the lab chief had left and he entered the office, Joe was holding the audio cassette, and Mark was painfully aware of what it contained.

"Mr. Wallingford? Excuse me for just dropping in. I'm Dr. Mark Weiss. We met at the hospital in Kansas City last week. I'm the one who wanted to join the investigation."

"Oh. Certainly, Doctor, come in. Sit down, please. What brings you to town so soon?"

Joe noticed Mark looking at the cassette in his hands, but given his intense interest, identifying it might not be wise. Without comment Joe slipped the cassette into his desk drawer, looking back at Mark with a subdued, friendly expression, acutely aware of what the psychologist had lost. "What *can* I do for you?"

Mark told him about his probing of the North America pilots. "I'm convinced that Timson was under intense pressure, and the people I talked to indirectly confirmed what I told you in Kansas City about his being scared for his job and very insecure, though he masked it effectively with stern forcefulness. The point is that such pressure, and lack of self-assurance, are often some of the major warning signs of an impending human-error accident, especially where authority figures and managers are concerned." He outlined his professional experience with airline pilots under stress, watching for any crack in Joe's resolve to keep him out of the official probe. Unfortunately, there was none.

"This is tough, Doctor."

"Mark, please."

"Okay Mark. This is tough, because I know you're qualified, but we do have psychologists on staff, and even one on the Board." Joe moved forward in his chair. "And in fact, with what we learned on Friday, human error probably played no role in this. Nevertheless, Andy Wallace, whom you've met, *is* a human-performance expert who needs to hear these things you're telling me, but he's back in Kansas City this morning to do a more in-depth interview of Captain Timson."

"Oh? When is that scheduled?"

"Around one, I believe, their time."

"Will that be public record?"

"Sure, in a few weeks, when we get it filed. Actually, I can get you a copy probably within a week. I'll be happy to help you with anything that's officially releasable."

Mark looked him in the eye with an intensity Joe found disturbing. Had the man not lost so much, Joe thought, I'd really resent his pressure. "Mr. Wallingford, I . . ."

Another investigator interrupted them, asking Joe to step into the hall for a quick conference on an unrelated matter. Mark was left alone in the office while Joe's voice echoed from the hallway, then mixed with two pairs of footsteps and receded into the distance.

The tape was inside the top drawer. He could pocket it and be gone in an instant, make a quick copy somewhere, and return it later, sheepishly, apologizing for acting on impulse. There were probably no laws other than petty theft governing such a thing, and the answer to what had happened to Kim and the boys might—just might—reside in the timbre and the meter and the tonal qualities of the voices on that tape, elements which he would never pull out of a written transcript.

Mark stood up, only marginally in control. He reached over and nudged the drawer, and as expected, it gave, moving a few millimeters as he struggled with himself. He was a professional and a principled individual who valued his reputation. But he valued his family more, and the need to know was overwhelming. But if he took that tape . . .

The sound of footsteps and voices made the decision for him. They were too close. There was not enough time. Quietly he nudged the drawer back in place and sat down, a few seconds before Joe Wallingford swung back through the door with an apology and sat down.

"You were saying, Doctor, when we were interrupted?"

Mark nodded. "Just this. Please keep me in the loop. Don't write me off just because of my family. I can be very useful to you."

There was no thought in Joe's mind of throwing some platitude back at the man. He was probably correct.

He shook Joe's hand and left, the urgency of a rapidly emerging plan swimming through his thoughts, the need to check into a hotel and use a phone becoming a burning priority.

Mark reclaimed his small bag from the guard in the main lobby and took a cab to the Hyatt, checking into a room on the twelfth floor.

Andy Wallace would be interviewing Timson in midafternoon, and since the transcript of that interview would be available within a week, everything Timson said could be examined in detail. Wallace had not heard the cockpit tape—no one had, except, perhaps, the technician who delivered it. He had overheard Joe lamenting the fact that it had arrived after Andy left for the airport. So if Andy couldn't tell Timson what was on it, and Timson couldn't hear it, and no transcript existed, then with the copilot gone, there was a small window of opportunity for a very specific, if risky, test.

Before leaving the eighth floor, Mark had leaned into an office at random and asked for the name of the NTSB lab technician. Phil Baker, he was told, which was exactly what he needed to know.

Mark entered the hotel room and went straight to the phone. He opened his bag and took out a small cassette recorder and a telephone suction-cup pickup, which he carefully attached to the receiver before punching the record button and phoning the front desk.

"Could you tell me the date and the time, please?"

The desk clerk complied cheerfully, if in a puzzled tone of voice, and Mark thanked her and hung up, lifting the receiver then to dial the number of Truman Hospital in Kansas City, asking for room 940-E.

* * *

When the call from Washington was over, Dick Timson replaced the handset in room 940-E with a puzzled look on his face which changed ever so slightly to the shadow of a smile.

"Who was that, Dick?" Louise Timson asked quietly.

He looked at her at last. "Strange call, and a lucky break. So the controls *were* screwed up! I told the copilot to take it. I said, 'My stick's not responding. Take it Don, take it.' "

His wife sat up, alert, looking puzzled. "You *remember* that now?"

"No." He shook his head slowly, a confused look clouding his eyes as he fought to concentrate. "I don't remember saying that, but if it's on the tape, I better remember saying that."

"I don't understand." Her voice was strained as she sat down on the edge of his bed.

He looked her in the eye for a few seconds, not really seeing her, but pleading silently for an understanding he had never let her provide. "Why . . . why can't I remember, Louise? It's tearing me up."

"Because you've been through a terrible trauma and a skull fracture. Forgetting is normal."

She said the words firmly, then turned and left the room, upset and not wanting him to see. She was used to her husband being fully in control, and it scared her to see him searching.

Dick Timson sighed at her departure. He was getting somewhat used to his wife's sudden exits. In Dick Timson's estimation, his wife had always been flighty and unreliable and overly emotional. This was nothing unusual. He leaned back and closed his eyes, another wave of apprehension washing over him. Would they let him retire honorably? Or would he be faced with the same dilemma so many pilots found themselves facing as companies and jobs collapsed during the deregulation wars: and what do *you* do for a living? How could he possibly answer that if he didn't have North America?

Louise Timson was in an agony of her own, standing outside the room where Jill and Jimmy Manning continued their slow recovery from the disaster wreaked by her husband's airplane. She had stood there many times in the past week, never going in, but deeply moved, the enormity of the accident still sinking in. It was all a nightmare she couldn't quite believe, but it wouldn't go away. Whenever she awoke, it was still there: her husband's plane had crashed, and hundreds of lives had been permanently changed, and she could do absolutely nothing to change that reality.

The playing of the CVR tape was set for 2 P.M., and Joe was straining at the traces to get to it. He had wanted to listen to the tape by himself first, but the day's frantic pace had prevented it. He would have to wait like the others.

Andy had called from Kansas City just as Joe tried to leave his office. The Timson interview, he said, had produced nothing new, but he had been contacted by the FAA's tower controller, Carl Sellers, when he got back to his hotel. Sellers had been listening to the media's excited coverage of the Wilkins allegations and the military's denials that the radar tracking unit had been turned on.

"Joe, there was a strange power surge—a transient pulse of some sort—that Sellers thought he remembered just as the Airbus was making the final turn. His radar in the tower flashed and went blank for a few sweeps, and the radios all made noise, like a squelch going off and on."

"Is he sure?"

"He went back and reran the original tower tape. It's there, he says, big as life."

Joe had been silent for a few seconds.

"Joe? That sounds significant to me, how about you?"

"I'm trying not to jump to conclusions, Andy. There was lightning in the area at the same time."

"Agreed. I'll do some more probing around before I come home."

Andy rang off, leaving Joe with one duty yet to perform. Bill Caldwell had never returned his daily calls the previous week. Earlier, Beverly Bronson from public affairs had dropped copies of the *Washington Post* and *New York Times* on his desk, with several related articles highlighted. The first one from the *Times* reported an in-depth analysis of the Wilkins charges from Friday, and that while sabotage was probably nonsense, the fact remained that there was a major piece of radar equipment at the airport which might have been operating, despite Air Force denials. Even the Secretary of Defense had been trotted out over the weekend to assure the country that the radar had been off and to attack the "gross irresponsibility of those who made such groundless charges." But, said the *Times*, the module ". . . was there, is powerful, and even the FAA has in the past expressed concern about potential radio or radar interference with the A320.'' Shipment of such items through the nearest civilian airports is normal, the article said, confirming that Kansas City International is the closest major airport to the factory. "According to Air Force sources, there are stringent safety precautions for shipping military transmitters through civilian airfields that require such a unit to be shut down at all times. The key question, therefore, is whether those precautions were followed.'' In their view, the whole thing hinged on whether or not the Air Force's word could be trusted, the implication being it could not.

Submerged within their front-page coverage, the *Washington Post* had run an article reporting the FAA was considering grounding the A320 because of the alleged vulnerability of the flight controls. In quieter times, the article would have been above the fold, but Wilkins's staff had eclipsed it with their Friday accusations. There was no question in Joe's mind the article was a Caldwell leak. Bill Caldwell was doing as he had threatened a week before—drawing his own conclusions.

Caldwell was behind his desk when Joe entered. He looked up at his own pace and extended his hand, lifting himself from his chair just enough to make a decent effort, but not enough to permit Joe to reach him without leaning over the desk. The man should get an Academy Award, Joe thought. The best actors are definitely not in Hollywood.

"What can I do for you, Joe?"

"Well, I've been trying to get you on the phone, as you asked."

"Sorry. I've been very busy."

"I can't give you that assurance you asked for. I can't guarantee that the flight controls aren't involved, though we still have no evidence they are."

"Doesn't matter, Joe. We're satisfied up here at FAA, and the task force has been disbanded."

"*What?* But what about all that . . . those veiled threats you threw at me on the phone last week about possible groundings?"

Caldwell had not smiled once. Now his face changed to a positive scowl as he took off his glasses and put down his pen. "Joe, I do not recall making any so-called threats to you or anyone else, but since then—in light of the allegations made the other day regarding that Air Force radar unit—we have satisfied ourselves through military liaison channels that the unit in question could not have been turned on, so therefore there could have been no sabotage, and thus no flight-control problem."

Joe sat back in his chair and stared at Caldwell. The administration's official line has found its voice at the FAA, whether true or false, he thought. "Just like that?"

"No, after careful investigation."

"Mr. Caldwell, your dismissal of the possibility of flight-control involvement is as premature as last week's consideration of grounding. Hell, we haven't even played the voice tape yet! That comes within the hour, and the smoking gun may be there."

"I'm glad you finally found that tape, Joe."

"So am I. But my point is, while it's certainly okay at this stage—and in the absence of contrary evidence—to blindly accept the Air Force's statements on the radar unit, there are still other possibilities. We still don't know what caused that aircraft to pitch down."

"Well, we do know it wasn't sabotage, by radar or any other means."

"Are you sure? One of my people has reported within the past fifteen minutes that one of *your* people in the Kansas City control tower has confirmed the presence of a pulse, or transient electrical interruption, at the precise time the Airbus was turning to final. Are you aware of that?"

Caldwell shook his head condescendingly and looked exasperated. "Of course I'm aware of it. Power fluctuations occur all the time during electrical storms. Were *you* aware there were lightning strikes in the vicinity at that same moment?"

"Yes. But my point is we don't know whether that glitch was caused by lightning, some transient electrical load through the local power grid, or perhaps a powerful source of electromagnetic energy on the airport property suddenly coming on line."

"Well, Joe, you chase your theories to your heart's content. This branch of the United States goverment is fully satisfied that the representations of the Department of Defense are true, and that the Secretary of Defense is not a liar."

"I wish I could share your confidence," Joe replied, his eyes boring into Caldwell's, "that the secretary and his generals haven't made an honest mistake, but I can't. By the way, did you see that *Washington Post* article this morning quoting un-named FAA sources and mentioning possible grounding?''

"Yes.'' Caldwell nodded his head and sat back, trying to look relaxed. "Leakers everywhere. I'm trying to find out who was responsible for that one. Of course we're not in any way thinking about grounding the 320, and by the way, you misinterpreted what I said last week.''

The two men regarded each other in uncomfortable silence.

"One other thing, Joe.'' Caldwell moved forward and leaned on his desk. "My people were not responsible for leaking the tower tape. I got the report a while ago. Now where do you suppose that leaves us?''

Joe bit his tongue as he tried to affect an unconcerned look, meeting Caldwell's hard gaze. "I don't know. The only member of my team that had a copy swears he never let it out of his possession.''

"Well . . .'' Caldwell was drumming his fingers. "Well, that means we've got a liar loose in the woodwork somewhere. It's your people or mine, but someone's guilty, and I intend to find out who and fire him.''

There was silence for a few seconds before Caldwell spoke again, still looking at Joe with the same expression. "Gardner, isn't it?''

"Beg your pardon?''

"Your man on the ATC group. Nick Gardner? A former air traffic controller of ours. He had the NTSB copy of the tower tape, right?''

"That's correct.''

"Tell him I want the tape copy back. I'm going to have it analyzed against the radio broadcast. Each tape copy has its own characteristics.''

"Fine with me. I'll relay the message.'' Joe got to his feet thoroughly disgusted, but left with just a nod, heading for the elevators and the conference room on the eighth floor, where the group was assembling to listen to the cockpit tape—unaware that Bill Caldwell at the same moment was angrily scrambling to get the Kansas City tower chief on the phone. No one had told him about the electrical pulse, leaving him to get blindsided by an inferior bureaucrat from the NTSB!

Kell Martinson had phoned Joe first thing Monday morning to ask whether the IIC had talked to the FBI agent, and what had been said. "Noncommittal attitude" was the phrase Joe had used to describe the agent's reception of the relatively insignificant news that the NTSB was satisfied. They talked about the Wilkins allegations, and when Joe mentioned that the CVR tape had been found, Senator Martinson asked to attend the first playing of the tape.

Now Kell was waiting for Joe as the NTSB man emerged from the elevators on the eighth floor, unflattering descriptions of Caldwell's duplicity echoing in his head. Joe had made the decision to include the senator, knowing it would be questioned—and probably criticized—by everyone. While Dr. Mark Weiss was simply too interested to be legitimately included, the head of the oversight authority for NTSB in the senate was not. And something undefinable—some gut instinct—had told Joe to do it. Martinson might somehow turn out to be even more helpful to the investigation than he had already been.

In the meantime, his presence on the eighth floor at Joe's invitation was only a career threat as long as neither Dean Farris nor the congressional affairs people knew about it.

"Senator, before we get started, let me walk you into the chairman's office for a second, and"—the two men began walking in that direction—"if you wouldn't mind, I'd appreciate it if you didn't volunteer the fact that I invited you."

Kell held up a hand. "Don't worry, Joe, I fully understand the drill. I forced this visit on you, and neither you nor your chairman have much choice—if you want to keep your funding, that is." Joe glanced at Kell, slightly relieved to see a broad smile on the senator's face.

Joe knew the chairman was in. He also knew the magnitude of the shock that was coming—and that brought a smile to Joe's face as well.

15

Joe's hopes were higher than they should be. The key to the entire puzzle of the Kansas City crash might—just might—lurk in the magnetic particles of the mylar tape he was about to play in the NTSB conference room, but such hopes could be easily dashed. The problem was time, and which way to focus the efforts of his people. The public hearing—formally called a Board of Inquiry—would be held in six weeks in Kansas City to help answer the main questions surrounding the crash. But first, they had to decide exactly what the main questions really were.

Senator Kell Martinson's presence on the eighth floor had astounded Dean Farris. The chairman had fallen all over himself to be friendly, and Kell had acted as if Joe were a brand-new acquaintance who had dutifully marched the senator to the head man. "If the IIC, Joe Wallingford, here, has no objections, Senator, we'd be glad to have you sit in," Farris had told him.

With Kell in tow then, Joe joined Susan Kelly, Nick Gardner, Barbara Rawlson, and two of Andy's staff members in the conference room. Dean Farris, for some reason, declined.

Joe had tried to get select members of the official parties to come in if possible, though it was on very short notice. North America vice-president John Walters had responded, having already been in town for a meeting with the airline's insurance carrier, and an FAA flight standards representative on Barbara's systems group—one of Caldwell's men—had shown up, as had one of the Air Line Pilots Association's accident investigators. The room was small and crowded as a result.

"First," Joe began, "let me introduce the chairman of the Senate subcommittee that nurtures us financially and legislatively, Senator Kell Martinson, who is following this investigation's progress. The senator has agreed to confidentiality restrictions. He's here to see what we do and how we do it.'' Joe glanced at John Walters, who looked alarmed. A senator meant political dangers, and Walters would certainly find reason to complain. There were nods and smiles from the rest of the group.

"What you're about to hear are the last thirty minutes of Flight 255 as it approached Kansas City a week ago Friday night. I assume everyone understands the strict nondisclosure rules, the delicacy of this tape in terms of the rights of the pilots and their families and their airline, and the effect it may have on your personal feelings. This tape starts thirty minutes before the accident, and I will be roughly timing the tape against the printout the lab sent of the flight data recorder's digital flight information. I'll try to periodically give you an idea what the airplane was doing from this readout and sequence it with the tape as best I can.''

He snapped on the recorder and a stopwatch simultaneously, the scratchy sounds of the airstream outside Flight 255's airborne cockpit from ten days before immediately filling the room. As they became absorbed in the sounds—the sporadic comments of copilot Don Leyhe and Captain Dick Timson along with the radio transmissions to and from the airplane—a secretary remained outside the door on Joe's instructions, making certain no enterprising newsman tried to listen in.

The descent had been rather routine, the handoff from the FAA's air route traffic control center (called "center" for short) to Kansas City approach control handled with professional brevity. The shortness of Timson's answers to Leyhe's checklist-induced questions was not unusual, nor was the sharpness and sarcasm of Timson's response to Pete Kaminsky's radioed warning.

"North America 255, this is North America 170 on the ground," Kaminsky had radioed. *"That's pretty wild weather you're getting into. We just had a lightning strike along the runway. Recommend you wave it off.''*

Joe Wallingford had heard that transmission before on the tape recordings made by the control tower. What he had not heard was the exchange that followed in the cockpit of 255.

"Who the hell is that, some Navy pussy? Where do our pro-

cedures give that sonofa bitch the right to play mother hen? Wave off indeed!" Timson had growled the words rhetorically, it seemed, as he keyed his microphone to reply in more friendly tones to Kaminsky. *"Thank you 170, but I believe we can handle it!"*

"I think he just wanted to make sure we knew about that cell, Dick."

Copilot Don Leyhe's voice was distinctive and quite different from Timson's low register. Leyhe's vocal tones were sharp and in the range of a tenor. Timson's, on the other hand, had a deeper rumble which nevertheless could be heard clearly through a noisy crowd with little effort.

"Who is that guy, Don?"

"I don't recognize his voice."

"Well, I'll find out later. Flaps to position one."

It was always eerie, listening to the words of pilots who had not survived. For a moment you could find yourself mentally and emotionally in that doomed cockpit with them, knowing what they didn't know, but unable to communicate, watching the sequence unfold inexorably toward tragedy.

"There may be some windshear in here, Captain," Leyhe had said, followed by silence from Timson as they approached the outer marker, the point on the instrument landing approach where the airplane should have its flaps and landing gear properly positioned for landing, be at a stable approach airspeed for the conditions, and begin descending.

Joe stopped the tape as he looked at his stopwatch and at the digital flight recorder's readout, a sheet full of digits, columns of them, all from the computer readout of the A320's flight data recorder, and each of them giving another parameter of the flight: airspeed, bank angle, engine speed, and many others.

"At this point," Joe said, "they were about 8 miles out, slowing through 145 knots, flaps at 20, gear down, descending at 700 feet per minute, and at an altitude of 2,400 feet." He restarted the tape, nearly forty seconds passing before the next words crackled from the speaker.

"Captain, if there's a microburst up here, we're too slow." Leyhe's voice sounded distant on the tape, but the words were clearly audible, as was his concern. For a few seconds there was no response from Captain Timson, then a sharp *"What?"* rang out.

"That exchange," Wallingford began, "started at six miles out and 1,760 feet, 135 knots."

There was just enough time for Joe's statement before Captain Timson's voice could be heard again. *"Oh for Christ's sake, Leyhe! I think this bird can handle a few gusty winds, don't you? That's what the kid in the Metroliner said: gusty."*

Joe Wallingford reached over and stopped the tape, freezing his stopwatch at the same moment. "Okay, now the way I read this, at this point they were 5⅓ miles from the runway at 137 knots and 1,570 feet, just a hair below the normal visual glide path. Remember that the ILS had been knocked off the air by a lightning strike and they were doing a visual approach—had accepted a visual approach. Now the note I have here from the lab indicates they think the aircraft entered a microburst at about 5 miles, and it probably had a diameter of 1 to 1½ miles. At exactly 5 miles out they were stable at 135 knots of indicated airspeed, but their speed over the ground was, according to the radar track the air traffic control group has been working with, 114 to 115 knots. So they were flying into a 20- to 21-knot head wind with an equal tail wind on the other side. At 4¾ miles their vertical velocity drops to 1,000 feet per minute descent, and by 4 miles out they are down to 1,500 feet per minute rate of descent, 98 knots of airspeed while still at 112 knots of ground speed, and less than 600 feet above the terrain."

Susan Kelly shook her head. "In other words, they were dropping like a rock at that point, within the space of 1 mile."

"According to this readout, yes," Joe replied as he reached over and turned the recorder on again, punching his stopwatch at the same time.

It seemed to Joe that the background wind noise changed suddenly, but it was hard to tell. Neither pilot said anything for nearly thirty seconds, then the voice of the copilot could be heard in an urgent cry.

"Captain! Windshear! Go around!"

The sound of engines increasing in power filtered through in the background, and that would have been very hard to measure if there had not been a digital flight recorder readout. In many other crashes there had been perpetual disagreement over just when the crew pushed up the throttles because there was only an old-style flight recorder which couldn't tell the investigators the exact power setting. Even when the accurate digital recorders became available, the FAA refused to order airlines to install them in place of the old ones. Joe had fought that battle years before with the FAA, and lost.

Joe stopped the tape and the stopwatch again. "At this point, they are about 4 miles from the runway and five minutes, fifty seconds from collision with Flight 170—provided I've calculated this correctly. They are dropping now at 1,500 feet per minute, the readout shows 75 percent engine power on both engines and rising, and they are several knots below stall speed. Okay, ready?" They all nodded, the tenseness in the room building. They all knew the Airbus had not crashed on this approach, but they were on the edge of their seats anyway. Joe reengaged the recorder and the stopwatch.

The distant sound of engines reaching full power raised the background noise level as the seconds ticked by.

"Climb, goddammit!" Timson again.

Joe stopped the tape again. "What this readout says happened during the period we just heard is this. At about 3 miles from the runway, they were showing, uh, 100 knots airspeed, full power on both engines—actually somewhere above maximum RPM, so they must have firewalled them—and they're at 100 feet above ground level on the radio altimeter readout, and sinking still at 160 feet per minute."

"Jeez." The voice belonged to Barbara Rawlson.

"Yeah, I agree," Joe said. "Okay, they keep sinking until they are 40 feet off the ground, I see a very high angle of attack here, the elevator channel shows a hefty up-elevator command, and their airspeed is hovering around stall speed, perhaps a hair above it, and they're clearly close enough to be in ground effect."

"Joe, weren't there trees out there? I thought I heard a thump, but I could be mistaken."

"We'll go back over it. Now at 2 miles they had come back up to 72 feet and had started climbing, speed increasing, and by 1 mile they were climbing at 500 feet per minute at 110 knots and had reached 200 feet. After that they go up to about 1,500 and level off, over the runway."

"That's the strange go-around that many of the witnesses saw."

He restarted the recorder once again, noting there were no cockpit sounds of rain or hail similar to what had been clearly audible on voice tapes from several other weather-related crashes such as Delta in Dallas in 1986. No further words were spoken on the tape as they listened to over a minute of various sounds, finally punctuated by the radio call.

"255's going around."

Joe looked at the faces of his colleagues as he stopped the tape and the watch this time. No one was moving or saying a thing. "Any thoughts so far?" Several of them looked at Joe, then at each other, before Barbara spoke up. "Are you kidding? They almost bought it. That was unbelievably close! I want to see that in a simulator."

"Agreed."

North America vice-president John Walters, who was in fact an official member of Andy Wallace's human-performance group, had started shifting uneasily in his chair, his face a mask of grim discomfort. He had been silent and motionless before, but the last comment was too much. "I would appreciate it if we could get on with the tape and not spend time interpreting or characterizing actions that are going to take a great deal of study to understand."

Joe nodded at Walters, understanding the defensiveness. "We're not here to pass any judgments, least of all at the first playing of the tape, but Mr. Walters, I'm afraid some comments are natural at this stage."

"Well, I'm not prepared to sit here and listen to you people conclude that they, as she put it"—Walters jerked a thumb in Barbara Rawlson's direction—" 'almost bought it.' "

Barbara bristled instantly. "How would you characterize 40 feet off the ground 6 miles from the runway? Is that normal North America approach procedure?"

John Walters turned and glared at Barbara Rawlson as Joe raised his hand. "Okay! Not here, and not now. Let's continue. I'll restart the tape, and we'll pick it up with them now over the end of the runway and at five minutes and one second before the crash."

The cockpit sounds filled the room again. Normally the lab would send a copy of only the cockpit area microphone channel to the IIC, but Joe always requested they add the channel that picked up the radio transmissions to and from the aircraft. Having both to listen to at the same time made the task of tracking the flight sequence a much easier process. Radio calls often overlapped cockpit conversations in such a complex web that only by listening to the same sounds that the pilots had heard could an investigator meticulously piece together what had really transpired. Apparently, the lab had also included the intercom channel to the flight attendants.

"What in hell are you two doing? What happened?" A female voice, obviously a flight attendant, had called on the intercom.

Leyhe had answered, *"Windshear. We nearly bought it."*

Joe noticed as Barbara threw a triumphant nod at John Walters, who did not react.

"Good Lord!" The voice was Timson's, heard only in the cockpit, Joe figured. His reaction had been instantaneous. *"Don't tell that dumb broad something like that! She and her fellow cats will spread that all over the airline in fifteen minutes!"*

"Well, however you cut it, Captain, we nearly—"

"No. Do NOT tell her that. Now correct it, tell her you were joking!"

"I'm informed," Leyhe's voice began again on the intercom, *"that we did not almost buy it . . . but in fact we did."*

"Leyhe, goddamn you!"

"North America 255, what are your intentions?" The radio voice of the tower controller followed by a fraction of a second.

Timson had apparently taken over the radio calls—his voice replaced Leyhe's in the next transmission. *"Tower, North America 255 would like a closed pattern. We'll come right back around for another visual approach to runway one-nine."*

"Captain," they heard Don Leyhe begin, *"we damn near died out there. We were down to 40 feet, and that microburst is still there. I think we'd better go out and hold until this blows over."* The voice was barely controlled, a few words seeming to shake slightly as they emerged from the copilot. One did not, in the cockpit traditions of North America, speak that way to one's captain. Though many airlines had been teaching an entirely new way of training crews to talk openly and frankly with each other in just that manner, at North America it was heresy, as Timson himself had said at an industry conference on human performance a year before. Heresy to talk back to a senior captain, let alone the chief pilot, and heresy to suggest that maybe

his decision was wrong, or, heaven forbid, dangerous. Leyhe had neatly violated all applicable courtesies.

Joe raised his hand for everyone's attention, but did not stop the tape. "At this point they begin a right turn to reverse course and fly a downwind pattern. They're just south of the far end of the runway here."

There had been a pause after the copilot's recommendation, but now Timson's voice could be heard again, tinged with what sounded like sarcasm.

"Damn control tower should have warned us, but I told you this ship could handle it. I'll admit that was a helluva lot closer than I ever want to see again, but . . . that microburst will be gone by the time we come back around. It's blowing east."

"Sir, you didn't hear me."

More seconds ticked by without a response from the captain, each of the NTSB team members sitting in absolute silence, listening to every sound as if the most subtle one might hold the key. The captain's broadside against the tower controller was by itself enough to provoke a major legal battle—North America's lawyers would try to prove the FAA contributed to the crash by failing to warn the crew properly.

"I heard you, Leyhe!" The snarl in Timson's voice was clear enough, the response sudden enough, that several of the occupants of the room jumped. *"And if I want your goddamn advice, I'll ask for it. I'm not going to discuss it further."*

Eight more seconds passed before the copilot responded, apparently refusing to drop the issue. *"Captain Timson, we don't know for sure that it isn't right off the end of the runway now. Please, let's go wait it out. I'm very uncomfortable with this."* Joe could hear a shakiness in the copilot's voice again. The words that followed validated his apprehension.

"Don, goddamn it! You're just like all these other weak sisters I've got to nursemaid around this fucking airline, scared of your own shadow. The goddamned windshear is NOT *over the end of the fucking runway!"*

There was silence on the tape and silence in the room as the team members looked around at one another, wide-eyed and startled by the exchange. All except the North America executive, Walters, who had his arms folded and his eyes welded to a spot on the desk in front of him. The tension in the man's expression was painfully obvious. What on earth was next?

"What do you want me to do, Captain?" The copilot's voice had dropped in volume. He sounded resigned, defeated, all the fight beaten out of him.

"I want you to shut your goddamn face and let me fly my airplane!" Timson's voice replied.

There were no further words from the copilot as the seconds ticked by. The sound that was probably a flap handle being activated was heard several times, followed by the landing gear cycling down, but if there was any copilot participation they could not hear it. There was no repeat of the before-landing checklist, no copilot call out of airspeeds and sink rates—nothing. It was as if Leyhe had simply left the cockpit.

The sounds of Timson's radioed exchange with the tower filled several seconds, then silence.

"At this point they are one minute from the end of the tape, from impact, and the flight recorder shows them beginning a tight right turn to final and descending out of 1,500 feet, airspeed 135 knots," Joe added.

Nothing but background noises filled the tape.

Joe raised his finger again, "Thirty seconds to go. They are coming through a heading of zero-nine-zero magnetic, 650 feet in altitude."

"Fifteen seconds, heading 130—" Joe stopped in midsentence. The sound of a quick burst of static, as if there had been a momentary power surge in the radio squelch circuits, instantly riveted his attention. "Wait a minute." Joe stopped the recording and his stopwatch, rewinding the tape slightly, listening again to the short, transient sound.

"Anyone have any idea what that might be?" Joe looked at each of them in turn. Barbara spoke up.

"Sounds like the noise you get in the radios when you switch electrical power in the airplane, Joe."

Several of them nodded. "We'll need to research that—see if there's anything similar on the tower tape. You all realize why I'm making a point of this?"

"The radar unit?" Barbara asked.

"Exactly." He restarted the tape and his watch then and resumed the narration. "Now at exactly this point is where the turn began stopping, the rate of descent suddenly increases . . . all the parameters change here. This is where the elevator suddenly goes to nose down." Joe stopped, listening intently as Leyhe's voice rang through on the tape.

"Captain! What are you doing?"

Several unidentifiable sounds could be heard which might be controls being positioned rapidly, punctuated by a computer voice which said simply, "Priority right," followed by the rising pitch of the engines.

"At this point, the elevator comes back to nose up, engine power increases steadily all the way to max power, the ailerons command a roll to the left back to a wings-level posture, and the aircraft finally stabilizes just above the surface on a heading directly for the 737. All that's from the flight recorder." Joe had stopped the tape and now reached to restart it. Susan stopped him. "What did that mean? Priority right?"

Barbara answered and Susan looked in her direction. "This airplane's two side control sticks are not physically linked together, they're electrically linked. The last pilot to press the priority button—which is located on each stick—controls the airplane and disconnects the other pilot's control stick."

"And that's what we heard on the tape?" Susan asked.

"Right. When you have to use a priority switch to gain control, the computer voice tells you 'priority left,' meaning the captain has seized control, or 'priority right,' meaning the copilot has seized control."

"And in this case . . ."

"In this case the copilot seized control from the captain, and the captain's side stick was definitely not in the neutral position, which means"—Barbara glanced at Joe to make sure he wasn't disapproving of her narration—"which means that the captain was actively flying the airplane and operating the controls when the copilot took over."

Susan looked amazed. "You can tell all of that just from the presence of that computer voice?"

"Absolutely."

"And," Joe said, "the flight recorder indicates that at that exact moment, when we hear 'priority right,' the elevator began moving back to nose up."

Joe looked around at the group as they absorbed what they had heard. "Let me restart this, now, within ten seconds of impact."

Joe's eyes were glued to his stopwatch, but instead of speak-

ing, he held up a final show of fingers counting down to the end.
Five . . . four . . . three . . . two . . .

"GODDAMMIT!" punctured the air as the muffled roar of
colliding metal dropped to silence, marking the point where the
cockpit voice recording had lost power as it was suddenly decelerated from 145 knots to zero and violently thrust into the
baggage compartment of the disintegrating 737.

There was silence in the room again, this time for nearly a
minute; it was broken first by Barbara Rawlson after an audible
intake of air.

"Was that Timson's voice at the last?" The voice had been
a significantly higher range than normal, but there was a gruff-
ness to it that sounded like Timson, the word *goddamn* and its
variations an overly familiar Timson usage by the end of the
tape.

"Mr. Walters, what do you think?" Joe asked, but there was
no response. He glanced at Susan and Barbara, then back at
Walters. "Sir? Mr. Walters?"

John Walters looked up suddenly, an accusatory look on his
face, as if rudely disturbed. "What?"

The reply was sharp and rude in and of itself, and Joe hesitated
before asking, "Was that Timson at the last? The last word,
goddamn, was that Timson?"

Walters nodded again. "I think so. It sounds like him . . .
like his voice, I mean."

For a second time John Walters shot a series of hunted looks
around the room before seeming to regain his confidence, this
time without the anger. "I'm sorry, everyone. I guess I'm
stunned. Would you please excuse me?" Without waiting for a
reply, Walters was on his feet, and just as quickly out the door,
leaving the rest of the group in uneasy silence.

They played the last five minutes again, making notes and
going over several times the last word Timson had uttered, before Joe Wallingford took the cassette out of the recorder, noting
the dead silence in the room, several of them staring into the
distance and a few heads shaking slowly, as if rejecting what
they had heard. Joe felt ill. There was no key, only more questions—including the sinister radio noise as the flight controls
began to change position, with or without pilot input. Once
again, it had gone from impossibly complicated to totally Byzantine.

Nick Gardner spoke first. "Joe, uh, am I reading all this right? The copilot did take over, but too late to save them?"

Joe nodded. "That's the way it seems to me."

"So the question, or one of them," Nick continued, "is why did he have to take over? What happened to the captain? He asks, 'Captain, what are you doing?' Could the captain have been flying them into the ground?"

Joe shook his head with a consternated expression and a sigh. "The captain says he was flying it properly. He says the airplane didn't do what he told it to do."

Barbara nodded at that and shifted forward in her chair. "That makes sense, though, Joe. He would have been pulling his stick, the airplane's not responding, the copilot finally takes control, but recovers too late. But when the copilot seizes control, his stick *is* working. That tells me the problem was probably electromechanical and in the captain's control stick—or radar interference with that same left side."

The implication of that sank in: a dreaded flight-control problem. Joe knew the FAA member would be telling Caldwell about it within a half hour, even though the associate administrator had already summarily dismissed flight-control problems as a potential cause because the political wind was blowing in the other direction. This should at least make the little bastard nervous, Joe thought to himself.

"Excuse me, could I add some ideas?" Kell Martinson had been studying the faces of each member, apparently trying to decide whether to jump in.

"Certainly," Joe said.

"Logic would dictate, I would think, several consistent possibilities from what I've just heard, but I'm sure there's a lot I'm not seeing, so please blow these comments out of the tub at will. First, the captain's stick could have malfunctioned as mentioned. That would explain the sudden flight-control change when the copilot took over. Second—the possibility we don't really want to face—the captain's control inputs are overridden or cancelled by electromagnetic interference from outside, from the SDI radar, which our military people say could not have been turned on. Third, they could have been caught in a small microburst, or downdraft, and come out of it at the same instant the copilot took over, sort of coincidentally. And fourth, the captain may have, for some physical or psychological reason, pushed his stick forward at the wrong moment. Not with intent, you see, but a momentary lapse.'' Kell sat back and waited, and Barbara spoke first.

"The third is probably not possible, Senator, because the flight recorder shows no airspeed variations or rates of descent not explained by the aircraft's attitude.''

"Okay.''

"But your fourth proposition . . .'' She looked at Joe, who shrugged, and at several others in the room, who were equally unsure what to say. "I guess that just flies in the face of what we expect of a pilot, you know? What could cause an experienced captain like this one to make such a mistake?''

"I have no idea. I'm just following the logical implications that if the captain's control stick was the source of the nose-down input, then either a malfunction of the stick or a malfunction of the human controlling it must be present. That takes in, of course, a wide range of possible behaviors, but human failure would, it seems to me, be one of the possible mechanisms of failure.''

Joe was nodding. "Your logic is impeccable, Senator. Upsetting, but impeccable.''

"Of course, you have possibility number two and the fluctuation you mentioned, Joe,'' Barbara added.

Susan had been leaning back, an elbow propped on the arm of the chair, her chin resting in the palm of her hand. She moved forward now and sighed, examining the table before looking at Joe across the wooden surface. "Joe, maybe it's just me, but I'm more confused now than ever. We're back to control failure, control interference, or pilot mistake. That's where we were when we came in the door forty-five minutes ago!''

Several were nodding as Joe answered, his right hand gesturing palm up. "I . . . I can tell you I'm somewhere between disappointed and stunned. I didn't expect the diatribe against the copilot, but having said that, I'm not sure it's material. The fact that the copilot eventually took control, though too late, indicates that the key to this entire crash is what happened at the left side control stick. Mistake or malfunction or accidental interdiction? It could be anyone of them, especially with that curious noise on the tape. And with the hysteria out there about the radar unit, if we can't prove it wasn't on . . .''

One of Andy Wallace's staff members had raised a hand, or

more precisely, an index finger. "Have you considered the possibility that if the copilot had taken over sooner, he might have saved them? There's quite a period of time between his asking, 'Captain, what are you doing?' and seizing control."

"I don't follow you," Joe told him.

Susan was nodding, and cut in. "What I believe he means is if the copilot saw a problem, why didn't he act sooner? Did that broadside tongue-lashing from the captain intimidate him? Surely it isn't standard practice to treat copilots that way. Since this is the chief pilot, I'd say we've got some questions here concerning why he is intimidating his copilot, and whether that's accepted cockpit style for North America crews."

"That is, *if* the copilot *was* intimidated," Joe added. "There's one other inconsistency that's bothering me. Dick Timson, the captain, told Andy and me in our first interview with him in the hospital that he had been flying the airplane all the way down. Obviously that's not true."

"When was that interview, Joe?" Susan asked.

"The Monday following the crash."

"Oh. You probably shouldn't put any significance on that contradiction. With a head injury, he could easily be misinterpreting his memories. He could be telling you what he *tried* to do all the way to impact."

He adjourned the meeting then and took Nick Gardner aside, telling him of Bill Caldwell's demand. "He wants that tape of the tower radio transmissions, Nick. Take it up there this afternoon, would you?"

Joe was startled to see a wide-eyed look of surprise on Nick's face, and he resisted putting a sinister interpretation on it. Gardner recovered quickly. "I'll go see if I can get it."

"Don't you have it, Nick?"

"After . . . after that release, I wasn't terribly worried about its security. But I think I can lay my hands on it."

Joe fixed him with a questioning gaze for perhaps ten seconds, but Nick did not look away. "Joe?"

"Nick, I'm sorry to say this, but if you're not being straight with me—if you haven't been up to now—this is the last chance to do so."

"Are you accusing me of lying, Joe?"

"I'm telling you that in the hopefully unlikely event you are, beyond this point you'll get no help and no sympathy. They're going to find out where that leak came from, Nick, and right now all their evidence seems to point to you. I've taken your word without question. I'm not asking for reassurance, I'm asking for your reassessment. If there's anything you need to tell me, this is the last chance.''

"Only thing I need to tell you, Joe, is thanks for the faith. It's not misplaced.''

"Okay Nick,'' Joe said slowly. "Just find the damn thing and get it up there, and . . . better make a copy of it before you do.''

Nick Gardner nodded and left, trying to do so casually. The effort did not go unnoticed by Joe Wallingford.

All but Kell and Susan had filed out the door, and Kell Martinson waited for Joe to turn back to the mostly empty room before speaking to him. "Where do you go with this now, Joe?'' he asked, hands thrust deep in his pants pockets, leaning slightly against the table as Susan came around the other side beside Joe, who was scratching his head. "Senator, I think we're in a lot of trouble with this. Especially with the hubbub out there about the radar, and the blanket military denials.'' He told Kell and Susan about the call from Andy Wallace, and the corresponding power glitch in the tower tapes.

"Joe,'' Kell began, "I've had a three-star general assure me the thing was not operating. The White House, the Secretary of Defense, a dozen senators—everyone is saying for the record the thing was not operating.''

"Is that enough for you, Senator, given what you've heard?''

Joe watched Martinson's face as he thought over the question in stony silence for a few seconds. Susan was watching him as well.

"No. I see your point.''

"I've got the FAA upstairs ready to close the lid on even internal flight-control failure. Let me ask you, could the Air Force not have known the thing was on? Could somebody—a technician, for instance—have accidentally activated it?''

Kell's answer was very quiet, his eyes focused somewhere down the hall. "I don't know, Joe. But I agree we need to find out.''

"Well, you asked where we go from here,'' Joe said. "We've got to do a massive amount of deep detective work from now until the hearing, and that sort of investigation costs a lot of money and strains our budget."

Kell smiled at the not-so-subtle funding appeal. "Hearing?"

"Early December, in Kansas City. At least that's what I've tentatively recommended." He turned to Susan, who was nodding.

"That probably is going to be approved by the other members, Joe."

"I'd like to be there," Kell said. "Unofficially, of course. I wouldn't expect to do anything but observe."

Susan beat Joe to the punch. "We'd be honored, Senator."

Kell left them alone in the briefing room, finally, the door closing behind him, and Susan told Joe about the appointment she had made with Mark Weiss in an hour.

"He's been sniffing around North America in Dallas."

"I know," she replied. "I'm curious to hear more about his analysis, especially now."

"Oh?"

"Joe, let's assume the Air Force is right, and in addition, let's assume there was nothing internally wrong with the captain's flight-control stick. This captain was flying alone, effectively. He'd beat that copilot into silence and inaction. In my opinion, whether you ever find out what happened with the control stick, the question is how many captains out there would treat a copilot like that? How many airlines tolerate it and set that precedent? That's a valid area to probe, regardless of what happened to push the nose over."

Joe sat down again across from Susan, enjoying her company and the brief respite. "Remember, Susan, this was the chief pilot."

She smiled and nodded. "That's exactly my point. He sets the pace."

"Well, it's an interesting ancillary issue, but it's not primary."

"No?"

The edge in her voice halted a quick reply. Joe studied Susan's face, noting the sly smile. She had opened a small trap and was waiting for him to step in. "*You* believe it's primary?"

"Maybe. Consider this." She moved forward, gesturing urgently. "Regardless of what caused the nose to push over, if the copilot had taken over a little sooner, they would not have crashed, correct?''

''Probably, but these were grown men, experienced pilots. If the copilot should have taken over sooner and didn't, he was trained improperly or was insufficiently assertive, which are his own problems, not the captain's.''

''But you just proved my point,'' she said.

''How?''

''Whether it's training, defective personality traits for the job, or intimidation, the failure to take over in a timely fashion is a *system* failure, and that is always significant.''

It went against the grain, but it made sense to Joe. And in any event, he didn't want to counter her, which was an unprofessional response born of the realization that he really liked this lady. He could do nothing about it, of course, but he could enjoy being around her, and, perhaps, fantasize a little.

Susan's eyes were on Joe's right hand as he played, unconsciously, with a paperweight, carefully and precisely raising it a few millimeters above the surface of the table, and landing it again, over and over, tilting it back each time as if flaring an aircraft, a part of his brain still working on the aerodynamics of Flight 255.

''You know, there *is* something more here, Susan. There is something about this accident that disturbs me very deeply. With all the tragedy I've seen, and all the crazy accidents I've worked, it frustrates me. There's something wrong here involving Timson. It's just a vague suspicion, but while on one hand I'm all but convinced this is mechanical, electronic failure—you know, since radar interference is more than probable now—I've also got a gut feeling that something human happened. But with Caldwell upstairs outflanking this investigation and no doubt influencing the chairman, who in turn is hovering over every decision with a portfolio of hidden agendas, I don't know if we've got a prayer of unraveling this. Someone may get away with murder.''

''You mean that?'' she said at last, looking him deeply in the eye.

He nodded slowly. ''I do.''

16

Monday, December 3, Kansas City International Airport

Strange how lonely it looked. Joe Wallingford stood just inside the doorway of the huge main ballroom of the same Kansas City Airport hotel they had used for the field investigation, feeling slightly intimidated by the emptiness. In two more hours it would become a battleground of sorts, but at 7 A.M. it was nothing but an empty stage, the ranks of tables and chairs arrayed like silent ghosts in the gray light from a single lamp visible near the back.

The great ceiling of hanging chandeliers loomed dark above him, their mirrored panels with no light to reflect, their light bulbs unpowered. Joe realized he had nearly tiptoed into the maw of the room, moving with the respectful stealth of an Indian crossing through enemy territory. Yet this was anything but foreign territory. It was uniquely his forum.

Two months had passed since the crash and the five days the ballroom had held the frantic comings and goings of Joe's NTSB team in full cry. The table and chair arrangements were far different now, the long head table on a raised platform along the western wall providing places for the hearing officer—which was Joe's role—plus five additional chairs for other NTSB staff members. Dr. Susan Kelly, as a Board member, would act as chairman of the hearing, and Joe would run the questioning. Whether or not the hearing would produce any answers was another question. What seemed to be the central issue overshadowing all other possibilities—whether the Star Wars radar was off or on—would hardly be mentioned. If it had been on and caused the Airbus to pitch down, then almost everything Joe had scheduled for the hearing would be superfluous. If the radar had been off, however, the mystery was still deep and compelling, and the hearing would be vital. Joe had wanted the hearing to probe the question of the radar, but Dean Farris had forbidden it, on political grounds—as far as Joe could tell. The government's position was clear, and Farris saw no reason to contradict it. But even if Farris had approved, there was no one to question. The Air Force refused to provide witnesses, as had the contractor—and from the Defense Department there had been nothing but stonewalling. Without names of people to question, even subpoenas were ineffective.

Four floor-level tables sat at right angles to the raised head table, looking in the darkness like miniature fortresses—shields of cloth and plywood behind which the worried and warring parties would consult and scribble, listen and react, each of them trying to preserve the interests closest to their professional hearts. Airbus, the FAA, North America Airlines, and the Air Line Pilots Association were the four officially admitted parties to the investigation, and each had a table.

Joe sat on the edge of one of the tables and thought back over the conflicting events of the past few weeks.

Without evidence, the sabotage accusations of the Wilkins group had faded from the media, leaving in their place a dangerous undercurrent of public belief that the Defense Department was lying to the Congress and the American people—though the FAA had flatly announced that electronic interference was not a possibility, and Caldwell had washed his hands of the issue. Increasingly, all eyes were on the NTSB—and Joe Wallingford—to solve the problem once and for all of what, or who, brought down North America 255. Yet Joe had been blocked in so many ways, turning out of near-desperation to Kell Martinson, who could probe the defense establishment in ways Joe couldn't. Dean Farris had been angry and threatening when Joe kept pushing at the radar issue, but there was no responsible way to let it go. It woke him up at night and kept scratching at the back door of his mind.

At the same time, Joe knew that Kell Martinson and other Brilliant Pebbles supporters were under siege from congressional colleagues for what looked to many like a foiled, sneaky attempt to test the tracking radar, and high-level thunderbolts continued to pass over Joe's head daily in a battle of behind-the-scenes maneuvering between the Pentagon and Capitol Hill on matters too Olympian to concern a mere accident investigator.

"What if it *was* off, Joe?" Andy had kept reminding him. "We can't assume it was on. We have to keep looking at all possible causes."

"Already at work, I see." Joe turned, startled at the sound of FBI agent Jeff Perkins's voice as he pushed through the double doors and walked toward him, his hand outstretched.

"Jeff. What are you doing here? Some new development?" Joe got off the edge of the table and shook his hand warmly. He had known Jeff for—what was it?—at least twenty years. Yet the two of them were always passing in the night, so to speak. They had met at Quantico Marine Air Station in Virginia in the late sixties, both assigned by their respective agencies to a special antihijacking course. Despite Jeff's postings outside Washington throughout the intervening years, they had kept in touch.

"Naw. I live in Kansas City, remember? Just can't pass up a good show, and a good excuse to officially get away from the office."

"Well, we'll try to accommodate." Joe checked his watch, squinting to read the 7:05 A.M. displayed on its face. "With a good show, I mean. By 9 A.M. we should be ready to start the fireworks."

"Actually, Joe, I do have one small item for you."

"Oh?"

"The senator you accompanied to our offices in D.C.? The owner of the mystery car seen here on the night of the crash?" A look of astonishment crossed Joe's features. "Hey, don't look so startled."

"How'd you get involved in that, Jeff?"

"I was assigned to the crash, remember?"

"Oh. Right."

"Well, the word is they may turn the package over to local authorities here to prosecute for criminal trespass."

"Oh, no. Martinson's a helluva nice guy, and very sincere. I'd hate to see that. He came forward voluntarily. In fact, he's been following this investigation. I expect him here this morning."

"The law is the law, Joe."

"Is it certain?"

"Not yet. But you know, Christ, a *senator*? You can't push

that under the rug. Anyway, it's not rape or murder, and the locals may decline to pursue it.''

"If it hits the media, it could damage him.''

Jeff simply shrugged as Joe began moving toward the head table, both of them looking at the empty audience chairs set in multiple rows and the press platform at the far end where at least eight television cameras would blossom within the next hour. Wherever the NTSB held a public hearing of this magnitude, the room setup was almost identical.

"I've done so many of these now, Jeff, I sometimes look up and forget which city I'm in. Ever have that happen with what you do?''

"Only in shopping malls when I'm on the road. They're all the same. I get vertigo.''

Joe plunked himself down in one of the chairs, looking back at Jeff Perkins, waiting for him to catch up and pull out a chair of his own. "There are so many things I'm going to have to fight over to get the right information on the record in this hearing, yet it's not supposed to be adversarial. You've heard the opening statements we use on these things, haven't you?''

"What, you read them their Miranda rights?''

"Hah. Sometimes I think we should, but that's for you guys to use to help protect the guilty. We don't have guilty parties, you see. Crashes just happen, at least according to FAA, the airlines, the manufacturers, and the pilots.''

Joe paused and looked at Perkins, gauging how much to tell him. "Jeff, this is not to be repeated, but aside from the radar interference question, there have been some strange things going on at North America. It would be too easy to attribute some sinister intent to their actions, but something isn't quite right. Back in early November, a member of my human-performance staff noticed an odd gap in Dick Timson's FAA medical record.''

That was the Airbus captain?''

"Yeah. Even management captains need recertification by an FAA-certified doctor every six months. But several years back Timson went eight months between exams. Now, that's not a terribly big deal, but the man crashed an airplane, so we have to ask the question, did he fly illicitly during the two-month period? And, of course, the root question is why wasn't he recertified? Was he sick during that period? Was he on vacation? What was going on while the chief pilot was legally grounded?''

"What *was* going on?"

"We don't know. That's the problem. The FAA's records showed Timson to be in perfect health, with no sick periods. North America has a company flight doctor on the payroll—a guy named McIntyre—who has given Timson his exams for many years, and Andy Wallace just routinely called up and asked the doctor for his medical files on Timson, the ones which back up those medical certificates the doctor had issued every six months, but the next thing we know, North America is getting hysterical and threatening to go to court to get an injunction because we're harassing them!"

"And you weren't?"

"Hell no! But their reaction raised flags for us. It was like painting a red target on the file cabinet, and what had been routine suddenly became a matter of some urgency. When Andy Wallace tries to interview the doctor, the doctor leaves on a sudden vacation. Finally, this week, we get an envelope from Banff, Canada, with the requested records of those medical exams inside. Now, the flight records which North America had already given us showed that Timson had not flown during that suspect two-month period, so a temporarily expired medical was no problem. But Friday we find that Timson, who has green eyes and brown hair in reality, has brown eyes and blond hair on the records the doctor sent. In addition, on the doctor's records Timson's blood is O positive, when we already know from hospital tests he's B negative."

Jeff was wearing a knowing grin and nodding. "That would make *me* suspicious."

"Well, that's what it did for us. We want to know why Timson seems to have dual hair and eye colors, and a changeable blood type."

"*Was* he in good health?"

"That's the point. The records say yes. Are the records lying?"

Dean Farris had told his wife the trip was necessary, but omitted the part about having no official duties at the Kansas City hearing. He had left Monday afternoon, arriving very quietly, checking with the one staffer who had been his eyes and ears in what Dean had started calling "the Wallingford camp"—a faction Dean Farris couldn't seem to control. Wallingford was going to have a small coronary when he ambled into the hearing room in a few hours and found the chairman there. Susan would be insulted too, but she would just have to handle it. In Dean's estimation, she was giving Wallingford too much support. No, adult leadership was called for, and he intended to provide it.

For one thing, it was time to take Andy Wallace and Joe aside and read them the riot and sedition act over this doctor business at North America. No less than North America's chairman, David Bayne, had become involved in what had been shameless NTSB harassment of the airline's medical department. In fact, Bayne himself had called on Friday. Oh, he had been gentlemanly, but his point was obvious. A substantial supporter of the Republican party in northern Texas—a personal friend of the President of the United States who had helped substantially with his campaign—was upset with the "vendetta" that Joe Wallingford and his people were conducting against North America, and if the chairman couldn't correct it, the President might get someone else who could.

"Professor, or perhaps I should say Mr. Chairman?" Bayne had said.

"Dean is just fine, uh, David."

"Okay, Dean. Look, we're going to do our time in the barrel for this crash. But this team of yours seems determined to put Dick Timson on trial, paw through his entire life and management history, and savage our airline's reputation rather than dispassionately looking for the real reasons the crash occurred. Your investigators are not looking into windshear or air traffic control's culpability with any serious effort, in our view, and we can see this is becoming a pin-it-on-the-Air-Force or bash-North-America exercise."

"That's an excessive view," Dean Farris had replied. "Joe Wallingford, our investigator in charge, may have some pet areas which need adjusting in terms of emphasis and focus, but he's hardly conducting a vendetta. And remember, it is the Board that makes the final determination, not the staff."

"Dean, he's probing the so-called atmosphere of management in this airline, and that's unnecessary, insulting crap! No more, no less. It won't solve any crashes, save any lives, or gain the NTSB any respect. They've been sitting out here in Dallas wasting our time with endless interviews and prying questions about how Dick managed things in the flight department and why we run a tight ship and require our people to toe the line. I'm tired of it. I promise you that every airline in this country is going to have to take a long look at the role of the NTSB in the grand scheme of things if this goes where we see it headed.''

''And I can promise *you*,'' Dean had replied, ''that I will monitor this personally and make certain that our normal, balanced procedures, if breached, will be corrected.''

''I'm sure you will, Dean. My legal and legislative people have been chomping mad and ready to unleash a congressional broadside and a White House protest. I told them to stand down, that I'd talk to you, and I was sure you wouldn't allow this conduct to continue. By the way, I Fed Ex'd to you a chronicle of everything we've been hit with. I'm sure you'll agree it's pretty unreasonable.''

''As I say . . .''

''One other thing, Dean. One special item I'm really upset about. Your people in human performance have got a wild hair up their rear about our company doctor. They've threatened him for no apparent reason and scared the poor man to the edge of a nervous breakdown. We finally sent him off on a Canadian vacation to recuperate, and now I'm told they're trying to track him down up there. In addition, they even used an intermediary, some psychologist named Weiss who's undoubtedly going to sue us because he lost his wife and sons in the crash—they used *him*, believe it or not, to come sleuth around our airline. That is ridiculous! I beg you, call off your dogs on Doc McIntyre. Anything you need, Ron Putnam can get it for you, but for crying out loud, the doctor's a decent gentleman and he's being hounded. And if you want to use a crash victim's husband, at least have the courtesy to put him on the NTSB payroll and warn us, okay?''

''That will stop, I assure you.''

Farris had replaced the phone feeling a combination of anger, embarrassment, and fear. Damn Wallingford! Damn Wallace! And damn the fact that David Bayne could end Dean Farris's political ambitions as fast as they had begun.

Dean left his office that afternoon in a high state of upset, but aware that there was at least one bone he could ethically throw to David Bayne: Dr. McIntyre would be harassed no more.

It was 8 A.M. when the chairman stepped from the downtown Kansas City hotel into a taxi Monday morning to head for the airport Marriott. He would arrive unannounced about an hour ahead of the start of proceedings, and that was enough time to take the appropriate parties aside, he figured, though the size of the crowd when he arrived caught him off guard. It was nearly nine before he herded Joe and Susan and Andy into a private conversation.

"I've got a hearing to conduct, Mr. Chairman," Joe began acidly, "are you going to attend, or did you fly out here just to have this little get-together?"

Farris and Wallingford stood regarding each other in icy hostility as Susan looked on. Andy Wallace had come and gone, leaving the three in the small conference room just down the hall from the main ballroom where all the participants had gathered for the NTSB Board of Inquiry into the crash of North America Flights 170 and 255.

Joe was struggling to keep his voice and demeanor under control, but he was afraid the effort was showing. Nearly two months of nonstop political interference into every facet of Joe's conduct of the North America investigation had pushed him to the breaking point, and once again Dean Farris was shaking his head in condescending fashion, that superior, professional sneer of his becoming intolerable.

"Joe, I think I'll join Susan and you on the dais, but of course she is still going to chair the meeting." Joe could see Dr. Susan Kelly in his peripheral vision, arms folded, a flint-hard look freezing her features into abject dislike for what Farris had done in popping up unannounced, undercutting her position along with Joe's.

"Do we understand each other about Doctor McIntyre, Joe?"

"I understand you are requesting that we leave the man alone if we can get the records through other North America sources."

"No. That's not right. I'm ordering you to leave the man the hell alone regardless of whether you get those records. If you don't get them, you come to *me* and *I'll* take the appropriate steps to get them. You and Andy and his people are not going to harass innocent individuals. I have assurances from North America that they can provide whatever you want. I have given them assurances the harassment will stop. You leave the doctor alone, *and*, you get this man Weiss the hell away from your operations."

"Mr. Chairman, first of all, the doctor has not been harassed, and second, Doctor Weiss, who admittedly lost his family in this crash but also happens to be a trained aviation psychologist, is exercising his own rights as a citizen. He has never worked for us and is not now, although we have listened to what he had to say. But, sir, are you aware that you're interfering with this investigation by pressuring me?"

"Joe, let me see if I can make it simple for you." Farris shook his head as if dealing with a recalcitrant child. "I'm the head of the NTSB. This may, I realize, come as a shock to you, but I really am. Not you. Not Andy. Not even Susan or the other members of the Board. As head, I have the responsibility to—"

Joe slammed the folder he had been gripping against the wall. "Don't you dare give me a goddamned lecture, Professor. I was a professional at this Board before you even knew the damn thing existed! I know the rules and the regulations, and I'm trying to advise you that what you are telling me to do is dead wrong. You're prejudicing an investigation for what I can only assume are political purposes, and that is intolerable."

Farris was shaking his head again, side to side, his hands held behind him in a purposefully mocking pose, trying his best to imitate a disgusted Oxford don about to wash his hands of a student he considered stupid, his slight Oklahoma accent making the effort seem low comic opera. "Oh, by all *means*, Mr. Wallingford, sir. Let us follow your kind and gracious lead and toddle on to the hearing. Perhaps afterward we can check on exactly when you were appointed to head this Board and I was deposed, because if that has not occurred, and if you so much as breathe that physician's name again without my written permission, you can kiss your job with this Board good-bye."

Joe saw only mockery in Farris's eyes, and he recognized his own reaction as growing rage, which was dangerous.

"We have a hearing to conduct. We can sort this out later."

"There is nothing to sort out, Joe. I told you what I expect, and I mean what I say."

Joe had begun to turn toward the door, but the last words were too much. He turned back to Farris, raising an index finger slowly, deliberately, looking Farris in the eye, Joe's face a picture of grim determination, noting the chairman's recognition of his fury as Farris drew back ever so slightly, unsure of just how physically insubordinate his subordinate might become.

There were no words Joe could think of that would not emerge in anger as a mortal challenge. There were no trite phrases or threats which were appropriate either, so he simply turned away at last and pushed through the door, leaving Farris speechless— if somewhat relieved.

17

The start of any NTSB Board of Inquiry is an intimidating thing, especially for the parties involved, each of whom approach the forum with their own set of interests, hoping to leave that forum somewhat professionally intact. There are silent prayers among such participants, prayers that their testimony— or that of others they can't control—will do nothing to increase the monetary or moral liability of those they represent. And there is apprehension that buried somewhere within the proceedings is a media bomb which, once exposed to the light of day, will explode into damaging publicity, damning one party or another for what was or was not done.

As Joe made note of Senator Martinson's unheralded entrance and watched the various tables fill with the appointed members from North America, Airbus, FAA, ALPA, and the NTSB technical staff, he also noticed an odd feeling in his stomach when Captain Richard Timson entered the ballroom. As heads turned throughout the ballroom, it was clear whom most of the audience had come to see.

In the previous weeks, Andy had slowly and steadily come to the conclusion that the Board should focus on the copilot's role: why he had been too intimidated by the captain to take over in time. Andy had pressed hard against Joe's feeling that control failure or human failure on Timson's part were the only true central issues. Bit by bit he had pulled Joe across the line, while getting North America angrier and angrier with each passing day.

It was ten minutes before Susan joined Joe at the head table, without comment, having left Dean Farris down the hall. She smiled fleetingly at Joe when he caught her eye, but then turned her attention to her notes. Farris was nowhere to be seen until moments before she called the hearing to order. He entered quietly, then, sitting at the opposite end from Joe. There was no time to ask her what had transpired after he'd left.

Susan's introduction went rapidly, the television cameras feeding it to satellite dishes and tape recorders as the proceedings got under way. Joe knew that many of those watching through television would expect the NTSB to issue a verdict at the end. The public seldom realized that such hearings were just part of the investigatory process, though providing a cathartic public relations tool in the meantime. But there were never any end-of-hearing verdicts issued by the NTSB indicating which way the Board might be leaning.

The first two hours were given to testimony from the staff establishing the basic facts of the crash and the surrounding human aspects. Andy Wallace and Walt Rogers and then Joe took their turns, Susan then calling to the stand the ALPA pilot who had conducted the simulator re-creations for the operations group.

Captain Dick Rohr, an accident investigator for the Air Line Pilots Association, was a fifty-eight-year-old ramrod-straight pilot with a Steve Canyon jaw and a full head of silver hair who looked like Central Casting's image of an airline captain. Yet he was becoming well known as a human-performance expert of great sensitivity and intellect (an all-but-finalized thesis stood between Rohr and his Ph.D. in industrial psychology). Joe watched the man stride confidently to the witness stand, a gray business suit replacing the four-striped uniform he normally wore as a captain for another A320 operator. There were some preliminary questions on routine matters before Joe plunged into the heart of what Rohr had come to establish, eliciting the response they both wanted.

"Basically, we found that the situation was recoverable."

"Please explain that, Captain?" Joe prompted.

"Simply stated, if the copilot had taken control of the airplane up to seven-tenths of a second before the time he finally did, the crash would have been avoided. He would have been able to fly over the 737 without a collision."

The statement created a wave of reaction which visibly rolled through the audience, the press, and the North America table, as Joe had known it would. A number of whispered conversations had begun among various observers as people wondered why the focus of the hearing had already turned to the copilot of Flight 255. A print reporter had asked him that just before Farris had shown up, pointing to the summary of hearing topics in confusion.

"Because," Joe had told him, "regardless of why the captain let the nose drop, the copilot's role as the safety pilot becomes a very important issue if we find he could have saved the aircraft by acting sooner. We need testimony on that point, and if the answer is yes, then the question the Board has to answer is: what prevented the copilot from acting sooner? Was it training? Environment? Temperament? What?" In some ways Joe couldn't believe he was hearing himself say such things, but he had, in fact, come to believe them.

"Captain Rohr," Joe began again, "are there any physical control problems or difficulties with this airplane that would have delayed the copilot's ability to take control?"

Now the Airbus table was alive, one engineer flipping frantically through a thick manual while another watched Rohr for his response.

"Because the captain's and copilot's control sticks—Airbus calls them side sticks—are connected only by wiring, they do not move together like conventional aircraft control yokes do. Therefore, Airbus designed a system to permit either pilot to take positive control by simply pushing the priority switch on either yoke. It works instantly, and no, it would not have delayed the copilot's assumption of control."

Joe raised a finger to indicate a follow-up question. He had seen stirring at the Airbus and North America tables, and knew they would want the floor shortly. "And when the copilot of Flight 255 finally got on the control stick, he pushed that switch?"

"Without question. When one of the pilots takes control with the priority switch, there are several indications. First, a red arrow illuminates in front of the pilot who has lost priority, and second, a green light comes on in front of the pilot who took priority. Now, we don't have any record of those lights on the flight recorder, but there is a third indication, an electronic voice saying 'Priority right,' and in this case it tells us that the copilot did take control and precisely when he did so. It also tells us the captain's side stick was in use immediately before the copilot pushed his priority button, or the message would not have sounded.''

The North America vice-president, John Walters, grabbed his microphone then, moving the small sliding on-off switch to the on position and causing an audible "pop" in the overhead speakers. He asked for the floor, which Joe granted. "Captain Rohr," Walters began, "isn't it possible that it was Captain Timson who took control from the copilot after the copilot took control from him?"

Rohr looked at Walters impassively, trying to find a diplomatic way of telling the man he didn't know what he was talking about. "I don't understand the question."

"Well, you said the tape contained this voice message saying 'Priority right.' Couldn't the captain have regained control by pushing his priority switch after the copilot pushed his?"

"Yes . . . yes he could, but he didn't."

"Well, Captain, you don't know that for certain, do you?"

"Yes, Mr. Walters, I do know that for certain. We know the system was working because we have heard the 'Priority right' message. Therefore, if the captain seized control back, we would hear 'Priority left' on the tape. There was no such message. And in any event, that's immaterial for our simulator tests. Whichever control stick was used, if the recovery attempt had been made seven-tenths of a second earlier, none of us would be sitting here now, because there would not have been an accident.''

"Well, you're just assuming, are you not, that the captain was doing something dangerous. Perhaps he was taking legitimate evasive action and the copilot's seizing of the aircraft interfered with his plan and caused the crash.''

Captain Dick Rohr stared at the airline executive in horror. The senior vice-president of operations was Ron Putnam, but the real day-to-day head of North America's flight operations— and Dick Timson's immediate superior—was John Walters, the man asking the question. Although there was no necessity for Walters to be a pilot, he should at least know the basics, Rohr figured, especially if he was going to sit there and ask questions of an A320 captain in an NTSB hearing.

"Sir, the flight path the captain was following would have impacted the aircraft into the ground about three hundred to five hundred yards short of the hammerhead where the 737, Flight 170, was sitting. If that had occurred, based on the distribution of wreckage that did subsequently occur, the remains of Flight 255 would have impacted the 737 broadside, at ground level rather than 10 feet in the air, and in flames. It is unlikely that anyone would have escaped from either aircraft. Therefore, the copilot's actions were, by our tests, a reasonable effort to salvage the situation the captain or the airplane had created. The only question in my mind is why did he wait so long to act?''

Walters and Rohr continued niggling the point and Joe let them go on for a few minutes. Walters was confused, but he felt he had to cast doubt on the theory that North America's captain and chief pilot had made no attempt to recover. If there was a possibility that Timson himself had begun the recovery, it could blunt the airline's image of negligence. The men at the North America table were well aware that the legal liability would be fought out in the courts, but they had to be consistent. It really didn't matter what the NTSB said about neutrality and nonjudgmental testimony. This was part of the overall fight to avoid liability, and one false move would bring millions in company damages—as well as David Bayne—down on their heads. They were, in effect, desperate men.

Dick Rohr remained on the stand for nearly an hour more as the NTSB technical panel and then the FAA, ALPA, and Airbus representatives picked through the findings.

Barbara Rawlson, the systems group chairman, was called to the stand then. Joe and Susan had agreed with the staff that there were loose ends in the public's perception of what had happened, and what had not—misconceptions and misunderstandings which needed a public burial.

"Ms. Rawlson," Joe began, "your systems group's factual report, which all parties have in the overall file of the investigation, mentions on page 7A-7 that no evidence of sabotage to the flight-control systems or anything else was found. Would you give us a verbal summary of that?"

"Sure." Barbara shifted in the chair, her fingers drumming the tablecloth lightly. "There was no bomb, or we would have found some evidence of outward tearing and ripping of metal structures along with explosive residue. Second, as to possible tampering with the flight-control computers, no foreign boxes or devices were found on or near the wreckage, and nothing was found in or around any flight-control system which was not factory installed. The only other established possibility of sabotage would be tampering with the factory-installed flight-control computers themselves, but other than the crash damage, the computers were in perfect condition.''

"Could radio waves directed from the ground, with or without criminal intent, have caused fluctuations in the flight controls?''

"It is possible. Whether it's probable depends on whether or not the only sufficiently powerful radar anywhere near the airport that night was operating.'' Barbara briefly outlined what they all knew, the ominous presence of the so-called Star Wars radar. "The FAA's experts have been very cautious about the possibility of radio interference, and have set minimum distances to safeguard against military ship radars bothering the 320 with what's known as EMI, or electromagnetic interference. We have to admit that it is remotely possible for the A320's flight-control system to be subject to EMI influence if the FAA-prescribed minimum distances are not maintained.''

The Airbus table came alive again, and Joe indicated that they would have their turn when he had finished.

"Ms. Rawlson, would you, for clarity and the record, explain the fly-by-wire system for us?''

"In brief, most modern transport-category aircraft use a system of metal cables which connect the control yoke and the rudder pedals in the cockpit with hydraulic control units out on the wings and in the tail. To climb, you pull back on the control yoke, and that motion is physically transmitted by the cable all the way to the tail, where it operates a system of valves on a hydraulic control unit, which in turn powers the hydraulic pistons which move the elevator surface. If there were no hydraulics it would be difficult to move those control surfaces because they're so big, and they would require a lot of brute force to move against the airflow. Now, all those cables create a lot of weight, so if you could use electrical wires instead of the traditional cables and pulleys—if you could electrically transmit the movements of the flight controls in the cockpit to the hydraulic valves in the wings and tail—you could save an enormous amount of weight, and maintenance over the years. In other words, you have fly-by-steel-cable, and fly-by-electrical-wire. The Airbus 320 uses the latter system—with computers making the decisions on *how* to translate the physical movement of the control yoke into physical movement of the control surfaces. You might say in the A320, the pilots are flying the computers rather than the airplane itself.''

"One more question, Ms. Rawlson," Joe promised. "Did you investigate the possibility that the flight-control computers malfunctioned, sending a false nose-down command to the flight-control surfaces?"

"Very extensively, we looked at that. The best evidence that there was no malfunction is this: the second the copilot took control with the priority switch, the flight-control surfaces instantly changed position to reflect a nose-up recovery attempt. If there *had* been a malfunction—even one not caught by the various flight-control computers running in parallel and constantly checking each other—the copilot's taking control would probably have had no effect."

The details were Byzantine, but the end result was the same. There was no evidence of an internal flight-control malfunction—though an externally induced EMI malfunction was possible.

Joe turned it over to Airbus then, letting their engineers take Barbara through nearly an hour of record-preserving testimony about the reliability of the 320's systems. As she spoke, Joe caught several indications from his right, from Susan Kelly, that they needed to talk, and of that he was already certain. It was during the lunch break that they finally slipped away, retreating to a far corner of the mezzanine, out of sight of the lobby and hopefully of Farris.

"Joe, after you left . . ." She looked at him in silence for a second before continuing. "Well, as I see it, Dean is about to commit professional suicide. He has absolutely no right to protect North America's doctor. I could not believe, I mean I really could not believe what I was hearing in there. Have you ever experienced anything like this? Has there ever been an NTSB chairman who tried to protect an airline to this extent?"

Joe sighed audibly. "In a word, no. Not in my experience. Susan, there may be *no* significance to the discrepancies in those reports that company doctor has given us, but we've got to find out. After all, the records involved are of the accident captain. The chairman is trying to prevent us from investigating the *accident* captain because North America is chewing on him."

"What are you going to do? He threatened your job. I can get the other members to intervene, but he has the power to do what he threatens, I think. I mean, I'm not a lawyer . . ."

"Neither am I. I don't know. I don't want to provoke him into throwing me off this case, or worse. I just want to get through this hearing. The doctor's gone to Canada right now anyway. We can't do anything about it until he gets back."

"I'm upset enough to resign, Joe, but that would leave you with even less help and it wouldn't solve anything." She reached out and placed a hand on his arm, but at first he didn't notice. The gesture was very much in character for Susan, not overly familiar, not improper, neither forward nor intimate, just a re-inforcement of sincere interest. Yet it suddenly sent chills down his back as he looked in her beautiful eyes, then yanked himself away from such thoughts. "What if?" did not apply to professional colleagues who happened to be women. If he had learned nothing else from the loss of Brenda to a career, he certainly should have learned that.

"Please don't resign on my account. We'll figure a way to handle him without destroying the investigation, the Board, or me, I hope."

"Well, I'm about ready to go outside the family."

He tried not to look startled, but he was exactly that. "I don't understand . . ."

"Joe, I didn't get this position by running the Junior League. I have been quite active in the political world. I do know a few people on the Hill."

"I never thought of you as political, I guess. I . . . not yet, Susan. We don't need to consider drastic action yet."

The sight of a newsman approaching with notepad in hand put an end to the exchange, and Susan turned to talk to him while Joe slipped away and headed back to the hearing room. Lunch would have to wait for dinnertime. There was much to coordinate before gaveling the hearing back into session.

Barbara Rawlson was waiting for him. "How'd I do, Joe? Are you happy?"

"With you, yes. Did you hear that Mrs. Wilkins was here?"

"No."

"Yeah. She just got through putting on quite a show for the media out in the lobby. Apparently we're all communist dupes working within a grand conspiracy with the military to rid this nation of its only true guardians of freedom and kill Star Wars in the process.''

''Lord!'' Barbara shook her head and smiled.

''I know.''

The cameramen and print reporters were already in place when Joe and Susan resumed their seats at the head table, waiting for the name of Dick Timson to be called.

The chief pilot still looked wan and fragile. He had not returned to work as yet, but there had also been no known attempt to remove him as chief pilot or as a staff vice-president. To do so at this stage, Joe knew, would look like an admission of guilt on the part of the airline.

Joe walked Timson through the routine questions of name and residence and experience and qualification, then opened his notebook to the list of questions that would form the heart of the testimony.

Yes, Timson said, he had been forced to fly the October 12 flight because he had suspended the captain originally scheduled for it, and scheduling couldn't get a last-minute replacement. No, he was not excessively tired, nor on medication, nor had he had anything alcoholic to drink. He was perfectly capable of serving as captain on that flight. Yes, he *had* snapped at Don Leyhe, and he *had* flown blindly into windshear, thanks, he said, to the control tower's failure to warn him of its presence.

''Captain Timson,'' Joe asked, ''tell us in your own words, having seen the flight recorder readouts and read the cockpit voice recorder transcript, and having been there as no one else in this room, what happened on that final turn?''

Timson had his hands clasped together on the table. He looked down for a second before beginning, his voice steady but slow. ''Everything was normal as we came around, descending on airspeed, looking to roll out right over the end of the runway and land. Somewhere in there, even though I was holding the same amount of back pressure on the control stick as before, somewhere in there the airplane suddenly pitched down. Don, my copilot, yelled something—I see from the transcript he asked what I was doing—and I was too busy pulling on that stick to answer him. It didn't respond for what seemed like an eternity, the nose stayed down and we were dropping, and we were no longer turning toward the runway. In other words, it was as if I had pushed the stick forward, and I was doing the opposite. I thought I had told Don to take it, but I guess I never got the words out. They were in my mind, though, but somewhere during that time Don did hit the priority switch and assume control, and the plane responded . . . only . . ."—Timson looked back down and dropped his voice to little more than a whisper—". . . only, too late."

"Captain, when you were first interviewed in the hospital by NTSB investigators, you said that you had maintained control all the way to impact. When you were next interviewed, also in the hospital, this time on October twenty-second, you stated that you said, and I quote, 'My stick's not responding, take it Don, take it.' In a third interview, after reading the transcript of the cockpit voice recorder, you said that you had meant to say those words, but apparently had not. Is all that correct?"

"Yes sir. I was quite mentally confused for many days after the accident. As you know, I had a skull fracture, and at the first interview, I was under medication. I don't even remember you people being there. The second interview, I told you what I thought I had said. That's what was in my head. I thought I had said it. The tape proved me wrong."

In the audience, Dr. Mark Weiss made careful note of Timson's words, a thin smile and a shallow nod the only outward indications that something of special significance had reached his ears.

"But you never pushed that stick forward or let it go?" Joe continued.

"Of course not. Why would I do something . . . something suicidal like that?"

Joe concentrated on the notebook for a few seconds, his brow deeply furrowed. The statement Dick Timson said he had made to Don Leyhe, but hadn't, really puzzled Joe. He had repeated the words to Andy during that second interview with so much force and assurance, as if he'd heard it on a tape recording. Then he'd seemed perplexed and even angry when they showed him the transcript weeks later, convincing him finally that in fact those words were *not* on the tape. The discrepancy probably was exactly as Timson claimed, the result of his head injury. But it still bothered Joe. The man had seemed so sure.

"Captain, you say you did not push the stick forward, but the airplane's nose dropped. How *do* you explain that?"

"There's only one explanation I can think of, Mr. Wallingford. The side-stick controller or the flight computers malfunctioned, or were influenced somehow from the ground.''

"But, sir, you've heard testimony from NTSB staff investigators here this morning that there is no evidence of that happening.''

Timson looked Joe in the eye and nodded evenly. "I know, but I also heard your people say that electromagnetic interference is still a possibility. Look, I was there, and I didn't command nose down. Therefore, the airplane did it for me. What made the airplane disobey me, I don't know. That's your question to answer, not mine.'' Timson shifted in his chair and studied his hands, his mouth open, on the verge of adding something. "I . . . I've flown airplanes for a lot of years, Mr. Wallingford, and I've heard airplane manufacturers and engineers and instructors tell me for years that it was impossible for a particular piece of equipment to fail. Yet that very item would later do just that— fail—and only then would we find their faith in mechanical perfection had been . . . misplaced. I was there, sir. My life, and that of many others, has been completely altered by this horror, which happened in spite of my best efforts as a pilot. It may be hard for you to accept, but the control system malfunctioned. Plain and simple.''

"There is, then, no chance you pushed it over even for a second to correct your flight path, or some other reason?''

"No sir. I did not.''

An idea flashed through Joe's head, from where he wasn't sure, but the question just seemed appropriate all of a sudden. "Captain, were you fully conscious all the way down?''

Timson's eyes widened slightly at that, but there was no other visible response. The same flat, controlled vocal tones carried his answer. "Of course I was. I wouldn't remember any of this otherwise.''

He had a point, Joe conceded. Plus there was the final word. "There is an epithet on the voice tape just before impact. Some-one said, 'Goddamn it!' Is that your voice?''

"Yes it is.''

To the media it looked like a dramatic pause, but Joe was trying to shift gears, pawing through the list of questions, steeling himself to probe into the foreign areas of human factors he had accepted so reluctantly.

"Captain, you have seen the transcript of your statements to copilot Don Leyhe. Would you characterize those exchanges to be an argument?''

"Of course not." The reply was quiet and even. "I'm the captain. I do not have an argument with a subordinate, though I may tolerate a discussion. When that discussion is over, if he doesn't know it, it's up to me to tell him. Don did not understand what I was doing, and he mistakenly thought we were running a risk of flying back into windshear. He was wrong, but he wouldn't let go. I had to speak sharply to get him to quiet down so I could concentrate on flying. It's as simple as that."

The man's eyes were boring into Joe's. Timson obviously felt strongly about this, but his words conveyed an amazingly archaic attitude.

"Sir," Joe began, "what is your philosophy of flight management in an airline cockpit? Are there two pilots up there, or only one pilot and an assistant who follows orders blindly?"

Timson smiled, and Joe thought he heard a small snort of derision. "Of course there are two pilots, Mr. Wallingford, and the FAA says they share responsibility. But there is only one captain, and he has the final authority. He should listen to recommendations and then make a decision, and when that decision is made, the other pilot should shut up and support it."

"Blindly?"

"Not blindly, but with respect and obedience."

"Are you familiar with a type of training called cockpit resource management?"

Now Timson did snort, audibly and with considerable derision. "Sure. You incorporate that, and you end up flying by committee, or by consensus, with a captain who can't make a decision without checking with everyone on board. That is a major mistake, and this industry will pay dearly for embracing it."

"Captain, did you hear the testimony this morning from Captain Rohr that if your copilot had taken control just seven-tenths of a second before he did, none of us would be going through this right now?"

"Yes."

"Do you accept that testimony as true?"

"Well, he said they flew a bunch of simulator flights, so I suppose it's accurate . . . in a vacuum."

"What do you mean, 'in a vacuum'?"

"They weren't there. It takes time for a copilot to recognize he needs to take over from his commander without being ordered to, and there just wasn't time for me to give that order. As I said, I thought I had, but apparently the words didn't clear my throat."

Joe stared at Timson, waiting without a word for several seconds, watching the captain's reactions. Was his resolve that firm, or was this well-practiced posturing? If Joe got too rough with him, there would be protests, and worse, there would be an outpouring of sympathy that might get in the way of the truth—whatever that might be.

"Captain, had you ever flown with Don Leyhe before?"

"No. I knew him, though. He was one of my pilots."

"Did you discuss with him when it was okay for him to take control?"

"Of course not. That's common sense."

"Is it?"

"Sure. You don't touch a captain's yoke unless you're asked to, ordered to, or it's obvious that the captain has no control."

Joe nodded slowly. "Okay . . . okay, let's pursue that. Let's say a copilot sees the captain is no longer able to control the situation. You would want him to take control at that point, right?"

"Of course. I expect it. *That*, you see, Mr. Wallingford, is what a copilot is really for. He's a standby entity in many respects, a captain-in-training under the complete control of the flight captain."

"All right. Now, the period of time it takes for a copilot to recognize a deteriorating situation which the captain, for whatever reason, has lost the ability to control, that period of time is not finite, correct?"

"What do you mean?"

"In other words, that time will vary from copilot to copilot."

"Oh. Yes."

"One guy may be more aggressive and self-confident and may spot the problem sooner and seize control sooner than a weaker or more tenuous individual, right?"

"Sure. That's logical."

"And in such an emergency, you would want the copilot to recognize the problem *as soon as possible*, wouldn't you?"

"I believe so."

"Otherwise, why is he or she there, right?"

"Right."

"So, is it a desirable state of affairs to train these copilots to be slower to act, or to be so uncertain of themselves that they may not act in time in the admittedly rare instance where they need to take over?"

"Of course not. We don't train our copilots to be slow, nor do we train them to seize control anytime they don't like what the captain is doing."

"Would it make sense to you, Captain Timson, as chief pilot, that you should step in and stop a form of training that seeks to make copilots so reluctant to act that they may not act in time in an emergency?"

"Yes. Of course."

"And, would you agree that a copilot who had been intimidated by a more powerful fellow in a superior position, intimidated and told to keep his hands off the controls, is going to be less likely to act in time?"

Timson stared at Joe, his face slowly turning red, having walked into a trap. "You're misconstruing that conversation."

"I wasn't talking about your conversation. I was talking generally. But now that you mention it, wasn't your statement on that downwind leg to a shaken Don Leyhe, your answer to him when he asked, and I quote"—Joe turned the page to find the line—"'What do you want me to do, Captain?' and your reply was, 'I want you to shut your goddamn face and let me fly my airplane.'" Joe looked up again and slowly removed his reading glasses. "Wasn't that statement, Captain, one that would intimidate any copilot into being much slower to act in an emergency? Didn't you intimidate your copilot right out of the loop? Wasn't he effectively removed from the cockpit?"

"He wouldn't stop blathering. I had to correct him. I had made my decision and he wanted to question it. I was in command, and he did not have the right to keep questioning my decision. It was time to get him out of the loop. I . . . I . . ." Timson was sputtering, his direction lost, his mind grappling with the fact that he had been painted into a corner.

"Thank you, Captain."

"No, I'm not through."

Joe leaned forward instinctively, the phrase just slipping out before he could think about it. "Yes, Captain, I'm afraid you are. You've answered the question.'' It was more the type of editorial remark Susan could make, but there it was, and Timson suddenly was silent. Joe felt sorry for him, which he hadn't expected to do. The man really didn't understand why his method hadn't worked, didn't work, couldn't work. Andy had been absolutely right. Whatever had happened between Timson's left hand and the flight-control system, the methods he used as a captain and a chief pilot were vital to the investigation.

From the second row in the audience, Mark Weiss watched Timson's head drop. He watched the man take a deep breath, and once again he tried to hate the man, hate him for what he'd done. But it wouldn't come. Just pity. Pity Dick Timson, and pity those like him who couldn't accept the responsibility for what they'd done. And pity those pilots who kept clinging to the idea that real pilots must always fly alone, even in a two- or three-pilot cockpit.

Dick Timson fielded questions from the technical panel and other parties for two more hours, his North America boss John Walters trying to repair the record and make up for the answers elicited by Joe's questions, and doing more damage in the process. It was crystal clear that Dick Timson, and officially North America, had their feet set in concrete on the issue of how to fly airliners: the captain was God, and that was that. They were fighting the NTSB's right to question the philosophy, rather than debating whether it was the correct philosophy.

Mercifully, Susan marked Timson's dismissal with a fifteen-minute recess, and Joe lingered a minute to watch him as he left the stand, expecting his wife to rush forward to him. She was nowhere to be seen, which was odd. Louise Timson, Joe knew from Andy's research, had spent almost every waking moment by her husband's side at Truman Medical Center for the entire two weeks he had been hospitalized, sleeping mostly in his room on a chair. And, as he also knew, her actions had raised concerns for her mental health, concerns Andy had found out about but had been unable to pursue. Whether they were related to any information about her husband useful to the investigation, Andy didn't know. Dick Timson had refused all NTSB requests to interview his wife.

Mark Weiss took Joe aside as he poured a glass of water at the rear of the room. ''There's something I've got to lay out for you, Joe. This afternoon or evening. Something I can only show you in private.''

"Can you give me a hint?"

"Only that it concerns Timson's testimony. I can't say more here." Mark patted Joe's elbow once, turned, and disappeared into the corridor, leaving Joe with unanswered questions and a piqued curiosity. In his limited experience with the man, Dr. Mark Weiss was not normally so secretive.

Andy was beside him then, and Susan approached, all three of them huddling to one side, discussing Timson's statements, agreeing that the answers were pivotal. Timson wasn't backing down a millimeter from his insistence that he never relaxed his back pressure on the control stick. He had thrown a direct challenge to the NTSB to prove equipment failure wasn't the cause, and Joe knew with a sinking feeling he'd been entertaining for weeks that they probably couldn't rise to the challenge.

"Who's next?" Andy asked.

"We're going to get the tower controller up there and let North America chew at him awhile."

Carl Sellers was precise and impressive once he began his testimony, piecing together each and every act of his life on that Friday evening, adding convincing explanations to match and even documenting the time and exact duration of the momentary power spike in the tower which had attracted so much media attention. He had no idea, he said, whether the power glitch had any connection with the machine being loaded by the Air Force C-5B. No, he was not exactly distracted in the tower cab that evening. Yes, he was aware of the windshear monitors as North America 255 approached, and no, they did not go off. It wasn't until North America's vice-president John Walters had tossed every have-you-stopped-beating-your-wife? question he could possibly think of that one finally found a nerve and Sellers began emerging from his cocoon of precision, his temper building as he considered the questions, and at last passed his personal critical mass.

"Mr. Sellers," Walters had asked, "the pilot of the landing Metroliner obviously meant windshear when he used the phrase 'gusty out there.' You were the tower controller, you knew there were thunderstorms in the area, why on earth didn't you correct him? Why didn't you ask him whether he really meant to say 'windshear' instead of 'gusty'?"

Sellers had leaned forward to the microphone, his hands formed into fists on each side of its base. The sound of his overamplified voice boomed through the ceiling speakers in the ballroom, slightly distorted and startling. "Mr. Walters, I've been sitting here all afternoon putting up with your snide and sarcastic insinuations that I'm too stupid to know what I'm doing, and now you're implying that I should have edited the pilot's statements. This may be hard for you to understand—"

"Mr. Sellers, please contain—"Joe began.

"No, let me finish. This desk jockey has had his opportunity, Mr. Chairman, and I demand mine."

"This is not a personal confrontation, gentlemen," Joe interjected, all but unheard as Walters bowed with a little flourish, saying, "By all means, Mr. Sellers, fire away."

"The point is this. It is not now, nor has it ever been my job, or the job of any controller, to think and speak and act for the goddamn pilots. When these people come down final, they should be trained adults able to call a spade a spade, and a microburst a microburst. The fact that jerkwater commuters like this one hire greenhorn children and put them in the cockpit without training them is not *my* fault, nor is it that of the FAA!"

Susan and Joe both could see the frantic look on the face of the FAA men at their table as Sellers spoke, pleading with him by expression and hand signals to simmer down. Walters, however, pulled the plug on their attempts.

"Are you quite through, Mr. Sellers? Can I continue now? Or would you like to snarl a bit more at me and the world in general for your demonstrated incompetence?"

Seller's mouth came open as Susan rose from her chair and shouted at them both, banging the palm of her hand on the table for emphasis.

"GENTLEMEN! THAT . . . IS . . . ENOUGH! This is supposed to be an orderly proceeding, and I will not tolerate such behavior in here again. Is that clear?"

There was no response, the veins in Sellers's neck standing out a quarter inch as he struggled to keep control as he watched Walters, who had painted the most witheringly disdainful sneer he could manage across his face.

"Mr. Walters? Mr. Sellers? I'm talking to both of you!" Susan said.

"I'm sorry, Madam Chairman, I shall contain my comments," a surprised Walters said as he turned to her. Sellers nodded as well. "I apologize for the outburst."

As Susan regained her seat, the barely concealed smiles on the faces of the television cameramen betrayed their analysis of the exchange: that was great camera! The choice of a sound bite for the evening news was now a foregone conclusion.

Joe avoided Farris entirely when Susan adjourned the hearing for the day. He assembled the staff for a planned briefing twenty minutes later, but kept it short so everyone could unwind and get sufficient rest. There had been enough emotion for one day, but Tuesday's session had everyone worried.

Jeff Perkins found Joe as the staff meeting broke up and shanghaied him to dinner, trying unsuccessfully to keep his obviously worried friend off the subject of the next day's agenda.

"It's going to be one of the toughest I've ever dealt with, Jeff. The 737 captain is the second witness. He asked us to let him testify. Demanded, was more like it, and ALPA underscored the request. We all want to get a clear record on Timson's management style, but their eagerness frightens me a bit, since this is supercharged emotionally already."

"You set this witness list up yourself, Joe?"

"I supervised. My human-performance group chairman, Andy Wallace, did most of the work, and he's promised not to make a circus out of it—promised to keep it from looking like an exercise in airline bashing—but there are four other North America pilots whom we'll put on tomorrow."

"This is on the question of why copilots can't monitor captains?"

"Yeah, as well as why oppressive management styles can adversely affect safety. You heard Captain Timson's testimony today, and that from the ALPA pilot who said the copilot could have recovered?"

"That shocked me."

"Well, it shocked *me* when I first heard how clear-cut the simulator tests had turned out. God, there was no doubt."

"Joe, I'm no pilot, but it seems to me that this is really a simple matter if you deal with people like machinery."

"That's what we're trying to *not* do, Jeff. Or do I miss your point?"

"Well, what I mean is, most of these airplanes have main

hydraulic systems, and backup systems in case the main hydraulics fail, right?"

"Yes."

"All right, Timson was like their main hydraulic system, okay? And the copilot was the backup system. When the primary failed—whatever the reason—the backup should have worked. So if I understand what you guys and gals are up to, you're saying you don't know why the primary system failed, but you're damn well going to find out why the backup system didn't work so it won't happen again. In fact, you're saying the failure of the backup is at least as important as the failure of the primary, and maybe more so. Am I close?"

Joe looked at his friend with admiration. "That's a hell of a good summary, Jeff—for a cop."

"Thanks, I think." They were both laughing, and Joe was glad he knew Perkins could still be kidded.

"Joe, by the way . . ." He glanced around, assuring they were not being overheard. "Our office has been asked to get a copy of the leaked control tower tape from that radio station and ship it to D.C. The lab wants to electronically compare it to the original . . . see where the copy came from."

"How can they do that?"

"Each recorder tape head leaves characteristic sounds and errors on a tape unique to it. So if the station's tape came from the NTSB's copy, they'll find it out."

"Meaning?" Joe asked.

"Meaning, just a friendly heads-up. You might want to question your man again, just to make sure he's telling it like it is."

Joe nodded slowly, chilled by the thought that he had trusted Gardner too much. He had begun to seriously suspect him a month ago.

"Jeff, is it possible—and permissible—for you to look into who holds stock in a public corporation? Is there an easy way?"

"I can do that. Who?"

"Bill Caldwell of the FAA. I'm curious whether he owns any aircraft manufacturer's stock."

"I'll call you," Perkins said simply.

"Bill?"

"Yes. Who is this?" Bill Caldwell's phone had been ringing as he turned the key in his front door in the Georgetown district of Washington, D.C. He figured it had gone through at least ten rings by the time he got to it, which meant someone really wanted to find him.

"This is Jake McIntyre, Bill."

"Doc! Well how the hell are you?" Memories of Dr. Jake lounging and laughing with his father in the Caldwell family home back in Texas flashed across his mind. Doc had been a guardian angel after Bill Caldwell senior had died, leaving behind a confused eight-year-old boy. Doc had been like a father after that, paying for his college, guiding him, and even keeping him out of the military draft through a few back-door manipulations of his medical record. He realized suddenly that the familiar voice on the other end of the phone was shaking. "Are you okay, Doc?"

There was a long pause, filled with the hissing static of a long-distance line, before the answer came. "No. No Bill, I'm not. I'm sorry to call you, but I don't know what else to do. I guess I'm spooked."

Caldwell shifted the telephone handset from his right to his left ear, his right hand instinctively uncapping a pen and adjusting a yellow legal pad he kept on the small rosewood desk with the telephone.

"Tell me about it, Doc. What's the matter? And where are you?"

"Canada. I'm in Banff, or near it. Kananaskis. Bill, there're a couple of people at the safety board trying to get my license, and I haven't done anything wrong. They're after me, and the local police up here are now asking me questions and want me to talk to the NTSB people again. I'm too old to go through this, Bill. I can't . . . I mean, I'm not responsible for Dick Timson's crash. I—"

"Whoa, Doc, please. One thing at a time." Caldwell questioned him slowly, making notes as the panicked physician related the NTSB's attempts to question him about the Timson medical records, his protests that all the exams were properly done, and his belief that Captain Richard Timson was in good shape.

Bill Caldwell wondered if there was something more. He had taken a chance once before for Doc when the agency had suspected him of giving class I medicals without all the proper tests. Bill had administratively "fixed the ticket," as he called it,

crushing the violation filed by the FAA Air Surgeon which would
have suspended McIntyre's certification as a doctor licensed to
administer FAA medical exams. He had done it aboveboard by
forcing an internal review, but it was sticking his neck out, and
for a surgically careful bureaucrat who had become a professional survivor, it amounted to a career gamble. Yet his loyalties
to Doc ran deeper than for any other human being. When Caldwell had engineered the ouster of the FAA's federal Air Surgeon
a few years back—a doctor who refused to take the associate
administrator's orders—he had thought about recommending
Doc McIntyre as a replacement. Doc would have done his bidding and been totally devoid of ambition or initiative. The realization that Doc was also very lazy had canceled the idea. If
he failed, it would reflect badly on Caldwell.

"Doc, please understand, I have to ask you this. Have you
complied with all the regulations on this man's exams? Have
you been keeping your nose clean like you promised me? Was
everything done properly?"

It seemed the doctor hesitated too long, but the answer came
at last. "Yes. Yes, Bill, it's all been done right. I'm just scared
of these people. Since I'm a company doctor, I'm afraid they're
out to get me in order to get North America."

"Why don't you just talk to them and find out what they want?
I mean, if everything was done right, then maybe all they want
is your impression of Captain Timson."

"No, Bill! No! They're after me. You've . . . you've got to
believe me. I've heard things. I've heard they want to prove I
didn't do a good job of examining Timson so they can say his
medical was no good."

"Was it, Doc?"

"Yes. I mean, he was in perfect health. My records show
that. Bill, is there anything you could do to get these people off
my back without endangering yourself? They've been calling
and calling, and the company told me to go on vacation to get
away from them, at least until the Kansas City hearing is over
. . . so the company knows they're after me. Please, Bill. I don't
want to put you in jeopardy, but if there's anything . . ."

Caldwell sighed quietly and thought. Since it involved the
NTSB, and that was headed by Dean Farris, maybe there *was* a
safe way to protect him.

"Doc, give me your number, then sit tight for a few days and don't worry. There is one guy I can get hold of and find out what's going on. If I can help, I will, but this problem doesn't originate within my agency like last time.''

"I know.''

"I'll do what I can.'' He took down McIntyre's number and hesitated for a second, a merged image of Doc's chronic laziness and the various duties of an FAA-certified company doctor coalescing in his mind, ready to ring caution bells and sound career alarms. Caldwell lifted his eyes from the legal pad suddenly and arrested the thought in its tracks. This was a matter of loyalty, and besides, he could be sufficiently circumspect and careful to avoid personal danger.

18

Tuesday, December 4

Pete Kaminsky's entrance had not gone unnoticed. The second day of the NTSB hearing had been under way for fifty minutes when the captain of the doomed Boeing 737 entered quietly at the back of the ballroom, his six-foot-four-inch frame moving like a huge shadow toward the first empty chair in the last row as Joe Wallingford watched from the head table. Even at a distance, the grim determination and the pain were visible in the pilot's face. Reliving the crash would clearly be an agony for him.

Ten minutes before Kaminsky arrived, Dr. Greg Phillips, a well-known aviation psychologist, who was the first witness, had been asked how likely it was that a captain could set up an accident by intimidating his copilot into inaction.

"It's happened many times before. Intimidated crewmembers permitting captains to do dangerous things are quite common. The Air New England Twin Otter crash in 1979, for instance. The captain apparently went to sleep on final approach, but he was the director of operations and a tough ex-marine, and his copilot was a brand-new employee who was so intimidated that he sat on his hands and let the airplane fly into the ground rather than take a chance of offending the captain by stopping what had become a clearly dangerous descent short of the runway. Before that there was the copilot in a Texas International Convair near Mena, Arkansas, in 1973 who finally got around to asking 'how high are these mountains?' as his captain blundered through valleys at low altitude, in the blind, in and out of clouds. The question was his last, however. They slammed into a hillside the split second the words left his mouth. We also had

communications and copilot-assertiveness problems in the Eastern Airlines Charlotte, North Carolina, crash in 1974, the Air
Illinois crash near Pinckneyville, Illinois, in 1983, the Pan Am
and KLM takeoff collision at Tenerife in 1977, and, of course,
the real classic, Air Florida's crash in the Potomac in 1982. All
of these and many more have involved breakdowns in cockpit
communication partially or fully based on pilots being too reluctant to speak up and be assertive. We call it the 'iron-pants
captain' syndrome, and it's cost thousands of lives and hundreds
of millions of dollars in losses.''

''And,'' Joe interjected, ''cockpit resource management
courses can solve it?''

''No.''

''No?'' The response startled Joe.

''It's merely a start, but a necessary and vital one.''

''Madam Chairman.'' The voice belonged to Dean Farris.
Joe had been aware of some movement on his far right, but
Farris's interjection was unexpected. Susan had been caught off
guard as well and was looking now at Farris as he more or less
hunched over his microphone on the far end of the head table,
looking back at Susan.

''I'm sure all this is very interesting, but I think we've heard
enough from this witness. His testimony isn't really relevant.''

At North America's table, John Walters was nodding vigorously as he chimed in, ''Madam Chairman, we too would like
to say that this testimony is totally irrelevant. The place of such
courses as cockpit management training in a modern airline is
very much a disputed and debatable issue, and even the FAA
has not mandated such training as yet. North America specifically rejects the concept as useless undermining of a captain's
legal authority, a concept which in some circumstances could
be dangerous.''

''That's outrageous,'' Joe muttered, close enough to the microphone to be heard.

''Let's take a ten-minute recess, please,'' Susan said without
warning, looking first at Dean Farris, then at Joe, then back at
Farris again. Before either of them could say more, Joe noticed
Susan glaring at him, her face hard and angry. ''You,'' she
hissed in a stage whisper, turning the other way toward the
NTSB chairman, ''and you. Come, please.'' Susan was out of
the chair and off the back of the platform in an instant, and both

men found themselves following her out the door and into the adjacent small conference room, where Susan was waiting with folded arms. Joe closed the door carefully.

"Now would you two boys like to put up your fists and duke it out on national television?"

Dean Farris's mouth was open as he groped for a dignified reply, but Susan was not in a listening mood. Hands on hips, her eyes flaring, she paced to one side of them, then another, like an angry teacher confronting two students caught fighting in the hallway.

"What a grand, dignified, appropriate display *that* was! It's not bad enough that I've a battle keeping Walters under control, now you two have to go ballistic."

"Now Susan, let's—" Dean Farris's right palm was in the air, a gesture to stop, but she continued.

"Dean, that remark was totally uncalled for. If you don't realize the significance of that man's testimony, you have not done your homework. I intend to create a record in this hearing which includes enough testimony about human performance to enable a clear decision on whether or not it applies. I resent and refuse to tolerate your prejudicial remarks." Susan's arms flailed the air in the direction of the ballroom. "You saw what that did. That sparked Walters off again and gave everyone the impression we're making premature judgments."

Farris tried a shallow bow in her direction. "I am very sorry, Susan, I was merely—"

"And *you*, Joseph Wallingford, know damn well better than make such a remark with your microphone on." She had turned to Joe suddenly, leaving Farris in the midst of a conciliatory bow to her back.

Joe raised both hands. "I'm sorry, Susan. You're right, of course."

She was out the door in a flash, leaving an embarrassed Dean Farris staring at an equally embarrassed Joe Wallingford, a brief standoff which ended immediately as they both moved toward the door, Farris startled by her ferocity, and Joe deeply impressed.

John Walters spent the next half hour trying unsuccessfully to put some distance between North America Airlines and Dr. Phillips's flat statement that a captain-oriented airline was always less safe, but finally gave up, clearing the way for the FAA's lawyer, who dragged out the fact that cockpit resource management training would become an FAA requirement very soon. Increasingly, however, eyes were shifting to Captain Pete Kaminsky at the back of the room as the questioning of Dr. Phillips came to an end with ALPA's questions about the effects of massive corporate losses on pilot safety performance levels.

And at last Pete was on the stand, Joe guiding him gently into the events of that Friday night, asking him to relate them as he remembered them, the occupants of the ballroom transfixed as the big man with the quiet voice told of his shock at finding his passengers gone, his craft in ruins, running from seat to ruined seat looking for someone to save. When he finished, there was dead silence in the room, and Joe could see tears reflecting in Pete's eyes.

"There was nothing I could do. There was nothing."

"Captain," Joe began, "do you know Dick Timson?"

"Yes. I know Dick."

"One of the things we are interested in probing is whether the management style of Captain Timson in his role as chief pilot was in any way a detriment to North America pilots maintaining the highest levels of safety, and whether it was intimidating in general."

Pete dropped his head for a moment, then raised it again, looking to his right and looking Joe in the eye.

"Dick ruled with fear and threats and intimidation—taught his junior chief pilots to do the same. His style reduced a proud group of self-respecting professionals to a divided, warring camp—an us-against-them war zone of distrust and company hatred in which we regarded the future as bleak and hopeless. In that atmosphere, coming to work was like taking a beating, each and every time. Did it affect our performance? How . . . how on earth could it not? Do *you* do your best work tied up in a knot or deeply angry? Could you reason as well if told by word and deed that you're worthless, mediocre, and easily replaceable?" Pete dropped his eyes again to the tablecloth, the fingers of his right hand playing absently with a fold in the fabric.

"Captain, let me ask you if—"

"Just before we pushed back," Pete began again suddenly, seemingly unaware of Joe's question, "my copilot and I were discussing a cut in a tire that should have grounded the aircraft. I mean, I should have told them to change it. It would have been safer. As it turned out, if I had—if I'd had the damn courage to say, 'I am the goddamn captain and I want the goddamn tire changed right now, and I'm not flying or pushing back or anything until it's done'—all those people would still be alive. But I was too tired of being sniped at for exercising a captain's authority, so I took the coward's way out. And . . . well . . ."

Joe and the staff questioned Pete for thirty minutes in all, giving the other parties their opportunity to question Pete Kaminsky as well. The FAA had nothing to add, but ALPA's investigator asked Pete enough questions to establish that his decision to leave the gate with a cut tire was perfectly legal, and nearly an hour after Pete Kaminsky took the stand, Susan gave John Walters his chance to question him, an opportunity which, to everyone's surprise, Walters turned down. He would have a chance to take the stand himself later on. That would be the time to attempt to repair as much of the damage as possible.

What John Walters had bitterly opposed in the prehearing conference started then in spite of his protests. Four North America captains, a first officer, and two flight attendants took the stand, all qualified and currently flying the Airbus 320, and all of them subpoenaed to attend. The picture they provided of life inside North America Airlines had convinced Andy Wallace, and in turn Joe Wallingford, that the story must be aired at the hearing. One by one they told of excessive pressure for on-time performance and a distrustful management who thought all employees were out to "get" the company.

"If you mean," began one of the pilots, "do I feel compelled to fly passengers in airplanes I'd rather have maintenance fix, or in weather I'd rather not chance? Yes, I do. If you mean, does the fact that every time I've grounded an airplane for reasons I felt valid, I've been forced to drive 50 miles on my day off to be chewed out by a junior assistant chief pilot masquerading as a captain, does that impinge on my go-no-go decision the next time when I sit in that cockpit with a broken fuel gauge or a marginal tire? Yes it does. If you mean, am I getting sufficiently tired of this job that sometimes I catch myself daydreaming when I should be answering checklist items? The answer is yes." The man paused and looked at the desk, wondering whether to continue, and Joe waited patiently until he looked up again.

"You know, sometimes the pressure comes from inside. We're professional people—technicians, yes, but most of us are aware of business realities. We know that our company, our careers, and our bank accounts are all welded together, and we know this airline is losing its ass financially. I'm sorry for the language, but it's true. When you know that, you also know that if we ground a flight, we all lose money. So sometimes the pressure to fly in less than optimal conditions comes from our own desire to have our company survive.''

Joe leaned forward and turned on his microphone. "One question, sir. Have you ever heard of, or witnessed, a situation in which a copilot or flight engineer was disciplined or chastised by the company for speaking up to a captain in flight?''

The man nodded and smiled. "You joking?''

"No sir, Captain, the question is quite serious.''

"That's very common around North America. You don't cross a North America captain, and that's a barrier between me and my crew I don't want. They're afraid to speak up even when I want them to.''

Finally it was John Walters's turn, and Joe watched with a disconcerting mix of empathy and hostility as he took the witness chair. Joe questioned him for forty minutes as Walters dodged and parried with argumentative pugnacity any queries about North America's methods of handling pilot operations and training. He was interested only in reading his corporate version of reality into the record. There was nothing wrong with Dick Timson's methods, he said, no morale problem in the North America pilot ranks—despite Pete Kaminsky's impassioned statements—and no reason to consider Don Leyhe, Flight 255's copilot, an intimidated man.

"You're saying Captain Kaminsky is lying?''

"I'm saying Captain Kaminsky may believe what he's saying, but that's an isolated, inaccurate view. Just because one wrought-up man, who I admit has been through hell, remembers his work environment as being terrible, does not make it so.''

"All right then; then, Mr. Walters, let's move on to Don Leyhe. Having heard the voice tape, why do you believe Don Leyhe was so slow to act?'' Joe had asked.

"I don't know that he was slow to act. That's an unjustified conclusion.''

Joe sighed all too audibly. "The nose had dropped, sir. They were aimed at the ground short of the runway, yet it took nearly ten seconds for him to seize control by pressing the priority switch. Don't you consider that excessive slowness?''

Walters had shaken his head vigorously. ''Not unless you have the unwarranted, preconceived notion, Mr. Wallingford, that the captain was doing something wrong. We have the captain's testimony, right here from this seat. He told you he had the proper back pressure and the plane nosed over on him. That's the only appropriate area for inquiry.''

Susan was shaking her head ever so slightly as she looked at Walters, noticing the stir of activity and angry faces at the Airbus table. Even Dean Farris, still seated at the far end, was watching Walters closely, and not interfering. Joe had heard that Walters had been chosen to handle the hearing simply because he was upper management, but it was obvious that had been a major mistake. David Bayne had sent a company attorney to sit next to Walters and advise him, but the operations vice-president was still far too brusque and technically uninformed. Maybe that's the problem, Joe thought. Maybe there's no one in the airline's management who *is* qualified, including Walters's superiors. Perhaps John Walters was the only candidate, but either way, he was putting on a very bad show.

Joe decided on one last attempt. ''Mr. Walters, was the amount of time the copilot took to seize control reasonable or extraordinarily lengthy in the view of North America flight-operations management? And, if it was extraordinarily long, doesn't that fact alone indicate that he was not guarding the aircraft, not functioning as an effective safety backup to the captain?''

Walters's face remained a mask of stern determination as he flipped through his briefing notebook and found the section he had been searching for. ''Mr. Wallingford, based on industry studies of subtle incapacitation of which this Board should be aware, the answer is no, it was not excessive, and in this case the copilot probably should never have seized control in the first place. But there is one other point I want to make. Our airline, which has many decades of safe flying to its credit, is a captain-oriented airline. That's one reason we're so safe. The captain is, as he should be, the commander, as Dick Timson properly indicated. He and he alone makes the decisions. When to fly, when to land, how to land. Copilots are merely captains-in-training, nothing more, and we certainly don't tolerate them hanging on to the controls during an approach, or for that matter seizing control or second-guessing the real captain.''

"Not even if the airplane is in imminent peril?" Joe asked, as evenly as possible.

"We don't know that it was in imminent peril," Walters snapped.

"But what if it *was* in peril? Treat this as a hypothetical situation, if necessary. Would you not concede that a copilot's duty is to try to save the aircraft?"

"A copilot's duty is to serve his captain, who is his instructor."

"And never take control?"

"Well, if the captain dies on the controls, or something drastic"—Walters's right hand swept the air—"then of course he's expected to take over. But we don't allow our copilots to stage a mutiny anytime they don't like the captain's flight technique."

"Are you a pilot, Mr. Walters?"

"Has nothing to do with it."

"The reasons for our questions are none of your concern. I ask again, are you a licensed pilot, Mr. Walters?"

"No. And that's immaterial."

Susan pulled her microphone closer. "Excuse me, but I have a question, Mr. Walters. Is that what you are saying happened here, that copilot Leyhe mutinied and seized control of Flight 255 without reason, authorization, or propriety? Are you saying that it would be the policy of your airline, as well as your opinion, that he should have sat with his hands in his lap and let this captain continue on a course that apparently would guarantee impact with the ground?"

John Walters realized too late that he had painted himself into a corner. There was no graceful exit. "Madam Chairman, what I'm trying to say is that all this blathering we heard yesterday, all the preconceived, prejudicial ideas that the people on your staff have locked themselves into, and some of Mr. Wallingford's questions this morning—all of them assume the captain was doing something wrong and the copilot had to take over. This is supposed to be a nonprejudicial forum, and I'm telling all of you that no one has yet *proven* that our captain was doing anything wrong, and he himself has testified under oath that he was not. Nor, I might add, is there any justification for involving management style in this investigation."

Joe knew Susan couldn't leave that challenge unanswered. "Mr. Walters," she said, "I think we're talking past each other. You're talking about proof in legalistic terms, but an NTSB Board of Inquiry is not a court of law, nor are we under rules of evidence. While that does not excuse any prejudicial conduct on the part of any of us, I'll say for the record I don't believe there's been any such conduct or questioning or any so-called preconceived notions here. I understand your desire to preserve the record for your company, but that type of posturing is best done in a court, not here. Now, I think Mr. Wallingford has additional questions, and I think all of us would appreciate a direct, non-argumentative response to each one."

Walters said nothing and Joe began again. "Mr. Walters, just a few more. Why, in your opinion, did copilot Leyhe seize control?"

Walters looked out at the audience, at the spot where Dick Timson sat impassively. He looked at his own people at the North America table, then back at Joe Wallingford before answering.

"We'll never know, Mr. Wallingford, but it had not a damn thing in the world to do with the way we manage our company."

That was enough. Joe dismissed Walters after polling the other parties and finding that no one wanted to question him further. There was no point.

Walters had placed North America's assistant chief pilot Dan Butler on the witness list the day before. Susan asked him as he left the stand if he still wanted Butler to testify.

"Yes, Madam Chairman, to rebut some of these scandalous and inflammatory lies that a handful of our dissident pilots spewed out earlier like poison onto this record."

Susan shook her head visibly while looking Walters straight in the eye. "Sir, another accusation like that and I will expel you from this hearing. Is that clear?"

"What about Captain Butler?"

"I call Dan Butler. Mr. Butler, if you please."

Dan Butler, slim, balding, and in his mid-thirties, got to his feet uncertainly as John Walters reached the North America table once more and turned on his microphone.

"Please refer to him as Captain Butler, Madam Chairman," Walters interjected, none too softly, as an obviously embarrassed Butler sat down in the witness chair.

"Are you a management captain, Captain Butler, without a seniority number, or did you come into management as a regular line pilot?" Joe asked, after they had read the usual name and position information into the record.

"I'm a line pilot who moved into flight management."

"If you had not gone into management, would you be senior enough to be a line captain today?"

"No sir."

"Do you know what position you'd have?"

Butler hesitated, looking at Walters for any signs of how to handle the unexpected line of questions. "With all the furloughs we've had, I . . . would probably be a senior flight engineer, a second officer, on the Boeing 727, which has a three-pilot crew, and maybe a junior copilot on the 737, which has two."

"But because you're in management, you've made captain?"

"I was given the chance to go through the training and qualify as a captain, yes sir. And I did."

"Madam Chairman," Walters began, "I object to—"

"To what, Mr. Walters? You have no standing to object. That is the last interruption I will tolerate." Susan was fuming, a wooden gavel in her right hand for the first time in two days. "Continue, Mr. Wallingford."

"Did Captain Timson start out as a line pilot too?" Joe asked.

"Yes, sir."

"How long was he on the line?"

"I think, uh, two or three years. He was a base manager for many years, then held my position, assistant chief pilot, and was made chief pilot about four years ago."

"How about yourself? How long were you on the line as a regular North America pilot?" Joe asked.

"Seven years."

Joe shuffled through his notes, watching Butler out of the corner of his eye. There was something very wrong about his nervousness and the way he kept looking at Walters, who was trying to avoid looking back.

"Captain Butler, John Walters is your immediate supervisor, right?"

"Dick Timson, uh, was, as chief pilot. At the moment—while Captain Timson is out on medical leave—Mr. Walters would be my immediate boss, yes."

"Do you have a shot at the chief pilot's job if Timson steps down?"

Butler looked stunned. "I . . . why do . . . I don't know."

"I ask that to gauge your answers. If Mr. Walters has your future position in his hands, then a good performance here would help, and a bad one would hurt, correct?"

"Sir, if you're implying that I'm going to lie . . ."

"Captain, no one is expecting you to lie, but the way you see things may be colored by whatever career pressure you're under."

Butler merely shook his head. "I don't agree."

"Okay, let me ask one other question before I get into the heart of this matter. Has John Walters, or any other superior at North America, coached you on what to say or how to say it on this witness stand?"

Dan Butler looked like he wanted to run from the room. His eyes riveted on John Walters, who was not looking, and then on Joe, who could read the uncertainty in them. "I would rather not try to answer that question," he said at last, "because we've talked about so much, I'm not sure whether you'd call that coaching or not."

Clever answer, Joe thought to himself. But let's see how long it holds up. "Okay, you realize that one of the things we are probing here is whether an oppressive management style can intimidate pilots into not acting in the interests of safety when they should act, and whether your airline's management style or atmosphere could be considered oppressive. We have noted that North America objects to this characterization, but we are still going to ask the question. So let me ask you, was Dick Timson's management style intimidating to pilots?"

"No," was the rapid reply from Butler.

"Well, could you elaborate?"

"Just no. It was not intimidating."

"You mean to you?"

"To me, or to the pilots under us. I mean, it shouldn't have been."

"Captain, you heard the previous pilot witnesses describe Captain Timson's management style as being very forceful, characterizing him as a man who would not tolerate dissent or disobedience, or late departures. Do you agree with their analysis?"

"No, I don't." Once again Butler answered, then fell silent. No elaboration, no passion, no support.

Joe cocked his head and looked at Butler, who was looking back nervously. "Well, Captain, would you tell us why you don't agree?"

Butler cleared his throat, his eyes darting over the panel and over the various tables. "Well, uh, they may have a different point of view, but the fact is, we simply ran a tight ship under Captain Timson."

Joe waited for him to continue, but in vain. "Captain, let me get specific, then. I'm handing you a copy of a memo posted in all the crew rooms on the night of the accident, in which management is telling all captains forcefully to, in effect, be very careful how they exercise their authority as the final determining factor of whether or not a flight is safe to operate. Have you read this, sir?"

An assistant handed Butler the memo. "Yes."

"Was Captain Timson the real author of that?"

"Yes sir."

"It would seem that this removes much of the captain's discretionary authority, perhaps illegally, by providing a penalty—that of explaining his actions in writing under threat of dismissal—for disagreeing with maintenance. Do you read it that way?"

Butler's hand was shaking as he held the memo, hesitating as his eyes darted back and forth over the paper, as if afraid there was a trick in the question. "No, I don't. It's just telling the captains to be responsible."

"And you don't think a line captain could construe that to mean that he's got to fly regardless of maintenance conditions?"

"No I don't."

"How long have you held the rank of captain, Captain?"

"About eight months."

"And how many hours do you have as a captain flying passengers in the real world?"

"I guess about one hundred or so."

"Only one hundred."

"Yes sir."

Joe sat back and looked at Butler, realizing Walters had to have been desperate to risk putting him on the stand. There was obviously no one else to help shore up their viewpoint, but the move had hurt them. Yes and no and limited answers would do absolutely nothing to help the investigation, nor, for that matter, the company's image. Joe leaned forward again, a risky decision made.

"Captain, how long have you held your *position*, as assistant chief pilot?"

"About one year."

"Did you enjoy working with Captain Timson?"

"That's really meaningless to me, sir, I just did my job. It didn't depend on enjoyment."

"But was he easy to work with?"

"Timson?" Butler asked.

"Of course, Timson. Was he easy or difficult as your boss?"

"He was tough, but fair."

"Was that a rehearsed line, Captain?"

"I don't know what you mean."

"I think you do, sir." Joe paused, his mind racing ahead. If he was any judge of human nature, this man had not been comfortable under Timson and had probably considered leaving the office and returning to the line. Joe had no hard information to that effect, but it was logical—and it was worth a shot. "Captain, isn't it true that you were thinking of leaving your position and going back to the line?"

Butler's head jerked toward Joe, a very puzzled expression on his face, his eyes searching Joe's for an indication of what had prompted the question, and for a second, Joe thought it had been in vain.

"I . . . well, I had been considering it, yes."

Bingo! Now to see how far I can go with this, Joe thought. "You'd done more than consider it, hadn't you? You had discussed it with several friends, telling them you couldn't stand it anymore. Right?"

There was no answer. That was probably too much gambling and guesswork, but he had already started down the path. "Captain, am I right about that? I should remind you that you're under oath here."

Butler's head dropped as he began studying the tablecloth, and his answer was so quiet Joe almost didn't hear it.

"Yes."

"Sir?"

Butler turned toward Joe again, this time with a different expression, a resolve, his eyes closed and head nodding. "Yes, Mr. Wallingford, your information is exactly correct."

Joe could feel Susan's questioning glances, and he knew the staff was stunned. There was no time to explain, but he could see he was beginning to chip Butler out of the company mold. "Did you hear the cockpit voice recording of Flight 255, Captain?"

"Yes sir, I did."

"Now, this is of the utmost seriousness. You're a man who worked with and under Dick Timson. We're trying to find the causes here of a disaster that took just under two hundred lives. The only loyalty is to the truth, and to the principle that aviation-safety responsibilities transcend companies and are the responsibility of all of us. In that spirit, Captain Butler, as a certificated airman yourself, I ask you to tell us without reservation whether the voice, the demeanor, the attitude, and the words of Captain Timson on that tape were or were not typical of the man as you knew him on the job, in or out of the cockpit?"

No answer. Butler's right hand was rubbing his mouth, his left fingers drumming the table, his eyes absently on the far wall.

"Captain? Was that Dick Timson's management style or not?"

Slowly Butler's head came around as he looked at Joe, took a deep breath. "Okay, Mr. Wallingford. You want the truth? I'm under oath? Fine. You were right, that was a rehearsed line a minute ago, a carefully rehearsed line. You're right, too, that I wanted out before this crash occurred, but I . . . I supported my company's viewpoint when I walked into this room yesterday." He paused and looked over at John Walters, who was looking at Butler with great alarm.

Butler looked back at Joe. "I wasn't even a small wheel in that office. Dick Timson didn't want an assistant—resented having to have an assistant—but they said he needed one, so I was brought in, given the bone of upgrading to captain, and told to stay the hell out of the way. Basically, I was a $140,000-a-year gofer."

"Captain," Joe began, but Butler's hand came up to stop him.

"Let . . . let me get this out while I can. No one can please Dick Timson. I thought at first it was just me, you know, maybe I was too new to know him. Then I figured the man was just cold and calculating, and he was—on the surface. In the last few months, though, I was around him long enough to see something else. Dick Timson, in my opinion, is not really in control. Oh, he makes you think he is, with blustering and tough discipline and unyielding decisions, but I've seen him with his guard down, which is rare, and he's struggling. I don't think he really knows how to do the job—how to be a manager—but he's afraid to go back to the line, afraid he'll lose the perks and the money. Management style? A reign of terror.'' Butler looked to his left, searching for Dick Timson's face and finding it turned away. Timson was listening, but he would not look at him.

"In my opinion, Dick Timson is running scared, but he won't let anyone into his personal feelings, and he'll beat you to death if you try to get close and friendly—which I've discovered the hard way several times.'' Butler's gaze had wandered over to Susan, Dean Farris, and to the staff table. Suddenly he refocused on Joe.

"You were right. I hated it in that office, especially since I was effectively useless. I found I had made one hell of a mistake, and even though it meant going back to flight engineer, I was ready. But I put in my request three months ago, and Dick told me, 'You leave, and you'll never pass your next checkride.' ''

Joe sat back in his chair, stunned. He had expected he might trigger a trickle of a response, but apparently he had broken the dam.

"Dick is very good at putting on a show, looking polished and professional and in control in front of his leaders. I doubt John Walters over there ever saw the real Timson that I saw. How did he regard line pilots? As lackadaisical goof-offs—his words, not mine—yet I think he envied them in many ways. What kind of a manager was he? The worst I've ever been around. He couldn't just sit and talk to you, or even give the impression that he cared about you as an employee, let alone an individual. Whether he did or not, he couldn't show it, so everyone below us got the impression—as you heard accurately here today—that we were at war with the rank and file. I wasn't, and I don't think Dick really was. He just didn't know how else to act. Being a manager meant having to be a tough drill sergeant to please the corporate leaders, but it also meant intimidating everyone. His memos were downright hateful.'' He fell silent again, and a loud noise of disgust could be heard from Walters as the North America vice-president shook his head and scowled at the back wall of the ballroom.

"There's a question you haven't asked me, Mr. Wallingford, but I'll answer it anyway. Why have I stepped out of the mold? Why have I angered my leader over there and, as he will see it, defected? I sat here, Mr. Wallingford . . . I sat here yesterday and especially today, and it finally sank in how much damage has been done. No, I don't know what happened in that cockpit, but I agree the copilot should have been able to recover and was intimidated out of it. I knew Don Leyhe. He was scared to death of Timson." Butler paused, his eyes searching the audience again, this time for the captain of Flight 170.

"Look at Captain Kaminsky out there. It's not just the fact that Dick Timson crashed into him, the fact that wrenches me is that because of this crash his world has become so dark. I never knew . . . I never wanted to know . . . that what we did in that office could have such an effect that . . . that . . ." He looked down again, shaking his head slightly. "I . . . haven't slept very well in the past few weeks knowing that even though Dick wanted me to stay out of the way, I was part of a management operation that could have contributed to this . . . *did* contribute to this. I just can't be a part of that anymore, even if I do flunk my next checkride." He looked over at Walters again. "I'm sorry Mr. Walters."

There was sudden silence in the room, John Walters sitting back in his chair, tapping his pen on the table with increasing vengeance, glaring daggers at Butler while Joe, Susan, Dean Farris, and the entire staff sat there effectively speechless.

Joe leaned forward at last and began guiding Butler through more questions, fleshing out the picture of Timson's methods and his day-by-day management of North America pilot matters. Susan permitted the ALPA and FAA members to continue the questioning until around 4 P.M., when there was simply nothing more to say.

Joe took the microphone again and thanked him, but before Susan could begin the rituals of closing the hearing, Dan Butler stepped off the platform and walked past the North America table, stopping by John Walters, who refused to look at him.

"By the way, Mr. Walters," he said, "I'm going back to the line. I'll save you the trouble of firing me." Butler moved on to the ALPA table, where he pulled out a chair and sat down as

Susan read her closing statement and brought the hearing to an end.

Joe got up from his chair and looked at Susan, who was looking back, both of them obviously galvanized by what had transpired. Joe glanced around at his other colleagues, reading the same shocked, destabilized look on each face. Seldom had any of them experienced as dramatic a change in the middle of a hearing as the sudden crumbling of Dan Butler's facade. Butler's words would force the entire Board to deal with copilot intimidation, and the fact that Don Leyhe hadn't acted in time. Even if the Star Wars radar *was* responsible for the crash, Dick Timson was responsible for deactivating the most important emergency system he had, his copilot, by creating an operational environment of intimidation throughout the entire airline. Having the consequences come back on the perpetrator in such an unpredictable and fatal way was somewhere beyond ironic.

The immediate aftermath of an eventful hearing is always the same, as people crowd forward to talk to various individuals, the staff and Board members included. Dean Farris had his glut of people, Susan hers, and several were pressing for Joe's attention—which was difficult for Joe to deal with, his mind spinning around a quick review of the previous half hour. Joe realized with a start that one of the people pressing forward to speak to him was Dan Butler. He started to thank Butler, but the pilot stopped him. "Don't. I should have come forward sooner, but I have one more thing to tell you. It may be nothing, but he acted so secretive about it."

"What?"

"Dick was supposed to be in perfect health, and I've seen his first-class medical come down without restriction from our company doctor, but I tell you, Timson took aspirin constantly. He always had a bottle in his briefcase. You might want to take a close look at that."

Dick Timson had remained motionless for much of the previous hour, his hands in his lap, his head down, listening impassively. There had been no one sitting with him, and Louise Timson was nowhere in sight. As soon as Susan gaveled the hearing closed, Timson got to his feet slowly and walked from the room, utterly ignoring a couple of reporters who tried unsuccessfully to talk to him. His eyes were on the carpet ahead, his pace leaden.

Pete Kaminsky caught him by the door, physically stopping him with a big hand on Timson's sleeve, forcing him to look up. Pete saw a haunted look there, an emptiness accentuated by the dark circles under his eyes. Dick, he knew, had a way of jutting his lower jaw out and hunching his shoulders when he was angry, but Pete saw only defeat.

"Dick, would you like some company?"

Timson just stared at Kaminsky.

"I . . . I wanted you to know . . . I had to say what I believed to be true."

Timson's right hand came up in a gesture of dismissal as he looked away. "Don't worry about it, Pete." He sighed deeply and slowly pulled away then, disappearing down the hotel corridor, Pete watching him go and thinking him in many respects the saddest victim of all.

19

Joe Wallingford walked into Dean Farris's office with the fatalism of a Roman gladiator facing the lions, having been warned by Andy Wallace a few minutes before that Farris was going to attempt to take him off the North America investigation. The odds were impossible, of course—Farris was the boss—but Joe wasn't about to surrender without a fight. The note to report immediately to the chairman's office had been affixed to his door for the staff to see, and that alone was infuriating.

"Well, Joe, you just couldn't take a hint, or an order, could you?" Farris was grinning ruefully as he motioned Joe to a plush chair while he moved to his throne behind the desk. "You hadn't been back from Kansas City for ten minutes yesterday before going after North America's doctor again, right?"

"First, Mr. Chairman, I don't appreciate the public note on my door."

Farris shrugged and smiled as Joe continued.

"Second, as the hearing broke up two days ago, Dan Butler came up and said that Timson was using medicine heavily, perhaps aspirin, perhaps not, and that John Walters has been guarding the files since the crash. Now that, to me, raises flags I can't ignore. There was no mention of medication on any of the medical records we received, nor on any of the FAA medical forms Timson filled out each year."

"I told you to leave the doctor alone." Farris's voice was even and threatening.

"We did, for heaven's sake. All we did was renew our request to talk to him."

"I told you to come to me first. I ordered you to lay off, Joe.

I've spent half the damn morning on the phone listening to David Bayne yelling at me and then Bill Caldwell upstairs griping at me.''

"What . . . ?" Joe cocked his head. "How does this concern Caldwell?''

"Bayne says you're harassing him, and Caldwell, who's an old friend of the man, agrees.''

"Harassing Bayne? North America's CEO?''

"No, the doctor. McIntyre.''

"That's not true, we—''

"Dammit, Joe, I told you not to call them again.''

"Wait a damned minute here, Mr. Chairman! We did *not* call the man in Canada yesterday or today. All I did was authorize Andy to get on the phone to John Walters after the hearing and demand to see *all* of the files, and to talk to the doctor in person, on the record, when he gets back. I don't know what they're saying to *you*, but it looks to me like it's not the doctor that's scared, it's North America.''

Farris had turned toward the window, ignoring Joe's response, and merely waiting for him to finish.

"In addition, Joe, I told you that it is the policy of this Board that there will be no further probing into the presence of that Air Force plane or its cargo." Farris whirled around to face him. "That, too, was an order. It's a closed issue! Yet you've had Andy Wallace running all over the landscape behind my back asking questions about it.''

"Mr. Chairman, how the bloody hell can I conduct an investigation if you're going to keep second-guessing me?''

"You're not.''

Joe looked at him. "What? I don't understand.''

"I know you don't understand. You don't understand who's in charge around here. Your conduct at the hearing was inexcusable.''

"In what way?''

"In terms of respect for the chairman of this organization, Joe. You're not going to have to worry about this investigation because I'm removing you." Farris had sat down and was leaning back in his chair, looking imperious, enjoying the upper hand. "I've had it with your insubordinate, I-know-everything-I-was-here-before-you attitude. You are hereby removed as IIC. I'm directing every department not to talk to you about any aspect of it. And, as to whether I let you keep the position of chief of the aviation accident division, or even keep working here at the Board, depends on whether you can learn to follow a directive from your superior.''

Joe set his jaw and stared at Farris. "Fine. Fire me. But what are you planning to do about the medical records, the doctor, and what's beginning to smell like a cover-up of some sort? In addition, what are you going to do to satisfy the bulk of the American public who aren't going to believe us any more than they now believe the Air Force if we don't make an honest effort to find out about that damned radar?" Joe was leaning forward in his chair, tapping the desk, looking Farris in the eye and trying hard to keep hold of his temper. It would be very satisfying to throttle that sanctimonious son of a bitch, he thought.

"We're not the FBI on the trail of a murderer, Joe. In due time. In due time, we will address the North America issue formally with them. There will be no addressing of the other issue. The radar unit was turned off. Anyway, none of this is your concern now.''

Joe stood up, his finger still touching the desk. "While you're worrying about your political reputation, Mr. Chairman, consider this. In this town, those who know about and fail to expose a cover-up, become part of it.''

Joe returned to his office in a dark mood, and equally shaken. Intellectually he knew he could take retirement—the ultimate revenge of a professional bureaucrat. But what the hell would he do? He was an accident investigator. A technical detective with a government ID. He didn't want to do anything else. In fact, he wasn't sure he *could* do anything else. Life without the NTSB was, quite simply, unimaginable. But Farris had embarrassed him and might even fire him. And that was reality staring him in the face.

"Joe, d'you get the word?"

He looked up to see one of Andy Wallace's people in his doorway.

"About what?" he said acidly. It was starting already.

"The crash. In Florida. Just came through, and we're scrambling the Go Team.''

All his instincts came back on line in an instant, even though he wasn't on the team this week. "Who, what, when, and where?"

''In the Everglades, a Miami Air Boeing 737. It was a charter flight of some sort, and the initial word is that it came apart in the air while climbing out of Key West northbound. It came down in pieces near Naples, Florida.''

''No survivors, then?''

''I don't know . . . probably not. It killed people on a highway, too.''

''Miami Air, did you say?'' Somewhere he had a vague memory about Miami Air, but what was it? ''Who's going?''

''John Phelps is in the IIC position this week. I'm not sure of the others yet. This just came in.''

''Thanks for telling me.'' The usual adrenalized rush of excitement had hit him, then as quickly escaped. Thanks to Farris, he was truly a man without a mission.

In his FAA office one floor above the NTSB, Bill Caldwell took the news of Miami Air's crash with a stoic expression, calmly closed the door to his office, and immediately picked up the phone to send one of his more trusted subordinates to Miami. That task complete, he sent his secretary on an unnecessary errand, and once she had gone, quickly took her telephone log to his desk, flipping through the pages looking for two specific telephone-number entries, a pen of the same color ink poised in his right hand. The man who had elevated him to associate administrator had left the FAA several years back, but was still a close friend. In fact, there was a network of recent alumni from the senior executive service positions of the FAA with whom he kept in touch. Two of them had gone to work for Frank Lorenzo's Texas Air group as instant vice-presidents. Two others—including his mentor—had ended up in control of a small airline in south Florida. An airline called Miami Air.

It was snowing lightly when Joe arrived home. He loved snow, and the dusky beauty of a snowy afternoon. But only the gray of the darkening skies matched his mood. He had never been truly in professional jeopardy from the Board's chairman before. He had disagreed occasionally with whoever occupied the office, but he had never been threatened. True, as a government worker he would be hard as hell to fire. He could always find another government position with his GM-15 rating, but he realized, perhaps too late, that for him there was only one right answer to the question: "And what do you do?" "I," he had always said, "am an accident investigator for the National Transportation Safety Board." Could that really come to an end?

Damn that stupid egomaniac academic anyway! He needed to think, but first he intended to destroy a bottle of wine. The radio tower lights from nearby Cheltenham Naval Communications Station were a welcome sight as he took the nonmilitary fork in the road south of Andrews Air Force Base and motored the final mile to his house, looking forward to a fire in the fireplace and a view of the countryside through the sliding glass door onto his patio.

The thought of Susan Kelly's offer tugged at him a bit, but he wanted to lick his wounds in private—which was more or less what he had said to her when she had stormed into his office with the assurance that she and the other Board members were going to confront Farris and try to reverse his decision.

"Susan, I really appreciate it."

"We need you, Joe."

"Farris doesn't."

"We're going to change that."

"Susan, at least make sure Andy doesn't drop the medical matter. I'm not supposed to even talk to him."

"That's bull. Farris can't issue such an order."

"Well, he sure did."

"We'll see. Meanwhile, let me take you out to dinner tonight, Mr. Wallingford."

Joe had struggled with the decision. He was exhilarated when he was around her, and the offer was tempting, but the harpoon from Farris had lodged too deep to enjoy an evening with her properly. Susan confused him, his feelings about her uncertain, his conduct around her becoming more guarded lest he treat her like something other than a colleague. Not tonight. Not when his guard was down. She would be too easy to turn to for solace of a more physical kind, and that could wreck their friendship.

"Not tonight, Susan," he said, trying to force a grin, "I have a heartache."

She had laughed easily and then stopped, looking him in the eye with her head slightly tilted, as if trying to fathom a deeper meaning behind that line. "Okay, then come to my place and I'll try to remember how to cook something. I make some of the best TV dinners this side of the Monongahela River."

"No. Really. But a rain check would be appreciated."

"You've got it, Joe." She got up and headed out the door, stopping then and turning back to him. "Do me a favor. Promise you won't make any rash decisions until we've talked, okay?"

"Like shooting Farris? Don't worry, I won't."

The memory of that brief conversation kept playing in his mind as he uncorked the bottle of German Moselle wine he'd been saving for nearly three months and listened to CNN's latest coverage of the Miami Air crash while he worked on building a fire. The media's facts were subject to change, but the accident aircraft was apparently one of the older 737s, and that was a problem, since by now they should all have been rebuilt. The FAA's change to a stringent philosophy of rebuilding certain parts at predetermined times in the life of an older jet was supposed to solve the problem, and had—until now. One hundred twenty-one dead, scattered over the countryside just like the Pan Am crash in Scotland back in 1988, but this time no initial indication of a bomb.

Once the fire caught, Joe closed the damper slightly to smoke up the room a bit, giving it the aroma of a smoky mountain cabin—a procedure Brenda used to hate. He turned off the TV then and settled into the recliner chair, the curtains onto the patio open, facing the snowy scene outside—a scene which suddenly included a figure emerging from the shadows and moving to the glass of the sliding door to stare in, her form feminine and her breath fogging the glass.

"Susan!" Joe was on his feet in an instant, fumbling slightly with the balky latch, sliding the glass open for her then as she stamped the snow off her boots.

"Hi. I'm not very good at taking no for an answer," she said, holding up a large paper bag emitting delicious aromas.

"Apparently." He closed the door and took her coat, a stylish camel hair, ankle-length affair with fur trim around the sleeves, collar, and hem. She looked like a fashion model in it, he thought. Especially with her snow-flecked auburn hair.

"Dinner, in case you're interested. I hope you like Chinese food."

"Sure."

"Good. Where is your kitchen?" Joe pointed and Susan disappeared in that direction, her voice bending back around the corner.

"I see you're a good housekeeper, Mr. Wallingford."

"It used to bother Brenda."

"Your wife?"

"My former wife."

"I knew that." She popped her head around the corner to look at him. "Or, of course, I wouldn't be here."

She was back in minutes with a loaded tray, the open wine bottle he had left on the counter, and a glass for herself.

"Aren't you going to ask the lady why she's invaded your privacy?"

"I'm just glad you're here. Being alone ain't all it's cracked up to be."

"Sometimes it is," she said, licking a dab of spilled sweet and sour sauce off her finger. "I like my privacy, part of the time. But I like to share my privacy, if that makes any sense." They sat on the couch and balanced the tray between them, digging at the individual cardboard food containers.

"By the way, I, ah, have never asked you about your husband," Joe said, having heard she had lost him years before.

"Story of my life, you mean?"

"Love to hear it."

"Only in brief. I've other things we should talk about, too." Susan sipped her wine and looked at Joe until he felt slightly uncomfortable, the eye contact downright intimate.

"My husband never was, Joe. People just assume I was married. But I was only engaged."

"I didn't know."

"Course not. Anyway, my fiancé and I were childhood sweethearts back in Des Moines. We met in grade school, always best friends, grew up together, more or less always knew we'd get married, but weren't in a rush. He looked around, I looked around, but we always came back to each other." She paused, watching him, gauging his interest.

"So what happened?"

"Vietnam happened. His family was an Air Force family. Father, uncles, everyone former Air Force flyers. He had to do the same thing, and when he graduated from pilot training, he was assigned to F-105 Thunderchiefs and rotated to Da Nang. I was really proud of him. Later he flew F-4s with Chappie James and Robin Olds, before they became generals, in what was called the Wild Weasels."

"I'm familiar with that mission," Joe said. "They're the ones who went out looking for North Vietnamese antiaircraft missile installations, getting them to fire, then flying back down the radar beam to wipe out the control trailer."

"That's right. As happened to too many of them, that big twin-engine jet didn't get him home one night, and he punched out somewhere around the DMZ. His backseater never got out, as far as we know. His wingman picked up an emergency beacon and a brief voice message indicating he was safe on the ground, but before the rescue choppers could get in the next morning, the beacon, and my fiancé, were gone."

"Killed?"

She sighed, her smile drooping slightly. "I'm convinced now that I'll never know, Joe. I rather hope so, but we got word he had been captured. This was in 1968, mind you. All those years I watched with his parents for his name to be on a list somewhere, other than the missing-in-action list. It never showed up. There was never an accounting. To this day I don't know, although I've asked many returnees, and some were convinced they had seen him in the same compound in Hanoi. Anyway, we finally got his name on the memorial, and I still have trouble visiting it."

Susan was looking out at the snow, her legs pulled under her as he had seen her do before, much as a cat curls up before a warm fire. "In some ways I've never given up." She looked at him suddenly. "But don't get the impression that I'm carrying an eternal torch, Joe. I felt cheated for the life we never had, but he belongs to the past."

"Susan, you're . . ." Joe caught himself for a moment, but decided the caution wasn't necessary. After all, she was here. "You're such a warm, caring person to be around—not to mention a real knockout, lady—"

"Sure, Joe. I bet you say that to all the Board members."

They both laughed easily. "No, just the sexy ones. But I had wondered why you weren't married."

"That's not the reason, Joe. Oh sure, the first few years after Operation Homecoming, after the prisoners came home, I held out hope and just wasn't interested in anyone else. Since then, it's simply been a case of the right guy never coming along, a growing career, and miles to go before I sleep . . . with anybody." She was looking up at him slightly, a sultry look, he decided, smiling, her beautiful eyes saying very disturbing, very provocative things to him, whether she knew it or not. And he had the unsettling feeling that she did indeed know it.

Susan carried the empty boxes back to the kitchen then, searching for coffee and figuring out how to work his grinder and coffee maker while he stood in the doorway and watched her, his eyes following the contours of her well-proportioned body beneath another of her flowing, silky dresses that were at once businesslike and revealing. She obviously kept herself in good shape, in trim shape. Seldom-used logistic and procedural strategies for maneuvering a date into more intimate positions were replaying in his mind, the thoughts amusing as well as disturbing. That surely wasn't the way she meant the evening to go. They were just friends, colleagues, right? But she was so comfortable to be around. No, not comfortable, invigorating. Inviting. Seductive.

"I rounded up the other three members this afternoon for a war council, Joe," she was saying as she worked on the coffee. "I gave them a rundown of what had happened, how I've watched this thing unfold, and the things that Dean said to me when I confronted him earlier in the day with the question of why he was pounding you."

"What did he say, by the way?"

She looked over her left shoulder with a knowing smile. "He told me too much. He told me, basically, that he's allowing external pressure from the airline and the FAA to massively influence our investigation. He's told me enough to nail him to the wall." She turned back to the coffee. "So, that's just what we're going to do. Tomorrow, all four of us have requested the dubious pleasure of his company at an eleven o'clock closed Board meeting, and I intend to rip him a new tail pipe."

"Are you sure your fiancé wasn't in the Navy?"

She laughed at that. "Seriously, he's still leader, but we have some leverage, and not the least of that is a mutual trip over to the White House, although I think that's unprecedented. He's scared of the White House staff. Thinks they'll block his reappointment next year."

They took the coffee back to the couch and talked awhile, watching the snow, Susan finding the switch for the yard lights, discovering that they illuminated the snowstorm better than the porch light, painting a wintry scene of soft beauty, especially with the interior lights off. When she returned to the couch, it was to sit beside him, touching his leg with her knee, looking at him so long without words that there was no longer a need to wonder what to do. The feel of her hair in his hands as he pulled her gently to him, the taste of her, was like waking from a long sleep. Susan pulled away slightly after a while, her face aglow with the reflection of the fire, her hand on his cheek, a chuckle in her soft voice. "This is going to get complicated, you know," she said, smiling.

"I sincerely hope so," Joe replied.

20

Thursday, December 6

In his parents' North Dallas home, Ron Timson quietly pulled a chair up to the folding doors separating the living room from the den, straining to hear the worrisome conversation filtering through from the other side. The 9 A.M. visit had caught him off guard, but he had recognized the chairman of his father's airline, David Bayne, from pictures and television coverage. Ron had never seen such a powerful man in his parents' home before. He was at a loss to know what to do—how to protect his folks. What *could* a nineteen-year-old college student do, anyway, other than provide moral support, which he knew in advance his father would reject, as always. Dick Timson needed no one, and neither should he. All his life that message had been hammered into Ron.

The level of the voices rose momentarily, making the words easier to understand, the effort blocking for a moment his concurrent urge to be with his mother, who had entered Baylor hospital two days before. Bayne was questioning his father, probably about the crash. He didn't seem mad, he seemed worried. And his father had been pensive, almost resigned, when Bayne had appeared on their doorstep.

". . . a lot riding on this. We took a hell of a beating . . . Kansas City hearing this week. Are . . . your assurance, without question . . . order to stand behind you." It was spotty, but Bayne's words, what he could hear of them, were painting a picture of wavering trust.

His father's voice was even harder to hear.

". . . everything I know . . . remember about it. It had to be the . . . whether Airbus acknowledges it or not."

At long last the sounds of chair legs scraping across a hardwood floor and leather shoes striding toward the front door were unmistakable, and Ron hurriedly got up from his listening post, replacing the chair, waiting for the doors to open after Mr. Bayne had left.

The sound of their grandfather clock blended with the sound of a powerful car engine and tires on gravel fading into the distance. It was a cold day outside, and the central heater clicked on suddenly, the rushing air masking all other noise.

There was no sound from the front hallway, and Ron forced himself to move in that direction, opening the den door at last, seeing his father standing with his right hand still on the knob of the closed front door, head down, saying nothing.

"Dad? Are you okay?"

Dick Timson didn't answer for the longest time, leaving his son in a quandary before turning slowly back into the lushly decorated interior of the colonial house his father had paid for and his mother had lovingly made into a warm and distinctive home. "I'm fine," he said simply.

Ron followed him back into the living room, standing and feeling awkward as his father sat heavily in the armchair his mother had purchased years ago over her husband's vitriolic objections. They couldn't afford it, he had raged. But we must have furniture if we're going to entertain, she had replied, and the argument that ensued had left both mother and eavesdropping young son in tears.

Ron moved forward a few steps.

"Dad? What's happening?"

Timson looked up and sighed, replying at last, "I wish I knew."

"I mean, why was Mr. Bayne here?"

"To see if I'm a bomb that's going to explode in their faces."

There was silence again as Ron worked up the courage to ask more.

"Are . . . is your job . . . ?"

"Are they going to fire me? Is that what you're trying to ask?"

"Yes sir."

"Eventually." Ron suddenly realized his father's face was down in his hands, and the man was actually crying . . . crying softly, but crying. A wave of utter disgust rolled over him for a moment, the memory of a thousand buck-up-and-act-like-a-man lectures ringing in his memory. Was this how a man acted? All the times he had choked back tears as a little boy so his father wouldn't rage at him, be disappointed in him, be disgusted with him, or stand him against a wall and yell at him—were they lies? Ron struggled to get past the feeling, sitting down finally opposite his father, studying him as if he had never before had permission to do so. His hair was a lot thinner than Ron recalled, as was his overall physique. It hurt to realize his father was looking old. Old and drawn and defeated, with none of the fire and determination he had always seen. He had always been terrified of this strong, dynamic, successful man. Terrified of his rages and his dislikes, of triggering his displeasure. As terrified as his mother had always been, though she was more anxious to please.

"Dad? It'll be okay. It'll work out."

The words were muffled, but the reply was clear enough because he had never heard such words from this man. "Do you really think so, son?" No sarcasm, no questions about who gave him the right to have an opinion, but a genuine question in return. What his father was feeling was fright. And he was asking his son's advice.

"Yes sir, it will. You didn't do anything wrong with that plane. Mom said you didn't, you told them you didn't. They can't blame it on you, they have no evidence. And even if they were to push you out as chief pilot, you can go back to the line."

Timson shook his head in the negative.

"Well, you have your retirement, and possibly medical retirement. We'll be okay. You'll be okay. Dad, please don't worry."

Dick Timson looked up and saw a thin young man with a tortured expression staring into his soul. "It's more than the crash, Ron. They tore my performance as chief pilot apart, they . . . they destroyed me as a manager, and that's what I've tried so hard to be. They destroyed the way I tried—one guy even claimed I was tough because I was scared and in over my head." Father and son looked at each other, in some ways for the first time.

"Were you, Dad?"

Dick Timson started to respond with knee-jerk phraseology.

But it didn't work anymore, it wouldn't come. Ron saw him shake his head sadly. "I guess so."

"The plane crash, it didn't have anything to do with . . . with our accident?"

"No!" The intensity of the response was a shock, his father's volume too loud. His voice quieted again, Dick Timson diverting his gaze out the window. "No, it didn't. No connection. Impossible." He looked back at Ron, pleading, not demanding. "And don't, son, don't ever mention that incident again . . . please."

"Are you going to see Mom?"

Dick Timson looked away again, holding his chin in his left hand, elbow propped on the chair arm. "A little later. I've got to call her doctor. He told me this morning it was nothing but hyperventilation, but they want to keep her a few days for observation."

"I know it wasn't her heart, but I couldn't believe she just hyperventilated. She was out cold, chest heaving, cold and clammy . . ."

"She's been under a lot of stress, son. I guess I've put too much pressure on her for too long." He looked back at Ron. "Keep that in mind when you marry. Women are weak. Your mother is weak. Always has been."

Ron Timson had grown disgusted with that attitude. But he had also grown up with it. Females are weak, females are incompetent, females can do nothing right without constant male guidance. But somewhere deep inside he had always known it was a fraud. It had been, he had finally realized, his mother who had held everything together singlehandedly for so long, and that had taken more strength than either her husband or son could muster. Slowly, too slowly, he had come to see it, but it took being away at college and looking back—as well as the horror of the last two months. What was that quotation from Thoreau? The "mass of men lead lives of quiet desperation"? Most women too, he figured. Especially his mother.

But what on earth was the matter with her now?

At that moment thirteen miles to the south at the sprawling Baylor Medical Center in Dallas, Dr. Mark Weiss was consulting a scrap of paper with the number of Louise Timson's room as he walked toward the main entrance. His wife, Kim, had been born in this hospital, and they had once rushed Aaron to its emergency room with a deep cut on his leg. How clearly he remembered that night! Mark found himself casually wondering what they were doing at that moment, Kim, Aaron, and Greg, his mental guard down, as if there had been no crash, and the flames of Kansas City had been only a nightmare from which he had now awakened.

The crushing reality settled in again, all the more painful for having been pushed so far away for a fleeting second. The most innocent things could trigger that painful cycle of forgetting, then remembering. Many times in the previous weeks that recurring mental jolt had shattered his self-control, forcing him to find a quiet corner on a bench, or to pull off to the side of the road. He had dealt with that reaction in patients many times over the years, always—he knew now—too glibly. He had never really understood the depth of the pain, the heart-stopping suddenness of the mental impact, until now.

But they weren't waiting for him at home, nor would they be ever again. He had to remember that clearly enough to be able to deal with it . . . and go on.

Mark fought the memories down faster this time, thinking instead about the economic disaster his psychology practice had become in Kansas City, and of his harassed receptionist who'd had to cancel two months of appointments with no end in sight. His accounts were running dry, though Kim had held some life insurance. He would not worry about the money. This was a quest, not an obsession, and he would have to get back to a professional schedule sometime.

The antiseptic aroma of hospital corridors met Mark Weiss's nose as he made his way through a surprisingly thick throng of people to the bank of elevators, bound for the sixth floor. It had been a stroke of luck that his call to the Timson residence had been answered by their son. He doubted Captain Timson would have told him anything.

He got off on the sixth floor and walked resolutely to and past the proper door, noting that it was open and only Mrs. Timson was within. He had expected to see her at her husband's side in Kansas City at the hearing. But she had never shown up, which deepened the mystery of what was going on in the woman's mind.

Mark walked to the nurses' station and identified himself as Dr. Weiss, here to look in on Louise Timson. The bored young woman handed over the chart without further question, several other people vying for her divided attention simultaneously.

He examined the records and the negative findings of coronary damage, steady EKG, pathology and other parameters, all the time feeling his stomach tighten. The woman had collapsed from an apparent heart attack at home, But it wasn't a heart attack. It was hyperventilation, which could be many things, including an attack of acute anxiety.

He replaced the chart and walked to her room.

"Mrs. Timson?"

The voice was slow in answering, but firm and controlled. "Yes?"

"I'm Dr. Mark Weiss. May I come in?"

They chatted amiably for a few minutes about innocuous things, Mark trying to anticipate her eventual reaction to his real purpose. There were a few flower arrangements in the room, but otherwise she was alone and unacknowledged, and she confirmed that her husband was not due to visit for several hours.

"Louise, I need to tell you who I am and why I'm here. You probably don't recall, but I met you in Kansas City, in the hospital, when I came to talk to your husband just after the accident."

She stayed quiet and studied him, only mild concern showing on her face. "I'm sorry, I don't . . ."

"That's all right. I'm a psychologist who has worked in commercial aviation, and I've been looking into this tragedy, into why it occurred, and staying in touch with the NTSB, although I don't represent them."

Now there was alarm on her face, her eyes darting to the door and back to the chair where he was seated. "I do remember you. You . . . you lost your wife in the crash. Oh my Lord! Your wife and little children. I'm so sorry, Doctor." Tears began to fill her eyes as Mark held out his hand, surprised that she grasped it tightly. "I'm so sorry for your loss."

They sat in silence for a bit, Mark finally breaking it. "I desperately need to understand what happened, Louise."

She nodded, her lips pursed tightly together, saying nothing.

"I need, especially, to know why you are so very deeply upset." He kept his voice calm and even, hoping for an even reaction from her, but expecting worse. Her calm reply caught him unprepared. "I can't."

"I'm sorry, I don't understand."

"I . . . I can't tell you the reason, Doctor Weiss. But I can tell you that my husband did not cause the crash."

"You can't tell me the cause of the crash, or why you've been so badly affected?"

"Neither."

More silence, Louise Timson closing her eyes, still gripping Mark's hand tightly. They fluttered open at last, her voice a whisper. "I can't. I can't tell you . . . it's . . . it's . . ."

"What?"

Her eyes closed again, her head starting a series of back and forth jerks, slowly at first, then more rapidly. "No. I can't. Only my priest."

"Are you telling me, Louise, that somehow you're responsible? That you did something? That's how you've been acting."

Her hand pulled away, both hands folding over her breasts protectively. "I can never tell you. It would hurt Dick. But he's not responsible. I am."

The need for professional balance competing with the burning personal need to know fought a rapid battle in Mark's mind, the professional training winning out.

"Okay. I'll stop asking." Mark took his business card and placed it in her hand, folding her fingers back over it.

"Keep this in a safe place, please. When you're ready, I'll be here. I'll come back, anytime, day or night."

She nodded finally, and Mark got to his feet with great reluctance, all his gut instincts crying out for more questions, crying out that he should yank the answers from her if necessary.

"One more thing. And you remember this, please. You're not responsible. No one person can be responsible for such a thing. It is a chain of causes, okay? Whatever it is you think you did, the crash might have occurred even if you were not involved."

There was no nod, just her sad and tear-filled eyes.

"Do you want me to go now?" he asked, hoping she'd say no. But Louise Timson nodded slowly.

"You'll call me when . . . if . . . you're ready?"

"Yes."

On the way back to his car Mark thought about calling Joe Wallingford or Andy Wallace, or perhaps Susan Kelly again. She certainly understood the situation from his perspective. Working with her had been a pleasure, but both she and Andy had warned him that Joe would be hard to convert, or to convince that human motivations and breakdowns were the most important key in the aviation-safety equation.

He had not been able to get Joe alone during the Kansas City hearing. Suddenly, the idea of driving straight to DFW Airport and flying to Washington made as much sense as anything else. When he stopped and thought about it, he really had nowhere else to go that wouldn't bring back the same wrenching cycle of memories. Mark stopped at a phone booth and phoned Wallingford, making an appointment for Friday morning, then checked to make sure the tape cassette and supporting papers from a certain telephone call to Kansas City were still in his briefcase. It was time to show Joe what they were really dealing with.

It had been a genuine effort all day long to keep his mind on business, the sweet memory of Susan Kelly in his arms the night before drawing him away from even the panic he felt over the threat to his NTSB job. She had caught him awake in the middle of the night, leaning on one elbow, studying the curves of her face as she slept in satisfied warmth. Her eyes had fluttered open, meeting his, a sly smile painting her features as she asked, "What are you doing, sir?" in a sensuous voice that brought him to attention again.

"I almost can't believe you're real. I don't want to miss a moment of this," he had said, melting into her smile, and her arms, once more.

Senator Martinson had invited Joe to a late lunch Thursday morning, and without checking to see how Susan's confrontation with Farris had turned out, he left the office at 2 P.M. to meet him, driving the short distance to a quiet restaurant north of the White House in a little under an hour, Washington midday traffic and scarce parking places taking their toll on his patience.

Kell greeted him with genuine pleasure and escorted him back to a private dining room where the two of them could talk in obscurity. Normally being entertained by a senator would have been a cause for quiet pride, but too much was happening, and Kell had already become a friend and a professional asset in Joe's estimation. He had called the senator a week before the hearing to plead for help penetrating the stone wall the Defense Department had thrown up around the Brilliant Pebbles project and the radar tracking unit.

"Any word, Kell, on the radar?"

Martinson shook his head. "Not yet. I'm pushing hard to find out, though. But that's not why I called. I want to bounce some ideas off you, totally off the record for both of us, of course."

He had, he said, been fascinated with the hearing, the investigation, and the dedication of the staff members. But he saw problems, and needed help in defining them.

"Such as?"

"Well, North America is only one investigation among many you're running, Joe. There are, at last count, about three hundred of you at the Board, both in Washington and in the field. How on earth can you take care of all these aviation accidents, as well as handle all the rail, sea, pipeline, and whatever else—"

"Highway."

"Yeah, highway accidents. How can you keep up?"

Joe looked at Kell, smiling. "It's very simple. We can't and we don't. We give most of them as much attention as we can, concentrate on the spectacular ones, and the rest go begging. A lot go begging."

"Give me some details."

Alarm bells had gone off in Joe's head as soon as the subject had come up. This was Dean Farris's area of responsibility. He would have a fit if he saw Joe lunching with the very senator that helped control NTSB purse strings, let alone heard what Joe had just said.

"Kell, uh, I've got a problem talking about this stuff."

The senator looked surprised. "Why? I'm cleared for security."

"It's not that. Look, I'm already in trouble with Dean Farris." Joe told him the story of the past few months and the rising tensions between them, leaving out the details of pressure from the FAA and North America. "Basically, he's interfering at will for reasons I don't consider valid, but he is the boss, as everyone keeps pointing out to me. He was madder than hell that I invited you in as an observer without going through normal protocol—"

Kell had smiled at last. "I hate normal protocol. Gets in the way."

"Yeah, I agree, but he doesn't. But what I'm getting to . . . if he found I'd been criticizing the Board and exposing the internal workings to you, I'd be gone for sure."

"Hmmm." The senator stared at the wall in thought for awhile, tapping a half-eaten breadstick on the table. He turned back to Joe at last. "I appreciate your position, Joe, but your Board needs reform, and though I can't guarantee I can protect you, I would sure try."

"I understand, but I'm not political, Kell, I'm just an investigator."

"Okay"—Kell had his hand up—"okay, but I want you to think about this. If you love your job and this Board as much as I think you do, you know damn well there are a parcel of things that need to be changed. Not just more money. You see, I'm considered a liberal Republican because I think certain problems can only be solved by a combination of governmental restructuring *and* money. You need more money, but I need to figure out what else. The NTSB hasn't been restructured in sixteen years, and I personally think you're in trouble."

"You have good information sources."

"Well, part of it is from observing your operations these last few months, and part of it is the work of one part-timer on my staff who knows a few things about accident investigation."

"Who?"

"Not yet, Joe. I want you to promise you'll consider helping, with the understanding that you could lose your job despite my protection."

Martinson was sincere, he was sure of that, but the invitation was too dangerous. If he could outlast the problems he had already created with Farris and stay in his position, with Susan Kelly's scintillating presence just down the hall, well, that was as close to a heaven as he could imagine. Politics and changing the world was for others, like the energetic and impressive senator across the table from him.

"I'll promise only that I'll consider it," Joe said at last.

"Good. Very good. I should add that if you did help us, Farris would probably not find out, though I can't guarantee that either."

"Uh, Kell, I should tell you Farris pulled me off the Kansas City investigation yesterday."

"Why?"

"Because I won't ignore the strange reaction of North America to our probing of the captain's medical records, nor will I simply ignore the unanswered questions about the radar unit."

"Joe, I promised I'd get an absolute answer on the radar unit, and I'm trying. But I really don't believe they're lying. The risks

would be enormous, lying to Congress, I mean. I can't imagine
why they'd do it. I'm assured, by the highest Pentagon authorities I deal with as a member of the Armed Services Committee,
that the unit was not operating.''

Joe looked him in the eye, knowing the senator was sincere.
''I guess I just need to be . . . sure beyond, you know, a shadow
of a doubt.''

''Give me time. I'm also fighting one hell of problem with
the Pebbles project and the SDI purists, and . . . there's still the
ticking bomb of my presence at the airport.''

''What's happening with that?'' Jeff Perkins's words echoed
in Joe's mind, but that was a private communiqué.

''They may prosecute me, Joe, which is small potatoes compared to what's going to happen when this leaks to the media.
So far, as Cynthia points out, I've been very, very lucky no
enterprising newsman has picked up on it and done a little home-
work. But it's just a matter of time. Hell, when the other mem-
bers of the committee find out, they're going to come unglued.
Cynthia wants me to hold a press conference and come clean.
I'm not ready to commit political suicide quite yet, but I guess
I'm toying with the inevitable. I just don't know how my con-
stituents will react, nor my colleagues, for that matter.'' Kell
Martinson sighed, raised his eyebrows, and sat back in the chair.
''I guess I should have also said that my offer depends on whether
I remain in office. I could be destroyed for reelection if it hits
the fan. I tell you, to have something so innocent blow up so
completely in my face, literally and figuratively . . .''

A waiter poked his head in the room with a full coffeepot, but
Kell waved him off. ''The only good thing was finding my aide—
the young lady—had *not* been on the plane.''

''I'd like to meet her someday,'' Joe said with thoughts of
Susan dancing through his head.

Kell smiled a broad smile that kept widening until he realized
he was beaming and pulled it back down a notch. ''Make a deal
with you, Joseph. You come help me, and I'll introduce you to
my second-wife-to-be.'' Provided, he thought to himself, I can
pull her off the fence and up to an altar somewhere.

21

John Tarvin had commuted the forty miles from his home near Leavenworth, Kansas, to the NTSB hearings at Kansas City Airport for both days of the proceedings on Monday and Tuesday, sitting anonymously in the audience each day, hoping to hear something in the testimony that would defuse his growing anxiety. He had read every news report he could get his hands on since the night of the disaster, and was painfully aware of the suspicions that the mobile radar tracking unit—the 90,000 pound oversized vehicle built by the defense contractor that employed him in Leavenworth—had caused the crash. Tarvin had hoped it was all a ploy by Larry Wilkins's radical group, almost convincing himself that the Air Force and Department of Defense denials were believable. But then there had been the article about the suspicious power interruption recorded in the control tower, and Tarvin had read those words with sinking heart and knotted stomach. The time of the interruption couldn't be coincidental! He was devastatingly sure of that.

Only a handful of people in the world knew he had been in the driver's compartment and was the operator of the mobile radar unit the night of the crash, and not one of that small group knew the whole story—his wife included. The dilemma of whether to tell someone else, breaching security and losing his job, was tearing him apart. Tuesday and Wednesday nights had been sleepless as well, as he had paced his way into the early hours of Thursday, deciding at last to wait one more week. If it had not been solved by then, he told himself, he would have to act.

* * *

With morning sunlight penetrating the bedroom, Susan Kelly stretched luxuriously, an unseen smile caressing her face, a soft hum of contentment masked by the sounds of rustling sheets as she rolled over and reached for Joe—who was not there. Susan opened her eyes suddenly, emerging reluctantly from her sultry dreams of Joe Wallingford and realizing a day had passed since she had left his bed. She was alone in her apartment, and regretting it.

Within an hour Susan was turning her car into the entrance of the FAA building's underground parking garage, negotiating the 90-degree left turn and pulling up in front of the parking attendant's station. Two members of the perpetually unsmiling and unfriendly garage staff took her keys without comment, one of them plunking himself disgustedly in the front seat. That usually irritated her, but not this particular morning. In a far corner Susan had already noticed the familiar car she had been unconsciously searching for when she entered the garage. Its presence meant Joe was already in the building, and that was a happy thought that eclipsed any other. For someone as meticulous as she, the unstructured jumble of her feelings for Joe and what had developed between them should have been upsetting. For one thing, no one at the Board could know—the gossip would be ferocious. But she was aglow, not, perhaps with love, but she was definitely falling "in like"—a term she used to hate. Yes, she admitted to her pragmatic self, her infatuation with Joe was unstructured, directionless, in part sexually motivated, presumptuous, perhaps improper, and definitely professionally dangerous, but the truth was, she hadn't felt as good—or as feminine—in many years.

Susan checked her watch, clearing her head, noting the fact that she was uncharacteristically a half hour later than normal, the careful drive through snowy, commuter-clogged streets from her apartment now blessedly behind her, a major showdown with Dean Farris ahead of her. The chairman had postponed yesterday's meeting, but this morning she and the other Board members would corner and confront him over his scandalous and unprofessional handling of Joe.

And somehow the apprehension she expected in anticipation of that showdown wasn't there. Instead she felt calm and content and optimistic, especially when she entered her large corner office on the eighth floor and noticed the small object sitting squarely in the middle of her desk blotter: a tiny crystal vase delicately holding a single red rose. There was no card, and none was needed.

At that moment the former IIC of the North America investigation sat in his office halfway across the building reading through a pile of newspaper clippings supplied by Beverly Bronson. North America had suddenly filed suit against Airbus on Wednesday, claiming the flight controls had caused the crash and trying to gain the upper hand in the public relations battle over who to blame. The announcement came late Thursday afternoon from Dallas. Either the captain's control stick, the suit charged (according to the *New York Times*), was defective, or the system had not been "hardened" against outside electromagnetic interference, and in any case Airbus had failed to warn them of the risks. North America had voluntarily grounded all its nineteen remaining A320s as of Friday morning for inspections of the system. What fools, Joe thought. Not a shred of evidence or even a clue where to start looking for defects—what to inspect—and they jeopardize their entire investment to hit back at Airbus for public effect. Joe was thoroughly disgusted, not that he hadn't seen such corporate maneuvering before. North America's leadership had obviously decided to build a wall around Captain Timson, who, of course, could not be at fault. Joe had shared that opinion at first too, but now . . .

The phone broke his train of thought.

"Joe?" The voice was John Phelps's, the line obviously long distance. Joe had to race mentally to recall that John had just deployed on the Go Team to the Miami Air crash in Florida.

"John? That you?"

"Yes. Joe, go to Dankers Bar and Grill, and tell Karen you're there." John Phelps fell silent.

"What? Say that again, John?"

"Joe, trust me, and do exactly what I'm asking. I'll explain later. Dankers. And Karen, one of the waitresses. The one I took to that party last year . . . ?"

"Yeah, yeah, I remember Karen, but why?"

"Just go." And the line was dead.

Joe sat back in his chair. Now what? His eyes roamed over the bookcase to his left, the space between two looseleaf folders catching his attention for some reason. There should be a book there, a book someone had borrowed. Oh yeah, he thought, that's the aging fleet material. I lent that to . . . John Phelps.

Joe was out of his chair in an instant, grabbing his topcoat and heading for the nearby watering hole through another light snowfall. He wondered what Susan was doing and found himself longing to tell her about John Phelps's curious request. First, however, he'd comply with it.

"Oh yes, Mr. Wallingford. There's a message he had me write down." Karen handed Joe a slip of paper and a glass of water and disappeared.

"Please call J. P. immediately at 305-463-9667," the note read. "Bill it to your home number only. Do not use an agency credit card."

Curiouser and curiouser, Joe thought. There was a pay phone near the rest rooms through the doors on the Sixth Street side, and Joe headed for it, punching in his personal telephone credit card number, listening for the first ring. The phone was answered immediately.

"Joe?"

"Yeah. John, is this you?"

"Yes."

"Why all the secret agent stuff? Where are you?" Joe could hear cars in the background.

"At a pay phone by a highway near the crash site. Joe, I've got a big, big problem. In fact, we may all have a big problem."

"Explain that."

"I heard about what happened between you and Dean, but you're still division chief, so it's still proper to report to you, right?"

"Of course, John. But I . . ."

"And you're now the last person who's going to go running to the chairman, right? I need your word on that, Joe."

This was getting exasperating. "Get to the damn point, John. Of course you've got my word."

"Okay. Joe, you remember that I came down here when this airline had a cabin-pressure failure on another Boeing 737 a few months back?"

"Vaguely."

"The same day North America crashed. I was worried because the blowout was caused by really poor maintenance, and

I wanted to find out more, but the FAA local office in Miami began blocking me, and then Dean ordered me off of it, claiming the FAA had it under control.''

"Had what under control?"

"Quality control inspections of how well these people in Key West were repairing their old 737s. Okay, then I heard the repair work was being done offshore, in Bogota, Colombia, at a repair station recently certified by the FAA to do the rebuilds ordered after the aging fleet inspections. You know, where the FAA decided that certain parts of the airplane will be completely rebuilt and refurbished when it hits a certain age, rather than letting the airline just watch it for deterioration?"

"Yeah, I'm familiar with all that, John."

"Okay, Joe. We've got a bunch of folks dead down here and a 737 that came apart in the air at 24,000 feet on climb out. No indication of a bomb, and, in fact, it's beginning to look a lot like the Far Eastern Airlines accident in Taiwan in 1982, where the bottom blew out because they're been sloshing salt water down there from fish tanks carried as cargo."

"Okay. So?"

"So, the FAA-inspected maintenance logs on this airplane—which I retrieved when I got down here yesterday—show this airplane was rebuilt according to the FAA's airworthiness directives issued in 1988 and 1989, and the work was done in Colombia and signed off. The FAA team in Miami has supposedly been inspecting the work on Miami Air's planes once they got back here, but as we know, that mostly means looking at paperwork, which appears to be in order. Now, bear with me."

"I am," Joe replied, intrigued but wishing he would get on with it.

"The skin at one particular location in first class, station 390, should have a brand-new piece of metal behind it. That's required to be installed during the major teardown and rebuild of that section. Now, I've got that very piece of metal in my hand this second, Joe, picked up at the crash site. This piece of metal should be two years old, no more. Joe, this piece is at least twenty-two years old, and so are all the other pieces I've found that should be brand-new!"

"Are you sure?"

"Yes. There's no way this type of severe corrosion could occur in less than two years unless they'd been floating the damn plane in salt water and mooring it to a dock. No question. The paper airplane was rebuilt, the metal airplane apparently was not.''

Joe thought for a second, ignoring the sound of bathroom doors opening and closing beside him. "John, that's a major find, of course, but again, why the secrecy?''

"I was told," Phelps began, "when I kept pressing the Miami FAA office, to lay off. Finally I took a friend of mine who works there out to dinner. That was two months ago. I asked him off the record, where is the heat coming from? He told me the next highest level of the FAA, which is Bill Caldwell. This guy says that he and all his people have to be very careful in dealing with Miami Air because the chairman of that company and their operations vice-president are both former FAA officials from Washington, and good buds with Caldwell. Anytime the rank-and-file FAA inspectors out here get after Miami Air for violations of any significance, they get called on the carpet by their boss, and he tells them the heat originates from Washington.''

"That would be hard as hell to prove, John.''

"God help me, Joe, I've actually got a memo of theirs to prove it. And God probably did help me with this one. Joe, listen to this. I don't believe it myself. I forced Miami Air to give me copies of their operations and maintenance manuals, and one of the executives personally delivers his copies when he realizes I'm gonna tear the place apart until they comply. Anyway, I'm sitting there last night in the hotel, and I open one of these large binders and this handwritten memo falls out that's from Miami Air's chairman to his operations VP, talking about this connection, Joe, *and* saying that Caldwell is putting the screws to, quote, 'that professor at the Board' to call off his dogs. Obviously this wasn't meant to be seen, but I've got it! I didn't even put my fingerprints on it, because when it fell out, I had this odd premonition. So I picked it up with latex gloves on, which means the latent fingerprints of whoever wrote it and handled it are still there, and those can be lifted off, probably, by the FBI lab. There is some technique involving ninhydrin that will do it. Joe, this thing was written one day before Farris did, in fact, call me off the case in October.''

"Jesus, John. Those guys haven't been away from the FAA long enough to escape the laws prohibiting that sort of pressure, have they?''

"I don't think so. But Joe, what the hell do I do now? None of the rest of the team knows anything, and I know Dean has his stoolies, so I don't dare trust this memo, or the information, to anyone down here with me. The other head of the structures group is already on the trail of the fraudulently certified repair paper work, but I'm sitting on a bomb."

"Can you copy the heck out of that memo and Fed Ex several to me, then lock up the original?"

"Already done regarding the copies and the original. I'll Fed Ex two copies to you this afternoon, Saturday delivery to your home."

Joe made arrangements to phone John Phelps at his hotel in Naples, Florida, during the evening, and rang off, his head spinning slightly. John's last statement had seemed absurd, but Joe found himself looking around cautiously to check for anyone listening. "Watch yourself, Joe," he'd said. "Watch your backside. There's no telling where this leads."

Joe left Dankers hungry but not noticing as he headed back to his office. Farris was probably involved only as a dupe, which would not be unexpected. So, I'm no match for Caldwell, eh? Well, Professor, neither are you.

The short walk back through the cold air that had blown into the city felt good, but he hardly noticed. There was too much to think about, and in spite of the deeply disturbing overtones, Joe realized there was a certain exhilaration in facing such hidden undercurrents.

The only connection between Miami Air and the North American crash was Caldwell, but a problem obviously existed. The question was, how deep, and what could—or should—he do about it?

Joe slipped behind his desk and immediately dialed Jeff Perkins's number in Kansas City, getting the FBI field office's noncommittal secretary, who took down Joe's name and number.

Agent Perkins himself, however, called him back within ten minutes from somewhere "in the field."

"Joe? Strange timing."

"Which means?"

"I was going to call you. Are you alone?"

"Yes. Why?"

"And no speakerphone, right?"

"That's right. Just my worn out, government-issue telephone

handset and me. You're not going to play secret agent too, are you?''

There was a pause as Perkins considered the non sequitur, then ignored it and continued. "You asked me to look into stock ownership in aircraft manufacturers for one particular individual, and I have—though it took a while to get to it."

"Good . . . I think."

"Well, Joe, your FAA man Caldwell owns no Boeing, McDonnell Douglas, or any other applicable shares, nor did he report any on his federal disclosure forms."

"Okay. Well, I just . . ."

"Hold on. There's more. There *is* an individual rather close to you there who *does* show up on the computer run as owning quite a block."

"Who?"

"First let me tell you what and how much. Not to stretch the suspense, but I want you to understand that I did not get this from the stock records of the companies themselves with any degree of currency, so the information could be out-of-date or faulty. This guy owns five thousand shares of Boeing, and twenty-five hundred shares of McDonnell Douglas, and two hundred shares of Lockheed, and he did *not* list them on his disclosure filing."

"Who, Jeff, who?"

"Dean Farris. Your chairman, buddy."

That stunned him, and Jeff had to ask if he was still there.

"Yeah. Yeah, I just . . . can't believe that . . . if I'm interpreting it correctly."

"If you want me to, Joe, I'll try to verify that with the current company lists, though I could get myself into deep trouble with the Bureau if I go too far with this."

"Please, Jeff. I think I need to know for certain."

"There's another round of incoming fire, Joe. Your man Gardner, the guy with the copy of the FAA tower tape?"

"Uh-oh. Now what." Joe had his hand to his forehead.

"The Bureau ran an analysis of the radio station's copy of the tape and compared it to tapes produced on the cassette recorder the tower chief used to make the copy for Gardner. There were sounds there that matched, but did not come from the master tape."

"In other words . . ."

"The leaked tape was your NTSB copy. I don't know who did it, but it was definitely your copy."

So Gardner had been lying to him. The stupid bastard! "Does Bill Caldwell of the FAA know?"

"I should think so. He asked for our help, I'm told."

Joe thanked his FBI friend profusely, hanging up then as he thought about Gardner. Farris would have to be involved. Since the FAA and the FBI were involved, Joe would have to take it to Farris. Goddamn Gardner! He lied to me. Joe tossed a pencil across the room at the bookcase, knowing Gardner would be finished when this hit the fan. It was no innocent act or white lie, that was certain. Joe knew Nick's background with air traffic control, and he also knew how he'd always had the tendency to want to skewer the FAA for what he felt they had done to him. The other problem was personal. Joe had been in command and had lost control of Nick too. Another debacle that would be credited against Joe's ledger with Farris. The thought canceled what had been the returning hint of an appetite.

Joe was ready to storm from his office in search of Gardner when Mark Weiss appeared in the doorway, explaining there was something very important he needed to discuss, and then shutting Joe's office door behind him as he handed over a sealed mailing envelope.

"What's this, Mark?"

The psychologist studied the edge of Joe's desk for a moment, working on phraseology. Joe noticed he wasn't even removing his topcoat, and the office was warm. Mark looked up at last. "Remember I told you I felt Captain Timson was hiding something?"

"Yes."

Mark raised his hand to forestall protest. "I know you didn't— *couldn't*—officially believe me without proof. I was hoping the hearing would unravel the mystery—"

"Weren't we all."

"Yes, but I mean as to whether Timson made some terrible pilot error and was trying to rewrite reality. Okay. I still don't know what he could have done, but he says he made no error and the airplane is at fault."

Joe held his palm up. "Mark, I'm afraid, despite all the revelations at the hearing, I'm privately convinced the Air Force is lying. All my instincts point to electronic interference and an attempted cover-up, though I'll deny it if you say anything outside this room."

"Maybe, Joe, but I've got proof that Timson has materially misled you on at least one occasion, and I think—"

"What proof? This envelope?"

"Yes. Let me finish. I think I can prove to you that Timson has not regained his memory and is making up what he says happened, or, he knows what happened and is trying to change it."

Joe was intrigued. Proof he could deal with—*relate* to, as they'd say in California. But what sort of proof could Weiss have that would do all that?

Mark explained his frustration after his first visit to Joe's office, omitting the burning temptation he'd had to steal the CVR tape. He told of setting up his recorder in the hotel room, how he had appropriated the name of one of the NTSB lab technicians, and how he knew from Joe's own statements that Andy Wallace would be interviewing the captain within a few hours after his call.

"I knew, Joe, that if the man was making up reality or trying to change it, he would grasp at the phrase I gave him, and it would show up in Andy Wallace's interview." Mark placed a page from the transcript of the interview on the desk, a heavy black circle around a particular Timson answer—one containing the phrase: "My stick's not responding, take it Don, take it!"

Mark opened the envelope then and retrieved the tape. He placed it in the small cassette recorder he had brought and punched the play button.

The sounds of Mark asking the hotel operator for date and time came first, then the sounds of a new number being punched into the phone were followed by a deep, subdued male voice answering on the other end.

"Hello?"

"Is this Captain Timson?" Mark had asked. There was a worrisome hesitation, then a slow response. Not suspicious, just hazy. The man had probably been under pain medication at the time.

"Yes . . . yes it is . . . um . . . who's calling?"

"Captain, this is difficult. I'm Phil Baker from the NTSB laboratory in Washington."

Joe shot Mark a disapproving glance, receiving a determined shrug in response.

"Yes?"

"Well, Andy Wallace is on his way out there to see you, isn't he?"

"Mr. Wallace . . . yes, he's supposed to call when he gets to the airport. Why?"

"Well, it's kind of embarrassing, sir. See, we're the people who transcribe the cockpit voice tapes, and I've been working over the last two days to do just that. I'm under a deadline to have that by this evening, but I'm stuck on one thing, one area where I can't quite make out the words. Now, normally we'd just take more time, but I've already said I could do it by tonight, so I'd like to ask your assistance."

More silence as Timson thought through the words. "What do you need?"

"Captain, the very last of the tape—and I know this is painful for you—but in the last fifteen seconds or so, I think I'm hearing you say, and I quote, 'My stick's not responding, take it Don, take it.' That's the best I can make out. Does that mesh with your memory? Is that what you recall saying?"

Timson was slow responding, but when he did there was more energy behind his voice. "Give . . . give me that again, please."

"Okay. It was, 'My stick's not responding, take it Don, take it.' At least, sir, that's what it sounds like. You'll save me half a day's work if you can confirm that."

"Well . . . I think that's right. I know I must have . . . ah, I know I remember saying that because my controls, you know, weren't doing what they should have . . . should have been doing. Yes . . . I'm sure I remember saying that."

"Excellent. Now I have one more favor to ask."

"Yes?"

"I'd very much appreciate it if you would *not* mention this call to Andy, or Joe, or anyone else. I won't tell you I'd lose my job, because that's not true, but it would be embarrassing."

He heard Timson clear his throat with some effort. "Don't worry. I won't mention it. That's no problem."

"Thank you, Captain. And I hope you're out of there soon and feeling better."

"Thanks." There was the sound of plastic against plastic, the hollow sound a telephone makes when the receiver is being banged against the cradle as someone struggles to put it back on the hook.

Mark snapped off the tape recorder and leaned back. "I figured at that point, Joe, now we'll see what he does. It was the perfect time to plant the seed. I made up the words, of course, using a phrase that would seem to get the captain off the hook— the words of a pilot doing everything he could to save his malfunctioning airplane. They were supposed to sound to Timson like the sort of thing he should have said. Yet a pressured individual like Timson would not realize how unlikely it would be to have such a phrase of helplessness and surrender—a cry for help—emerge from his mouth. Totally uncharacteristic for someone in Timson's position. I figured that if my analysis was correct, that exact phrase would show up word-for-word on the transcript of Andy Wallace's impending interview, and it would prove that Timson was playing games with the truth, grasping at straws, claiming to recall something he couldn't really recall. And you heard how fast he latched on to it."

Joe nodded, still in deep thought as Mark paused, then continued.

"I sealed the tape in a mailing envelope, which you just saw me open, and here's the hotel receipt with the call on it, and the Kansas City phone number, and you saw me take that out at the same time. Plus, remember you heard me get the date and time from the hotel operator before I dialed the call."

The sound of breath being sharply exhaled filled the room.

"Son of a bitch, Mark, you got him all right. I can't endorse your methods . . . that may even be illegal, fraudulently representing—"

"I'll take my chances, Joe. If you want to prosecute, I'll go willingly. But think about what this proves."

Joe nodded and sat back in his chair. "It proves, as you said, that the man is trying to rewrite the record. His reaction, Mark, when he finally did hear the CVR tape, tells it all."

Mark had not heard of Timson's protests to the NTSB that he had been supplied with a faulty transcript of the CVR tape, or his openly voiced suspicion that someone at the NTSB had monkeyed with it to "get" him. Andy ended up taking the actual tape to Timson's house to play it for him before the captain would believe the transcript was legitimate. "We need to talk to Andy about this, but he told me that Timson said he could've sworn he said more at the end. Then he and his airline start acting as if the copilot seized control without authority.''

''What are you going to do about it, Joe?''

Another sigh as Joe diverted his gaze to the bookcase, seeing only Timson's face. ''I don't know. I don't know if we can crack him . . . crack his story. But Mark, if the man's lying, that means he is, as you say, covering up something. Let's think this through a second. Either he's covering up the fact that his memory has not returned—which simply means that he *cannot* guarantee us that he maintained nose-up pressure on the control stick while the airplane was pitching nose down—*or*, he *knows* that for some reason he commanded nose down and the airplane's control system is blameless, which would confirm the Air Force's story.''

''You think North America knows about this?''

Joe shook his head vigorously. ''No way. Look at this.'' He pushed the newspaper clipping about North America's suit against Airbus and their fleet groundings over the desk. ''I can't believe they'd do this if they suspected. Timson's sold them a bill of goods too.''

Joe felt his thoughts racing up and down with different possibilities, knowing he'd have to reexamine every one before acting . . . provided there was anything he could do. I can't present Mark's tape as evidence, he thought, or can I? How can we use this? How can we let Timson know we've got him red-handed, at least as far as this interview goes?

''Joe?''

Mark had seen the investigator drifting, his eyes wide, his mind working and his fingers unconsciously beating a rapid, if syncopated beat on the arm of his chair.

''Mark . . . ,'' he said at last, ''let me think this through. I don't know how we'll use it, but you're right. It shows Timson is misleading us or out-and-out lying to us. Hell, he *is* lying. In any event, it proves to me we can't indict the airplane, or the Air Force, just yet.''

When Mark had left, Joe grabbed his topcoat from the old wooden hat rack he kept in the corner—an antique also furnished by Brenda—and headed for the door, apprehension as well as habit driving him out of his office. Sometimes he could think best just walking.

The clouds overhead were racing to the east before a swift

late-autumn breeze, the wind at ground level loud enough to
beat the roar of city traffic. There was still a thick covering of
snow on the ground, but the sun was out and the temperature
had climbed to the upper thirties. It was, in Joe's estimation,
cold and crisp but invigorating and enjoyable. So often D.C.
was too hot, too cold, or too rainy for comfort—or for casual
walks. He would miss days like today, though, even if they
came only once a year. He would miss them if he were no longer
at the Board.

He would have to go to Dean Farris about Nick Gardner,
knowing Gardner was professionally doomed as a result, and
that he, Joe, would be blamed by Farris for letting it happen.
Gardner had gone renegade on Joe's watch. That was all Farris
would grasp.

But what to do about Dean Farris himself? The man's stock
dealings created a monstrous, scandalous conflict of interest. He
couldn't survive the disclosure, either. Of course, Joe should
wait for confirmation from Jeff Perkins before doing anything
overt, just to be sure the stock really did belong to Farris, but
its ownership would explain some of Farris's behavior.

Yet, how could Farris not see the conflict of interest? The
man must be too naïve for words! And playing into Caldwell's
slippery hands the way he had. Or was there something more?

Joe stopped in his tracks suddenly, causing a young couple
who had been unconsciously keeping pace with him on the walk-
way to stumble trying to avoid a collision. The thought was too
horrific and dark and dishonest, but nothing else ever seemed to
really be what it appeared to be in high political office. There
was always something different lurking behind the facade. Farris
had acted to protect U.S. manufacturers ever since he took over
as chairman. Was that tilt an honest one, or could Farris have
other motivation? And what if Caldwell was involved?

Conspiracies began cropping up in his mind. Suppose John
Phelps had stumbled onto a rat's nest of intergovernmental corruption? What could he do about it? Protect your backside, John
had said. Joe was beginning to regard it as wise advice.

But I've done nothing wrong! He reminded himself of that
aggressively, knowing full well that even an innocent can be
professionally destroyed in the public riptide of indignation
which always follows yet another revelation of corruption in
high places.

And what of the North America investigation itself? There was a rising apprehension in his gut about that. Usually he proceeded like a detective against mechanical or operational culprits, chasing them resolutely through technological tunnels, through manuals and hearing testimony and reconstructed wreckage. This one, though, had been unique. He had felt sorry for Dick Timson, but Timson had broken the code and misled an investigation, and to Joe, that was a crime by itself.

The queasy feeling gnawing at him ever since Mark Weiss's visit was the simple frustration of an aeronautical sleuth confronting a cunning new foe. Whatever happened, he *had* to nail Timson. He had to, but could he? In other words, Joe thought in clear terms distilled from a kaleidoscope of thoughts and considerations, will he get away with it?

Joe realized he was pacing around on the grass to the north of the National Air and Space Museum, located just across Independence Avenue from the FAA building. He pushed through the main entry then, losing himself among the displays for a while, seeing nothing but the images of his own thoughts.

Should he take all of it to Susan? She and the other Board members would be in a meeting with Farris by now. No, better leave her out of this for the moment.

Joe paused beneath the Mercury 7 capsule in which John Glenn had orbited the earth, the first American to do so, but the second human, beaten by Yuri Gagarin of the Soviet Union. It took a lot of courage to climb into that garbage-can-sized capsule on top of a marginally proven rocket full of explosive fuel. Glenn had gone on to become a U.S. senator. In fact, there were quite a few aviation-knowledgeable senators now, many of them pilots.

Kell Martinson came to mind, as did his exhortations to Joe to have enough courage to take a professional risk and help him. Martinson had warned he couldn't protect Joe with complete certainty. Helping might accomplish nothing and lose him the only job he cared about. Why on earth should he agree to such a gamble? What would it accomplish?

Yet how could he handle what was now in his lap. It was way beyond his level. Way above his pay grade, as military friends would describe it.

Joe sat down on a bench in the main hall, totally oblivious to the throng of people coming and going just in front of him. The lighthearted feeling which had enveloped him since Susan sailed out of a snowstorm and into his life—and his bedroom—had been replaced with fear. And on top of everything else, if he played this wrong and ended up fired, he might lose Susan as well.

The logical choices all began to converge on one course of action—the only course of action—and in response Joe left the museum and hailed a cab at the corner, giving the Hart Senate Office Building as the destination, showing up ten minutes later in Kell Martinson's outer office totally unannounced, which led to some negotiating before the senator's administrative assistant emerged.

"Mr. Wallingford? I'm Cynthia Collins. What can I do for you?"

"I need to see the senator as quickly as possible. He'll understand."

"He's on the Senate floor at the moment in a vote. But I expect him momentarily. Unfortunately, his calendar is crammed."

"Please, let's talk privately."

She looked him over thoughtfully, then nodded, and Joe followed her to an inner conference room with traditional leather chairs and bookcases full of ancient, leather-bound tomes which no one there had probably ever read.

Joe explained his position at the NTSB and his investigation of the North America crash, leaving out for the moment Farris's dismissal of him as IIC.

Cindy Collins nodded. "I know that crash only too well, Mr. Wallingford." She was sitting next to him, her legs crossed, a beautiful young lady in every way. "You had no way of knowing, but I was booked on that flight. Except for last-minute changes in my schedule, I would have died in that crash." The statement startled Joe, but one thing was clear. This was the friend Kell Martinson had been waiting for the night of the accident.

"I'm certainly glad you missed it."

"Me too!" she said with a laugh.

"Has the senator mentioned me, by any chance?"

"Absolutely. We try to keep track of where he is, and he's been spending an awful lot of time with you folks lately. Frankly, we need him back here on the job."

She left Joe then to check on the progress of the vote, and returned in a few minutes with the senator in tow.

"Joe. A pleasant surprise, sir. Come into my office. You've met Cynthia then?"

"Yes. She told me your schedule was crammed, and I'm sorry to barge in, but it is urgent."

Senator Martinson ushered Joe toward the couch in the sitting area of his office, indicating Cindy should close the door and join them, which she did.

He laid it all out. Mark Weiss's visit, John Phelps's information on Caldwell, the FBI report on Farris's stock holdings, and his dismissal from the North America investigation.

"I guess this is self-serving to a fault, Kell, but I promised you I'd think over your request for my help, and if you'll help me figure out what to do with all these scary pieces to the puzzle, I'm your man. What I've got in my lap is far above my ability to handle."

"On the crash, and as a lawyer, Joe, I'd say North America's going to be hung out to dry on this. Gross negligence will not be too difficult to prove, I would think."

"Of course, as an accident investigator, I have no interest in that aspect," Joe replied.

"I understand. But the observation was begging to be made."

Joe then launched into the Miami Air crash, Kell's eyes watching him intently as he told him everything, including John Phelps's name.

"So what it comes down to," Joe told him at last, "is an out-of-control NTSB chairman who may have a massive conflict of interest or worse, a man appointed by the president, who is from your party, and the FAA's second-in-command is playing games with the rules for suspicious reasons. You see why I feel like a mouse at a cat convention?" Joe said.

"I can indeed." Kell fell silent almost instantly, staring at the small glass coffee table in front of the sofa while obviously deep in thought. He looked up at Joe suddenly. "As you well know, this is a very serious situation. Part of what you've told me may involve federal criminal violations—the Miami Air stuff. As for your man Farris . . . good Lord, he's either horribly naïve or loves taking chances. Does anyone on the White House staff know any of this?"

"I doubt it, but I have no way of knowing. You don't think they'd tolerate it?"

"I would certainly hope not. Look, I think I've got an idea." He sat on the edge of his chair with his hands folded under his chin, elbows on his knees, looking at Joe for a few seconds before speaking. "If I handed you a legislative paintbrush with which to paint a new NTSB, if you could rebuild it just the way you, with your experience, know it should be structured, how would you do it?"

"I don't understand."

Kell's hands came down and he sat back. "What I mean is this: I could help get rid of Farris, but without a change in the way chairmen of the NTSB are picked, the next chairman could be worse. So, we need a more permanent fix. We need, in other words, to concentrate on how we could fix the *structure* of the NTSB so this sort of thing would be impossible, or at least much less likely, in the future."

"All right. Yes. But how . . . you mean a bill of some sort?"

"That's the starting point, Joe. A bill to restructure the NTSB. That would be controversial in my party because we're in control of the White House, and why rock the boat? But, it gives us two major advantages. One, we get people up here on the Hill focused on what's wrong, even if they're not willing to vote to change it; and two, we get a license to hold hearings, through which all this nefarious skulking around can be hauled into the sunshine, perhaps on national TV."

Joe looked at the senator with a mixture of admiration and concern. This had started out as a cry for help. Suddenly the man was talking about national television. Alarm bells were sounding in Joe's head.

Martinson chuckled and held up his hand. "Don't panic, Joe, I see the look on your face. Let me take this step by step."

Kell explained what it would take politically to get the chairman of his Senate committee, which was above Kell's subcommittee, to approve expedited hearings on a bill to restructure the NTSB. "To a certain extent it could be the fishing expedition we would need to expose these immediate problems, but it could also do a lot of good in sending a warning to others that any future attempt to influence an investigation will blow up in their faces." Kell turned slightly toward Cindy, watching for any cautionary reaction. There was none, and he continued. "We could even get the chief pilot here to testify, and perhaps pull the truth out of him. Sometimes it's far more difficult to lie to Congress than to a governmental agency such as yours. Now, if I can pull the right levers, so to speak, we could set this up just after the New Year, a little less than a month from now. Cynthia? What do you think?''

She thought about that for a moment while checking a notebook on her lap. "Difficult, but not impossible. I think we could do it.''

Kell turned back to Joe. "We'd give no warning to your chairman, of course. We'd let him walk into the crossfire thinking this was a routine matter. That would be far more effective than giving him time to prepare explanations and circle his wagons.''

"I don't follow you there,'' Joe said.

"I mean we'll want to ask him on the record and in public just who he's been talking to about NTSB investigations, and how those conversations might have influenced those investigations. We'll also want to ask him about his stock ownership—provided, as you cautioned, that tip is accurate. But that follows naturally, don't you see, from our stated purpose of examining how well today's structure works in isolating the board politically, as we tried to do with the Independent Safety Board Act of 1974. You remember that bill, by the way?''

Joe nodded. "Sure do. A good friend of mine blew the whistle on the Nixon gang's efforts to influence the Board, and that led to passage of the bill. He was effectively forced off the NTSB staff as a result.''

"I just read a summary of the story, Joe.'' Kell tapped the folder he had retrieved from his credenza. "You remember I told you just yesterday that I've been wanting to do this for quite a while. This is the ideal time. And for me, politically, this is an important issue.''

"Really? Why?''

"The inability of the field offices to do more than a two- or three-day investigation—without additional support, mind you—into general aviation crashes. I come from a general aviation manufacturing state, as you know, and some of the accidents the NTSB field people have ascribed to mechanical and structural failure have probably in truth been human failures. I've got manufacturers in my state who've literally been put out of the small-airplane business because of soaring liability costs, and poor-quality accident investigation only makes that problem worse.''

''I'm impressed,'' Joe said.

''I saw one, firsthand, involving a Beech light twin which crashed for no apparent reason on an evening approach. Single pilot operation. Your man came out, did his best, couldn't find a cause, couldn't get Washington's authorization to probe further or do extensive lab tests or probe the pilot's life-style and background, and he just had to close the book. It took a safety consultant nearly six months to uncover the cause, which was chronic fatigue of the pilot.''

Now Joe was moving to the edge of the couch. ''I do have some ideas.''

''I knew you would,'' Kell told him. ''And we've got quite a body of staff work around here which I helped to spark several years ago, Joe. As I mentioned, I do have a man who's done some work for me on this, and the reason I want to keep his name out of it for the moment is because he's still with the Board.''

Kell had a hand up, as much to stop himself as to trigger Joe's response. ''You were going to tell me your ideas, Joe.''

''Well, we too are somewhat prepared, not just from bull sessions and scuttlebutt among the staff—though there's plenty of that—but because of a staff group formed by a number of us very quietly two years ago. We made it a semisocial sort of thing, get together and brainstorm what the ideal Board would be. Never produced a written report, but I know the proposals by heart.''

''Go ahead, please. Cynthia? Could you take some notes?''

''No problem.'' She had already been scribbling incessantly, in a steno book.

''Okay,'' Joe began, ''for starters, we need to break it into two boards, one just devoted to aviation. The current work load in aviation is enough for two NTSBs. Bogging us down and diluting our aviation expertise with all these rail and pipeline and highway and ship accidents is idiotic. We try to do a professional job on the aviation accidents, but we don't have the time or the funds. We're supposed to monitor safety trends as well, but who has time? We're almost totally reactive. There should be a separate board, perhaps called the National Surface Transportation Safety Board, to handle all that. Separate staff, separate board members, separate funding, everything." Joe felt himself getting enthusiastic.

"Let's look at that," Kell replied. "What else?"

"Well, the chairman problem is because of two things. One, the current guy is a political hack without sufficient aviation experience. Yes, he was on the blue-ribbon panel, but he had no credentials for that, except being a loyal party man. Sorry, your party again, but the lesson would be the same whether Democrat or Republican. The chairmanship of the NTSB—and for that matter all the board positions that are appointed—should not be political patronage plums. I may be stepping on your toes saying that—"

"No. It so happens I agree. Go on."

"It just creates trouble. The staff has to try to educate the Board members who want to be educated, and work around the ones who are just biding their time till they get a cabinet position or ambassadorship, or whatever they want out of the White House. The rules were changed several years back to require technical experience in two of the five Board members, but for the chairman in particular, there are no requirements for technical knowledge. I'm convinced that Farris is one of those just biding his time. He should never have been appointed."

"So, we should change the appointment process? Or just the criteria for selection?"

"Both." Joe nodded. "Make certain only highly knowledgeable aviation people are eligible, preferably people with a technological pedigree and substantial experience in aviation-accident investigation. And as for the appointment process, there should be a technically qualified board appointed to pick the NTSB members and the chairman, and a longer term for all involved so they'll outlast the president who picked the board that picked them, and therefore they won't feel the need to check which way the wind is blowing before watering down our findings."

Kell didn't answer, but he was agreeing, and Joe went on.

"And perhaps the most important thing, Kell, the charge of the Board, or both Boards, must be changed. Right now, we're charged with finding the 'probable cause' in every aviation accident. But there is almost never a single probable cause. We should be charged with finding the various causes that contributed to the occurrence of an accident, and with addressing each and every one of them. With trying to correct each one of them. With kicking the FAA to correct each one of them.''

"You want authority to compel the FAA to do the things you think are needed?''

"Some want that, but I don't. That ties our hands. Then we get into all the legal cautions and political problems of rule-making.'' Joe watched Kell for a second, deciding finally to mention a hotly debated idea. "We might benefit by having standby authority whereby, if some future FAA administrator tried to ignore us completely on an emergency matter, we could take this statutory shotgun down from the shelf and force the issue legally.''

"Good. Good list, Joe.'' Without warning Kell turned to Cindy. "Other than the session tomorrow, anything on my agenda I can't clear for the weekend?''

She flipped through a notebook on the table, mumbling to herself. "Just a minute.'' Cindy jumped up and moved behind the senator's desk, punched some keys on his computer, looked at some sort of calendar, then turned toward the two men. "No problem. We can clear everything.''

"Excellent.'' Kell turned back to Joe. "Can you come by here about nine in the morning and, in effect, spend the weekend here hard at work?''

"I . . . I guess so.'' Susan's image flashed in his mind. They had made no plans, but somehow committing the weekend without talking to her now seemed wrong, and that was disturbing. Already he was measuring his commitments in reference to her. "Sure, I can be here.''

"Well, it's lucky this came up on a Friday.''

"What are we going to be doing?'' Joe asked.

Kell Martinson rocked back in his chair with a broad smile. Joe had seen a picture of John Kennedy in that exact pose, in a rocking chair in the Oval Office, a room Joe had always wanted to see in person.

"We, Mr. Wallingford, since we want to hold a hearing and extract eyeteeth, we need a bill. You and I and Cynthia and at least two of my staff members who are good legislative drafts-men are going to write one.''

Joe was out the door and down the hall when he remembered the question—and the idea—that had imposed itself early that morning. He retraced his steps, startling the receptionist by sailing past her back to Kell's office.

"I think I may have a solution for your Kansas City car problem."

"How?"

"First, where do things stand?"

Kell shook his head and sighed. "I wish I knew. The suspense is driving us all crazy, and Cynthia . . ." Kell looked out the office door, but Cindy was nowhere to be seen. "Cynthia is quite upset that I have not gone public with this, and I can't believe it hasn't leaked yet. The FBI turned it over in the form of an information packet to both the Kansas City Airport authorities and the FAA, but I'm told the FAA dumped it back on the FBI's desk like a hot potato, saying they weren't interested in prosecuting me. I don't know about the airport's attitude. What're you thinking, Joe?"

"You held a hearing on security this year, right?"

"Right."

"And you have a security clearance for classified military information, right?"

"Yes."

"Okay, whether it was your intent or not to probe their security defenses at Kansas City, your actions did just that, and could be viewed as a somewhat unorthodox test, for which no prosecution should ensue."

"That's stretching it, Joe."

"Have you made any recommendations as a result of slipping in?"

Kell broke into a smile, slowly. "How'd you know that?"

"I assumed. It fits your character. You'd be concerned enough to want to plug the hole. I'd say the fact that you've taken steps to do just that means that there was a legitimate purpose in going through that gate, or at least that a purpose has been served. And certainly your security clearance would attest to your qualification *to be* trusted, if you had applied or asked for an escort."

Kell nodded. "I don't know if the folks in Kansas City will buy it, but it's . . ."

"Let me call them," Joe said.

* * *

Dr. Susan Kelly leaned out of her office doorway, catching her secretary's attention. "Any word from Joe Wallingford yet?"

"Not yet."

"Thanks." She moved back to her desk, anxious to tell Joe that Farris had been buffaloed. With the other three members in agreement that the chairman's so-called firing of Wallingford as IIC of the North America crash was ridiculous and maybe even in violation of civil-service regulations, Farris had backed down. "I'll reinstate him myself," the chairman said, none too happy. "This is a disciplinary matter. I started it and I'll finish it."

Like hell, she thought, am I going to let Joe walk in there and get treated with condescension without advance warning.

That had been around noon. It was now 2 P.M. and no Joe, despite messages on his desk and one on the windshield of his car. Susan was almost ready to go guard the elevators in the lobby when an animated Joseph Wallingford walked briskly into her office, shutting the door behind him. "I got your note, and I've got some things to tell you."

"Good. Me first. We won, you're IIC again, but you've got to bite your tongue and let Dean tell you that himself in his authoritarian tones."

"I see. How'd you do that?"

Susan noticed the guarded response. "You haven't done anything rash, have you, Joe?"

"Rash?" He looked worried. She seemed amused.

"Rash. Like slashing Dean's tires."

He smiled thinly. "No. Nothing like that."

"Which," she began, more guarded and curious now, "implies that something has gone on. What's up?"

She looked even more beautiful than on Wednesday night, he thought, though her position on the other side of an imposing desk reemphasized the distance between them in professional terms. He had worried about telling her of the meeting with Kell, let alone the call from John Phelps or the visit from Mark Weiss. The worry that she would be upset with his actions, upset enough to hurt their blossoming relationship, had eaten at him all the way back. But he launched into the story anyway, relating the entire sequence of events—his lunch with Kell, his trip to the Hill, and thus his betrayal of the bureaucratic code against consorting with known legislators. When he finished, Joe noted with dismay that Susan's jaw was set, the happy look gone.

"Well, you *have* been busy. You know what you're doing?"

"I hope so, but I'm not sure. I'm not sure I should involve you with this information."

She pursed her lips and laughed, a singular sound, then got up and moved to the window, looking at the Capitol in the distance. "Joe, I'm not sure what you've just started. I agree Dean is way out of line, but you just moved to politically assassinate him, do you realize that?"

"Yes."

"Not to mention open up a congressional investigation. Did the good senator explain where that can lead?"

"To some degree, yes."

"And did he tell you that your ability to function here may be destroyed if you don't win this battle?"

"You mean the Ernie Fitzgerald syndrome? Exile or freeze out the whistle-blowers?" he asked.

"Something like that," Susan replied, turning to him suddenly with an edge in her voice. "God, Joe, couldn't you have waited a few hours? Couldn't you have trusted me with this first?"

Joe's eyes wandered to the rose he had left for her when he arrived a few hours back. It was sitting to the right of her blotter, in a place of honor. Obviously she had been pleased with him then. He wished that was still the case. "Susan . . ." How to go about this? What to say? "Susan, here I am with a ticking bomb or two in my lap, not knowing whether it would be ethical to reveal them to you and feeling like I needed to move right then. I owed it to Mark Weiss and to John Phelps down in Florida. I'm not a political animal. You know that."

"You are *now*, fella—although we've got to keep this absolutely quiet." She had resumed looking out the window. Now she whirled back to him, angrily. "You could have at least waited until I finished fighting the battle for you, for Christ's sake."

"I'm *sorry*, Susan. But what would you have advised?"

"Well, let's see." She walked back behind her desk to consult a notepad. "First, Dr. Weiss came to see me too, with a copy of the same tape. I agree Timson's lying, but there were things we could have talked about that could have been done other than creating a Senate hearing, which isn't going to smoke the man out."

"I didn't know he . . ."

"Of course you didn't. You didn't bother to ask me." Susan picked up a piece of paper and came back around the desk in front of Joe and leaned against a chair, her eyes on his.

"And, Joe, this intriguing message was on your desk. Perhaps I shouldn't have picked it up, but I figured I'd see you before you got back to your office. I wasn't sure I understood it before. Now that you've told me about your FBI friend's call, it makes sense. You let the stock ownership panic you, right?"

"Well . . ."

"It contributed, at least?"

"Yes."

Susan's face was grim. She handed Joe the small piece of pink paper bearing Jeff Perkins's name and a cryptic message: "Cancel stock ownership allegation—different D. F. Jeff."

Joe was silent for a minute, running over the different possibilities. There were none. Perkins had turned up another Farris. The chairman owned no such stock.

"I guess I'm relieved."

"I am too," Susan said, "but you've still started something you can't stop."

"Susan, think about the rest of it, please. We've got an airplane down in Florida with evidence of fraudulent noncompliance with FAA airworthiness directives, a cover-up of which may reach to Caldwell at the FAA and Farris of the NTSB. The stock thing may have fizzled, but the other seems valid. We've got confirmation of lying by the pilot of the crashed North America airplane, which may have led to a mistaken lawsuit and unwarranted damage to the reputation of what may be a perfectly sound airplane. I've got a panicked inspector in Florida telling me to watch my backside and making clandestine phone calls through local bars, for heaven's sake, and on top of that you've had to go in to try to get my position back for me against what seemed like heavy odds. What *would* you have advised on those matters? That we confront Farris? What about Caldwell? And, as Martinson said, what about the greater good? Doesn't the NTSB side of this mean we need to change the way the Board is picked?"

Susan looked back at Joe. "Including me, remember."

That stunned him. "Hey, Susan, any criteria for selection I would want to see, you would qualify for just as easily."

"I'm not worried about that, Joe. It's just . . ." Her voice trailed off as she walked behind the desk and picked up the vase with the rose, looking at it lovingly. "We work so well together, you and I." She looked up at him and smiled. "We, uh, do well together in other ways, too." Susan turned away and walked to the window. "We ended up being a good team in Kansas City, Joe. We're a good team here. You may have done the right thing, I suppose. I just guess I felt that anything of that magnitude, we would do together. This surprised me."

"You'd go over there with me? Jump ship?" he asked.

"At the very least, I would have supported you."

"Would have?"

"Will." She put the vase down. "Will, of course, Joe. You're right, there are more issues here than just Dean trying to get you off the case. Maybe this thing with Martinson will have an effect."

"Well, if it doesn't, and I get booted out, I still wouldn't leave Washington. As tough as it would be to leave the Board, I suppose in some ways . . . uh . . . it might be easier with me on the outside." He forced a smile and she finally returned it.

"It? What's this 'it' you're referring to?" she asked, her voice now absent the hard edge.

"Us. You and me."

No reply.

"Susan, you're the one who said this would get complicated."

"I did, didn't I?"

"You did. I heard you. I was there."

Susan gave him a sidelong look. "Yes, now that you mention it, I do seem to recall keeping company with a gentleman of your description and saying those words."

"Would you be at all interested in, um, getting together with that fellow again tomorrow night or Sunday?"

Her smile drooped a bit as she looked down, fingering something on her desk. "I think not, Joe. You're going to be busy with the senator."

"Susan?"

Her eyes met his, her expression a disappointment. "We'll see, Joe. Maybe I need to define the full range of what 'complicated' means."

The short walk back to his office was painful, his thoughts on

Susan, but his eyes catching the course reversal of one of Andy Wallace's people when she saw Joe coming down the hall. He had already noticed a coolness on the part of some staff members in reaction to his removal as IIC. Suddenly getting too friendly with him was dangerous to one's career. When *this* story finally broke, he thought, they would be diving into broom closets to avoid passing him in the hallways. Such was the self-protective instinct of bureaucratic life.

The note from Farris was there, as he expected. This time it was done more correctly, a folded piece of paper on his desk. The meeting was as expected: ten minutes of professorial, face-saving lecture. "I'm sure you've learned your lesson," Farris had the gall to say. Joe took it, made the right noises, and left, feeling no better or worse than when he'd left Susan's office, but inwardly chagrined that he was ready to believe the worst of Farris. Joe took the time to call Cynthia Collins to relay the word that Farris held no aircraft company stock.

Things were happening too fast, and Susan's rejection—although temporary, he hoped—stung badly. Joe gathered the notes he and the other staffers had made in past years about reforming the Board's structure—the if-we-had-our-druthers file named after the song of L'il Abner fame—and headed to the elevators, relieved to find himself the only one waiting.

The doors of the elevator had barely opened before a figure punched through them, obviously in a hurry to get somewhere in the NTSB's eighth-floor complex. The look on his face was one of controlled seriousness, and Joe recognized him immediately and with a start: it was Bill Caldwell. The close encounter with a man he had just targeted professionally was unsettling. Farris was one thing. This powerful, almost brooding presence from higher up in the hierarchy of bureaucratic power was entirely another. Caldwell disappeared around the corner in the direction of the chairman's office as Beverly Bronson held the door and then joined Joe in the elevator.

"Joe, I was trying to catch you."

"Beverly. How are you? Thanks, by the way, for the clippings."

"You're welcome, and I'm fine. Joe, I have to ask you, why were you in the Hart Building this morning?"

The question froze Joe in his mental tracks. Did Farris have spies on the Hill? Had something happened? Had Kell gone public already? Oh, Lord, now what?

"Uh, what prompted that question, Beverly?"

"I was there on business and saw you go by in a rush, and I wasn't aware of anything going on involving Senate business and us right now other than a few inquiries I'm working on."

Joe just looked at her, trying to show a calm countenance, disturbed that they had stopped on a lower floor and several chatty FAA employees had carried their conversation into the elevator.

"Beverly, I was simply dropping in on a friend of mine."

"Oh? Who was that, Joe?"

Her voice was friendly and her tone warm, but the lady wanted to know why the head of the aviation accident division was snooping around in her territory. Joe knew she worked closely with Farris, although he had long since discounted the rumors of how close. She must know of his suspension and reinstatement on the North America case. She must know he was madder than holy . . .

The doors opened again and more people entered, pushing Beverly against Joe as they stood at the back of the elevator. Under different circumstances a lovely person to be pushed into, Joe thought, but not now. Definitely not now!

Her voice was low, almost intimate, but her intent was deadly serious. "Joe, I'm sorry to pry, but I'm responsible for keeping the Board in balance in the eyes of the Hill. If any of our people are engaging in outside forays, for whatever reason, it is my business."

"I'm well aware of your position, Beverly, but a personal call is a personal call. Don't worry about it."

"This person, was he in Senator Baccus's office or Senator Martinson's?"

Joe looked at her with a scowl. "What'd you do, follow me down the hallway?"

"No, but when I saw you, those were the offices you were heading toward, and Martinson worries me because of his subcommittee, and because I know you've had him over here a few times lately. Dean knows too, and is none too happy, as I think he told you. Joe, you aren't going off campus, are you?"

Strange way to put it, he thought, still frowning as the doors to the main floor opened and everyone but Joe and Beverly and one FAA staffer got off. "You going to the garage, Beverly?"

"I am if you are. Would you please tell me what you're up to?"

"I should probably let you think I *am* up to something. It might be fun to get known as a man of mystery around here. But at the risk of disappointing the ranking colonel in Dean's KGB, I was there simply to chat as a friend with the senator and to see Cynthia Collins, Martinson's AA, who, it so happens, was originally booked on North America Flight 255 into Kansas City, but missed it."

The door opened to the basement garage and Beverly made no move to leave. Joe caught the door and held it open. "I had promised another mutual friend I'd discuss the situation as we currently know it, just for her personal use, and for his part, the senator has simply been curious to know more about how we work. That's why he was over here."

"Okay. That's no problem, then. I know Cynthia, but I didn't know that had happened. Sorry to pry Joe. By the way, that wasn't fair. I am *not* Dean's KGB!"

He stepped out and looked at her silently, trying to keep a disapproving look on his face, letting the doors shut between them without a word before heading for his car. He would have to call Cynthia and warn her about a potential inquiry. Good Lord! One solitary visit in the past ten years to the Senate office complex and the NTSB's governmental affairs officer is standing outside the door!

At the same time Beverly had been engaged in cross-examining Joe, Bill Caldwell had arrived in Dean Farris's office, finding the chairman on the phone and making it clear he would wait *in* his office until Farris was through. Farris hurried to finish the call. "What's up, Bill?"

"I just want to confirm something. You and I have been able to have some pretty frank, and I think useful exchanges over the years, Dean. But I want to make absolutely certain—and I apologize if you consider this so obvious as to be presumptuous—that whatever we say to each other regarding government business is privileged information which will never be divulged to others."

Farris shrugged and puffed out his cheeks. "Sure Bill. No problem. I don't discuss what we talk about."

"If we've made requests of each other in the normal course of business, you know, person-to-person, those requests are equally privileged, right?"

"Of course. What's the problem? Something bothering you?"

Caldwell's mind rapidly calculated the odds of Farris remembering his phone call about Miami Air. He would certainly remember the North America calls, but Miami Air was some time ago. Farris got to his feet and wandered around his desk to face Caldwell, a friendly expression on his face. "You worried 'bout calling me on the Miami Air thing, Bill? Hell, all you did was tell me they were headed up by friends of yours and that's why you knew they were well-managed. Nothing wrong with that."

Dammit, he had underestimated Farris. "I would not use the word *worried*, Dean, but conversations like that, just like some of your questions to me, could be misinterpreted by others despite being perfectly proper and legal." Caldwell knew there must be something Farris had asked, some favor, some information, *something* which would compromise Farris as well. But he couldn't think of anything on the outer limits of propriety. Nothing usable, at least.

"Well, don't worry, Bill," Farris said, obviously enjoying the situation and understanding none of it. "I have a high threshold of pain. They'll never torture it out of me." Farris was laughing and Caldwell forced himself to act equally lighthearted as he shook the chairman's hand and left, even more worried than he had been before.

Friday traffic was always terrible inside the Beltway, but given a little snow and slush to spice things up, it became a nightmare. For once, however, Joe didn't care. His mind was somewhere else as he poked along in bumper-to-bumper intimacy with the majority of bureaucratic Washington, heading southwest over the Potomac with only a vague idea of where he intended to go. The Fourteenth Street Bridge behind him, Joe headed toward Alexandria on the George Washington Parkway, diverting to a fast-food drive-through for a chocolate shake he knew he shouldn't have before continuing on. There were Christmas decorations everywhere now, but they didn't register on his consciousness. Driving sometimes was the best relaxation, the anonymity giving him time to think, yet there was a place he loved to go, especially on moderate spring or autumn days, which this decidedly was not. The Army's Fort Belvoir, near Mr. Vernon, with its wide boulevards and central parade grounds. It was snow covered now, of course, but a welcome sight. Joe parked across from the headquarters building of the Army Corps of Engineers, cinched up his topcoat, and began walking, thoughts of Susan mixing with the memory of his impulsive visit to Kell Martinson's office and the encounter with Beverly Bronson. Her report, he figured, had already reached Dean. There was much to worry about, so why wasn't he worried? Joe ran the various threats and concerns and problems and challenges past his mind's eye again, expecting his stomach to tighten and his mood to change. Neither happened. Strange, he thought. It couldn't be his growing feeling that he had found a true and powerful ally in Kell Martinson, despite the warnings that his protection was limited. There was something more making him happy and content and confident and optimistic all at once, and when all other possibilities had been exhausted, there was only one left.

Joe looked back to the east through the old oak trees lining the parade ground, his car a distant speck, his footprints marking a meandering path through the snow. It was beautiful here, he thought. He would bring Susan here in the spring.

22

Friday, December 14

It took an article in *Time* to push John Tarvin over the edge. The investigation of the North America crash had stalled, it said, with the NTSB focusing its attention on the role of the copilot only because they had nowhere else to turn—the inquiry into possible radar interference with the airplane's flight controls frustrated by government and military stonewalling. The accident, in other words, would never be solved—unless John Tarvin came forward, or so he reluctantly decided.

He had tried to go through the normal channels at his defense-contractor company, but they didn't want to listen—nor, apparently, did the NTSB or the FAA. If the government wouldn't hear him out, then he would go instead to the institution most affected by the tragic events of October 12: North America Airlines. Early Friday he drove to Kansas City International Airport to talk to a startled North America station manager, who immediately put him on a flight to Dallas, where he was met at the airport and whisked to the downtown headquarters of the airline.

By 11:30 A.M. John Walters had been pulled away from a meeting to listen to John Tarvin. Irritated at the interruption and upset at the presumptuous move of the Kansas City manager in sending the man to Dallas, Walters bustled in to give the affair a maximum of five minutes. Within two minutes, however, his attention had locked on nothing else but Tarvin's words.

It had been wet and chilly that Friday night, Tarvin told him, and he was cold as he waited in the cab of the mobile radar vehicle for the Air Force loadmasters to start the loading procedure, but he wasn't supposed to idle the unit's huge diesel engine just to keep warm. So he had plugged the unit into an

337

aircraft ground electrical outlet instead. With electricity supplied to his cab, he could operate a small electrical heater and keep from freezing. It was all very routine—until he tried to turn on the master ground power switch.

"I got the wrong switch, I guess. I wanted to power the electrical panel for my cab, but I got hold of the master switch for the radar module instead. I could see everything dim instantly— the power it was sucking out of those lines must have been incredible. Even the sodium-vapor floodlamps around the ramp flickered and dimmed too, and I nearly broke my finger turning the switch off. It was only on for ten seconds or so. I don't know why a circuit breaker didn't blow somewhere."

"When did the crash occur?"

"Within a few seconds . . . no more than, say fifteen seconds. It seemed like almost, you know, immediately. I was so shocked! We all ran forward to see. I didn't think about that switch and the reaction until much later—a week later—when I heard the news people talking about the radar unit, some saying it may have caused the crash, and the Air Force swearing it wasn't on. Well, they're right to a point. It wasn't *supposed* to be on." Tarvin looked at John Walters with a tortured expression. "Then later they started talking on the news about this strange power interruption, and I knew exactly what had caused it. Immediately, I knew. I went to my supervisor, told him the story. He told me to forget the whole thing, that I had done nothing that could have affected the airplane. About a week later I asked to talk to him again, and both he and *his* boss took me into an office and said to drop it immediately, and that if I didn't, I would be fired. They said that if I went to anyone else, I would be prosecuted for giving away classified information. I signed an oath, you see." The man lowered his head and rubbed his temples, looking up at last. "I don't want to do anything wrong, but I can't live with this, and they don't want anyone to know. I told them the NTSB must be told, and they told me the NTSB and FAA already knew. I guess they had all decided it didn't occur, so they wanted me to shut up." Tarvin stopped and sighed deeply. "I didn't mean to turn it on, but, I did. The power it took was so great . . ."

Walters got a cassette recorder to tape Tarvin's account, ordering a secretary to type it up for his signature, and sent him then to a nearby hotel at company expense with an escort of two lower-ranking executives with orders to keep Tarvin in sight and under control.

"We'll take it from here, Mr. Tarvin," Walters said. "The NTSB will need to talk to you too. You get some rest. We can talk tomorrow." After we get the jump on things, that is, Walters told himself.

As John Tarvin left the North America offices in Dallas, Walters placed a call to David Bayne in New York. Bayne was grateful to be rescued from a joyless meeting with the airline's investment bankers which had droned on for hours. Things had been going badly in their attempts to find a way around corporate annihilation, and whatever the news from Dallas, the day was already a loss. The investment group trying to take over his airline was composed of circling financial sharks, looking to dismember the company for quick profit. Bayne's only chance was to find a white knight—a friendly company willing to take a chance with billions of borrowed dollars to buy North America and save it as an independent entity. There were some possibilities, but North America, quite simply, was running out of time, and David Bayne's erudite and professional overtures to the chairmen of the potential rescuing companies were becoming a bit shrill and urgent.

"Yes?"

"Mr. Bayne? John Walters in Dallas. I've got everyone looking for Ron Putnam, and I'll switch him into this call when we can find him."

"What's up, John?" Visions of airplanes in pieces on the ground filled his mind's eye. With such a buildup, the news must be terrible.

"It might have been radar interference that brought down Flight 255 after all," Walters told him, filling in the details of Tarvin's galvanizing visit, and the implications.

Ron Putnam was located in Tampa and hooked up to a conference call, the three of them urgently exchanging details and ideas.

"I've got to tell you two," Bayne said at last, "I'm very relieved, because I was getting damned worried that you fellows had lost control of your people." Bayne said it almost lightheartedly, but his words chilled both Walters and Putnam.

"What do you mean, David?" Ron Putnam asked, caution flags fluttering in his mind.

"Well, I was beginning to think, after that disastrous hearing, that the mistake you two made in hiring and not supervising Timson had caused it all. I was about convinced he'd caused the crash, God knows how. But now, the flaws of our chief pilot will be eclipsed when this breaks . . . and I want this to break immediately."

"Shouldn't we take this to the NTSB first, David? John's got the man on hold here in Dallas." Putnam's voice sounded tentative.

"Hell no! We've got the goods. Call a news conference and let's go for it! That bastard Farris and his people can read about it in the *New York Times*. Or, better yet, call someone we want to cultivate on the *Dallas Times Herald* and give them an exclusive for their afternoon edition, then break it on the evening news for tonight. Don't worry about the NTSB. They should have found this poor SOB before we did."

By 6 P.M. the nation was hearing North America Airlines' senior vice-president Ron Putnam announce that new evidence had all but solved the crash of Flight 255. The phone calls began immediately between members of the NTSB and Joe's staff in particular, lacing an urgent web of communication among startled people instantly venting feelings of outrage against North America. "The damned airline didn't even have the common courtesy to call and let us know the media had this story!" Andy railed at Joe. "And I don't even know who this man Tarvin is."

Within an hour of getting the news by phone from Joe, Dean Farris had told the IIC to do nothing while he, Farris, called David Bayne. Only John Walters could be located, however, and his attitude was disgustingly smug, in Farris's estimation. He had been authorized, he said, to pass along the information on just who John Tarvin was and where he could be found, but the NTSB would have to ask their own questions.

"You realize you people have breached traditional duty and courtesy in accident investigation by taking this to the media first, don't you?" Farris was almost sputtering into his home phone. "We have rules against this sort of thing, and you are a party to this investigation."

"Mr. Chairman," Walters answered, laconically, "I did what I was told to do. You'll have to take that up with *my* chairman, David Bayne. He apparently assumed you should already have known about Tarvin." Take that, you sanctimonious bastard,

Walters said to himself, his treatment at the hands of the NTSB at the hearing burning for redress.

In different parts of the Washington, D.C. area, Joe Wallingford, Susan Kelly, Andy Wallace, and Barbara Rawlson—among others—sat stunned before their telephones and tried to adjust to this latest twist. As Joe had moaned to Andy, "I suspected it was the radar unit, but goddammit, this investigation keeps playing out on the national news! If we don't like this conclusion, just wait another twenty minutes and someone will uncover another one."

Dean Farris called Joe back by 7 P.M., Washington time. "Joe, I want you to get someone to Dallas to talk to that man, but do not say anything to the media. I've talked to a very highly placed source in our government in the last ten minutes who assures me the man is mistaken, that the unit couldn't have been transmitting anything harmful. They say North America went off half-cocked, and is going to look ridiculous."

"Andy's already headed for the airport, Mr. Chairman. There's a nine P.M. flight from Dulles to Dallas. He'll be on it."

"Good." And Farris hung up.

Kell Martinson took it even harder. He had invested a substantial amount of personal capital in assuring his fellow senators—including the angry proponents of the full SDI project—that the Defense Department was telling the truth. Everyone he talked to in the Pentagon had assured him that there was no way—"*No way*, Senator"—that the mobile radar unit could have been activated. He had accepted the assurances at last and gone back to his angry colleagues on the Hill with a "Trust me!" approach. Now those assurances—along with a lot of his credibility—were in danger of being blown away. And the American public would probably conclude the Pentagon was incompetent, and Kell Martinson was, at best, an amiable, gullible dupe.

"Kell, keep in mind it was not sabotage. You told them it wasn't, and this doesn't contradict your assurances," Cindy had said by phone around 7:30 P.M., trying to calm him down.

"Yeah, but I asked them point-blank if it *could* have been physically possible—electronically possible—that the radar was transmitting as the North America Airbus approached the airport, and all I've gotten is a resounding and apparently fraudulent no."

Cindy's counsel was to be cautious, but Kell immediately punched in the unlisted home number of Lt. Gen. Roach's superior, the four-star general heading the SDI program. The resulting exchange was rather one-sided and vitriolic.

"Once and for all, General, I want a straight answer, and this senator's support for anything you people hold dear hinges in its entirety on getting an honest answer. You dance around this one, General, and your people will be spending the rest of their natural lives testifying before committees up here with a galaxy of angry senators—including this one—as your constant inquisitors."

"Senator, we have not lied to you. I'll be back to you in an hour."

Instead, he was back on the line in twenty minutes.

"Senator Martinson, I say this to you for the record, and with my full belief that it is indeed absolutely true. I stake my personal and professional reputation on it, sir. Despite the statements of this man Tarvin, the mobile tracking radar unit's main antenna was retracted, and because of an intricate system of interlocks and other safeguards in the design, as well as safeguards built into the physical unit, if the antenna is not fully shaped into its normal 25-foot dish on top of the unit, the unit cannot—I repeat—cannot—transmit a single watt of radio frequency energy. It is a physical impossibility. It *is* possible, Senator, for someone to switch power into the main radar module and have a tremendous power drain, but that drain does not go to producing radio, radar, microwave, or any other sort of radio frequency radiation."

"What *does* it produce? Electrical energy has to go somewhere."

"That part's classified, Senator. But it doesn't produce radio waves."

"In other words, General, the man may be telling the truth about what he did and what he saw, but there could have been no radio interference with that Airbus?"

"Exactly."

There was an ominous silence, and the general was prepared for it.

"Senator, would you consider a midnight flight with your Air Force?"

"What?"

"To clear this up beyond a shadow of a doubt, would you forego some sleep and meet one of my people at Andrews in, say, two hours?"

"I suppose so. To go where?"

"Just stop at any of the gates, Senator, and identify yourself. Someone will escort you to the right location. Bring a change of clothes and your Dopp kit, but expect to be back within, say, fourteen hours."

Kell was somewhat shocked, but accepted immediately, and by midnight found himself strapped into a tiny cabin seat of an Air Force Learjet, the general himself sitting in the next seat.

"All I'm going to tell you right now, Senator, is that what you are going to see and hear is classified Top Secret, and you are authorized to receive this information subject to your security clearance. You may not divulge anything classified outside of normal cleared need-to-know channels. This would be the same as if you had convened a closed session of the Armed Services Committee for presentation of Top Secret classified national-defense testimony. This is definitely a matter of national defense. Do you agree and reaffirm your understanding and acceptance of the limitations?"

"Yes sir. No problem."

"I've discussed my appraisal of your need-to-know status through the chief of staff. We're in agreement that you do, indeed, need to know this, though it's only for your reassurance. You can't divulge."

Kell was consumed with curiosity as the small twin jet lifted off Andrews and turned west, climbing rapidly to 41,000 feet. Both of them settled back and slept through the next three hours, the sounds of throttled-back engines finally announcing a descent into—somewhere.

"Holloman Air Force Base, New Mexico, Senator," the general said simply when Kell's eyes came open.

They touched down and taxied at what seemed to be excessive speed straight toward a lighted, distant hangar, the doors of which opened as they approached. The Air Force major in the left seat rolled his craft through the doors and to a stop in the interior. It was just before 4 A.M. in Washington, and 2 A.M. in New Mexico, the stars showing brightly in the clear desert sky as the huge doors were motored closed again behind them.

Kell stepped out into a world of metallic echoes and soaring open space within the walls of the cavernous hangar, facing the most ungainly monstrosity of a vehicle he had ever seen.

"This is it, Senator, the cause of our mutual discomfort. Ninety thousand pounds, two complete antenna sets, automatically deployable and retractable within two minutes, on-board diesel generators for stable, rectified power, multiple transmitters, on and on. Unlike the main SDI plans which, as you know, have varying dependence on ground-based radar, this is merely a tracking test unit, so when you gentlemen on the Hill give us the money and the go-ahead, we can start flying the equipment and proving what the space-based hardware can do."

The general looked rumpled. He had arrived at Andrews wearing a full dress blue uniform. The blouse, bedecked with ribbons, now hung open, revealing a wrinkled shirt, his tie askew, and a half day's growth of unshaven stubble on his chin—quite in contrast to the spit-and-polish neatness of the Air Force security police watching the four-star general's every move with respect and anticipation. Yet his voice was sharp, his words precise, and Kell noted almost a pride of ownership in his description of the radar unit. The general brought Kell around to the front and they climbed into the cab.

"This is the switch Tarvin got by mistake. You can see it's a bad design—I could have screwed it up myself on a cold and boring night."

"You *knew* about this?"

"Within an hour of the time he reported it to his supervisor in Leavenworth more than a month ago. We already suspected something had happened to power up the unit, because of the power surge reports."

Kell bristled. "Why didn't you tell me then? Damn it, you knew the thing was operating."

"Wait, Senator, hang on. Let's have you look in the back first before you take a swing at me."

They climbed down and walked the 85-foot length of the unit, climbing up the rear entrance steps to the main radar unit, where the door already stood open.

"Okay, Senator, step in and take a look at the most powerful mobile radar unit on the planet."

The interior was lighted by incandescent lamps, and the pristine walls and ceiling were in contrast to the tightly packed electronics he had expected. The module was approximately 55 feet long, 10 feet wide, and 8 feet high—and except for several large concrete blocks on the floor, it was completely empty!

"What . . . where . . . ?" Kell began.

"Where is everything? Is that what you're asking?"

Kell saw the general had played him like a violin, but for a purpose. He let him continue.

"It's still being developed, Senator. This unit couldn't transmit a single watt of radio energy because there's nothing inside the sucker. Nothing has been installed yet, and this is exactly what it looked like when we loaded it at Kansas City to fly it to Kwajalein, and then back here."

"How about the power drain?"

The general reached over and lifted a floor panel, revealing a series of large transformers.

"Power sinks, you might call them. They suck up a tremendous amount of power and convert it into nothing but heat. That way, somebody plugs it up, it will appear to be operating at phenomenal power-requirement levels. But nothing related to radio or radar is happening."

"Why, General?"

"You haven't figured it out yet? I don't mean to twist your arm, because you've helped keep peace on the Hill for us to continue development, but because of the budget restrictions and test restrictions, we've put our resources into research, not testing. That's what you wanted, that's what we've done."

"But . . ."

"The Soviets, Senator. Our adversaries, despite the democratization of the Warsaw Pact, *perestroika, glasnost,* wholesale troop withdrawals, German reunification, and the declaration of a blessed state of peace between us. All of us in the military are praying for Mikhail Gorbachev's reforms to permanently change the Soviet Union to a nonthreatening friend, but the process, at best, will take a decade. There is still a terribly powerful Soviet military over there, led by hardened senior officers who watch the direction of the political winds in their government from hour to hour. As long as things could change internally—as long as there are Soviet missiles pointed at us and missile-carrying submarines out there—we can't afford to drop our guard for a split second, any more than they can, despite hail-commies-well-met and constant exchanges of warm fuzzies between us. Don't forget, we watch each other constantly with our surveillance satellites. We want them to *know* we're prepared for war as well as peace as this process continues. We want to remind them constantly how costly this arms race will continue to be until we disengage, and that means ongoing development.''

Kell leaned against the encumbered wall of the module and looked at the general, who was smiling. ''This was all a show, then?''

''That's right. It was showtime. The CIA picked up indications of extraordinary Soviet interest in the progress of one particular aspect of Brilliant Pebbles—a facet of the program that we really hadn't made as much progress in as we wanted them to think. Well, we can't very well trot out one of the Pebbles vehicles and disassemble it on an outdoor picnic table for their cameras, but if they see us getting ready to test it, moving a piece of equipment even our own Congress has forbidden us to move . . .''

''I get the picture.''

''So did they. We monitored the transmissions. Beautiful. We moved it through Kansas City Airport to make sure at least a ground-based agent would find out and report it to Moscow, but their satellites caught it too, as we'd hoped. They caught it leaving the factory, sitting on the ramp in Kansas City, and even had the C-5B pictured in flight on the way to Kwajalein. They also got the North America accident moments after it occurred. Most of it imaged on infrared, of course. You can see that whole careful setup would have been destroyed if we'd said anything more after the accident.''

''You didn't have a cover story?''

''We never anticipated an airline crash. Even now, no one outside of secure channels can know this—and that includes what I told you about their surveillance satellite capability. We're only telling you because *someone* has to champion us as something other than rotten liars.''

''What *can* I tell the other members of the committee?''

The general's face changed instantly to a look of dead seriousness.

''This circle can't widen, Senator. Tell each of them that if they absolutely insist on jeopardizing national defense, and they refuse to take your word, I will reluctantly show them the same thing in the same way with the same restrictions if they will take the time to fly here with me, but otherwise, they must take your word that this unit could not have been transmitting that night because the antenna was not deployed. That's all you can say—a half-truth, of course, but it's necessary.''

The flight back to Washington was spent sleeping, the daylight streaming in the Learjet's windows before they were past Memphis. Kell knew he looked like hell, but he headed for his office anyway, a long series of calls to each member of the committee ahead of him, all with essentially the same message: ''Trust me, I've seen it, it is electronically impossible for the unit to have transmitted, although the power surge was normal.'' And amazingly, there was little resistance.

Kell thought of calling Dean Farris. Protocol made it the proper course of action, but he called Joe Wallingford instead, finding the NTSB investigator almost too shell-shocked to accept anything on faith.

''I want to believe you, Kell, but I've got a man in Dallas talking to Tarvin right now, and the entire NTSB is up in arms about North America's method of releasing this.''

''What does that have to do with believing me, Joe?''

Kell heard a snort from the other end. ''You're right. That made no sense, did it? You say you physically saw this thing?''

''Joe, I was there, I saw it, I touched it, and although I can't tell you the details why—because it's a matter of national security since this an important piece of defense equipment—it could not have been transmitting. You simply have to trust me. I'm telling you the truth.''

''Okay, Senator. I didn't mean to doubt you. Of course, this means we're back in the woods with respect to what caused the accident.''

''Sorry, Joe, but radar interference was never in my equation.''

There was momentary silence from Joe's end as he struggled to decide whether to ask.

''Uh, Kell, could I ask a favor?''

''Certainly.''

''I appreciate your calling me first, but if I give you his home phone, would you call Dean Farris too, and not let on you've called me? Otherwise the tenuous truce between us will probably come apart.''

''Consider it done.''

Kell replaced the phone momentarily, thinking not of the

promised call to the NTSB chairman, but the calls he needed to make to the media. The general had asked for help as they taxied in at Andrews.

"Senator, since the media and the public don't believe us, and since you're the only other person who really knows the truth and can assure the public we were telling the truth . . ."

"Would I go tell the media in a press conference?"

"Something like that."

"Something *exactly* like that indeed. That was part of the plan, wasn't it?" Kell asked it without rancor and delivered it with a smile. There's no sense denying a tiger his stripes, Kell thought to himself. The top military brass could be just as politically astute as the elected masses on the Hill. And in fact they had to be. It was a matter of survival if their programs were to be funded with any consistency.

"Well, we kind of figured—the chief of staff and I—that you would volunteer to help once you knew the truth." The general was grinning, and Kell shook his head in mock despair.

"The hell of it is, General, you're right. *After* I try to make peace with the committee members, I'll do it."

Kell checked with Cindy before calling the networks to see if they would be interested in his presence on the Sunday morning news shows. They were, of course, and before leaving the office he alerted Joe.

"Watch 'Face the Nation' tomorrow morning, Joe. They've got David Bayne on from New York with me by satellite, and he doesn't know what's coming. This should be interesting."

"I wouldn't miss this one for the world," Joe replied.

23

Fred Sneadman checked his watch in the light of oncoming traffic as he pulled up in front of Washington's refurbished Union Station with his boss, Senator Kell Martinson, in the passenger's seat.

"It's 9:55, sir. Your train leaves at 10:30 so you've got a few minutes."

"I sure appreciate your staying late to get the agenda together, not to mention the taxi ride, Fred."

"No problem."

"You'll get those papers I gave you over to Joe Wallingford at the NTSB for me tomorrow, won't you?"

"Yes sir."

"Hand them to him personally, now, and only to him. Make him show you some identification." Kell looked at Sneadman. "I'm serious about that. He's taking a big risk working with us on this."

Sneadman nodded. "I understand."

"And"—Kell rummaged through a file folder as he talked—"tell Mr. Wallingford I'd appreciate it if he'd study the background material over the holidays, and reconfirm with him that the hearing begins at nine A.M. on January eighth, and give him the room number and all that."

"Yes sir." Sneadman had put the gearshift lever in park and was struggling to write on a steno pad balanced on the steering wheel.

"That drafting session two weeks ago really worked well. Tell him that. Tell him I said that thanks to his ideas, I think we've got a good piece of legislation. Have you heard any reaction, by the way?'' Kell closed the folder and stuffed it into his briefcase.

"From Wallingford? Only chuckles over the way you embarrassed North America last Sunday on network TV. If you mean committee staff reaction about the bill, we're going to have an uphill battle convincing everyone this is needed right now, but so far no one's throwing mud balls philosophically. The problem is, it's not revenue neutral.''

"But the funding plan was clever as hell, don't you think? It's almost neutral, even though plugging it into fuel taxes does constitute a bit of a tax hike.''

"Oh, I think it will wash, sir, but we'll need public pressure.''

"That's the other thing, and I only mentioned it in passing back at the office. I want you to get hold of Wally on the committee staff. He's the best congressional subcommittee publicist in the business. Tell him we need this to explode nationally on the day before the hearing starts, and I want to meet with him sometime next week if possible to plan the strategy, provided he'll do it.''

"Yes sir. And he will. He owes us a favor.''

"Should I ask what?''

"No.'' Fred grinned at him.

"Okay, Fred. I'll trust you—this time. By the way, you were planning to stay in the District over Christmas, weren't you? You're not changing any plans on my account?''

"No, no. My parents are driving in from Philly on Sunday and we're going to observe Hanukkah right here. Holding down the fort is no problem, and in fact, I was going to show them the office and even sit in your chair.''

Kell laughed at that. "Be my guest. Just don't swing on the chandeliers.''

"You don't have any, Senator.''

"Okay. Make a note to buy some chandeliers.'' Kell leaned back, chortling, while Sneadman shook his head.

"You're in an extraordinarily good mood tonight for someone about to risk his life on the open rails.''

"It's good to get away. It's good to see us go into recess after that marathon budget battle and the filibuster. Am I not entitled to one good mood a year?''

"According to the ethics committee, no, not if you enjoy it.''

"Oh. Well then. Officially I'm in a somber and serious mood, but Merry Christmas anyway."

"Happy Hanukkah to you too."

"Hanukkah. Yeah, you said that. I knew that." Kell looked at his watch again. "About time, I think. I hate running for planes and trains. By the way, has Cynthia left for Missouri?"

"I think so. She bustled out of the office around four."

"There was an item I needed to go over with her, but it can wait."

Kell got out of the car with his briefcase and wrestled his portable computer and bag from the backseat, placing them on a folding baggage cart and strapping them down as Fred watched. "You sure you don't want me to help you, sir?"

"No," Kell said, smiling. "No, you're already into the above-and-beyond-the-call-of-duty roster here. I let you do any more, I'll have to start treating you better."

"You mean, like paying me too?"

"Now cut that out, Sneadman." He laughed. "Seriously, Fred, thank you very much. Please relax and have a good holiday."

"I will, sir. You, too. Please don't break anything skiing."

"All I patronize are the bunny slopes, Fred. I'm in more danger around the cabin. By the way, did I give you the phone number?"

"Yes sir, you did."

He waved his aide good-bye and pulled the baggage cart into the beautiful interior of the proud old terminal, marveling at how effective the facelift and remodeling job had been. The bright floodlights illuminating the stark white facade of the classic, columned front, gave it a grandeur which rivaled any of the great public buildings of the world's capitals. It was a government project he had been proud to support.

Kell looked at the departure screens as he entered the terminal, searching for Amtrak's Night Owl, Train #66, and finding the track number at last. He entered the gate area at 10:05 P.M., enjoying the walk between the railcars and the sound of powerful diesel engines in the distance as he searched for car number 6705, an old but refurbished Pullman. Kell folded the baggage cart and slung the computer's strap over his shoulder, picking up bag and briefcase and trundling aboard, moving laboriously down the narrow companionway to compartment 8, a full-size bedroom he had reserved. He opened the compartment door and struggled inside with the luggage, banging a knuckle in the process, finally closing the door behind him.

"Just get into port, sailor?" A honeyed female voice enveloped him from the top bunk, and he held out his arms as Cindy came to him, giggling. "Mission accomplished? Or were you followed?"

"The only thing missing from this scene," he said, "is having the train pull out of King's Cross Station in London."

"Fred doesn't suspect a thing?"

"Probably thinks I've been drinking. I wished him Merry Christmas."

"Kell!"

"Well . . ." He kissed her deeply. "I was being ecumenical."

They held each other for a while, Cindy talking over his shoulder. "I never thought I'd ever drag you away from here for an entire week."

"I never thought you'd give up Christmas with your folks."

She pulled back, an impish look on her face. "You have your cellular phone in the briefcase?"

"Yes."

"The battery, please." Cindy had her hand out.

"Don't worry, it won't ring."

"The battery, or you go alone." Kell saw her smiling but serious. "Okay, honey." He kissed her once more and then pulled his briefcase onto the bed, retrieving the phone and sliding the battery out, which he handed to her with mock ceremony.

"Thank you." She stuffed it in her bag, zipped it up and sat down in a small chair. "Now. The itinerary."

"Okay."

"First, the tickets are to be placed outside the door. The porter has already made an extra fifteen dollars for agreeing not to disturb the very fatigued gentleman in room 8. Second, we get into Boston South Station at 8:35 A.M. I get off there, proceed to the taxi stand, take a cab to the rental car place, pick up said car, drive straight to the main station, where I find you looking confused on the curb. I pick up said confused lawmaker and proceed across state lines to Stowe, Vermont, where our prerented, prepaid, prewarmed cabin awaits."

"I thought transportation of pols across state lines for immoral purposes was illegal?"

"But fun."

"What about dinner? How are we going to handle the dining car without being seen together?" he asked.

"We're not," she said, pointing to a large tote bag. "Dinner is already here, sir. But first, a little music." Cindy reached down and produced a small tape recorder, which she snapped on, the sweet sounds of a string quartet playing Bach's Double Concerto in D filling the room. "Next, le tablecloth." Out came a checkered red-and-white plastic tarp, which she draped over the small table by the window. "And, the menu includes hamburgers à la golden arches, pommes frites from the same source, a naïve little white wine with great pretension and screw-top cap, and enough cheese to feed an army of rats—but why discuss the House of Representatives tonight." They were both laughing as Kell tried to pull her out of the chair with carnal intent.

"No, no, no. Not yet!" she said in mock alarm, her index finger in his face.

"Why not?"

"Your suit. Your suit is wrinkled."

"So?"

"We should hang it up. Out of your suit, please."

"Okay . . ." He began taking off his suit coat. "But what should I get into?"

Cindy smiled as she undid the top button of her blouse and slowly rose from the chair, moving to him and touching the tip of his nose very lightly with her finger. "Did the honorable gentleman from Kansas ask what he should get into?"

Kell looked amused but puzzled. "Yes."

"Me." Cindy began undoing his tie. "Dinner can wait. I can't."

An hour north of New York City in the dead of the night, Kell awoke alone and startled for a second, rolling over to see Cindy standing at the window in the darkness, watching the lights go by, the evocative sound of railroad crossing bells approaching, dropping in pitch as the train shot past, the volume dying rapidly in the distance behind them, the sound of heavy steel wheels clickity-clacking occasionally over unwelded rail sections beneath the car. What a beauty she was, he thought, the changing lights and flickering shadows playing off her breasts, the lightness of her tawny hair cascading over tan shoulders, the deeply provocative shape of her stomach and buttocks the essence of femininity. How lucky to be with her, to have her love and her trust.

Cindy's plan worked, as usual. In wartime, he had told her, the Army would need her as a logistics expert. They were in the cabin surrounded by snow by 2 P.M., and on the slopes by 3, having a ball, Cindy leading him on merry chases through the snow on rented skis. In the interest of anonymity, Kell kept a pair of dark glasses in place into the evening as they mingled with the après-ski crowd in the restaurant, but no one seemed to notice who he was, or even care. They watched a movie at the lodge, a well-acted love story with Matthew Broderick and Jodie Foster set on a space station in near-Earth orbit, and ended the evening in front of a roaring fire back in the cabin, wearing little but contented expressions, debating the finer points of what lovemaking would be like in a weightless environment.

The phone woke them at 9:30 A.M. on the twenty-third, the sun shining through the front windows, the day full of promise. Kell was surprised to hear Fred's voice, and more surprised when Fred explained he was patching through a call from the White House assistant chief of staff.

"What is it?" Cindy rubbed her eyes and snuggled up to his back as Kell propped himself on his left elbow and tried to sound professional.

"Shhhh!" He said it softly over his shoulder, holding the mouthpiece, waiting for a voice on the other end.

"Senator Martinson? You there?"

"Yes. How are you?"

"Fine Senator. I'm sure sorry to bother you, but the President asked me to chase you down. King Hussein is flying in on short notice to discuss his initiative for Beirut. Since we know you two are friends and fellow pilots, the President was hoping you could come help us out."

"Entertain him, you mean?"

"Not entirely. There are some substantive things we'd like you to help us present. Anyway, could you make it?"

"Yes," Kell said without hesitation. "Just tomorrow?"

"That's right, Senator. You could get back on a plane by two."

"What time do you want me there?"

Kell felt Cindy's warmth diminish as she moved away slightly, her hand leaving his chest, her arm retracting.

"Call me through the White House switchboard when you get in this afternoon," the voice said, "and I'll have the final itinerary. The king's coming into Andrews, and we'll shepherd you out there for the arrival."

"Fine. See you then." Kell hung up the phone and rolled over, his eyes spotting the obvious disappointment on Cindy's face.

"Presidential request, honey. I'm sorry. Hussein is coming to town, and it's a privilege to be asked. I should not refuse."

"You didn't, in any event," she said, smiling rather weakly.

"I'll be back tomorrow night, and then nothing will get in the way till we come back on the second."

She said nothing for a few seconds, kissing him lightly then and slipping out of bed and into the satin robe he had given her. Her words were spoken to the far wall, her voice very quiet. "I'll make us some coffee. We'll need to get you moving." Kell watched her glide into the kitchen in the chill of the morning air, worried that she was truly upset by something politically unavoidable. But she would understand. She always did. After all, she was a pro at this business.

She kissed him good-bye at noon before opening the door, a hurry-and-get-yourself-back-to-me send-off which kept him smiling all the way down to the interstate and over to Burlington. While Kell stepped on a Boeing 737 bound for Washington National, Cindy tried to lose herself in a book back at the cabin, deciding then to pull out the box of tinsel she had brought and decorate a tiny Christmas tree. At least they would have Christmas Eve, she thought. He was a senator. She wanted him to be successful and powerful and summoned occasionally by the President of the United States for state functions. So if she wanted all that, she asked herself, why was she crying?

The snowstorm began in Washington at 2 P.M. on the twenty-fourth, as King Hussein and Kell were leaving the White House for Andrews. They had become acquainted several years back at a state dinner when the king discovered that the senator was a fellow pilot. They had spent most of that evening telling each other pilot "war stories" while the diplomats fumed in the distance, and a friendship developed. Whenever Hussein came to town, Kell was called, usually by the king himself from Amman, Jordan. This trip had been too sudden for the normal call, and Kell had been unavailable—until the White House got involved.

The flurries had increased to a steady snowfall by the time the motorcade arrived at the Air Force base, and the king, a qualified Boeing pilot with a personal Lockheed Tristar 1011 and a type rating to command it, directed that his airplane be deiced. That complete, he and his American-born wife, Queen Nor, the daughter of a former FAA administrator, waved good-bye and lifted off the tarmac at 3:15 P.M. A White House limousine took Kell directly to Washington National, fighting its way through heavier and heavier snowfall, arriving at 4:20 for a 4:30 flight. Kell had called ahead from the car and was told not to worry, the flight would be delayed at least thirty minutes. By the time he reached the gate, it had been canceled. At 6 P.M., unable to keep up with the accumulation, the airport manager closed the airport, Dulles following close on its heels.

"Cindy?"

"Kell. Where are you?"

A pause, and too long at that. She knew by the slight echo he wasn't close. "Honey, we're snowed in here at National. Everything's cancelled. I tried to get an Air Force bird, and I'm still working on that, but even Andrews is having trouble. I'll take the first thing I can get northbound. Are you doing okay up there?"

"Yes. Just missing you terribly. How did things go with Hussein?"

"Very well." Kell filled her in on the day, and when her interest seemed to flag, changed the subject back to the obvious. "I'm going to stay out here for awhile, just in case."

"No. Go back to your apartment, Kell. Try in the morning."

"Well, I may at that. I'm so sorry, Cindy. Let's just pretend Christmas isn't for another day and a half. It'll be okay."

He replaced the receiver with a hollow feeling, more for her than himself. She could have been with her mother and father in St. Joseph. They were getting on in years, and it was a sacrifice for her to be with him. But when duty calls . . .

When it was obvious nothing with wings was going to fly

northbound until Christmas Day at the earliest, Kell checked into a hotel in Crystal City adjacent to the airport. Somehow it didn't seem right to go home. He phoned to give Cindy the number, then dove into a fitful, lonely sleep. It certainly didn't seem like Christmas. In the morning he phoned her as soon as he had rebooked his flight and the airport began the process of reopening. "I'll be there, if all goes well, by seven tonight."

"No, Kell. I've had some time to think. I want you to stay there. I'm coming back."

"What? Cindy, no! We've still got a week together. We . . ."

"Don't leave, Kell. You'll just pass me in the air. I'll call you back with my inbound flight time. I've already arranged transportation."

"Cindy . . ." But the line was dead. He tried again but she wouldn't answer, and when he at last found someone at the lodge to physically go check the cabin, she had left.

The maroon-and-metallic 737 was the very same one that had brought him back two days before. He recognized the tail number as it nosed into the gate at National. Cindy was all business, of course, when she came up the jetway. It was home territory, and they could be easily recognized. But the need to be circumspect was tearing him up.

"Why? That's all I want to know. Why?" he said, anguish in his voice.

She motioned him out to the concourse and in silence they walked toward the main part of the old terminal before she turned to him suddenly. "My flight to Kansas City is on TWA, Kell, in thirty minutes. Let's go down to their club room." She turned, leaving him stunned and rushing to catch up. "You're going home?"

"Yes."

"Why? Has something happened with your parents?"

"No."

"No? Then, *why* Cindy? Answer me!" He tried to stop her, to whirl her around, but she pulled away and kept walking resolutely to the southern section of the terminal and through the doors of the club room to a private upstairs alcove where she sat down facing him, waving him to an opposite chair.

"Kell, I tried to rationalize it. It was a political plus for you to be called back here. You needed to come. That was good."

"Then why . . . ?"

She looked at him sadly, tears betraying her attempt at control. "There I was, holding on to you, so close I could almost hear your thoughts. And you didn't even ask."

"Ask what?"

"You didn't even ask whether you should go. You just accepted."

"Cindy!"

"No, Kell. Remember when I said I needed to be sure who came first when the chips were down? If you can't even ask me, then Lady Politics owns your soul."

"I *had* to go."

"All you had to do was touch my face and ask if I minded. That's all. Nothing more."

He sat back, defeated, and looked at her, feeling her slip away. "I'm sorry, Cindy. I didn't think."

"I know."

"You're going back to St. Jo for awhile?" The look in return chilled him. "How long?"

She was too slow to answer, and his stomach was already churning when she finally spoke.

"I don't know, Kell. You'll have to put me on leave, or fire me. I don't know when or even if I'm coming back. Fred can pick up for me. I'll communicate with him on where everything is."

She saw the pain in his face, but knew it had to be part of the process. "I need you, Cindy."

"And I truly need you, Kell. That is exactly the problem."

It hurt to see him hang his head in such gloom. "Kell, I'm not saying it's over. But I'm less sure now than before. I know if I'm going to live with you, love you, be your wife, I have to take a backseat. That's hard for me. I don't know if I can accept it."

"God, Cindy, this is like a replay of the breakup of my marriage, for Christ's sake."

"Well, perhaps you understand why *she* couldn't adapt. Is it so hard to see why?"

"It's hard to even think about losing you. My God! It's Christmas. It's impossible to think about not being with you." He looked up suddenly, "What am I going to do at the office? Sneadman's a good aide, but he's not ready for prime time. How about that hearing? The NTSB bill? We did that together, how can I do that alone?''

"You may have to.''

"Cindy . . .''

She looked at her watch and got up. "I've got to go . . . or I won't.''

"Then don't. Please. I'm begging you not to leave.''

She started to reply, then shook her head, took his hand, and began guiding him to the stairway and the door. They walked in silence to the gate, Kell struggling against feelings of emptiness and panic as she handed the ticket to the gate agent and took the boarding pass.

They walked to the window next to the door before she turned to him. "Give me a week or so.''

"This was to be our week, Cindy.''

"As were the last two nights, my love.''

Her choice of words gave him a glimmer of hope, and he held her hands in his. "I love you, Cynthia Elizabeth Collins.''

"And I, you, Kell. Give me some time. It is I who has to adjust now, or not at all.''

And she was gone.

24

Joe Wallingford had just turned his desk calendar to the current day when Beverly Bronson charged into his office and slammed the door behind her, eyes flaring and mouth set. "So, Mister Wallingford. You only dropped by Senator Martinson's office for a social visit with Cynthia Collins, huh? Like hell you did!" Beverly slammed a copy of Senate Bill 323 on his desk—the NTSB bill—along with a copy of the subcommittee's letter inviting Chairman Dean Farris to testify on January 8. "You had a hand in this, didn't you, Joe?"

Joe looked at her and sat back in his chair, keeping an even expression. "Where would you get that idea, Beverly?"

"Oh, come on, Joe. The first proposed legislation in a decade affecting the NTSB and it just happens to whistle in out of the blue a mere three weeks after I see you at Martinson's door. Some coincidence!"

"Did you call Cynthia Collins to ask what I was doing there?"

"Not until this morning when we got this, but she's out of town somewhere, as I'm sure you already know. I'm equally sure she'll cover your story, Joe. But with you and Dean at loggerheads the day before, and this bill proposing new ways for appointing board members and the chairman, even a first grader could figure out what's going on." A wry smile broke through her apparent anger at him, and that was puzzling.

"You're jumping to unwarranted conclusions."

"Am I?"

"But I'm sure you've long since told Dean where you saw me."

360

Beverly looked at him in silence for a few seconds. "No, as a matter of fact I haven't."

Joe was surprised, and let it show. "Why not? I thought the very day I saw you in the elevator . . ."

"Yeah. You called me Dean's KGB. I *really* appreciated *that*."

"Well . . ."

"Okay, Joe, let's stop shadowboxing. It's just you and me in here—unless you've got us bugged." She shook her head ruefully. "Now *I'm* getting paranoid."

"Beverly, please sit down." Joe motioned her toward a chair across the desk, and she finally sat on the edge of it, as if ready to bolt.

"Joe, I am well aware that everyone around here thinks I'm merely an extension of Dean Farris." She sat back and shook her head slightly. "I'm also aware that people think my intellect must vary in inverse proportion to my bra size. However, I do happen to have a mind of my own"—she followed Joe's gaze and looked down at her blouse—"despite my big tits. Yeah, I know, you can't take your eyes off of them. Don't be embarrassed, you're not alone."

"I'm sorry Beverly, I didn't mean to—"

"You're male, I'm overbuilt, that's normal. But I am not Dean's mindless bimbo. And I happen to think this bill is a damn good idea. Does that surprise you?"

"In fact, yes."

"Okay. Good. It has obviously surprised you that I have not said a word to the chairman about your none-too-subtle involvement in this bill and this hearing. In fact, when he asked me about it a while ago I dismissed it. I told him such things tend to pop up every few years when committee staffs run out of other things to do. And he bought it."

"Why didn't you . . . ?"

"Why not tell him to raise his defenses?"

"Yes. Isn't that your job?"

"My job, Joe, is congressional liaison. I try to keep us out of trouble with Congress and keep our funding coming. Yes, I do try to put a good spin on our image over there, and yes, I am supposed to advise the chairman what to say and when to say it when he's called to testify. But nowhere in my job description does it say I'm also supposed to hide this chairman's abject stupidity.''

"What? So you're . . .''

"Setting him up? You might say that. That's why I'm pretty ticked off at you. You've apparently done what I've wanted to do all along, and when I tried to send you signals to tell you I wanted to join the effort, you just figured I was trying to protect Dean's interests. That hurt. The way you dismissed me hurt.''

"I'm sorry, Beverly, really, but the truth is, we don't know each other very well. I never suspected you might be fed up with Farris too.''

"He's damaging this Board, Joe. That's why I want to be on the team, on your team, whatever it's up to. You staging a mutiny? Hand me a cutlass, laddie, and move over. But you've got to trust me and tell me what the hell's going on. Now, is someone preparing an ambush over there or not?''

It was Joe's turn to stare at her, looking carefully for signs of duplicity. The North America investigation was still in disarray, and Joe was trying to keep the lid on until the subcommittee met, hoping to get some new answers. He had to be careful. If Beverly tipped off Farris with nearly two weeks to go before the chairman was due to walk into Kell Martinson's trap, it would give him time to burn the evidence and circle the wagons. But if Beverly *was* lying about keeping Farris in the dark, then the chairman would already know there were people gunning for his official hide, and telling her more wouldn't make much difference. Either way, with caution, he could probably fill her in.

"Beverly,'' he began cautiously, "how familiar are you with Dean's outside contacts on the North America investigation?''

She smiled and looked down before replying. "You mean, do I know about all the phone calls from David Bayne, North America's chairman, and the calls from upstairs—from Bill Caldwell—about the doctor? Do I also know something's up with the Miami Air accident which I can't quite isolate because John Phelps won't talk to me? The answer is yes, Joe. That's why I'm concerned about the damage he's doing to all of you in the trenches. This poor dolt may be a great college professor, but here at the NTSB he's in way over his head, and the thing I cannot forgive is his letting people reach in and manipulate us, sometimes in scandalous ways. In fact, I probably know of some you don't.''

"I wouldn't doubt it."

"Academically and socially he's smart. But politically and legally he doesn't understand how careful and circumspect you have to be."

"From my vantage point, Beverly, the main problem is he can't understand why his people in the trenches must not be interfered with."

She was nodding. "Okay, coconspirator, am I in the club now, or what? Is there a test? An initiation rite? As long as it's not kinky . . ."

Joe smiled at her. "Okay, you're in the club. There's someone in the Hart Senate Building I want you to talk to."

"Wouldn't be an elected official, would it?"

"How'd you know?" Joe asked, smiling.

Beverly got up from her chair and put a hand on the door. "Joe, I am sincere. Make an appointment for me with whomever you think I should talk to, and tell whoever it is that I'm willing to help. I do have Dean's trust for a little while longer."

"Will do." Joe felt stunned, but far less isolated.

As Beverly Bronson left Joe Wallingford's office in Washington, North America Airlines' government affairs vice-president Mark Rogers was on the hot seat in Dallas, facing North America's chairman, David Bayne, across his imposing desk—a copy of Senate Bill 323 on the blotter, along with the letter from the subcommittee asking for Bayne's personal participation.

"What do we think about this, Mark?"

"I think you'd better go, David. It would send the wrong signals if you didn't."

"Why?"

"Well . . . after Putnam and Walters went off half-cocked two weeks ago, and then got you broadsided and embarrassed on national television, our previous position of alleging that the Board's investigators were out of control has no credibility. Before that, though, we were sufficiently upset with NTSB actions that you had to complain and put pressure on people in D.C., right? Well, here's a bill to reform things, but if it passes, it will make the Board much more powerful and independent. We've *got* to have an opinion on *that*."

"You think we should oppose it?"

Mark Rogers snorted and shook his head. "Can you imagine an NTSB with almost as much power as the federal judiciary?

That's where this bill is headed. If a federal judge goes off the deep end and does something essentially stupid, we have to grin and bear it while we appeal. There's no one we can contact to apply pressure to a judge. Well, sir, if this bill goes through, the NTSB's people will be almost as insulated.''

''That's an extreme view.''

''David, what's the alternative? Support this bill? Don't forget why we fought them on Doc McIntyre: because they were on a witch-hunt. This bill licenses witch-hunts.''

Bayne leaned back in his chair and thought a minute. He had reasoned through the same logic, but listening to someone else present the case helped put it in perspective. ''Mark, how do I argue this in a hearing? I can't accuse them of staging witch-hunts.''

''True. But we want them to be accountable to the industry. That's the argument, just like we want elected officials to be accountable to the electorate. The way the Board is structured now, they can be pressured if they stray too far from reason. Even when there's not a crash we have some degree of influence currently to encourage them to face the realities of the business world, you know, when they want to demand hideously expensive safety features no one can afford. If this bill passes? No way. It might be a criminal act for you to even hint at having objections to their methods.'' Rogers got to his feet and gathered the papers from Bayne's desk, watching him for signs of objection. There were none, so he continued. ''I'll draft your statement and a briefing paper for you, if you're going.''

Bayne looked at him and nodded. ''Do it. I'm going.''

Mark Rogers left David Bayne's office at the same moment John Walters was facing professional panic in a small office at North America's operations base. On his right was Senior Vice-President Ron Putnam, on his left Doctor McIntyre, and teetering in the balance was his future as an airline executive—a future looking increasingly bleak. Before them on a small coffee table in Walters's office was a stack of medical papers from McIntyre's files. Walters had finally confronted the doctor on his return from the Canadian Rockies, and to his horror, the whole story had tumbled out.

Putnam shook his head slowly as he picked up some of the medical forms and let them drop, looking incredulously at

McIntyre, who was not looking back. "Not one time did you examine him? Not one godforsaken time? What the fuck were we paying you for, Doctor?"

McIntyre looked up slightly, talking to Putnam's shoes. "I *did* examine him in my own way. I watched him daily, I'd check his heart rate or blood pressure in his office at intervals, I just didn't bring him down to my office for a formal exam. I mean, this guy is a company officer and chief pilot and my superior, right? He shouldn't be treated the same way as some bozo line pilot. I knew Dick could be trusted! If there was anything wrong in the way I was medically supervising him, he'd tell me. Besides, he wasn't flying much anyway."

"Right. And of course God had given him authority to suspend federal rules. Jesus!" Putnam picked the papers up and slammed them down. "Now, tell me again, 'cause this is beyond belief. He'd just send you the signed FAA medical form and you filled out the doctor parts?"

"Yes."

"What'd you do, make up the blood pressure and temperature or whatever else I see on these?"

There was a long pause before the doctor replied, his face crimson. "Yes."

"And he obviously knew you were doing this?"

"I think so . . . yes, I'm sure he did."

"Wasn't he supposed to have an electrocardiogram each time?"

"Yes."

"But you didn't do that? And you didn't have any EKGs in his file, which is why you came screaming harassment to us and pulled us into your web of deception, is all that correct, you fucking idiot?"

McIntyre sighed and nodded, his head still cupped in his hands.

"So you put someone else's EKGs in Timson's file, didn't you?"

McIntyre simply nodded.

"For Christ's sake, man, you're an FAA-certified doctor. Those are federal requirements you were screwing around with. The goddamn FAA doesn't care how much you trust the man. They don't care if he's a vice-president and chief pilot. Before he gets a medical certificate, they want a doctor looking

at a warm body. Jesus, McIntyre, do you know the meaning of
the phrase *gross negligence*?''

There was no response, so Putnam continued, getting out of
his chair and stalking around the room, arms flailing, his voice
a barely contained shout. "When an airline crashes or an oil
company grounds a ship and oils up half a continent, one of the
things the lawyers do is try to prove that it wasn't just *ordinary*
negligence, it was *gross* negligence. Like a company permitting
an alcoholic sea captain to keep sailing supertankers, or an airline filing fraudulent company medical examinations to keep a
captain flying. And you know what happens when they find
gross negligence? That means tens, perhaps hundreds of millions of dollars more in liability. That means insurance premi-
ums off the chart. That means having the FAA paint a large
bull's-eye on the side of the company logo.'' Putnam adopted a
gruff voice. "Here's North America. Watch those sneaks! They
don't play by the rules!''

John Walters sighed and looked up at Putnam. "Even with this,
Ron, we don't know whether there was anything medically wrong
with Dick. I haven't asked him. I called you immediately.''

Putnam whirled on him. "Shall we talk about presumptions?
The sonofabitch nosedives into the terrain with a perfect medical
history, everybody *assumes* he must have had, at worst, a brain
fart. But when the man hasn't had an honest medical certificate
in ten goddamn years, they'll assume he's suffered some sort of
impairment, which means we shouldn't have let him fly, which
means gross negligence. Even if there's not a thing in the world
wrong with him right this minute, we're screwed.'' Putnam
walked to a far wall, closed his eyes, and leaned his head against
it with gritted teeth visible, hitting the wall hard with the fist of
his right hand, the *thunk* reverberating through the room. "Bayne
is gonna come fucking unglued! He'll probably fire all of us.''

Ron Putnam turned suddenly in Walters's direction, his face
a dark visage of rage and betrayal. "Okay, what else? Let's get
it all out. John, did you know this irresponsible quack was hangar flying Timson's records?'' Putnam pointed at McIntyre like
a harbinger of doom.

"Absolutely not.''

"You were defending him on principle alone?'' Putnam half
laughed, half sneered the question.

"Yes, believe it or not . . . that, and because he was panicked," Walters replied. McIntyre remained silent.

"There's another loose end," someone said. The voice was muffled, but Putnam and Walters recognized it was coming from McIntyre. He looked up at them and sighed a ragged sigh. "When . . . I sent them the records of the exams I doctored up? From Canada, you know?"

"Yes." Putnam almost hissed the last consonant.

"I pulled the records of another pilot about the same age and weight, and I carefully took his name off and put Dick's on it. So they had a full set of exam results for all those exams."

"So what's the problem?" Putnam asked, no less harshly.

"I . . . I didn't check some of the vitals, like eye and hair color, and blood type. They may not catch it, but they didn't match."

Putnam looked at the remorseful physician with utter contempt. "Don't worry, Doctor, I'm sure they caught it. I'll wager you your goddamned job that they've been trying to ask you about exactly that!"

January 8 dawned unexpectedly balmy for a winter's day in the nation's capital, and NTSB Chairman Farris was enjoying the 60-degree temperatures. He had never had the opportunity to sit before a Senate subcommittee and expound on the serious and important work he supervised, and he was looking forward to it. Beverly Bronson had briefed him that the bill stood little chance of passage, especially if the subcommittee members were left with the impression that the NTSB was running like a precision watch. That would impress the White House as well, and they undoubtedly would be watching. Dean turned to Beverly as they sat in the back of a taxi, headed across the quadrangle to the Senate office complex, where the hearing was already underway. "Who'd you say is televising this, Bev?"

She looked at the chairman and smiled, a picture of calm and self-assurance. "C-SPAN is broadcasting it live, and taping it too. I think all the networks will be there on tape, and I don't know who else. The newspapers stirred it up." Beverly watched him turn toward the front of the cab, a serene smile on his face. The *Washington Post* had broken the story just after Christmas, but the morning edition carried a lengthy piece on the inherently divisive problems of an aviation accident investigative agency trying to solve bus and pipeline disasters too, and the *New York*

Times had done a front-page article on the past conflicts between the Board and the Air Line Pilots Association over quality of investigations. No one in the media had devoted any ink to the possibility of internal scandal. None had seen the storm clouds on the horizon. And, fortunately, none of the briefing papers which could be sitting in front of the subcommittee members had leaked.

Dean Farris took his seat at the witness table as Beverly took a chair beside him, facing the curved, single-tiered dais which at varying times during the typical Senate hearing would accommodate from one or two senators up to a dozen, with waves of staff members ebbing and flowing behind them in accordance with the daily tides of Senate business.

The Air Line Pilots Association's president had already testified, supporting the bill, as had the Air Transport Association and the Regional Airlines Association. Executives from two commuter airlines had added their stories of truncated NTSB investigations due to budgetary constraints, and a senior vice-president of Amtrak had submitted a written statement in lukewarm support.

But the star the media had been waiting for—had been told in confidence they should wait for—was Dean Farris. And after some introductory niceties and Farris's formal statement, which had been drafted by Beverly and several other staffers, Farris looked up at Kell Martinson and four other senators. "I'll be happy to entertain any questions at this time."

"Chairman Farris," Kell began with a friendly smile, "first of all, let me call you Mr. Chairman, and for the sake of not getting us all confused, instead of you calling me Mr. Chairman, just use Senator, okay?"

"Certainly Senator," Farris replied, smiling. This was going to be easy.

"I might also add"—Kell looked to his left and his right, making eye contact with the three other senators present— "thanks to the generous agreement of my colleagues, and having studied this issue extensively in preparation for submission of this bill, I am going to do all the preliminary questioning, then give the other subcommittee members their chance." Kell looked back at Farris. "Now Mr. Chairman, are you familiar with the Independent Safety Board Act of 1974?"

Farris answered that he was, and outlined the general aim of the act as Beverly had carefully briefed him.

"Mr. Chairman, would you say that the NTSB as it operates today fulfills the promise and intent of that act?"

Farris looked puzzled. "I'm afraid I don't understand, Senator."

"Well," Kell began, "we agree the legislation tried to keep the Board from being influenced by outside political forces, or any other forces. It tried to make sure that interested parties would have no ability to sway the decisions on accident causation. So, Mr. Chairman, you're the head of the thing? Does it work that way?"

Farris smiled and nodded. "Certainly does, Senator. Our decisions are our own. There is no ability on anyone's part, whether in the political arena or the corporate community, to push us."

"Does anyone try?" Kell asked.

"Well, I'm sure from time to time in the middle of an investigation, since we have so many civilians actually working with us on these investigative groups, people attempt to argue from a parochial point of view, but in the end, with a well-balanced panel, we still get the truth."

"Do you now?" The sharpness of the question echoed like a rifle shot. Something about Senator Martinson's tone triggered a warning bell in Farris's mind, slowing his response ever so slightly. "Yes, we do."

"Well then, Chairman Farris, there are some things which have come to the subcommittee's attention which I'd like to ask you about, and the first concerns the tragedy in Kansas City, the North America crash."

"Okay."

"North America has a company doctor named McIntyre, is that correct, Mr. Chairman?"

"I believe he is a company doctor, yes, Senator."

"Now, within a week of the Kansas City crash, some of your investigators contacted Doctor Mcintyre, I believe, and asked him for certain records. Is that right?"

"Well, as I recall, probably."

"And Doctor McIntyre apparently asked his company to block that request, and at one point North America threatened to go to court to get an injunction against the NTSB's seeking those records, which, if I have it right, were the medical records for the captain that crashed Flight 255 in Kansas City, that captain also being the airline's chief pilot and a staff vice-president. Is all that correct?''

Beverly had been watching Dean Farris as the blood began to drain from his face. She could see his vocal muscles constricting, and she forced a look of puzzlement when he glanced in abject alarm at her as Kell continued in an even, friendly tone of voice. ''Now, Mr. Chairman, obviously your investigators wanted to see those records, which was probably a logical thing to want to do, and North America officially did not want to give them up, or they surely wouldn't have taken the extraordinary step of going to court. In a case such as this, isn't it important for the Board and their investigators to be unrelenting? Isn't it important that the public know they cannot be scared away from a legitimate inquiry when innocent passengers have died in a mode of public transportation? In other words, if the investigators in their wisdom think they need to see those records, shouldn't we have the assurance that no one will be allowed to block them?''

''Yes . . . uh, of course. I don't understand—''

''Bear with me, please, Mr. Farris. Now . . .'' Kell shuffled some of the papers in front of him and made some notations, letting Farris sweat. ''Do you recall a few years back when there was that terrible Amtrak accident north of Washington in which the Conrail engineer, who was found to be under the influence of drugs, ran in front of a high-speed Metroliner?''

''Yes, Senator, everyone does. What does that have to do with North America?''

''Well, let me just ask you a hypothetical question, Mr. Chairman. If you had been chairman at that time, and the president of Conrail had called you—which I do not suggest he ever would, this is a hypothetical question—but let's say he did call and said, 'Dean, please call off your dogs. You have my assurance that Conrail's personnel did nothing wrong. Don't harass the poor engineer anymore.' Now, would that be wrong, Mr. Chairman?''

''Of course. the man was, as you say, found to be on drugs, he—''

''Yes, but—'' Kell smiled and held up a hand to stop Farris, whose voice had risen in pitch a bit, ''what I'm asking, sir, is whether it would be wrong for the NTSB chairman to actually agree to do what the railroad leader was asking?''

Farris knew where he was being led, but it was like sliding on ice; he had no traction, no way to stop. ''It would, of course, be wrong, Senator, for him to actually stop his people from investigating, but in the normal civility of a conversation, you know, the railroad man might have the impression he had come away with some concession when he hadn't."

Kell tapped his chin with a finger and squinted. "You mean, he might make the railroad president think he'd back off, but not really do it? He wouldn't talk to his investigators?"

"That's right."

"I gather it would be wrong for him to actually talk to his investigators and say, 'Back off'?"

"Yes, of course it would."

"Would it be wrong of him to even relay the conversation to his investigators, knowing they might take that as a signal to back off?"

"Your hypothetical situation is getting rather deep, Senator. A Board chairman like myself can't know for certain how someone is going to interpret something."

"That's exactly my point, though, Mr. Chairman. Since the investigator who has to poke around this railroad may be too impressed with the power of the railroad's president for the investigation's good, wouldn't it be taking a risk to even mention the phone call to an underling because that could influence him to pull punches, not ask for records, not seek depositions, or even stop pushing for medical records central to the case?"

"Perhaps."

"Just perhaps?"

"No, I mean I do agree," Farris said.

"Good. I'm glad you do. But that, then, troubles me."

Farris gave Kell a puzzled look. "I beg your pardon, Senator, was that a question?"

"No sir, but this is: Isn't it true that among the many telephone calls you got in the days after the North America crash, one of them was from Mr. David Bayne, chairman and CEO of North America?"

Seconds passed with Farris frozen in place before he leaned into the microphone to answer. "Yes, Senator, Mr. Bayne called me. That's not at all unusual."

"His airline had two planes in that crash, of course, and his chief pilot might be the cause of it, and he calls you, and that's normal?"

"It's not abnormal."

"What did you two gentlemen talk about?"

"The general progress of the investigation, of course."

"I see. Did he mention Doctor McIntyre?"

"Yes."

"Yes he did, in fact. In fact, he asked you to call off your dogs, didn't he? He asked you to tell your people to stop harassing the poor doctor, who by that time they had sent on a hurried vacation to Canada because he had become so scared. Is that correct?"

Farris put his hand over the microphone and leaned toward Beverly with a whispered command. "Get the staff counsel over here fast."

"I can't. He's out today," she whispered back innocently. Farris turned again to the microphone, looking nervously at Kell.

"Senator, I don't know where you got all this but—"

"Oh, Mr. Farris, don't you worry about our sources. They will be placed under oath as necessary and their recollection of what you told them—and I emphasize the plural—will go on the record, too. We're talking about undue influence here. The airline chief calls you, asks you to call off your dogs, and what did you say?"

Farris's mind raced through possible answers. It was obvious he was alone, Beverly had made no move to help him, to whisper in his ear. How could this have happened? He should have brought the Board's lawyer, the staff counsel. He saw the TV cameras and radio microphones. He had seen David Bayne behind him in the audience. Martinson was talking about multiple sources for that story. How could he deny it? He couldn't just lie to Congress. In fact, wasn't it a crime? A glimmer of a possibility locked into his head, and he looked up at the senator and tried to smile, though he was shaking inside. "Senator, obviously some disgruntled employee or employees of mine have come to your staff with some gross misinterpretation, and perhaps misunderstanding, of what occurred. Yes, David Bayne called me, and yes he pressured me rather substantially to back off, saying his physician was really spooked and in a bad way because of the pressure. Now, I warned him I could not and would not call off my people, but I would certainly make sure that they were civil to the doctor. Since this was the very first week of the investigation and there was time, and since we want the general cooperation of the airlines in a crash investigation, I'm not going to tell him to go to hell. I'm going to do what I did, assure him that my staff will treat the doctor properly, or words to that effect.''

"Did you?''

"Did I what, Senator?''

"Did you instruct your staff to treat the doctor properly?''

God, how much does he know? Farris thought frantically. That's the problem. Wallingford had probably started all this, so anything he said to Wallingford would now be in front of the Senator. "I instructed my investigator-in-charge, Aviation Accident Bureau Chief Joseph Wallingford, to accept the reality that the doctor was out of town, and to wait for him to get back before they pursued the matter of the records. They had tried to track him down in Canada on vacation, for heaven's sake. I, well, now as I remember it, I believe Bayne said one of his people, John Walters, would provide the records, and so there was no need for the doctor.''

"Isn't it true that Mr. Wallingford, and the head of your human performance group, wanted to interview the doctor?''

"Well, in time I'm sure . . .''

"Isn't it true, Mr. Chairman?''

"Maybe at that time.''

"Isn't it also true that you told Mr. Wallingford, and I quote—''

Here it comes, Farris thought to himself. This is where all this originated, that goddamn Wallingford!

Kell continued, quoting from the paper in his hand: "You said to Wallingford, 'I have assurance from North America they can give you whatever you want and I have given them assurance the harassment would stop, so you leave the doctor alone'?'' Kell had been reading from a piece of paper, his half-frame reading glasses balanced on his nose. He left them that way as he looked up, peering over the top of them at Farris, watching the man squirm.

"Senator, I probably said those words, but you've got the whole thing out of context.''

Kell Martinson reached up with his right hand and took hold of his glasses, removing them across his face with a small flourish while staring at Farris, holding the glasses like a prop. He had watched so many excellent trial lawyers use the gesture, and it worked well. In one small movement he had told Farris and the world that the NTSB chairman's last answer was unbelievable. "Out of context, Mr. Chairman?''

"Yes.''

"You assured North America that the harassment would stop, and that's out of . . . well, let's go on, shall we?" Kell put the glasses on again and looked at the paper again. "Did you also tell Mr. Wallingford—just before the start of the December Board of Inquiry in Kansas City, by the way—did you also tell him that, and I quote again, 'If you so much as breathe that physician's name again without my written permission, you can kiss your job with this Board good-bye'?"

Farris sat stone still without answering.

"Well, sir, are those words yours, and are they out of context too?"

"Again, Senator, I may have said those words, but in the context of trying to keep my employees from going too far in pursuing this doctor."

Kell summarized the actions taken by Joe and Andy Wallace to talk to McIntyre and get his records. "You consider that harassment?"

"It could be considered harassment, yes."

"It could be," Kell said, "by a company that had something to hide."

"You could read it that way, yes."

"And since you're supposed to be looking for the truth, why were you saying these things to the investigator-in-charge?"

Farris took another deep breath, squared his shoulders, and slightly overboosted the microphone trying to sound confident. "Well, Senator, I don't expect any layman to fully understand how we do things, but a certain amount of discretionary authority is necessary in my position, and I exercise it even if I have to take the heat for it later on. Now, you're characterizing all this as if I were trying to help North America hide from responsibility. You can twist it however you like, but all I was attempting to do was rein in some overzealous investigators of mine who were, in fact, harassing an honest doctor." Farris swept his right hand through the air. "Dr. McIntyre's friends were just concerned that we'd been too harsh with him, okay?"

"Oh, okay, I see now. Then these were people simply concerned that you'd overstepped the bounds of *propriety* . . . people other than David Bayne?" Kell asked him in a conciliatory voice, as if the problem had been solved by that revelation.

"Yes, you've got it, Senator." Farris said, visibly relaxing.

"I mean, even Bill Caldwell of the FAA, who's a friend of his too, called and pleaded with me to call off my dogs."

Dean Farris's words had stopped echoing around the hearing room before he realized what he had done. The reaction from the subcommittee members, the staff members, the knowledgeable people in the audience, and a particular FAA associate administrator watching the C-SPAN broadcast from his office at 800 Independence Avenue, was subtle but decisive. Dean Farris had just stabbed Bill Caldwell in his professional heart.

"For the record, Mr. Chairman," Kell said, "that was William Caldwell, associate administrator of the Federal Aviation Administration here in Washington, who called you to intercede on behalf of an FAA-certified medical examiner, Dr. McIntyre, a North America employee, then under NTSB investigation as the flight physician who had for many years certified the medical qualifications of the captain whose actions may have been at least one of the direct causes of the terrible airline tragedy in Kansas City three months ago? Is all that correct?"

Cold fear had gripped Farris as he recognized the depth of his gaffe. It took two tries to get an answer out, the first one too soft for the microphone to pick up. "Yes, Senator." There was nothing more he could say that wouldn't make it worse. Damn, damn, damn, damn! Caldwell would never speak to him again, of that he was certain.

It went downhill for Dean Farris from there. Kell guided him into a rambling, revealing series of answers about North America's attempt to get the NTSB to back off probing the management climate at the airline. His statements to Joe, his trip to Kansas City, the transcript of his remarks from the head table—all wove a heavy noose of evidence and circumstantial presumption that Dean Farris had not only let North America influence him, but also had led him to whipsaw his investigators in general, and Joe Wallingford in particular, trying almost frantically to thwart a deeper probe into why Dick Timson had pushed the control stick forward in Kansas City.

Farris was almost inaudible by the time Miami Air came up.

"Mr. Farris, did anyone, and I do mean *anyone*, outside the NTSB call you or communicate with you in such a way as to request, directly or indirectly, that the NTSB should back off a deeper investigation of the quality of maintenance at Miami Air?"

Farris hesitated just long enough to raise eyebrows, and another senator jumped in. "Chairman Farris, with Senator Martinson's approval, if it would make you feel better about unhesitating truthfulness, we could have you sworn in. We don't like our witnesses to feel uncomfortable, sir, and I see you spending more and more time considering your answers to very simple questions. Now, since I'm sure you wouldn't be contemplating telling us anything but the truth, I can only conclude that perhaps it would help to be able to say to whomever you might need to say it to, 'I was under oath, I had no choice.' Would that help?"

Farris had shaken his head, a horrid scowl on his face. "I do not need an oath to tell the truth, Senator. I am not in the habit of lying to Congress or anyone else."

"I'm truly glad to hear it. I yield my time, Senator."

"To repeat the question, Chairman Farris—"

"I know what the damn question is," Farris snapped. "And the answer is yes. One person. But before you take it out of context, he simply called to tell me . . . to give me a quality rating on this airline, Miami Air, and assured me that they were a quality operation."

"This man called you?" Kell asked.

"Yes he did."

"Out of the blue?"

"Well, after the incident we discussed, where the hole was blown in the top of their airplane. Before the crash."

"And who would that caller be, Chairman Farris? Would that be Bill Caldwell too?"

"Yes."

"And did you call off your investigator?"

"Yes."

"And that was about a month before what appears to be an improperly maintained Boeing 737 crashed in Florida, killing all aboard?"

"Yes."

"And, Mr. Chairman, you came here today to oppose this bill, and tell us the NTSB cannot be effectively influenced from outside by political or commercial considerations?"

There was no answer.

"Mr. Farris?"

"Yes."

25

Tuesday Night, January 8, Dallas, Texas

Mark Weiss pulled his coat tighter around him, hunching his back against the biting-cold wind of a Texas blue norther as it lashed at his face and ears, making the short walk to the curb a painful trek through an alien winter landscape. The frigid air mass had thundered in from the northwest earlier in the day, bringing a Siberian winter to Dallas, an annual symphony of impeded human convenience and heavy coats accompanied by the cacophony of breaking pipes, roaring furnaces, and soaring utility bills.

Mark clutched the manila folder of medical records as he fumbled for the keys to the rental car, his hands numb from the freezing temperatures, his head in shock from what he had just heard. Louise Timson had just handed him the key to the crash that had killed his family.

He plopped quickly behind the wheel and started the car, putting the heater on full blast and jamming the shift lever into drive, anxious to get away—to head for the airport—as if a slower getaway might prompt Mrs. Timson to emerge from her house and retract everything.

The last flight back to Washington left in less than an hour, at 11:30 P.M. He already had a ticket, but there would be no time to leave the car in the proper rental lot and take their shuttle. He would abandon it at the terminal and call its owners tomorrow. Getting on that flight was far more important than a penalty charge. He had to be back in Washington for the second day of the Senate subcommittee hearings.

Wednesday, January 9, Washington, D.C.

"Our first witness this morning is Captain Richard Timson, staff vice-president and chief pilot of North America Airlines. Captain Timson, would you come forward please?"

Kell Martinson watched Dick Timson get gingerly to his feet, a North America attorney at his side. The airline had protested the subpoena, but finally decided it would look better to comply than make a messy public battle of it. After all, they were only investigating the NTSB.

"As the captain is coming forward, it would be appropriate to mention, since Captain Timson was pilot-in-command of one of the airliners involved in the tragic North America accident in Kansas City on October twelfth, and since that crash is still under active investigation by the National Transportation Safety Board, we should make it clear that this forum is not trying to supersede that investigation, nor search for the cause. We have asked Captain Timson here today because we are probing undue political interference in NTSB investigations, and a prime example of that has been the attempts from various parties within and without the government to prevent NTSB investigators from probing certain medical records pertaining to the Kansas City crash. Since the records involved are those of Captain Timson himself, it is appropriate that he be deposed under oath in this forum to establish why a probe of these records might be important to the investigation."

Kell administered the oath to Dick Timson and let him take his seat. The early morning phone call and meeting with Mark Weiss and Joe Wallingford at Dulles Airport had left Kell sleepy, and he shook his head slightly to clear the cobwebs. It was inordinately warm in the hearing room, and that always made it difficult to stay awake when hearings droned on and became boring. This one, however, would be lively.

Copies of Timson's medical records had been made and distributed, but Timson had seen nothing as yet. He was walking into an ambush carefully laid.

The normal preliminary questions of name and job and other establishing items out of the way, Kell paused, looking directly at the captain, who was keeping a neutral expression and a steady voice.

"Following the accident, were you aware that your company

was seeking to block NTSB access to your medical records held by Dr. McIntyre?''

"No, sir."

"Do you know why they would have made such an effort?''

"No, sir. I learned about it later. I believe they felt the method of pressuring the doctor was wrong . . . not that there was any problem with the records.''

"What is your blood type, Captain?''

"Ah, my blood type is B negative. Why?''

"Let me ask the questions, please. Our committee staff is handing you copies of the medical records the NTSB was sent finally by Dr. McIntyre. These have your name written on each page, is that correct?''

Timson studied them quickly before looking up. "Yes.''

"And a stack of some ten FAA medical forms is included, each one representing the form you and every pilot must fill out each time your medical certificate is renewed pursuant to a medical exam, is that correct?''

"They're all here for about five years, yes.''

Kell thought he saw Timson's jaw muscles working as he realized the significance—and the danger—of the five-year time period.

"Now, Captain, would you look in the block circled in red on page one of Doctor McIntyre's internal office forms—the ones on which he records the results of his examinations each time—and tell me what blood type is listed?''

Timson was puzzled, but he complied, looking at the page Kell had indicated, and stiffening a bit in response.

"Uh, it says O positive, Senator. But that's not right.''

"Have you ever been O positive?''

Kell suppressed a smile. The question had befuddled Timson.

"Wha . . . what?''

"Have you ever had a blood type of O positive?''

"Senator, I'm not a doctor, but I don't think you can change blood types.'' Timson was looking at him as if he were dealing with a dangerous fool.

"So happens, Captain, that I agree, though I, too, am not a doctor. What color are your eyes, Captain?''

"Uh, green.''

"And would you describe your hair color as brown?''

"Yes sir.''

"Now, would you look at the stack of FAA forms you filled out every six months."

"Okay."

"Those forms all have you with green eyes and brown hair, right?"

"I . . . of course. What else would they have?"

"Indeed. You filled them out, they should be accurate, right?"

"Yes. Right."

"Now, look at Doctor McIntyre's office examination forms for the same period. Tell us what your hair color and eye color is on each one."

Timson started rifling through the papers again, finding the notations, his face turning crimson slowly but steadily as he realized something was wrong . . . something not of his making.

"What," Kell continued, "do you see notated there over a five-year period each and every time the doctor filled out his report?"

"I . . . it says brown eyes and blond hair."

"And again, each of the doctor's forms has you as an O positive blood type, right?"

"Yes. I guess so." Timson kept rifling back and forth as if the entries were going to change.

"Could you be mistaken about your blood type, Captain?"

Timson shrugged. "I guess I could. I always thought I was B negative."

"Captain, our staff is now handing you a copy of the hospital blood report from Kansas City's Truman Medical Center, the workup done just before you were admitted the night of the crash. What is your blood type there?"

Timson looked, then looked again, small beads of perspiration showing around his receding hairline. "Uh, this says . . . B negative."

"So, you *were* right after all?"

No answer as Timson kept his head in the papers, looking for the trap he knew was there somewhere. Finally he looked up. "I don't understand where you're going with this, Senator. If there's a question you want to ask me, please just ask."

"Okay, sir. We've established that the FAA application forms are your work product, and the other forms are Dr. McIntyre's. Both sets, though, reflect a perfectly healthy individual with two different hair and eye colors, and the doctor's forms have the wrong blood type. The FAA forms, of course, don't ask for blood type. Could it be that somehow the doctor got the wrong medical records mixed up with yours?''

"I don't see how . . .''

"Captain Timson, when an FAA-certified doctor fills out these forms, he usually does so while he's giving the exam, right?''

"I suppose.''

"Well, I'm only a private pilot with a third-class medical certificate, but that's how my doctors have always done it, progressively: height, weight, pulse rate, eye color, hair color, et cetera. Now, were you present when each of these medical exams was filled out by Doctor McIntyre?''

"I'm not sure.'' The voice was tightening. Kell could hear the tension level increasing as Timson fought for control.

"Now, Captain, tell me, how did a busy executive like you handle the biannual medical-exam routine? I mean, at your age you needed an electrocardiogram each time, as well as the full physical.''

Timson leaned into the microphone. "Senator, our company doctor was completely equipped in his office near mine to give those exams. I would simply go to him.''

"Physically?''

"Beg your pardon?''

"You physically, each and every time, went down to the doctor's office and had him give you the exam in person?''

"How else would it be done?''

"Again, Captain, let me ask the questions. And, please don't be offended, but you are under oath here. Were these FAA medical exams given to you personally in Dr. McIntyre's office each and every time?''

Dick Timson just stared at Kell for a minute, calculating the odds. The import of the questions was clear. If Martinson knew enough to ask such questions, he knew the exams had been pencil-whipped. Therefore, if he lied about them, he could face perjury charges of some sort for lying to Congress. They put people in jail for that sort of thing.

"Senator, let me explain how this worked. I kept in constant touch with Doc McIntyre. He knew my physical condition. I would fill out these medical applications every six months, and he would make his own decision on what, or how much, he would need to do in person to examine me. Sometimes he took my blood pressure in my office, for instance. I trusted his medical discretion. If he'd needed me in his office, then I would have gone."

Twenty feet behind the witness table, David Bayne's entire defenses had gone on full alert. Overnight he had coolly calculated how to put a reasonable spin on his calls to Farris, which were decidedly not illegal, but what the hell was coming now? Sitting beside him, Ron Putnam was dying a slow death inside, his decision to keep from Bayne McIntyre's falsification of medical exams obviously a fatal mistake. Somehow they had found out. He had based his decision on the once-reasonable hope that nothing more would be discovered, and that hope was crumbling.

In Dallas, glued to the C-SPAN broadcast on a television in his den, John Walters was oblivious to anything else, including the questions from his wife. Walters could see that something was very wrong. Something was coming, but what. Timson was coming apart! The feeling of impending doom almost blocked the senator's next question.

"You never, shall we say, pressured him to just fill out the forms and issue the license?"

"Of course not!" Timson was trying to be firm, but his resolve was slipping. Kell could see his jaw trembling slightly.

"But isn't it also true that not once in five years did you ever get a traditional, complete personal physical exam from Dr. McIntyre?"

There was a long pause before he answered in a quieter voice. "Yes sir. During that period, he always elected not to do it in person."

"Did he, Captain, have you send in a urine sample?"

"I . . . what?"

"Each of these exams has a lab workup of some sort, and at least one over that five-year span has a blood workup with the blood type listed as O positive. We just talked about it. Or could those workups be those of some other individual?"

"I wouldn't know."

"In fact, Captain, I think it's obvious, isn't it, that all the lab slips attached to your medical forms, and probably every single entry made by the doctor on those medical forms, was for someone else and not Richard Timson. Isn't that right?"

"I don't know that!"

"Okay, let's turn to something else. When you fill out the FAA forms, they ask a long list of medical questions. One of them asks if you've ever had frequent blackouts, another whether you've had a significant injury since the last report, and yet another whether you're under medication. Right?"

Timson knew he'd been nailed. He didn't know how, but he knew it was all crumbling. The defense, the facade, everything. But how? How could they know? "What are you getting at, Senator?"

"Captain Timson, do you know anyone by the name of Joseph Thompson?"

Timson gasped audibly, then caught himself, but he knew instantly he'd been discovered, though his whirling mind could not grasp how on earth. No one knew! No one in the company knew! How in God's name could they know about *Thompson*?

Fifteen feet behind him in the audience, Mark Weiss realized he'd been holding his breath, in some ways, since leaving Dallas. There was a chilling reality to this hearing: the truth would not be unfolding without Louise Timson's call. Kell Martinson's precisely targeted questions would not have been possible without her confession.

She had phoned Martinson's office yesterday during the hearing, her plea coming in the form of a folded yellow slip handed to Weiss by one of the senator's people. "Urgent you call Louise Timson immediately," it said, giving her Dallas number. The senator was still dismembering Dean Farris at the time, and Mrs. Timson had been watching the process on C-SPAN back in Dallas, aware that her husband would face the same questioning the following morning. Apparently she had reached the breaking point.

"Mrs. Timson?"

"Dr. Weiss. Thank you for calling me back. I . . . you said anytime. I saw you in the audience, on TV." There was a pause. "I know what they're going to do to Dick if I don't stop it. Can you come here?"

He had hesitated, but only for a second. He had indeed told her anytime, anywhere. . . .

"To Dallas?"

"Yes. Please. Please!" The voice broke into sobs, then recovered. "Dick left this afternoon. He's on his way there.

Please, I need to talk to you. I'll pay for the ticket, Dr. Weiss, but I need to tell you what . . . what happened. Why they mustn't blame him.''

It had been a mad dash to National Airport, but Mark was on a 5:30 P.M. flight to Dallas, arriving at the Timson home before 8 P.M. local time, carrying his tape recorder and consumed with questions.

Louise Timson had seemed rock-steady and calm when she met him at the door, and almost relieved as she showed him into the living room. She had taken the time to dress elegantly, Mark noticed, an expensive jade bracelet dangling from her wrist as she served him the coffee she insisted on making, the flash of a substantial diamond wedding ring catching his eye as she smoothed the skirt of her carefully selected outfit. The elegant house and the taste of the lady within were typical earmarks of North Dallas opulence.

She had seemed distraught and near hysteria on the phone. Now, however, she had pulled herself together, proceeding along a set course, her mind made up about what she had to do and exactly how she must do it. There was massive tension behind the facade of her composure, a tension Mark could feel, like the tiny vibrations of an overwound spring barely restrained by failing bonds. Had she walked into his office, he would have fought to remove those bonds. But this meeting must obviously proceed her way, and he decided to follow her lead.

Her hostess duties done at last, Louise Timson sat primly on the edge of a beautiful wing back chair and handed Mark a thick folder of papers, silently asking him not to open them just yet.

"My husband, Dr. Weiss, is a good man," she began, "but impatient and very competitive. Even with our son Ron, who is our only child. Dick never knew much about raising children. None of us do at first, but he didn't have a good childhood, so he had no base of comparison. He was tough on our son—too tough—and Ron had always fought back, fighting especially to win his father's respect, to impress Dick, most of the time without success.''

She paused and again smoothed her unwrinkled skirt, as if the success of her meeting with Mark Weiss depended on absolute perfection in the trappings of domestic tranquility.

"Ron has always loved sports, and he's always been very good at them—better than Dick ever was.''

She painted a complex picture then of a man progressively eclipsed and alarmed by the superior abilities of his own son, who could shoot more baskets, run faster, catch a baseball better than most—abilities that deeply threatened the father.

"About five years ago, when he was fourteen, Ron won a dirt motorbike in a contest. He became good at riding it, even started coming home with . . . with . . . trophies for rallies and . . ."

"Motocross?"

She nodded and studied her hands, which were gripping each other.

"Dick stayed out of it. He was always busy anyway, so he paid no attention, until one Saturday I made a terrible mistake. I asked Dick to pick up Ron from a race in a hilly area north of here." She had been looking beyond Mark, but now she looked him in the eye for a moment. "He couldn't drive the bike on city streets, you see."

She looked away again and continued. "Anyway . . . I knew better, but I . . . I was selfish, and busy, and I thought, just this once, maybe they won't get in an argument. He went and he found Ron, watched him ride for awhile, and then ordered him to hand over the bike so he could demonstrate to Ron how it should be done."

"Had he ever—?"

"No!" Her reply was sharp, and she studied her hands briefly before looking at the wall again, struggling constantly for control. "Dick had never ridden a motorcycle. Ron tried to give him his helmet, but he refused. He took off across the dirt course jumping the bike over every hill, and Ron saw him crest three of them, but not the fourth."

"He fell?"

"Headfirst at high speed into a pile of large rocks. He was unconscious for a half hour. Ron was scared to death, and the bike was badly beaten up. Ron ran to his father and found him unconscious and bleeding. There were others there offering help and someone called an ambulance, which took a half hour to arrive—they were out quite a ways from town. Dick finally came around, and when he regained his bearings on where he was, he refused the ambulance, got to his feet, and insisted on driving Ron home. He even picked up Ron's bike."

"They didn't go to an emergency room?"

"My husband, Dr. Weiss, is impervious to physical injury or

illness or any incapacity . . . or so he thinks. But he was bleeding badly, and he looked horrible when the two of them walked in. The thing was, within ten minutes he blacked out, for the first time, staying unconscious for two, maybe three minutes.''

"For the first time. It happened again?''

She nodded. "I've had some first-aid training. Dick thinks I'm too stupid to tell him anything, but I knew he must have a concussion, and I knew the blackout—the blackouts—meant he needed medical attention fast. But he yelled at me and screamed and threatened every time I tried to get him to the hospital that evening and Sunday. Yet . . .'' Her voice caught and she closed her eyes momentarily, the memories vivid, the feelings fully recalled. "Yet he was blacking out every hour or so.''

Louise Timson turned to Mark suddenly, her eyes boring into his. "You must understand, Doctor, he was terrified that if he sought medical help, the FAA would suspend his medical license and not reinstate it. He wouldn't be able to fly again. He . . . he kept raging at me that if a pilot ever once checked the 'yes' block where the medical form asks if you've ever blacked out or been unconscious, you were a marked man forever.''

She broke eye contact and looked down again, the silence so hollow that Mark had to fill it. "What happened, then? Did he go finally?''

"The headaches were blinding. Hot packs, cold packs, aspirin, we tried everything. He was in agony. Finally . . . finally after he'd thought it out, he agreed to let me take him in, but he had specific instructions. First he took out all of his identification from his pockets. I was to drive him to Parkland Hospital and admit him as Joseph Thompson, and never, ever tell anyone his, or my, real name. I gave them a false Social Security number and paid a cash deposit, because of course we couldn't use his normal insurance under a false name. That was sufficient, since Parkland is a public hospital. The next day I withdrew several thousand dollars and paid it in advance on his account, so no one would start asking questions. I hated sneaking around, but Dick was terrified the company would find out he was having problems, so I also had to call his boss at North America and say he was going in for a series of routine tests and needed two weeks off.''

"And this folder?''

"The medical records from that hospital stay . . . two weeks. As Thompson, plus copies of the prescription."

"What was the diagnosis? Louise, how does this relate to the crash? You kept saying when I visited you before—"

"Give me time. I need for you to understand this fully. It's very important to me that you understand why—as well as how—this is not Dick's fault. It was mine." She had approved his use of the tape recorder, and she pointed to it now. "You're sure that's on."

"Yes."

"Good. Dick came out of the hospital two weeks later and spent two more weeks at home before returning to his office, and returning to flying. He was, after all, chief pilot, and he took great pride in being able to fly on the line even though he was in management. When he got back, he knew his medical clearance certificate had expired. You may know a captain's is only good for six months at a time?"

"Yes. I'm a private pilot."

"Okay. Well, there is a company doctor Dick used to joke about, Dr. McIntyre. Dick got McIntyre to recertify him without an examination. I remember because he came home and told me with great glee how he'd manipulated the man to where all Dick had to do was send him the paperwork, and the license would come back. He never had to show the doctor the hospital records, and the doctor never knew about the accident, and Dick's boss, John Walters, never asked him any questions. I guess no one there really cared."

Mark was puzzled. Where was this going? Had he flown fifteen hundred miles just to hear the woman's overwrought story compelled by misplaced guilt over her husband's illicit manipulation of the medical licensing procedure? Was that all?

"What no one knew, Dr. Weiss, was that Dick had not fully recovered. The blackouts—the tiny seizures, I suppose you could call them—continued even after he left Parkland, and the doctor—'Joe Thompson's' doctor—finally got them under control with phenobarbital. Dick was in a panic until he found the drug would keep the blackouts from happening. That's why he stayed home two more weeks. He found if he took three a day, he never had trouble. But if he failed to take one just once . . ."

"They would occur again."

"Yes. Without fail."

"So . . . so this continued to the present day? When he crashed, he was on that drug? It wasn't found in his system, according to the toxicology reports. I studied them carefully."

"No."

"I don't understand."

She raised a hand, pleading for patience. "All these years, Dr. Weiss, all these years Dick has kept it under control and never had a problem because he takes his medicine with religious precision. You see, he found out . . . phenobarbital pills are very recognizable as prescription medicine, but there is another drug called Mysoline the doctor had told him about that worked even better, and that had a great advantage: it looks like an aspirin. It is still a prescription, though, and in our case the prescription was for Joseph Thompson, so it was my job . . ." Her voice caught and she looked down, wrestling with herself again before continuing. "It was my job . . . to always keep the prescription filled. I bought it from a pharmacy near Parkland. I always drove over there every second Thursday afternoon of the month to get a fresh bottle. I always paid cash—because of the name, you see."

"He didn't carry that bottle with him, did he?"

"Oh no! As I say, they look like aspirin, taste like aspirin . . . exactly like little white aspirin tablets. Dick figured out that if he carried them in a small aspirin bottle in his briefcase, no one would ever find out. He'd take one before leaving in the morning, one at two P.M., and one at eight P.M., religiously."

"I think I see where you're going with this. He failed to take his tablets when he went on that flight?"

"No! No, he would never do that. He was very, very responsible, don't you see? He understood that he absolutely had to take them on schedule, and that if he did, he was just as medically sound as anyone else. So, that was the price he paid to stay certified. It might not have been technically legal, but as he explained it, you see, it was his responsibility to take his medicine, and as long as he fulfilled that responsibility, he was entitled to be treated like any fully healthy pilot."

"Louise, I—"

"Let me finish. You don't understand yet. The Thursday before the crash I got way behind, and by the time I got to the pharmacy, it had closed. I couldn't get the prescription, and there was only one tablet left in Dick's bottle. I was panicked!

I couldn't tell Dick, he would have been furious with me! But I knew I had one left, so I figured a way around the problem. I decided I would give him the remaining tablet in the morning, and put a substitute bottle of real aspirin in his briefcase. It was my responsibility to make sure that bottle was full and in his briefcase. As soon as he left for work, I would run down and get the prescription, put it in the bottle, and while he was at lunch, I'd replace the other bottle in his briefcase at his office. He never took the second daily pill until two P.M.''

"It didn't work?"

She looked at Mark with a pleading expression, tears glistening at the corners of her eyes. "I didn't know he was going to fly a trip. I . . . I got there with the replacement bottle, and he was gone! I nearly fell apart. I tried to find out which gate he was leaving from, but he was already in the air. I didn't know what to do! I decided to leave messages for him to call me, and his secretary didn't understand, but she finally helped. I left messages at every station, but he didn't call. He was like that. If I wanted him to do something, he felt I was trying to control him. He . . . he didn't call. I waited in agony all day. I figured he'd . . . he'd keel over somewhere for a few seconds, realize something was wrong, and get off the flight.''

Louise Timson looked down at her hands, now visibly shaking. "I got the call from the Kansas City hospital about midnight. I had already heard the news on the radio.'' She looked at Mark suddenly, her voice strong. "Do you understand now? *I'm* the one who caused the crash. *I'm* the responsible party who failed. Not Dick. He did everything right. But he had no way of knowing that wasn't his prescription in that bottle. I know he blacked out during that approach. I know it. That was only aspirin. I killed them, Dr. Weiss. I killed them all!''

She broke then, his attempts to limit her guilt totally ineffective.

Mark looked at her long and thoughtfully. "Louise, does he know?''

"That you're here, that I'm telling you this?''

"No. Does your husband know what was in the briefcase bottle?''

She didn't answer. She merely thanked him for coming, reverting to the part of perfect hostess, the smile, the gestures, and the practiced movement to the door telling the tale.

Mark didn't argue. He promised to call the following day, to take her on as a patient if necessary, knowing how much she needed professional help.

Having the key to the accident was all that had mattered at the moment. Having it and getting it back to Washington with it. Regardless of the hour, he had resolved to call Joe Wallingford from the airport, and Senator Martinson's people as well.

Yet, there were disturbing thoughts tugging at his professional conscience, nagging mental alarms that he had refused to acknowledge as he shoved them all into the background and raced to the airport. There had been one element of confirmation looming ever larger in his mind as he thought of how to summarize things for Wallingford. As he had told Mrs. Timson, he had studied the toxicology report carefully. There was only one foreign substance found in her husband's blood at the hospital. Salicylic acid. Plain aspirin.

Mark's focus returned, the familiar image of the Senate hearing room where it was all coming to a head filled his eyes once again. Dick Timson's back was still before him at the witness table, and Mark watched as he sat up straight and took a deep breath, reacting finally to the last question.

"Captain, I ask you again," Kell was saying evenly, "do you know anyone by the name of Joseph Thompson?"

Dick Timson nodded slowly, and in a controlled tone of voice began relating the story of his injury, his hospitalization, and his careful taking of the drug Mysoline. Kell let him confess in detail, Timson's voice the only one heard for nearly ten minutes in the excessively quiet hearing room as he built his case: he knew what it took to be a whole pilot medically, and he had complied with that. The fact that he had violated the rules was, essentially, immaterial.

David Bayne looked at Ron Putnam and knew by his expression that he had withheld information, permitting his boss and his airline to be ambushed. Putnam was in complete confusion. He had known nothing of the Thompson-Timson subterfuge, or of Timson's head injury, but he knew only too well why McIntyre's records on Timson were so pristine, and he knew David Bayne. When it all came out it would add up to the same thing: Ron Putnam was as good as fired. And in Dallas, John Walters simply turned the TV off and sat staring at the wall, his worst fears confirmed.

When Dick Timson finally fell silent, Kell leaned forward. "Captain, is it possible that the crash of North America Flight 255 in Kansas City on the night of October twelfth was caused because the captain—you—were suddenly rendered unconscious?"

"No!"

"It's not possible that the same malady you'd been fighting for years, the same one for which you took three Mysoline tablets per day at careful intervals to prevent—there's no possibility that could have occurred on final approach?"

"Absolutely not! That had nothing to do with this." Timson's voice was loud and angry, but the tone was warbling, the tension and fear modulating it clearly.

"Captain Timson, do you in fact really have a memory of those last few seconds? Or were you unconscious?"

"Yes I have a memory, and no I wasn't unconscious. And I'll tell you why, Senator. For five full years I never had any variation to this truth: if I took my pills, I never—and I repeat, never—blacked out! On the day of the crash, I carefully took my pill at eight A.M. before leaving for the office, a second one at two P.M. while in flight, and the third promptly at eight P.M. Dallas time while on the ground in Washington. Since I had the proper medication, I could not possibly have blacked out."

"Captain, you kept your medication in an aspirin bottle, didn't you?"

"Yes."

"And your wife was responsible for keeping it filled?"

His eyes widened, the connection made: Louise had betrayed him! It was she who had spilled all of this, ruining him, ruining herself. He'd kill her . . . he'd . . . he'd *leave* her! *Goddamn* that bitch!

"Yes," he replied.

"Captain, look at the hospital lab report we handed you, at the green circle. Read what it says."

He read out loud the confirmation that only aspirin had been found in his bloodstream, his hand waving it off. "They probably missed the Mysoline, that's not a common drug."

"They didn't miss it Captain, because it wasn't there," Kell told him, seeing the puzzled expression showing through the feigned defiance on Timson's face.

Suddenly his hand closed into a fist as Timson came halfway

out of his chair, his face purple, banging on the table for emphasis with each word. "I . . . TOOK . . . MY . . . PILLS! I told you that!"

"Yes sir, you did," Kell replied calmly, determined not to acknowledge the ferocity of the outburst. "But you had run out of them that morning. The eight A.M. pill was the last of the bunch, and your wife had forgotten to pick up the new bottle the night before. She was terrified you'd find out about her failure and be furious with her, so after you had taken the last of the real Mysoline tablets at breakfast the next day, she substituted regular aspirin in your briefcase, intending to come to your office and secretly replace the bottle while you were at lunch. But you left on a flight instead. What you took later in the day, Captain, as verified by the lab report from the hospital, was aspirin. Nothing more. At the time of the crash, you had virtually no operable levels of Mysoline in your bloodstream."

Never had Kell Martinson seen such a look. Timson's face went through an indescribable range of emotions betraying his total internal upheaval as the man slowly realized what must have happened and that Kell's version was correct. The memory of those messages from Louise at every station, and his sneering comment to Don Leyhe, "Let her stew, whatever it is . . . I call no woman before I'm ready" now rang like a death knell in his head. The senator was asking him something again, but he hardly heard it, and when he asked for the question to be repeated, he could barely recognize his own voice.

"I said, Captain, I'd like to ask you to rethink your answer now to my question of whether you have a clear memory of the last few seconds of Flight 255. Do you really remember, or did you construct a memory?"

"I . . . I don't . . ."

Kell saw the man was thoroughly broken, and he softened his tone. "Captain, just answer yes or no. Is it possible that you fell unconscious on that final approach, and that your hand may have pressed forward on the controls, causing the airplane to dive? Is that possible?"

"Yes."

"And you don't to this day *really* have a memory of those last few seconds, do you?"

There was a long, interminable pause before sound emerged from Timson's bone-dry throat. There was no sound from the spellbound audience, and only the whirr of videotape recorders as the vibrations finally reached their ears.

"No," he said simply.

The small envelope had fallen from the stack of Timson's medical records as Kell Martinson was examining them, and Mark hadn't noticed at first. The envelope was addressed simply "To Dick," and when they realized what it was, Mark decided to hand it to Timson later.

Halfway through the questioning of Dick Timson, the final mental tumbler in Mark Weiss's subconscious fell into place, and with a start he faced the question of why Louise Timson would say what she had said, in the manner she had presented it. The jewelry, the dress, the neat house—it all added up, and he felt an ice cube in his stomach, the adrenaline pumping suddenly, his professional responsibilities to a hurting human having been totally breached.

Mark fumbled for the envelope, tearing it open.

"Dear Dick," it began. "I can never tell you how sorry I am for what I've done. The crash was my fault, not yours. I hope somehow you can forgive me. I'll love you always. Louise."

Mark got to his feet suddenly and pushed his way over several sets of toes to get out of the room, heading for the closest Senate office and commandeering a phone from a none-too-friendly secretary.

There was no answer at the Dallas home of the Timsons. Exactly what he had feared. He dialed the operator then, gaining her help in searching out the telephone number of the Dallas Police, who agreed to send a car to the house and phone him back if there was anything amiss. He called an ambulance service as well, giving them a credit-card number and begging them to send an aid unit immediately to the same address, just in case. Only then did he return to the hearing, his own feelings of guilt rising precipitously.

Dick Timson had left the witness table and taken a seat on the end of the second row, his head down, when the same secretary found Mark. He retraced his steps, calling the number given.

"Doctor, no one answered when our people arrived, so we forced entry. I'm sorry to say you were right."

"Where?"

"Upstairs. It looks like an overdose. Her pulse was very weak.

We transported her immediately and almost lost her twice on the way. She's in extremely critical condition, but she may make it. There was no note, by the way.''

Oh yes there was, he thought. She had, in effect, dictated it to him in person last night.

Mark trudged back to the hearing room as everyone was streaming out, Martinson having called a fifteen-minute recess. He watched Dick Timson simply ignoring the press—and everyone associated with North America ignoring him. The simple logistics of how to get a man who had become an instant pariah from that room to the anonymity of the parking lot and beyond was excruciating. Mark watched the pilot from a distance, following as Timson reached the hallway and turned, alone, scorned, and broken. There would be more than one duty to perform before he could walk away from the captain of Flight 255.

This was the man who had killed Kim and Aaron and Greg by pure self-interested negligence, violating the rules systematically, drawing his own family into the web of deception, bastardizing the medical checks and balances, and lying, lying, lying to cover it up. As in Kansas City, he fought to hate Timson, hate him enough to kill him.

But he could feel only pity.

Timson needed to be told about his wife—to go to her side, however angry he might be with her. He would undoubtedly be fired and prosecuted and reviled, and as the horror of what he had done to his life began to unfold, he would be in great need of psychological help. He probably had been for decades.

Dr. Mark Weiss put on a burst of speed suddenly, catching up with the hunched form of the slowly departing former chief pilot, stopping him and forcing him to look up, his vacant eyes red-tinged mirrors of despair. There were ethics involved. There was his basic humanity involved. And there was duty. He had failed Louise Timson, but there was yet another human life in the balance. And in the final analysis, he had the training to help.

26

Wednesday, January 9, Washington, D.C.

Beverly Bronson tightened the belt of her long black coat and stepped into the teeth of a stiff wind as Joe Wallingford held the door of the Hart Senate Office Building for her, the din of late-afternoon Washington traffic instantly assaulting their ears. A cab screeched to a halt in front of them, the cigar-chewing driver having sensed an impending fare as they approached the curb, but Joe waved him on, having concluded an unspoken agreement with Beverly that they needed the fresh air, however laden with carbon monoxide it might be.

They walked halfway to the Capitol in deep thought before Beverly found her voice, her words emerging as a sigh amidst a sudden explosion of condensed breath in the crisp air. "Other than Watergate, or Iran-contra, I don't think I've ever seen so much come out in a congressional hearing. That was amazing!"

"Are we going to survive?" Joe asked. "Will Farris resign?"

Beverly smiled and watched the sidewalk disappear beneath her feet for a few paces before glancing over at Joe to answer. "I saw him stop you in the hall, Joe. What did he say?"

There was a masculine snort as her companion shook his head in short staccato bursts. "Something on the order of, 'Where are you working next week, Judas?' "

She resumed her perusal of the sidewalk until Joe was tempted to repeat his question, burning to know just how she assessed the damage.

"Well," she said at last, looking in the distance ahead, "he told *me* that he might not get reappointed next year, but no one was going to run him out of Washington. He may stay, Joe, and I don't know how—"

395

"How I'm going to work with him?"

She nodded before continuing. "The rest of it . . . good grief! Not only did Martinson destroy Dean yesterday, he solved the crash for you."

"We have Mark Weiss to thank for that, Beverly. He had Timson figured out from the beginning, which, I suppose, is what a trained psychologist should be able to do. I just can't believe the poor woman blamed herself. That's ludicrous!"

"I know. And such a tragedy."

"I hate to say it, but I don't think we would have figured this out without her."

They turned right at the southeast corner of the Capitol and walked westward for awhile, trending back toward the FAA building.

"What was fascinating to watch today," she said, "other than Timson, of course, was David Bayne of North America, and how fast he figured out how to blow with the wind. I mean, here's the chairman of the airline that's just been exposed as grossly negligent in several ways, including its misuse of influence with the government, and the man sits there with a straight face and forcefully tells us he is in full support of the senator's bill, that the NTSB should never be manipulated this easily, and, Joe, that if your people had been allowed to do their job without interference, he, David Bayne, would have then had some way of finding out that *his* executives were lying to him! That is unprecedented."

Joe nodded. "Talk about me being in professional jeopardy, I've never heard a senior corporate leader fire so many people in a public hearing before. Let's see . . ." Joe held up the fingers of one hand and began counting them off. "He fired John Walters, Ron Putnam—who was there in the audience, by the way—Dr. McIntyre, Captain Timson, of course, and two names I didn't recognize on Walters's staff."

"Appearances and public perception, Joe. And guess what? It'll work. A lot of people out there watching on TV will feel great empathy for Bayne. The poor chairman! No one told him that his people were lying, cheating, and drawing him into the web. But he's a good moral individual who won't stand for such things, and here are the heads of the miscreants to prove it." She shook her head. "I will give him this: he did at least say that as CEO he was fully responsible for failing to know what was happening. Those are the right words, but I know the positive impression he left with the public. Clever, clever man.''

''Yeah, but you know, maybe I'm naïve, but I think the man's truly sincere. I think he was amazed . . . watching him . . . that he had lost control.''

''You'd be surprised how few corporate leaders really know what's going on in their companies,'' she said, remembering her time in the corporate world, trying to advise CEOs who simply refused to listen to things they didn't want to know.

''Beverly, I'm worried about *you* . . . your position, you know? Does Dean have you targeted?''

''He thinks I'm a mindless bimbo. I'll be fine.''

''What are my chances?'' Joe asked, not certain he wanted to hear an answer.

''Joe . . . ,'' she began, then hesitated, her tongue massaging her upper lip as her mind raced ahead, looking for the best way to tell this professional investigator about the dangerous, shifting world of shadowy alliances and ever-changing prospects he had blundered into. ''I don't know. A lot depends on . . . well, outside events we can't control.''

Joe looked over at her, trying to fathom her meaning, then deciding that ignorance would help him through the night.

''You going home, Joe?''

''No, I'm—'' He caught himself before uttering Susan's name. ''I'm meeting someone for dinner.''

They parted at the FAA garage and Joe drove the few miles to Georgetown, irritated with himself that he was running late. They had made the arrangements at noon, as Joe called Susan to report on the Timson testimony. Six-fifteen P.M. at her favorite French restaurant.

He didn't feel like dinner. In fact, he felt like hell, his stomach in a knot, his palms sweaty, and his prospects dim. Instinctively, he knew Farris was determined to get him, but it would probably take the form of a Chinese water torture—slow, excruciating moves to keep Joe from any substantive work, embarrassing him a thousand times over. Yet what could he do but take it? The Board was his home. He'd be lost without it.

The question of whether he should have gone to Martinson in the first place was moot. Whatever the cost, the process had brought him the answer to the Kansas City crash.

Susan was running even farther behind. It was 6:45 P.M. before she appeared in the doorway of Michellene's, looking, Joe thought, like she had stepped off the cover of a fashion magazine, her face aglow, responding with an electric smile when she spotted him fumbling to get up from the table to come greet her.

"Where do we go from here, Doctor?" he asked, tapping a breadstick on the tablecloth, still struggling to look happy, struggling to hide the apprehension and turmoil he was feeling.

"Was that an institutional 'we,' or a personal 'we'?" she asked.

"Let's start with institutional, 'cause on a personal level, you may be fooling around with an unemployed bum before long."

"Sexiest bum I've ever slept with," she said.

That embarrassed Joe, which tickled Susan. She watched his color rise as he glanced around them furtively to see if anyone had heard the remark.

"Susan! Good grief," Joe said under his breath.

"Okay, you want to know what happens next? We see whether the chairman falls on his sword. If he does, you are completely safe. If he doesn't, then in the long term, as I warned you, I'm going to have a devil of a time defending you."

Joe tried to smile at that. "I wonder how many boxes I'll need."

"For what?"

"Cleaning out my office."

"Too soon. Don't give up yet. By the way, Joe, John Phelps came by to see me today with the details on the Miami Air situation and a copy of that smoking-gun memo. He said he didn't want to, but you told him he could trust the board member who wears pantyhose."

Joe smiled sheepishly. "Did he use those words?"

"Um-hum, and I wonder where he got them?" She was grinning—fortunately, Joe thought. "Watch what sexist remarks you make about me, boy."

"Yes ma'am. What did he say?"

"The FAA administrator called him personally just after Dean blew the whistle on Caldwell. Phelps went upstairs to meet with him, and took the house counsel. By the time he came back, Caldwell had been fired, and he's under criminal investigation for influence peddling."

"Oh boy."

"Yeah. And you may not have heard, but David Bayne lost the takeover battle for North America. That investment group from Miami won board approval for a buyout at fourteen a share. The way he fought it, Bayne will be out, too."

"Provided the Transportation Department approves the buyout."

"You kidding? DOT would rubber-stamp anything. United could sell itself to Aeroflot and get approval!"

Joe fell silent and just looked at her for a few seconds. "Should I come to work tomorrow?"

"Would you consider coming in together?" she shot back, "Not to be pushy, of course." She winked at him, watching him blush anew, and he smiled in spite of himself as he shook his head. "I'd be pretty nervous, distracted company tonight, and you deserve better."

"Judging from past performances," she said, smiling and munching a celery stalk as seductively as she could manage, "I'd say if I could command just a quarter of your physical attention, I'd be in heaven. But if you insist, a rain check, perhaps?"

"Absolutely," Joe said.

He battled the dragons all night long, sleeping fitfully, rising at 6, having finally concluded that there was nothing Dean Farris could do to him, politically or professionally—a refreshingly positive attitude which held until the elevator doors opened on the eighth floor and a uniformed security guard stepped forward to greet him.

"Mr. Wallingford?"

"Yes?"

"I'm here to inform you, sir, that you have been suspended pending dismissal by order of the NTSB chairman. I'll escort you downstairs, if you'd like."

Joe shook his head and looked at the man. Just doing his job, of course.

"I'll just get some of my things . . ."

The guard reached out to take Joe's arm. "Ah . . . no, Mr. Wallingford. Your office is sealed. Your belongings will be sent to your home after the investigation."

"What investigation?"

"I don't know sir. I'm just telling you what I was told to tell you."

Joe pulled his arm away and returned to the elevator, angry and confused and frightened all at the same time. He was halfway to his car in the basement when Beverly Bronson caught up with him.

"Me too, Joe. Dean fired us both, fired Andy, fired Nick Gardner—which we expected, of course—and he's on a rampage. He's not going to resign, he's talking of suing us all, and at this rate he'll self-destruct before dinner."

"What should . . . ?"

"Drive us to the Hart Building. I've already called Martinson's people."

"No, Beverly, I can't . . ."

"What? Ask for help? I'm talking about strategy planning, fellow. You helped start the process of changing the Board, you can't back out now."

Kell Martinson was waiting for them when they arrived.

"Sit down, Beverly, Joe. This has been a wild morning."

"For us, too," Joe said.

Kell sat down behind his desk, leaning forward, drumming his fingers. "Okay, here's where we are. The White House is in disarray about all of this. I was up half the night with . . . well, let's just say members of my party, okay? They're angry with you, Joe, they're angry with me, and they're infuriated that their man Farris has been exposed as an idiot, too stupid to even be on the take."

"Where does that leave us?"

Kell held up his hand. "Let me work through all this a minute. Now, so far this morning, the chief of staff has asked Farris for his resignation and been refused, has called me to see if I would amend the bill to sweep the Board clean and start over when the bill passes, if it passes, just so they can get rid of Farris— they're outraged he won't step down—and they've offered the chairmanship to another Board member, which is grossly premature."

"Who?" Joe asked.

"Dr. Susan Kelly," Kell replied, noting Joe's stunned expression. "You know her, of course?"

"Yes . . . I . . . ah . . . ," Joe stammered, angry with himself for breaking composure. "What did she say?"

"She said no and suggested someone else. But she's the only politically acceptable member of the Board right now. Okay, I was going to hunt you up, Joe, for a conference this morning, anyway, when I found out from Beverly's call that Farris is firing most of the Western world, and may have to be physically restrained, if I understand the pitch of his anger.''

''You do,'' Beverly told him. ''I believe the word is *apoplectic*.''

''Well, he's finished in this town politically, though he might succeed in hanging on until the end of his term at the Board. We'd have to have him criminally indicted to get him out of there otherwise.''

''What about the new bill?''

''We *might* be able to legislate him away, but it would take several months, in any event.''

''What a mess,'' Joe said, his head still spinning.

''Yeah. The good part is that the media is having a field day with what happened in the hearings, and we tipped them off early this morning about Farris's refusal to resign despite internal pressure. That means that by the time the papers come out in the morning, Farris will be barricading himself against public opinion and a media storm.''

Beverly and Kell talked with Fred Sneadman, who had joined them, notebook in hand, while Joe's mind raced around, looking for lifeboats. All he wanted was his job at the Board. How had all this occurred? Suspended, maybe fired . . . Farris on a rampage. How had it come to this?

The fact that Fred Sneadman and not Cynthia Collins was serving as administrative assistant finally caught Beverly's attention, and she asked where Cynthia was. Kell's expression changed ever so slightly, a flicker of distress showing for a moment before he caught himself.

''She's taken some much-deserved personal leave.''

''She is coming back?''

Kell stared at her for a moment before answering. ''Yes. Of course.''

''Well, if she ever decides not to, keep me in mind. I seem to be out of work at the moment.''

Kell worked hard to smile. ''I don't think that condition will last, but if the occasion arises, Beverly, let's talk.'' Kell's mind was elsewhere, and the sparkle of unfocused interest in Beverly's eyes which went slightly beyond the professional made no more of an impression on him than her statuesque beauty.

Joe's attention returned to the room suddenly, his head snapping up just enough for the others to notice that he'd been drifting from the conversation. "What should we do?" Joe asked, embarrassed at the lapse.

Kell Martinson looked Joe straight in the eye to the point of discomfort. The senator was trying to read something there.

"Joe, what do you want?"

"From you, Senator?"

"No, what do you really want to do professionally?"

"I just want to be an NTSB investigator. That's all."

Kell looked at him a bit longer before replying. "You may have to look beyond that, Joe."

Which means, Joe thought with sinking heart, that it may truly be over. He almost didn't hear Kell's call to action.

"Okay, let's go."

"Where?" Joe was confused.

"I'm sorry Joe, you were deep in thought a minute ago. We're going to go over to the Executive Office Building to meet with some of the President's people on this. I'd like you both to come along."

Joe followed Beverly out the door, trying to look engaged, but feeling dead inside. Kell asked him to hold a cab, that he had one phone call to make, and with that they left him and headed for the street.

Kell sat back down for a moment in troubled thought. Beverly's question had triggered feelings he was trying to hold at bay. His divorce from Julie had become final on the eighth, two days ago. He had hoped they could remain friends, but Julie's voice when she'd called about the final decree had been frosty and distant. He was truly alone now, and with Cindy still in Missouri, he was lonely as well. What was she thinking out there? he wondered. Had she watched the hearing? Was she thinking of him? Should he call her? They hadn't talked for a week, and even then it had been strained and she had been noncommittal. He was living in fear she might call to say it was over, yet he longed to hear her voice. God, how he missed her.

Kell Martinson got up and slowly pulled on his coat as he looked around at the impressive collection of framed plaques and certificates and pictures, shots of him with presidents and dignitaries, the sort of thing a U.S. senator collects as a visible record of achievement. Yes, he was proud of all that. Yes, it was his life. But it wasn't enough, and he knew that now more than ever. Without the right someone to share the victories, they were hollow. Kell sighed and stood up, grabbing his briefcase as he headed out the door to join the others.

For Joe, the short taxi ride to 1600 Pennsylvania Avenue served only as a distant and blurred background for the rapid progression of desperate thoughts of where he would go, what he would do, how he would live. It wasn't that life away from his position at the Board had never been considered, it had simply never been taken seriously. Ethereal thoughts of "What if?" were simply that: ethereal thoughts.

This, however, was reality—the result of a technician blundering stupidly into the maelstrom of the political world. In that game, Joe now knew only too well, he was no match for anyone.

As they got out, Kell motioned Joe aside for a moment.

"Joe, did you talk to someone at Kansas City Airport about the problem we discussed?"

"Yes I did. Over the weekend."

"Well, I want to thank you. It worked. I got a call this morning from their security chief, and the general gist of the conversation was, if I won't make a big deal out of which airport had the breach in security that would permit a car to roll through undetected, they won't make a big deal about the technical impropriety of my probing their defenses, especially since the FAA has declined prosecution."

"I'm glad to hear that."

"It can still blow up publicly, but I think now I could handle it. Thanks again, Joe."

A deputy to the chief of staff was waiting to escort them over to the White House itself. The domestic-policy group had become involved, given the embarrassing nature of the situation to the administration. Joe had always wished he could be invited to some nonpublic function within the walls of the world-famous building, but not in the present circumstance. Now they loomed more like the fortress housing the gallows than a place of awe and beauty and power.

"Mr. Wallingford, Senator Martinson . . ." The voice came from a small man with flint-hard features and eyes like tiny coals, both of them boring into Joe's. "We've got a difficult problem here."

The hearing, the bill, and especially the unmasking of Bill Caldwell at the hand of the NTSB chairman, who was appointed by the sitting administration, had been a political embarrassment that could only be handled by the departure of both men, along with Presidential support of a bill the President's domestic staff had originally thought unnecessary, but which now *would* be politically expedient. "We'll have to support it now to make it look like this was a Republican response to the very problems created by our Republican chairman."

They were mad as hell at Martinson and mad as hell at Joe for starting the entire affair, but they were also realists. "There are," the deputy said, ". . . solutions."

The man who entered the room at that point with profound displeasure showing clearly on his face was far too familiar to trigger the appropriate recognition response in Joe, until, as he shook the proffered hand, he realized it belonged to the President of the United States, who sat on the edge of a desk and regarded Joe in silence for a few seconds.

"Dean Farris has just given up. His resignation will be on my desk in an hour. I had to twist his arm nearly off, but he's out." The President's hand swept toward the door for emphasis, and he got up then and walked toward the end of the small office. "We offered the job to Susan Kelly this morning, on the supposition that Farris would leave. She turned us down . . . said she hasn't been there long enough. I know this new bill, if it makes it, will require the chairman to have technical expertise and since I'm now forced to support the damn shake-up, I might as well put us on the side of the angels with a qualified individual. Mr. Wallingford, for all the grief you've caused me so far, I should support your canning by Dean Farris as his last act on political earth. Instead, I'm going to appoint you chairman."

Joe just stared at him. That made no sense. "Of what, sir?"

The President laughed—a short, rapid chuckle replaced instantly by the same serious face. "Things been moving a little fast for you, Joe? Of the NTSB. I want you to take over for Farris and lead the Board into the new world you and my overly exuberant friend from the Hill here"—he motioned to Martinson—"have concocted." The chief executive's eyes were hard and none too friendly and they were aimed directly at Joe, cutting through any imagined defenses like a laser through butter.

"Sir, I'm flattered, but . . ."

"Goddammit, Wallingford, I'm not here to flatter you. I'm here to put you back to work. You got yourself fired this morning for going around your boss, and I don't, in principle, disagree with that. Federal employees must maintain some degree of decorum when it comes to a chain of command or we'd have anarchy. I'm sure as hell not honoring what you did in running to the senator here, but I have to admit two things: One, you were right that Farris was damaging your operations. The admissions that you drew out, Senator, at your subcommittee hearings made that clear. Two, there seems to be no better-qualified person at the Board to take care of it with the technical side in mind, especially if the Board is broken away as an aviation-only entity. Even if the bill fails, there's no better candidate around, since Susan won't take it. I have to tell you, parenthetically, that you are my second choice because I don't know you, and my people do know Susan Kelly by reputation. Now. The ball's in your court. You're not being honored, you're being given a serious assignment of great import. I expect a quick decision." The President looked at his watch, then at an aide who had materialized at his elbow. "About time, Fred?"

"Yes sir. They're waiting."

"Okay." He turned back to the thunderstruck former IIC of the Kansas City investigation. "Joe . . . may I call you Joe?"

"Uh . . . good Lord, of course, Mr. President."

"Good. Joe, I need a quick answer."

"Sir, I'm not a politician . . ."

"Which is exactly why I'm appointing you." The President turned and left, smoothly transitioning to a running discussion with his aide over another unrelated problem waiting in the Oval Office.

Joe hadn't seen Susan and didn't realize she was there, standing in the background. Now she appeared at his side. Kell had called her an hour before, knowing instinctively that she would be needed to reassure Joe that the appointment was appropriate. Kell had no inkling that the Board member and the investigator were anything other than professional friends, but he had dealt with men of Joe's sensitivities before. Since Susan had been offered the job, and even though she'd turned it down, only Susan could convince Joe he should accept it.

She motioned Kell away with a tiny flick of her hand and led Joe to the far end of the room.

"Why didn't you take it, Susan? *You* should be chairman, not *me*!"

"I'm still learning. It's far too soon. I'm not qualified, especially not for a proper, technically oriented Board with a chairman possessed of a seven-year term. Good grief, Joe, you helped design the way this new Board should be. You know I'm not sufficiently knowledgeable."

"Bull, Susan. You're a psychologist, the world is turning to human factors and human performance, and nuts-and-bolts guys like me are becoming dinosaurs—confused dinosaurs at that. Look"—he started counting off fingers—"I don't have a doctorate, I never got beyond a master's degree, I . . . I'm just not . . ." Joe put both his palms up. "Susan, I'm a *technician*, a technocrat. That's all I've ever wanted to be. I do *not* want this job. I don't have the slightest idea if I can *do* this job!"

She put her right hand on his arm, her eyes searching his, looking for the resolve she knew was there. "You can, and you must. Joe, it's not what you started that counts in this equation. It's the fact that he's right—the Board you just designed needs a Joe Wallingford on it. It'll be tough. It'll be alien terrain to you. There will be duties and requirements you are not used to, and a rank you have never dealt with. But I know you, and you'll do an honorable and excellent job."

Deep down he knew she was probably right, yet he was scared—so very scared. He had feared losing the job he loved. Now he feared taking the job he had loathed, yet, what was the choice? There were people depending on him. Kell Martinson was depending on him, and had probably helped engineer this. Andy needed his job back. Beverly, now sitting quietly at the other end of the room, watching Joe with apprehension, certainly needed hers. The President, who had cleverly turned the tables on him—the old that's-a-great-suggestion,-why-don't-you-form-a-committee-and-look-into-it? method taken to an extreme, also, he supposed, needed him.

But most of all his mind embraced the image of the beautiful woman before him and the advice he knew by instinct he could trust. Besides, he couldn't let her down if this was what she expected of him.

"You really think I could do the job?" he asked at last.

"No question. I've seen you work as a diplomat, a commander, and even as a politician, whether you believe it or not.

And you're certainly a consummate technical expert. You'll make mistakes, Joe, without question. You'll make mistakes, but in the long run, you'll be excellent.''

He sighed then, the exhalation sounding somewhat ragged, his heart beating an accelerated tattoo.

"You did say, Susan, that it would get complicated, didn't you?"

She smiled, sensing the crumbling defenses. "I did indeed."

"By the way, are there any rules about Board members . . . that is, against . . ."

"Fraternization among Board members?"

"Something like that."

She smiled a radiant smile as she withdrew her hand from his shoulder and cocked her head slightly to one side.

"If there are, Mr. Chairman, dear, you'll have the power to change them.''